First Edition: August 2025

ISBN: 979-8-9851081-7-0

Editor: Lopt & Cropt Editing
Proofreader: Beth Attwood

LAVISH

CALIFORNIA KINGS · BOOK TWO

tinia montford

Playlist

Dead Man's Arms – Bishop Briggs
Vertigo – Raphael Lake, Ben Fisher, Aaron Levy, Daniel Ryan
Murphy
Anxiety – Doechii
Me - OSHUN
Sugar – Zubi
Heartless – Kanye West
Cry Me a River – Justin Timberlake
Don't Hurt Yourself – Beyoncé
No Church In The Wild – Jay-Z, Kanye West, Frank Ocean, The-
Dream
Heaven Knows – The Pretty Reckless

Want the full Serena & Miles experience? Listen now: http://bit.
ly/4lcUbvz

Would you like to see deleted scenes, character interviews and

exclusive character art? Sign up for my newsletter: https://
tiniamontford.com/newsletter/

You can also connect with me on:
Website | Facebook | Instagram | Pinterest | Tik Tok:
@tiniawritesbooks

To Sean—
For becoming family in all the ways that matter. Thank you.

It is difficult to know at what moment love begins; it is less difficult to know that it has begun.

WADSWORTH LONGFELLOW

A **DEFIANT CRIMSON** stain spread slowly across the champagne silk.

Shit.

This dress cost four thousand dollars, and in less than twenty minutes, it'd been ruined. I let out a breath and counted down from five. Omar Whitmore—too loud, too smug, too drunk—had stumbled right into me with a glass of wine.

I smiled through it. Of course I did. I always smiled through the bullshit.

I smiled and excused myself without waiting for my mother's reaction or Miles's apology. I already knew how that conversation would go with him.

Serena, don't make a scene. Serena, he didn't mean it. Serena, calm down.

Something was wrong with Omar.

The whole town had seen this past month—maybe even longer than that. I thought his weirdness began after his father died. Rumor had it Woody had rewritten his will before he died, and Omar shouldn't actually be in charge.

But Miles wouldn't talk to me about it.

Tonight was meant to be a great night.

My fingers worked the zipper at my back.

If I focused on the details of the party, it was easier to not be embarrassed. Half the party watched as Miles's father spilled wine on me; Miles was shocked and didn't help.

I peeled off my dress and lifted my heels. I headed to my closet in my bra and panties to find another dress, enjoying the cool air.

Good thing my room was on the far left of the mansion; all I heard was distant music and mumbling. Laurene's upcoming wedding was probably the gossip topic. The women loved to talk about my brother. Another multimillion-dollar deal! Mama's already calling him the future of King Enterprises, conveniently ignoring who actually keeps the company afloat.

Give me a fucking break.

I placed my hand on my hip, pushing through the rack for a dress acceptable for tonight. The door creaked open behind me.

"You should knock," I said calmly without turning around.

"When did I start doing that?" Miles's voice was low, then the door closed.

"You shouldn't be here."

"I came to make sure you were okay."

I grunted without turning around and picked up a dress, then changed my mind.

"You really gonna act like that?" Miles said.

"How should I act instead?" I finally turned my head. Miles was closer than I expected—too close, really. His shirt was undone at the top, exposing just enough collarbone and hint of chest to make my skin tighten. That lazy, crooked smile teased the corner of his mouth like he knew exactly what effect he had on me.

"He didn't mean it," Miles added. "My father. He was trying to—"

"He's been like this for months now, Miles. Your father's been making scenes at events, which we could ignore, but not *today.* The Ashbournes are here, and Laurene's engagement means a lot to my parents."

His jaw twitched, but he didn't deny it.

"I handled it," he said. "Back then. Tonight too."

"No." I stepped closer, my thigh brushing against him. "You apologized before. That's not the same thing as handling it. You need to *do* something about him, Miles. What's wrong with him? What aren't you telling me?"

Miles shook his head. "Sunny, chill."

"I can't have your father embarrassing my family and ruining things. Mama asked me to help plan everything and you know how much this party means to me."

"Unlike your family, we don't worry about how we look."

I scoffed and rolled my eyes. "Yeah, it's been like that forever."

Miles came closer, pinning me against the closet door. He put his hand on my waist, his rough fingers making slow circles that sent shivers down my spine. He slowly licked his lips; his intense gaze had nothing to do with the party or the wine.

"What's that supposed to mean?"

"You know what I mean." I didn't break eye contact with him. "I've told you again and again: people in this town look up to your family just like mine. Mama said—"

Miles groaned and rolled his eyes. "I don't wanna hear what your mama said right now."

I chewed on my lip. I didn't want another fight with him about it. That's all we ever fought about.

"You should take it seriously. The Kings and Whitmores founded Lush. We can't lose that power. This is who we are, Miles."

"We're more than our last names," Miles said, getting serious, then he sighed and looked at me.

He let his hand drift down my hip, his thumb brushing the lace. My thighs squeezed together. I gulped.

"Is that why you won't tell them we're engaged?" he asked, voice low, almost teasing.

I didn't answer.

"You're a King. I'm a Whitmore," he went on, a sly smile tugging at the corner of his mouth. "People would be thrilled. Keeping the power in the family, hmm?"

My frown deepened.

"Do you ever take anything seriously?" I snapped, the words slipping out before I could stop them.

His smirk faltered—just slightly. But then he tilted his head like he was studying me, deciding whether to play or push.

"Only when you look at me like that," he said quietly, giving me those puppy dog eyes he knew I couldn't fight, and I hated how warm my face suddenly felt.

"You play too much." I hit him, smiling reluctantly.

I wasn't Laurene, but she had something I wanted, even though she didn't love—or maybe even like—Conrad Ashbourne.

She wasn't the forgotten middle child.

Miles didn't move, but I felt his energy shift. His hand was still on me, but the heat of it now felt different—less possessive, more…distant. Like he already knew the answer, and just needed to hear me choke on it.

"We can fuck in secret but can't hold hands in public?"

"We've been together six months. Who gets engaged that fast?" I still can't believe I said yes.

"We do," he said. "It's us. It's our business. Who gives a fuck what people say?"

"My family has a tradition—"

The Kings had been following it since my great-great-grandfather Augustus King founded this town after the Tulsa Massacre.

"That archaic arranged marriage rule? C'mon, times ain't that desperate, and the average life-span isn't twenty-five anymore.

We can be our own people now. Out of everybody you can break that rule."

Could I? There were a lot of things within our family I couldn't change. No matter how much I fought, my rules and boundaries were cemented.

"I know we were sudden and it's wild and feels reckless. But let go, Sunny. It'll be okay."

His voice was low and sure. His eyes burned—full of belief, full of me—and for a moment, it almost cracked something open in me. Almost. I wanted to reach for him. God, I wanted to want him the way he wanted me—recklessly, loudly, without calculating the fallout. But I couldn't.

Not yet.

I thought about the proposal. We were in his bed. No ring, no kneeling. Just certainty. I said yes before I even mapped the consequences. That was mistake number one. Love was messy—illogical. But being with Miles felt like stepping off a cliff: thrilling, terrifying, and utterly overwhelming.

"I need King Developments first," I whispered, more to myself than to him.

I saw his eyes blaze, and his hands slid down my thighs, cupping my ass, pulling my hips against him. "Why? You have me."

"You don't get it, Miles." I tried to push him back, but he was a brick wall. He reached between my thighs, his fingers touching the dampness through the fabric.

"I've listened to you talk about taking this company from Erik for months."

"That's not it!" I snapped. "You're an *heir*. Erik is an heir. You both just *get* companies handed to you. I'm not Laurene—I'm not the princess, nor can I do whatever the hell Gigi does. You don't know what it's like to have to fight for something. I've earned every inch of what I've got from my family, and I'm still not enough."

"You're enough for me."

"I love you—" I was serious. I'd only ever loved my family, but he showed me otherwise. "But I need and deserve *more*."

His jaw flexed. His fingers stayed where they were—pressed between my legs, claiming.

"I get that your mom's a lot," he said, shaking his head. "But you don't even realize you're in the best damn position. To do whatever you want and not have your fucking mama on your back like she is with Erik."

"Have you told Erik about us?"

He pulled back just enough to let air between us, not enough to leave.

"You haven't," I said.

"You're half-naked in my arms," he growled, "and you're asking me if I told my best friend about us? Now? We have other things to deal with."

"Erik's not gonna be happy, that's why you haven't told him."

Miles sucked his teeth.

"You're pressing me? Have a conversation with him. While you're at it, why don't you get your father in line."

He let out a dry laugh and finally released me. "You think families are supposed to fall in line like little soldiers," he said. "We don't march to the orders of one person in the family, and smile for the goddamn camera. That's not *my* family, Serena. We love each other. We *care*. I'll do it my way when I'm ready."

I frowned. "You're saying I don't care about my family?"

"You're fucking planning to usurp your brother. And for what? Yvonne is *never* going to hand you King Enterprises. When it comes time to pass the crown, it's going to go to Erik— just like it *always* was. He's the firstborn, even I know that."

I turned away from him, crossing my arms. I just wanted Mama to give me something, like she did for Erik.

He stepped closer, his voice lower now, bitter and honest.

"Just take what you can get," he said. "You and me—we can still start our lives, away from all this."

I went still.

"Take what I can get," I repeated, voice flat.

He blinked like he just heard himself.

"You mean settle," I said. "Shrink myself so I fit. Clap from the sidelines like a good girl? Be silent. Be a *mouse.* I should just be grateful I was born into this family and I have money? Is that what you think I deserve?"

My hands were fists now.

"You have privilege, Miles," I said. "That's why you spend most of your time playing around town and partying. If I don't get this—if I don't *win*—then what was all this for? All the pretending. All the silence. All the blood I've swallowed just to be taken seriously. I just want to be remembered."

He stared at me.

"You're right, I won't get King Enterprises. It will go to Erik. But I'm not going to be a housewife like Laurene, and I'm not gonna be lazy like Gigi. I know I'm meant for something bigger."

I finally just picked out a black dress and pulled it up over my hips with shaking hands. But when I reached for the zipper, my fingers fumbled uselessly at the small of my back.

"My mind's made up, Miles. King Developments first, then we'll see."

I stood there in silence for a beat, eyes shut, furious at myself for needing him in even the smallest way.

"It can't happen any other way."

Then I felt him behind me.

No words.

His mouth found my neck. Hot, soft, trailing down. I clenched my fists, trying to suppress the desperate urge to turn around and throw myself at him.

"I can't win against your family," he murmured against my skin, tongue flicking just beneath my ear. "I definitely can't change your mind. I would never try to change you or invalidate your feelings, Sunny."

"J-just let me finish my plan. Then…then we can tell them." I gasped.

I felt his breath on my neck, his lips brushing once more across the place where my shoulder met my throat—featherlight, like he was memorizing it.

Then, finally, he pulled the zipper up. Slowly. Excruciatingly slowly. Each inch felt like a thread unraveling inside me, a slow, agonizing pull. I turned slowly to stare into his dark brown eyes.

With a gentle touch, my fingers cupped his cheek, his beard, coarse and dark, scratching against my palm. He was all golden-brown skin and sharp edges softened by a mess of tight curls that looked like they hadn't been brushed, just pushed through with frustrated fingers. I traced the faint dusting of brown freckles across the bridge of his nose.

What did I do to be blessed by him?

I kissed him.

Slow. Firm. Deep.

I savored the sweetness of the wine on his tongue as it gently pressed against mine. His hand slid up, fingers grazing my spine, and I melted into the curve of his chest like I had a hundred times before. I fisted my hands in his suit jacket, pressing my body to him where there was no space.

With a breath, I released his lips and inhaled shakily, looking up at him.

"Handle your father."

Untangling myself from Miles, I headed downstairs to rejoin the party.

I spotted Mama and Daddy at the far end of the room, whispering vehemently among themselves. It was only when I got close that I heard Mama hiss, "He's on something, Vincent!"

I almost gasped as Omar Whitmore stumbled through the crowd, his champagne glass tilting dangerously in his loose grip.

That's not drunk. I know *drunk*. Drunk is falling into a gardenia bush after too many martinis or flirting with someone's husband.

What started off as a simple party was now becoming a *Jerry Springer* episode.

The day after the most beautiful night of my life. Of course everything went wrong.

"Relax, Vonnie. He's fine," Daddy said, but I could see he didn't believe himself.

"This is not the first time. Look! He's sweating like this is the Mississippi Delta! He's falling over, and his eyes look blacked out like an alien," Mama said. "He ain't been right since his father died."

"You weren't any better," Daddy reminded her. Mama glared at him.

I expected tonight to be low-key. Simple but luxurious. A big King party for the whole town before Laurene's engagement party next week, complete with rosé, twinkling lights, and that laidback summer feel that Lush brings.

"You saw him at the mayor's gala when the press was interviewing him. He looked unshaven and dirty like some drifter."

"That's just grief," Daddy said, standing up for his best friend.

Mama's glare didn't ease up. "I never let myself go like this when my daddy died. Omar gave a sloppy, rambling speech at the town hall. He crashed my Women of Lush networking brunch, and you know much time I put into that, Vincent, don't act dumb."

"It could be depression. Anxiety?"

"And? What does that have to do with him messing up my party?" Mama put her hands on her hips. "The Ashbournes are here. Lord knows we don't need to give them any more ammunition than they already have. All the families that matter in Lush are here. Mayor Johnson, the *Lush Chronicles*, investors, *donors—*"

I knew better than to interrupt when Mama was pissed. My eyes flicked back to Omar.

"He's our friend," Daddy said, wincing as he watched Omar fall into a guest who yelped.

Despite what Miles thought, Mama *had* been dropping hints about giving me King Developments. She wanted to add another venture to King Enterprises, but Erik was too busy with King Aviation. Laurene was obsessed with her art.

This was it. But one wrong move from me tonight, and she'd place it right back into Erik's lap without blinking.

So, I stayed still.

It was my job to ensure everything ran like clockwork tonight, and Omar was a variable I couldn't control.

"Omar, *stop!*" Audrey, his wife, cried. We all spun around to see Omar knocking a drink from a guest's hand. The woman gasped and leaped back, eyes wide with fear.

Mama would already be pissed off when I told her about the engagement. But maybe Miles was right. She loved Miles. He grew up at our house. He was the only one of us kids who could ever make her laugh.

I hoped.

"You think you're better than me?" Omar slurred with rage as he moved toward the group of guests clustered near the bar whispering. "You all think you're so *fucking* perfect. Always looking down on me..."

What could I do? I couldn't rush over and help—not without putting everything that I worked for at risk. But Miles... I had to help, didn't I?

"Pops!" Miles shouted over the crowd, walking toward him.

Omar shoved a passing staff member with a tray, sending the champagne flutes and canapés scattering across the marble floor. The server yelped as glass shattered everywhere.

"*Enough*, Omar," Daddy shouted as he and Mama rushed over to him. My heels clicked on the marble as I trailed behind her. My mind whirled with possible solutions, but nothing viable.

"Stay outta this, Vincent!" he slurred, voice all shaky. "This is all your fucking fault, you hear me? Your fault!"

"Look, man, we can discuss all that later, in private. Now ain't the time. Let's get you—" Daddy placed a hand on Omar's shoulder.

"No!" He jerked away violently, his eyes flashing with something that bordered on panic. "It can't be fixed! *They're here!*"

"Who?" Daddy's brows furrowed.

Then Mama turned, her eyes slicing toward me. "What are you *supposed* to be doing, Serena?"

"Well, I—"

It'll all be worth it when I'm finally CEO, I told myself, *when I'm not just cleaning up messes but building something that's mine within the family.*

"Pops," Miles said again, taking a step toward him cautiously.

"They're all watching," Omar muttered, his voice low, barely a whisper. His head snapped toward the corner of the room, then his gaze snapped to the left, locking on a group of guests who were watching, terrified. "They're all watching. *Everyone's watching.*"

"Omar, snap out of it! You're making a damn fool of yourself." Mama's voice was icy. The smell of her expensive perfume was sharp, almost bitter. Her manicured fingers snapped, summoning security.

I made eye contact with Miles. Inside, everything was a storm—between wanting the success I knew I was destined for and wanting what my heart yearned for.

If I said something, questions would be asked. *Why was I defending Miles? Why did I care?* Mama would look too closely, and I *knew* she would figure us out immediately. Erik would get angry. Scandal. Corruption. People would talk about me instead of Laurene.

If I spoke, I'd lose King Developments. If I didn't, I'd lose him.

How do you choose between a legacy and a love that could shatter it all?

"Handle this," Mama barked at the nearest security, snapping her fingers.

"Let's get you outta here, Omar," Daddy said softly.

One of the guards reached out, but Omar snapped—shoving the man so hard he went flying into the dessert table. Guests gasped.

"Stay the fuck away from me!"

Mama's grip tightened on my arm, her nails digging in like she needed an anchor.

A sickening thud reverberated as Omar's fists landed on Daddy's chest when he stepped forward to grab him, sending him stumbling backward and careening to the floor.

"Vincent!" Mama screamed. I jumped in front of her, gently shoving her back a bit.

Daddy hit the ground hard, groaning. Omar was on top of him, his hands clawing at Daddy's throat. It was terrifying how fast and strong he was. "Daddy!" I yelled.

Miles just stood there like a statue. His eyes were wide, not blinking, like he couldn't believe what he was seeing. He took a half step forward, then stopped. His hands twitched at his sides, but they didn't lift.

"Do something!" I yelled at Miles. "Move! Don't just stand there!"

A second guard tried to rip Omar off, but he stayed put. He was totally unaware of the hands on his shoulders. With a growl, he spun, throwing an elbow into the guard's face, sending him stumbling backward, his nose spurting blood. The guard collapsed to his knees, gasping for air, his vision likely a blur.

Everyone scattered, yelling, trying to escape from the hell unfurling.

Why couldn't Miles do something? My father was on the floor, and the man I wanted to marry was standing there stuck on stupid.

Daddy's body bucked beneath him, his hands clawing at Omar's wrists, his legs kicking out against the marble floor. His face reddened, veins bulging at his temples as he gasped for air.

I started to rush forward, but I was yanked back abruptly. "Don't you fucking dare!" Mama hissed at me, dragging me back with force. "You will not be getting hurt."

"But Daddy—"

Her grip tightened like a vise. Daddy's feet scraped the floor, his shoes scuffing the tiles as Omar's thumbs pressed into his windpipe.

Suddenly Erik was leaping through the crowd.

He crossed the room in less than two strides, and he hit Omar with a full-force shove, driving him into the floor so hard the impact sent a shock wave through the room. More security poured in, and I could see the lights from several phones recording.

Miles finally seem to jump awake, and rushed to Omar. "Pops!"

That didn't stop Omar.

He was back instantly, like a spring, lunging for Daddy again. But Miles got Omar in a rear chokehold from behind, yanking him back hard. He struggled wildly, trying to escape from his son's grip.

Omar let out a choked roar, his hands clawing at Miles's arms, his nails digging into his skin, but Miles didn't let go.

Erik was on his knees next to Daddy as he helped him up, eyeing Omar like he was bird shit on his windshield. Daddy coughed, his breathing ragged, his hand on his throat.

"Call the police," Mama barked to a staff member. "Get an ambulance here right away."

I ran over, grabbing Daddy's arm, shaking like crazy. "Daddy…"

Suddenly, Laurene and Gigi burst through the throng, their faces pale. Gigi's wail echoed over the murmur of the crowd, tears already streaming down her face as she collapsed onto Daddy and he groaned.

"I-it's okay. I'm okay…" Daddy coughed.

Miles kept wrestling with Omar. His grunts punctuated the sounds, and I saw him bite Miles's forearm.

"Damn! Stop!" Miles's voice cracked, his grip tightening.

This chaos would haunt every deal, every meeting, every family dinner we had.

With a sharp crack, Erik's fist met Omar's jaw. Omar went slack, his body crumpling into Miles's arms.

Miles held on to his father, but glared at my brother. "You ain't have to do all that. I had him."

"You didn't have *shit*. What the fuck is wrong with him?" Erik's voice was a hiss of pure venom. I could count on one hand the number of times I'd seen my brother that angry.

Miles squared his shoulders. "You think I wanted this?"

"You didn't stop it," Erik barked . "That's the same damn thing."

He took a step forward. Miles matched it. And just like that, the space between them vanished.

I moved fast, grabbing Erik's arm, tugging hard. "Erik, enough. Miles, get your father."

Miles's head turned, and the second our eyes met, I felt the shift. Not anger. Worse. Disappointment. Hurt, cold and quiet.

"That's it?" he asked, low. "Just 'get my father'? You're not gonna say something else?"

I swallowed, and Erik jerked his arm from my grip. "Why are you looking at her like that?"

Miles didn't answer. Just kept staring at me.

"Say it," he said, daring me now. "Just say it. Things can't get worse."

I blinked, my mouth parting slightly. For half a second, I thought about telling the truth. About saying I loved him.

But all I could think was, *Don't say anything. Don't give them a reason to look at you. Don't give Mama something to use.*

"I want him gone!" Mama shouted.

Miles tensed up. "Miss Yvonne—"

"Don't." Her voice was steely, firm. Her gaze flicked to Daddy, still struggling to breathe, and something in her face hardened even more.

"You think I'm going to let this slide? That I'm going to pretend like I didn't just watch him nearly choke my husband to death?" She gestured toward Daddy, toward the shattered glass, the discombobulated guests, the absolute fucking disaster of it all. "I will be pressing charges."

Miles's breath hitched. "Come on, you can't—"

"Yvonne, we're so sorry," Audrey said, tears in her eyes. Mama ignored her friend and shook her head.

"I can, and I will." Mama's voice never wavered. "This has been going on for too long."

"Honey…" Daddy's weak voice said.

"No! Audrey, we had a private conversation about your… situation, and I understood. I gave grace. But this? I can't allow that to happen."

Erik stepped closer to Mama, his hand catching mine as he tugged me gently to his side. My heels scraped against the stone as I stumbled into place.

I looked at Miles.

He looked *only* at me.

Mama shook her head. "Now get him the hell out of here before I have security drag him out like the animal he is. Our friendship? It's done. I never want your family in our presence again."

Miles's jaw clenched, his throat visibly working. Then Erik stepped in front of me like a shield—cutting the line of sight between us.

"You heard my mama." His voice was low and cold. "Get your father. Get out."

Miles didn't move.

Just…stared. Past Erik.

At me.

CHAPTER 1

Serena

PRESENT DAY

"THIS IS SLOPPY." I pointed my red laser at the crack in the ceiling. "Look at that crack."

The contractor blinked up. "I don't think that's a crack. It's a spider web."

"It's a crack," I snapped at him, and kept walking down the hall, frowning at every little imperfection I saw.

I can't believe we're still dealing with this shit.

The project was already two weeks behind schedule. Two million dollars sunk into this property. And I was losing control.

I couldn't let Mama know. Definitely not *Erik.*

I'd gotten what I wanted. King Developments was mine. He may run the empire—but this? This was mine.

Everywhere I looked, people wandered like dazed cattle like this wasn't urgent, like I hadn't already spelled out the stakes a hundred fucking times.

I stopped in the kitchen, eyes narrowing at a cabinet handle that was off center. "This isn't even aligned. Did someone eyeball this? I said three-point-two inches from the edge, not three-point-six."

The contractor flinched and scribbled something down.

Take a breath before you have a fucking stroke.

I couldn't. There were no breaks. No days off. Shit had to get done, and I had to make shit happen. I should have felt relieved. Instead, I felt…unfinished. Why wasn't this fulfilling anymore?

My jaw ached from clenching it. My temples throbbed with every heartbeat, and my shoulders felt like they'd been stitched into my ears.

It had to be perfect. *Everything* had to be perfect. Because that's what a King delivered. That's what Mama always said.

No excuses. No flaws. No weakness.

I was a goddamn machine now—a finely tuned, professionally polished, emotionless machine. The kind Mama had designed.

For six years, I hadn't made a single mistake. The only mistake had been giving my heart to something I knew was dead on arrival. I anticipated her every need. I made the company money. I didn't make anyone second-glance my way. I'd become invaluable.

I paused in the unfinished master suite, staring at the empty windows, the cold floor. If I let myself really feel, really let the silence sink in, it was always there, just under the surface.

The exhaustion.

No matter what I did, it didn't go away. No massage, or coffee, or LED light therapy could fix it. At this point, it was second nature to run on fumes. I was tired.

I couldn't remember the last time I took a real breath.

And then—like a crack in the foundation of my own thoughts—came the whisper:

What if I leave?

My heart stuttered, and I froze. What if I just…walked away? The thought was a live wire in my mind, too loud, too sharp.

But how could I leave when I'd spent years proving I could run King Developments?

I shoved the thought down before it could take root.

I wasn't going anywhere. This was mine. This was *me*. I

worked for this. I didn't miss him. I missed who I was when I thought I could have both him and King Developments.

I closed my eyes for a beat. Just one. Then I opened them.

"This backsplash is crooked," I said tightly, voice cool again. "Fix it."

It was all for a good cause. To make King Developments *untouchable*—not just successful. We would own all of California in real estate development. Was it right, what I did over the years for that goal? No. But brute force was necessary. I'd wiped all but one competitor from town.

That was my plan.

Plans kept things from slipping. Spreadsheets didn't lie. They didn't whisper behind your back or flip on you in the press. They didn't make your heart hurt. I could rely on formulas. People? Not so much.

If I got the Harrington estate, Mama would have no choice but to admit I was the future of King Developments. That's what I was looking forward to next.

It wasn't just a win. It was *the* win.

I wasn't fucking around anymore.

"We followed your specifications. I thought you—" the contractor said.

What I wanted was to take over King Enterprises. What I got was King Developments, our real estate arm of the enterprise, and hadn't I learned to do a lot with a little?

"You thought wrong," I cut him off sharply. "Now explain to me why I'm looking at this bullshit?"

His jaw flexed. He didn't answer fast enough.

Buzz.

Buzz buzz.

Texts. Emails. More things to sign off on coming through my phone.

The contractor stumbled out some piss-poor excuse.

"I'm not paying premium for fucking mediocrity," I hissed.

"You don't get to take shortcuts on *my* job. You understand that, right? Or do you need someone to draw you a picture?"

"N-no, Miss King…"

Buzz.

Buzz.

Buzz buzz buzz.

I exhaled sharply through my nose.

"You have twenty-four hours to make this right," I said. "Or I *will* make an example out of you."

I turned, shifting my Chanel purse on my shoulder, and then looked back at him.

"You will give me a *hefty, hefty* discount that will be on my office desk in an hour as well for my pain and suffering for all that I witnessed today."

"Miss King—"

"Get to fucking work," I demanded. Most of the workers who'd been nosy listening to our conversation scattered as I walked by.

Text messages continued to flood my phone, each notification a jarring reminder of everything else going wrong with my life.

Did he do this? Did he secretly pay Leonard to sabotage this place? I hadn't thought about it till now, but I believed it.

This had Miles over all it. This property had been nothing but trouble since we got it. Or rather, since I snatched it out from under Miles. God, I hated him. He'd said *nothing* when he left. Just like I said nothing that night.

He'd turned from my lover to my worst rival.

I chose this over him. I can't regret it now.

I made it to my Range Rover and pulled out my phone to see the family group chat going crazy with nonsense memes from Gigi, Laurene's constant pictures of baby stuff she'd bought, and Erik's thumbs-ups.

Didn't I mute this text thread?

It wasn't like I ever responded, and none of siblings cared to ask why.

Suddenly, the shrill ring of the phone made me jump. I checked the caller ID. Mama. I breathed deeply as I settled into the driver's seat.

"Serena, we gotta talk about Laurene's baby shower tomorrow," Mama said when I answered.

Great.

"Yes, ma'am," I said, trying to sound cheerful.

After the showdown between Mama and Laurene when she was in the hospital after her car crash last year, I thought maybe something had shifted in our mother.

Mama, the woman who ruled this family like a kingdom, had *softened*. Not with everyone. Just with Laurene. Now that Lu was pregnant, Mama acted like she was the second coming.

That softness? That grace?

She never showed that to me.

"You're responsible for getting us the perfect present," she said matter-of-factly. "I'm stressed enough dealing with Reese's mother and sister's tacky décor."

Buzz. Another text from the project site. I didn't look at it.

I rubbed my temples, my eyes fluttering shut as the pressure built up. A little throb in my head told me a migraine was brewing.

"Make sure it's something really special. We don't want to look like we're just showing up with any old thing," Mama continued.

"Right," I murmured.

"Also, I need you to coordinate with Erik. He's already had a brilliant lunch with that investor from Charleston—the real estate one with the vineyard son? He's lining something up with the Heritage Commission too. He's doing so well lately." She said it like it was news. Like it hadn't been the headline of every conversation since January.

I opened my eyes.

"I thought *I* was coordinating with the commission. Since when does he deal with anything related to my company?"

"You were," she said vaguely. "Either way, he's handling it now. That lets you handle the baby shower."

She said it so easy. Like it was nothing.

"Understood," I said, my voice smooth, unbothered. "I've got it covered."

Through the tinted window, I watched my contractor storm out to scream at the crew again. Another mistake. Another delay.

"And I need you to run to the florist and handle the new arrangements I made. The flowers they tried to give us were poor quality. Too…common. You know what I like. Make sure they're at the country club in an hour."

I opened my mouth to protest, but she continued.

"Make sure you're there early to help set up. And bring me a latte from Café L'Amour while you're on your way too. Oat milk, sugar-free syrup. We just need the right gift to tie it all together." Another pause. "Did I already say that?"

"Yes, Mama. I've got it handled."

"Good," Mama said, and the call ended without a goodbye.

I stared at the dark screen for a beat too long.

If I screamed, no one would hear it through the soundproof glass.

If I cried, it would smear my mascara.

My phone buzzed incessantly again. The screen was a chaotic mess of notifications—texts from my mother giving me more orders, messages from my assistant about urgent issues at the company, Gigi sending us pictures of Walter in a sweater.

As I scrolled through the onslaught, a new text notification appeared from an unknown number. My heart skipped a beat as I read the message: *We need to talk.*

Fuck.

I hadn't thought about *her* in forever. How the fuck did she get my number?

I blocked her number and quickly deleted the message, my fingers shaking a bit.

Miles entered my thoughts again. It wasn't real love. It

couldn't have been. Not if it ended that easily. I'd made the right call. I had to.

I shoved it down. Hard. I wasn't going anywhere. This was who I was.

This was *all* I was.

I screamed uncontrollably, overwhelmed.

My fist slammed against the steering wheel, again and again. The sting was nothing compared to the mess inside me. Tears blurred my vision. My breath broke into heaving sobs, and still, I kept pounding. Until my knuckles bruised. Until my throat burned. Until I didn't sound like myself anymore.

And then—silence.

I crumpled forward, forehead against the wheel, every muscle trembling. My temple pulsed with a sharp, familiar ache. I reached into the glove compartment with shaking fingers, fumbling until I found the bottle. No water. I didn't care. I tossed the aspirin back and swallowed it dry, nearly choking.

Then I sat up.

I smoothed my suit jacket, wiping my face with the back of my hand.

I stared into the mirror. And when I blinked—

Serena King stared back.

Unbothered. Untouchable. Unbreakable.

CHAPTER 2
Miles

"THIS IS BAD NEWS, MILES," Carlus, my second-in-command, told me the second I stepped into the hospital hallway.

I didn't even kill the engine. Left the Porsche idling out front. I did ninety across town, ignoring every red light. I needed this not to be true.

Was this as bad as when Serena mailed back the engagement ring?

Nah. That shit sucked. She might have burned it. Selling it would've been colder. But no—she mailed it. Efficient. Professional. Serena to the bone.

"How bad?" I asked, already adjusting the cuff of my suit, smoothing down nothing. I made sure to keep the smile on my face. Jokes typically made things easier. Hell, when we laid off a big chunk of staff a few months back, my smiles and jokes took some of the heat off my ass.

Not the typical CEO way, but it worked for me.

I caught sight of Reggie. One of our best guys. Built like a damn fridge, now laid out like a Jenga tower someone tipped over. Cast, traction, wires.

Fuck.

Carlus rubbed the back of his neck. "He fell off the second floor. Faulty railing. He's lucky to be alive."

"At least now he has time to catch up on all those HR safety videos he kept skipping." I nudged his arm.

Carlus didn't laugh, and I cleared my throat, wiping my face. No.

Nothing about this was remotely fucking funny, but it was all I could do to not show a panicked man watching his company bleed out.

I sighed, running a hand over my face as I looked in front of me.

A lawsuit waiting to happen. Insurance was already thin. This delay? It'd cost me six figures, minimum.

And more than that, my reputation. The comeback I was staging? The redemption tour for the Whitmore name? Slipping. Again.

"Let's not say 'faulty railing' out loud anymore," I said quietly. "Until we find out what really happened. Maybe Reggie tripped. Maybe he's clumsy as hell."

"This ain't a joke, Miles. This shit is serious."

I forced a chuckle. "Tough room."

My phone buzzed in my pocket for the third time. I ignored it. Whoever it was could wait. Probably someone else needing money, answers, miracles.

I watched Reggie breathe through the mask. Shit.

This was all Serena King.

Every time I rebuilt, Serena found a way to swing the wrecking ball with a smile on her face. Nothing says "I hate your guts" like stealing a $20 million development out from under you.

The woman knew how to grip me by the balls. Funny… How love quickly turned to hate.

I gritted my teeth, jaw ticking as I replayed the last few months in my head like a horror reel. She took the last beach-front property I'd been working on for *months*. In Lush, practically nobody fucking left town or sold generational property. I'd taken the owner—a sweet, stubborn old widow—*salsa dancing*. *Me*. Salsa.

But I was willing and able to do anything to save Whitmore Ventures. We belonged in this town, just like the Kings.

And just when I thought I had it locked, Serena swooped in like the fucking angel of death she was and stole it. Probably promised the woman a goddamn statue or a yacht or some bullshit. And poof. Paper signed.

Game over.

She'd been tormenting me for months, years, really—cutting off my suppliers, spreading rumors, cherry-picking my investors like she was harvesting grapes for a goddamn King family wine.

That woman was a walking apocalypse.

She'd been relentless. Ruthless. And sure, I used to admire that about her. Hell, I used to *want* her. Still kind of did.

She always wanted power. I just wanted her. I once thought we could have both.

The few times I'd seen her recently, that ass was looking tight in those old lady slacks she wore. But I also wanted to throw her through a window. Metaphorically. Maybe. Even now, I'd probably lose my damn mind if she walked through that door.

"I don't feel anything for you, Miles." She took a step forward, and I gritted my teeth when I felt my body heat at the brush of her against me. "But I will destroy you. Every. Single. Bit. Of you."

That's what she said to me last year at Café L'Amour. A part of me saw her cutting me down and thought, *maybe she's the only one who still sees me standing.*

But I was the roach she couldn't squash. The charming bastard who always managed to crawl out of the wreckage. Even now, with the building falling apart—literally—I still had pieces on the board.

"Are you even listening to me?" Carlus's voice jolted me from my thoughts.

I blinked.

"This is some *serious* shit. More shit than we've dealt with in the past. It ain't a game."

I pinched the bridge of my nose, head throbbing like it had been waiting for me to notice. "You don't think I know that? You think I wanted to get a call about this? It's been fucking shit show after shit show. You don't think *I* want a break?"

Calm. Be cool, Miles.

The company didn't need a saint. It needed a fast talker with a toolkit of backup plans and a bulletproof smile.

I was trying to make my last name mean something again. Trying to build a legacy out of the ash and cocaine residue my father had left behind. I was thirty-three and felt seventy.

I hadn't slept through the night in years. But I smiled. I shook hands. I gave speeches. Because people expected a Whitmore to stand tall even when the world was kicking him in the teeth. I had my instincts. And instincts had gotten me this far.

I glanced back at Reggie.

"You'll be alright," I murmured. For him or for me, I wasn't sure.

Carlus shook his head. "I don't know if it will be."

"We don't have the luxury of falling apart over it." My voice was sharp, but the weight in my chest was sharper. "We need a solution. Fast. Before this gets into the *Lush Chronicles*."

My family had been in that damn gossip rag so many times over the years, I think sometimes they just put our names in there when internet traffic got low.

"You know I'm here for you, big man. I'm not going nowhere. Don't panic. Don't we always figure a way out?"

My phone buzzing made me jump.

I'd been reaching out to some new investors, people I didn't think Serena had managed to touch. If we could get some new money in, that could help this go away.

Please let it be good news.

Disappointment flooded through me as I glanced at the screen.

Not the potential new investor, but a text from Gwyn, a name that I only vaguely remembered.

Are you free tonight, handsome?

I rolled my eyes. Fucking wasn't on my radar right now. Gwyn looked at me like most of the women in town did. Like I was still Miles, the playboy. People would always remind me.

My intention was to set things straight for my company. Not fuck up and make another mistake. Some things were beyond repair, regardless of my desire to change it.

Scrolling through my contacts, I found Serena's name.

Sunny.

I started calling her that because she was the most serious person I'd ever met.

Even when we were kids, she didn't smile. Not once, not genuinely—not unless she was scheming or sparring with me. Cold, composed, terrifyingly brilliant.

But I saw the fire under all that ice. The way her mind never stopped moving. Her curiosity and compassion. The rare moments when she let herself laugh—God, they were blinding. It felt like the sun came out just for me.

So yeah, *Sunny.* Because it pissed her off. But I never stopped using it. And I never stopped waiting to see her shine again.

Even after three phones, I still had her number.

"We can't let this get out," I said.

Carlus turned to me slowly. "You're saying cover it?"

"I'm saying *contain* it." I rubbed the bridge of my nose, trying to breathe around the tension. "If this ends up in the *Lush Chronicles*—'Whitmore Crewman Injured in Unsafe Conditions'—we're finished. I'll lose the next project before I ever bid."

Carlus folded his arms. "You want me to talk to his family?"

"Yeah. Just…soften it. Say we're taking care of everything—hospital bills, worker's comp, hell, I'll even cover the damn groceries for the month. But they don't talk to anyone until I say so."

Carlus nodded. "It's done."

"Get the site shut down for two days. Say it's for a safety review. Quiet. No press." I clenched my fists.

"It's already in motion." Carlus slapped me on the shoulder, then squeezed. "I'll go sit with him a bit."

I waited until Carlus entered the room, then let out the breath I hadn't realized I'd been holding. I wanted to punch something —anything to release the furious energy coursing through me.

This was supposed to be the comeback year.

I was so fucking tired.

Tired of smiling through failure. Tired of pretending this wasn't all one long free fall from grace. Every damn day, I woke up and tried to will this company—and my last name—back into respectability like it was a corpse I could drag upright. But no matter how many boardrooms I pitched in or palms I greased, the whispers always came back: *That's Omar's boy. You remember what he did?*

This situation was the kind of thing that would bleed out slow—one photo, one blog post, one ugly headline at a time. It wouldn't matter that I paid every bill or that I handled it in private.

Optics were everything in this town.

And the vultures would circle. Like they did when Pops was dragged out to the cop car in cuffs where all our friends and family could see. How the lights and press were in our faces during the trial. That was six years ago, but the way people in town behaved, you woulda thought it happened yesterday.

What the fuck was I really fighting for?

Everything. I had to. Because no one was coming to save us.

I knew above all I couldn't wait to watch everyone in this town—Serena, Erik, all the Kings—eat fucking shit and be shocked by the way I turned things around.

That was what the last six years have been about: proving everybody and their bald-headed aunties dead wrong.

They were wrong when they said the Whitmores would never make it again. They were wrong when they said we'd only hold our heads in shame. They were wrong when they said we would run from the town my relatives helped build with our tails between our legs.

Whitmores were petty above all.

But we didn't run. Never that.

One day, it won't be us ducking our heads in shame. It'll be them. All of them. Looking up at me from the dirt, wondering how the hell I did it.

Yes, my father fucked up. But I was turning this ship around.

So, if Serena wanted to fight dirty—sabotaging sites, stealing clients, sweet-talking people I danced salsa with, for Christ's sake—fine.

I'll admit, I wasn't going as hard as I could be. Now? Fuck feelings. Fuck these people. They meant nothing to me anymore.

I was coming for the Kings. I was coming for Serena. I was coming for *Lush*.

And they better hope they fucking survived.

And I knew there was one property she wanted in town that could make her. That *I* was going to take.

I couldn't *wait* for that moment. I couldn't wait to finally say it.

Told you so.

CHAPTER 3
Serena

"PERFECT," I mumbled, taking another sip of wine as I looked around the room.

It was a beautiful sunny day for Laurene and Reese's baby shower.

A low hum of conversation filled the air as I surveyed my hard work. Delicate pink roses and lilies adorned the table, their fragrance mingling with the baked goods from Laurene's favorite bakery in Paris I had shipped overnight as a surprise for her.

There were even more flowers set around a sign that took me nearly an hour to pin up against a backdrop of pink and gold tulle and a balloon arch that announced "It's a Girl!"

My task was simple: ensure Laurene's special day went off without a hitch. Keep everything in line. Keep everyone happy.

"Rena! Chill the hell out, have you had one of these macarons? They good as hell," Gigi yelled out to me, strutting in her pink wrap dress and too-high heels snacking on a dessert. "Imma need you to order me like a dozen of these after, okay? Have a shot of tequila, unwind. You got a joint?"

"I don't have time, Georgiana," I muttered to my little sister, rolling my eyes.

"Why you gotta call me by my government name?" She pouted, nudging me with a shoulder bump. "You been acting like you the one pregnant. C'mon, chill. It's a happy day. When was the last time you got some head?"

I whipped my head toward her. "What? Lower your voice."

Gigi could just float through life, pretty and messy and somehow still adored.

She didn't stay up until three a.m. arranging pink and ivory gift bags. She didn't double-check the caterer or make sure the press stayed out or redirect Aunt Eloise when she started talking about how Laurene "used to be so tiny."

No. That was me. Always me. No one else in the family besides Mama had the ability to be controlled and disciplined like me.

Gigi sipped champagne like it was juice and took another bite of the macaron while she shook her head. "I'm telling you. Keep frowning, you're gonna get lines that Botox ain't gonna get out."

I mentally reviewed the timeline for Laurene's gift opening and made a note to check whether the staff had brought in the custom bassinet.

"I'm serious. I got something in my flask that'll put some hair on your chest." Gigi leaned forward, showing the metal bottle stuffed down between her boobs.

"I don't want your warm boob flask liquor." I rolled my eyes at her, and she linked her arm with mine as we scoped out the crowd. It was just like with Laurene's first engagement party years ago. Everyone kissed ass to be here and be nosy. Vultures.

How did I get through mind-numbing events like this?

Miles.

He wasn't even here, and somehow, he still managed to hijack my thoughts. Typical.

"Are you suuure?" A sly grin spread across her face. She leaned closer, her voice dropping to a whisper. "I bought this absinthe when I was in Spain last year, and I swear I was hearing colors and smelling sounds."

"No."

Miles liked being the center of attention at these parties. He used to find me in corners like this. Slip me a drink, crack a joke, make me laugh when I wasn't supposed to. He could read me. Not in the way people pretend to. In the way that made it hard to lie—to him or to myself.

He'd made everything easy.

Now I couldn't even picture that version of me—soft, breathless, hopeful. She was long gone. Packed up and shipped off when he chose his father and I chose my family.

"For real? Let me show you a good time! I had it in Amsterdam, right after the sex show and me and my man—" I gave her a look, and she grinned sheepishly. "Save the absinthe for later? Gotcha."

We settled in silence, and our eyes followed Laurene as she laughed. Reese, our new brother-in-law and former enemy, was right next to her, his hand placed protectively on her protruding stomach. She was glowing, and it made me appreciate how much we'd achieved since she came back home over a year ago.

"She looks so happy," Gigi said with a sigh.

How did Laurene pull it off?

I couldn't just disappear for six years and come back home. I wasn't the one who could mesh seamlessly in and out of society. People here didn't extend the same grace to me as they did Laurene. She was the perfect girl. Someone fit for a town like Lush.

Laurene's return and arranged marriage to Reese Ashbourne had been the talk of the town for months. But somehow my older sister had found love in a crazy situation.

Miles used to look at me like I was something he couldn't resist, something he *needed*. Was it just because no one else looked at me that way that I fell for it? I gave in to those silly feelings of believing in the fairy tale. That his eyes were true when he looked at me like there was no one else in the room.

He *always* saw me.

That made me the perfect target.

Gigi continued and squeezed my arm tighter. "It's like we've come full circle, huh? We didn't know what was going to happen to her or if Mama would let her come back. I mean, it felt like a piece of us was missing. But now we're all here, together again. Both of my big sisters."

I kept my expression neutral, though her words stabbed deeper than she realized. How easy it was for Gigi to believe in that kind of simple, happy ending? I couldn't do that.

"Do you…do you think we'll be happy too? When our marriages get arranged? Or will it be all sad and shit like the ladies from the fifteenth century when they sold you for a goat and a pot of sugar?"

Unfortunately, that made me laugh, but then I shook my head at her and frowned.

The truth was love didn't belong to us. Or at least to *some* of us. I wished someone had told me the truth years ago about our position in this town. We were privileged beyond belief. But with that came restrictions. Gigi would have to fall in line someday.

"We all have roles to play when it comes to King Enterprises. Business first. Always. We don't get the luxury of a 'happily ever after.'"

Like I expected, Gigi's face fell.

You can lie about this, Serena. You've lied about so much else.

"But with your charm, wit, and boobs, I'm sure no man will resist you, G. They'll fall at your feet."

Immediately, Gigi perked up.

"You're right, men do fall at my feet. I'm sexy." She licked her lips and sat up straighter. "What the hell am I worried for?"

My phone buzzed in my pocket, but I just listened to Gigi go on about her good looks. Eventually, Laurene turned, and we watched her finally detangle herself from Reese, and wave to us.

She waddled toward us, her hand on her belly, and gave us the *look*. Who pissed her off this time? Pregnant, hormonal Lu was a new beast. "I need a favor."

"What, oil bleeding through your foundation? Need me to powder you?" Gigi raised her brow. "I will get that face *beat* in a minute."

Laurene placed her hand near her face. "Oh my God, do I look bad?"

"No," I said and gave Gigi a look. "Absolutely not. You look perfect."

Laurene seemed to calm down before exhaling deeply, looking over her shoulder.

"I've been watching the dessert table and people keep eating those raspberry tarts. I saw Mayor Castillo put three in his pocket. Don't cause a scene, but I want some for later, and if I don't, I might cry and that'll make Reese fight the mayor, then he'll go to jail, and my child won't have a father—"

I sighed loudly, and Gigi grinned.

"You want us to hide treats from the fine-ass mayor?" Gigi asked, and I just rolled my eyes. "I mean, I can do more than just distract him. Look at me."

"Stash a few away for me for when I get up snacking in the middle of the night, and baby girl here will think you both are the best aunts *ever*."

"Don't try to suck up," I told Laurene. She batted her brown eyes at me, and already I was mentally contacting the baker to get an entire tray delivered to her house tomorrow morning.

Gigi chuckles, digging into the front of her dress, taking a hit of the suspect absinthe. She passed the bottle to me, and I balked at the warm feeling of the flask before she gave her cleavage a little push-up.

"Glad to help, big sis." She swiped gloss over her lips. "Out of my way."

Laurene and I looked at each other as Gigi pushed past us and headed straight for Mayor Castillo.

He watched her like a panther eyeing prey. A slow smile touched his face when she stopped, all hips and attitude. He had that kind of smile that said *I know exactly who you are.* Gigi said something—too far away for me to hear—but it made Dante's brow arch. He moved in slightly.

Laurene sighed beside me. "Tell me you're seeing this."

"Oh, I see it," I muttered.

"I miss pâté," then she looked at my glass. "I miss wine. And sushi. I wish this baby would come out of me."

I glanced at her, studying the familiar contours of her face. Laurene had always been striking—tall, with warm brown skin that glowed even more now stretched over high cheekbones, and a sharp jawline. Her long hair, dark and thick, spilled past her shoulders in soft waves, framing her face in a way that made her look regal.

But there was something different now.

The roundness of her stomach, the slight puffiness in her face. She was still my sister, but she wasn't just Laurene anymore. She was someone's mother.

"How did you do it, Lulu?" I said it without thinking. "Come back home after everything that happened?"

Laurene had always been *the* Laurene King—perfect, admired, the one everyone gravitated toward without question. The first girl of the family. Erik, the hotshot, had his future laid out for him. And Gigi, well, Gigi had charm in excess, the kind of chaotic magnetism that made people want to be around her.

I'd learned to copy charm. Watched how Laurene tilted her head. How Gigi laughed at the right moment. I could mimic it, wear it like a dress. But it never fit.

Why couldn't I be like them?

I didn't need to be *liked*. That's what I told myself. That was what people like Laurene were for. I was the mind, not the heart. I didn't need the room to love me—just to follow my lead.

"It was tough." Her eyes softened. "It was a struggle, but Lush was always home, even when I fought it."

"But it's always been a breeze for you," I said. "After you left, Mama made me go to the galas and parties, but I couldn't do it right. You always made these parties so much fun. All the guys wanted to dance with you, and the girls wanted to be like you."

"It might've seemed like that," she said. "Didn't mean I was happy then."

"But at least people noticed and cared about you," I replied softly.

Laurene turned to me, her expression shifting—not defensive, not dismissive, just *watchful.*

"Serena." Her voice was quieter now. "What's going on with you?"

I chose my words carefully. "It's just…everything's shifted."

"Shifted?"

No. No. Immediately, I felt the resistance coil inside me, instinctual and unshakable. I didn't do this. I didn't share. I dealt with my emotions, neatly packaged them away, and kept moving forward.

"This is your baby shower. We shouldn't be talking about this." I wasn't about to steal her shine.

"Hey," Laurene said softly. "It's okay. We can talk about it. I'm here for you, no matter what."

I hesitated, my fingers tightening around the stem of my glass. The words were heavy, stuck in my throat. Admitting uncertainty felt like relinquishing the last bit of control I had left.

"I've just…lost sight of who I am, or who I thought I was supposed to be," I said. "It's scary, it's not like me."

"Are you sure it's about knowing who you are? Or is it about being scared to finally choose for yourself?" She sighed when I didn't reply. "You've always been the most disciplined out of all of us. The most controlled. But sometimes, Serena, control is just another way of following orders."

I hated how easily she could see it—how fast she cut through the layers I'd spent years perfecting.

That meant other people could see through me.

I wasn't supposed to be this tired. This angry. This…brittle. And yet, every win felt emptier than the last. Every headline, every closed deal, every fake smile at another industry gala—it all felt like feeding a machine that never noticed I was the one keeping it running.

"I *chose* this," I said, more to myself than her. "No one forced me."

Laurene didn't argue. She just looked at me like she knew better.

"Anyway," I said, voice cooler now, steadier, "none of that matters. I'm fine."

It was a lie. But if I said it enough times, maybe I could still believe it.

Laurene sighed and shook her head. "I don't want you to wake up one day and realize you built an empire for *her*, not for yourself. I think you're scared of disappointing her, of disappointing us because you aren't what we expect. Do you even know who you are?"

"You think I don't know what I'm doing?"

"I think you're great at what you *do*," Laurene said simply. "I just don't know if you ever stopped to ask if it's what you *want*, or if you're just eliminating competition, because that's how Mama raised us to survive."

The words hit deep, scraping against something I wasn't ready to acknowledge. "You're pregnant and suddenly full of wisdom, huh?"

"Motherhood does that to you."

Regret, regret, regret. It was beating in my heart and mind like a steel drum, and I couldn't silence it.

Because the truth was, I didn't know who I was if I wasn't winning. I didn't know what I offered if I wasn't delivering results. If I stopped being useful—stopped being *her*—what was left?

Who would stay?

All of a sudden, the doors flew open, and the room immediately went silent.

"Why…why are *they* here?" I was so shocked, the words came out before I could stop them.

Miles Whitmore had entered the room.

Damn him.

He stood tall, all lean muscle and quiet arrogance. Built like a swimmer. His shirt clung to a chest I once clawed at. Tattoos peeked from his right sleeve, ink curling down the forearm that had once pinned mine to silk sheets. Slacks rested low on narrow hips, hinting at a body I knew far too well.

His skin—golden brown, sun-kissed—held the warmth of summer, of long afternoons spent outside, of a man who never truly stayed still. His braids were pulled tight, framing the sharp lines of his face. That beard, trimmed just enough, only emphasized those full lips. The ones that used to say my name like a promise.

Then his eyes found mine—dark, unreadable, burning.

Mama's gasp cut through the room, snapping my attention to her.

"What the *hell* are they doing here?" she hissed through gritted teeth as she came over to us, fixing her glare squarely on Laurene. "They shouldn't be here!"

"I asked them to come." Laurene didn't look back at us as she squeezed my arm before letting it go, turning to go greet Miles and his family.

The room around us seemed to hold its breath as Mama's gaze remained locked on Laurene's retreating figure, her expression an open battlefield of emotions—anger burned brightest, but beneath it, there were traces of something harder to define. Pain? Regret?

I kept my eyes on Laurene as she greeted Audrey with a

wide, bright smile and a warm hug, Reese quickly joining them with an equally cheerful smile. She was now talking with Miles, his face open and unguarded in a way that I hadn't seen in years.

He still hadn't looked at me.

"We can't just let it go," Mama said again, quieter this time but no less pointed. "Right, Serena?"

My pulse ticked under my skin as I stared straight at him. He tilted his head back, the sun catching on his skin as he let out a low, unbothered laugh at whatever Laurene said. That smile—lazy, cocky, boyish—curled at the edge of his mouth like he didn't just crash my damn party.

I couldn't stop staring at his lips.

God, I remembered the way they felt against my neck. The way they moved when he called me baby in that voice low enough to crawl under my skin and stay there.

I hated him.

"Serena!"

"Yes, ma'am," I responded instantly.

Daddy appeared. He moved with quiet authority, his warm gaze landing on me first before flickering over to the Whitmores. The color drained from his brown skin.

"Serena," he said gently, placing a steady hand on my shoulder when he got to us. "You holding up okay?"

"I'm fine, Daddy."

"Vincent," Mama hissed. "This is exactly what I didn't want."

"I know, Vonnie," he said, his tone steady but firm. "But we need to handle this carefully. You, Laurene, and Serena put so much into this event, and the last thing we need is a scene. Today is about Laurene and our future granddaughter. Let's focus on that."

Mama seemed to deflate. Her lips pressed into a thin line, but she didn't argue. With that, Daddy gently guided Mama and me toward the Whitmores and Laurene.

"Vince. Miss Yvonne." Miles gave a smile so smooth it nearly slid off his face. "Well, damn. Y'all still look allergic to joy."

Nobody laughed, and I narrowed my gaze. "Still with the same bad jokes, huh?"

"Still uptight, I see," he snapped back.

Reese tried to reduce some of the tension. "Thanks for coming and bringing a gift. Please tell me it's that baby saddle I wanted."

Miles made everything a joke—because that's what feelings were to him. Punchlines. Deflections.

But that's what made us work, wasn't it?

CHAPTER 4

Serena

"PLEASE TELL me you didn't come to ruin this celebration. Haven't you done enough?" Mama snapped at the Whitmores.

"Can't ruin something we were *invited* to," Miles replied.

I'd been careful to avoid the places he haunted, to rewrite my routine in a town we once shared. Still, every now and then, he'd slip through the cracks. Like that night a few months ago—dinner, some girl on his arm, laughing. Before that, that encounter at Café L'Amour.

Here he was. Again. And damn it if my heart didn't remember how to ache.

"Excuse us for not rolling out the welcome mat. I don't forget how someone we trusted attacked us and ruined over thirty years of friendship," Mama continued. "Should I have security come now or later?"

"That's behind me," Omar snapped. "You don't need to keep bringing it up, Yvonne."

"I know you're not talking," Mama shot back. "Still snorting? Or just sticking to the pills now?"

I was so transfixed with Miles I didn't feel Erik come up beside me and stand next to Mama. He remained silent.

Instinctively, Miles and I stepped forward. He was sweating

and breathing hard; his cologne was strong and really familiar. Sharp. Male. Trouble.

Too close. Not close enough.

He still wouldn't look at me. *Why do I care?*

"This is my *baby shower*," Laurene hissed at Mama. "You're causing a scene."

"You know how important it is for us to look collected to the rest of the town." Mama pointed to a guest who was whispering and staring at us wide-eyed. "This is not looking cool, calm, and collected. Quite the opposite."

"Mama, *enough!*" Laurene said.

"Hell, everybody in here knows Omar was doing crack. It's not some secret. But why you insist on dragging us through the mud like it's a damn thrill ride, Laurene Elizabeth? I have no idea why, but you could have done this in *private.*"

"You need to get your mama up under control. She's talking real wild right now," Miles gritted out, and I saw his mom, Audrey, place a hand on his shoulder.

"Watch your mouth," Erik growled, looking Miles up and down.

I inhaled deeply.

"Serena, get security over here immediately. Get the drinks flowing. And make sure no one outside the room finds out they were here. I don't need this mess splashed across the *Lush Chronicles* if, God forbid, Omar wants a second chance at taking your father out." Mama stood closer to Erik as she glared at the Whitmores.

"You're embarrassing yourself," Audrey said tightly. "You're the one ruining everything, not us."

Mama's eyes locked on her. "Don't act holier than thou, Audrey. Smiling in my face back then while your husband was trying to kill mine."

"He didn't try to kill anybody!" Audrey barked. "He had a breakdown!"

Mama let out a sharp laugh. "Oh, is that what we're calling coke-fueled assaults now?"

"This is why I didn't want to come," Omar muttered.

"Well, then roll your ass out, Omar, and take your accomplices with you," Mama said.

"You act like you don't have skeletons, Miss Yvonne. Let's not be quick to call the kettle black," Miles said.

"Miles—" Laurene warned.

"Mama," Erik said. Not sharp. Not scolding. But enough to make Mama blink and lift her chin. He stepped forward, taking up the space like it belonged to him. "Not here," he said. "Not like this. You raised us to handle things with discretion, right? So let's honor that."

I waited for Mama to argue. To lash out. To remind him who ran this family.

She didn't.

She exhaled—slow and tight—and gave him a single nod. Just like that.

And I felt it, sharp and familiar, that stinging little knot of heat behind my ribs.

I understood her relationship with Laurene—at least now. She had set a boundary, and Mama didn't dare cross it with her. But Erik?

Mama *listened* to him.

"C'mon, Vonnie." Daddy grabbed her arm, leading her away. "Let's try some dessert."

"Oh, so I'm the villain now?" Mama asked.

"You are," Miles said.

Erik pointed at Miles as they were basically chest to chest. "I don't care what history we got with each other. You don't talk sideways at her like that again. Not while I'm standin' here."

"How about a drink, Mr. Whitmore?" Reese asked Omar and Audrey.

I'd forgotten he was standing there watching, his arm around Laurene, holding her close as his eyes flicked between the mess that was all of us. Omar looked at his wife, who nodded. "We could use one."

Reese led them off toward the bar, and Laurene squeezed my arm before following them.

I locked eyes with Miles.

"Rena," Erik murmured, and I jumped, feeling like I'd been caught, and turned to him.

"Don't let him rile you," he said, chin tilting just barely toward Miles.

I bristled. "I'm not."

"You are."

I folded my arms, defensive. "Since when do you care who I look at?"

Surprisingly, Erik smiled instead of getting mad. "If he does something, come to me. I'm here for you."

"I need some air," I mumbled.

I'd thrown the perfect shower. I'd accounted for flowers, food, lighting—every little detail. And still, the party was ruined.

Breathe, just breathe.

I paused, tilted my head back, closed my eyes, and soaked up the sun. If I had someone bring out more champagne, maybe people would focus on the drinks instead of Mama storming off and probably cussing.

A new playlist. Something softer. Distracting. And maybe if I gave an impromptu toast—no, too desperate. A game? Too childish.

Think. Think.

How can I fix this? My brain spun through solutions like a Rolodex. I needed to control the narrative before this made it to the *Lush Chronicles*. Before someone posted a video.

Damage control. Not panic. Not failure. Just…strategy.

So why did it feel like I was about to cry? Why couldn't I stop thinking about the past? I thought it was dead and gone.

"If they think they've won, you've already lost," Jenese once told me. *"Control the room before the room controls you."*

"Serena." Miles's low rumble chilled me.

"Didn't you hear my brother? What do you want?" I asked without turning around. My voice was surprisingly calm, despite the inner turmoil I felt. "If you came to piss me off, you did."

"Cold as ice, baby, always so cold as ice."

"Why the hell are you still here?"

Miles snorted. "To give you a good look at all this sexiness you been missing, of course. I got a six-pack now. Wanna touch?"

I gave him a look of disgust, but my eyes couldn't help but glance at his stomach, unfortunately covered by the shirt.

"That why you ran?" he asked, voice quiet now. "'Cause I embarrassed you? Or 'cause I still know how to get under your skin?"

"Don't," I said.

"Sure." He grinned. "That why your hands shakin', Sunny?"

Sunny. He often said it growing up. My special nickname. I felt a knife in my chest.

"Don't call me that."

I had to leave. He was overwhelming.

"What should I call you?" I snapped. "Liar? Backstabber? Two-face?"

"Damn, baby, say it with your chest," Miles said, smirking. "Why stop there? Add 'devilishly handsome' while you're at it. Talk to me real nice."

"Stop playing!" I hissed. "I hate when you do this."

It was just like when we were growing up. He never took anything seriously. *Wasn't that his appeal to you?*

"I'm glad I ruined your party." Miles shrugged. "Didn't think it'll happen so quick but...I'm pleased with the results."

"I have no idea why I'm even bothering talking to you." I

started past him. If he wanted to be an asshole, he could do it by himself. I needed to figure out how to salvage this party.

He suddenly reached out, grabbing my arm and pulling me in until we were touching.

Don't bend, Serena.

I felt a searing jolt from his touch.

Surrounded by his cologne; it was intense. I tried to draw in a breath but my heart stuttered and tripped.

"I came to tell you something," he murmured.

"Miles—"

"I want you to know *I* did it."

Dread, sharp and sobering, sliced through the heat. I met his gaze.

Dangerous. Deadly. Unforgiving.

God, he was beautiful.

"What did you do?" My voice didn't shake. Barely.

His smirk was deadly. "What I should have done a long time ago. Let's end this tit-for-tat once and for all."

His hand, warm and calloused, slid up my arm, over my shoulder, fingers brushing lightly against my bare skin, sending shivers down my spine, then up, until his thumb rested just below my throat.

Immediately, I was transported to us in the back seat of his car, the windows fogged, my fingers leaving streaks on the glass, my legs over his shoulders, his hand in the same position. His lips were close—so fucking close. His warm breath grazed my cheek, sending shivers down my spine, and a knot formed in my stomach. A head-turn and we're kissing.

"Should you be doing this?" I muttered.

"Probably not."

His thumb didn't move. Neither did I.

"You ruined my site, didn't you?"

Miles raised a brow. "Did you sabotage my worker?"

My spine stiffened. "What the hell are you talking about?"

"You know exactly what I'm talking about." He folded his arms.

I stared at him, waiting for the smug to melt off his face—but all I saw was confusion. Genuine, annoying confusion.

"You really think I did something to your employee?" I asked.

"You really think I messed with your site?" he shot back.

We stared at each other, something uneasy settling between us.

"I didn't touch your damn worker," I muttered.

His brow furrowed. "And I don't even know who's on your site."

"I asked my question first," I reiterated.

"Don't lie and don't try to deny it. You've been trying to sabotage me," he continued, voice silk-smooth and venom-laced. "Undercutting my deals. Taking my investors. Poisoning every opportunity before it even reached my desk. You really thought I would let that shit keep sliding?"

I glared at him, and tilted my chin up. "Business is business but I didn't hurt your employee."

His grip shifted, trailing down the column of my throat. *Move back. Why are you letting him touch you?*

"No, Sunny." He said it like a caress. "This is personal. We will always be personal."

He leaned in, lips brushing the shell of my ear.

"I'm taking the Harrington estate."

My stomach dropped.

The jewel of the market. A sprawling waterfront lot that had been the source of intense competition among developers for years. It was *mine*.

If I got the Harrington estate? Mama and Erik would have to acknowledge all my hard work.

King Developments would be at the top.

Maybe I'd get a say in King Enterprises as a whole. Years of work for the family would finally pay off. I would be unstoppable.

"You're barely scraping by. How do you think you're going to pull that off? It's worth forty million alone. Those two nickels in your pocket ain't enough."

"The ladies think what I have in these pants is good enough." He grinned.

I *hated* him.

I hated how much I wanted to *hurt* him, to claw at him, to make him *feel* something close to what I felt right now.

He released me and gave me his signature smile.

"Auction's tomorrow." He shrugged. "Just know I'm gonna walk away with it and have you looking sad."

He turned like he was done—like he'd already won—but then glanced back, eyes gleaming.

"I'll wave from the podium, Sunny."

CHAPTER 5

Serena

THE AUCTION WAS BUZZING, and all eyes were on me the second I walked in.

"Ms. King!" the attendant blurted out. He stumbled over his words before reaching out to hand me a paddle, which I quickly snatched. "Best of luck, Ms. King."

"Luck isn't needed." I didn't break my stride into the auction house.

I was up all night thinking of the auction. I had a meeting with Erik and Mama in a few days to report on King Developments' most recent quarter, and I *would* be telling them that I'd acquired the best property on the market.

Winning this auction could be my leverage to demand more control, more resources from King Enterprises as a whole.

If I failed, the ripple effects would crush more than just my pride.

No. *No.* I couldn't take this loss. I'd worked too damn hard for too many years to just have him slide in and take what was rightfully mine.

I couldn't be soft today. When I got soft, I gave him my virginity. When I got soft, I gave him power.

They wanted a cold-hearted bitch?

Well. They came to the right auction.

I saw some familiar faces—enemies, old friends, and sharks in fancy suits—but I ignored them. I was already scanning the space for one person.

He stood near the far end of the room, his suit tailored to perfection, and he had the nerve to look well rested and moisturized.

Why did you sleep with him all those years ago?

Desperation. That's why.

To be someone. To be wanted. To matter, even if it was just for a moment.

Because sometimes attention—even the wrong kind—felt like the closest thing to love.

I would never be desperate again.

His eyes met mine, and the air crackled with a strange energy, making the already cramped room feel claustrophobic. My pulse fluttered. His gaze was challenging, daring me to acknowledge him with a glint of steel in his eyes.

He wants to play, let's play.

"Miles," I said, my voice slicing through whatever bullshit the men around him were saying.

"Serena."

"Gentlemen." The group's curiosity turned to surprise. "Is this a bad time?"

"No problem," Miles said, but his smile didn't quite reach his eyes. "Just talking business."

"You know, Miles," I said, letting my tone slip just enough to carry a hint of mockery, "a little birdie told me your company's been having…some challenges lately." I inched closer. "Did your employee get hurt?"

There it was.

A brief moment where the mask slipped, and the panic couldn't be hidden fast enough. Jenese used to say timing was everything—wait until they think they're untouchable, then strike. I learned where to look from her. Never start with the target—start with who they're trying to impress.

I wasn't spying on his business, despite his belief. Not recently. I guess I should have paid attention because things were going to shit for him, and I honestly had no hand in it this time. It was pretty amazing that his employee's injury hadn't come out. I knew how to play this game, and I'd play dirty if needed. But despite his accusations, the thought of harming an innocent person was repulsive to me.

He looked like he wanted to strangle me, and I smiled.

"Go get 'em!" I said, and took off for the main bidding area.

The room filled up as people took their seats. The air crackled with anticipation. I stayed glued to my notes, my gaze flicking between the listings, forcing myself to concentrate.

The auctioneer stepped up to the podium, and the crowd settled.

The first property came up, but I couldn't make myself care. My focus was on Miles, across the aisle. His eyes were on me, with an evil expression. I laughed.

A little part of me wanted to remind him who I was. Another part told me to turn away.

I just pretended to pay attention to the other bids. The auction dragged on for what felt like hours.

My phone buzzed in my pocket. Another blocked number. I didn't even look at it this time. The calls had been constant, but I couldn't afford to be distracted.

"The Harrington estate," the auctioneer's voice rang out. "We'll start the bidding at twenty million. Do I hear twenty million?"

I raised my paddle.

Miles lifted his paddle with a casual "Twenty-one million."

I stole a glance at him, his nonchalance only fueling my resolve. The auctioneer continued, "Twenty-one million from Mr. Whitmore. Do I hear twenty-three?"

"Twenty-three." I raised my paddle again.

"Twenty-five million."

I felt everyone's eyes on us, but my eyes were only on him.

"Thirty million."

I had every intention of seeing him fall, and I would make sure it was hard. He never understood why I needed control, and I never understood how he let go so easily. Or maybe we just didn't want to understand each other.

"Thirty-one million," he said.

I didn't break my gaze. "Thirty-six."

His eyes darkened. A silent warning—or perhaps an invitation. I couldn't tell which, but it didn't matter. It was all part of the game now. I caught him tapping his pen just like I did—something I never thought I'd share with anyone.

My phone buzzed once more. I sent the call straight to voicemail. If I answered, I risked losing control of the auction.

"Thirty-seven million!"

Miles and I both turned to see someone in the back raising their paddle. *Who the hell?*

I raised my paddle, and other bids continued.

"Thirty-eight million!"

"Thirty-nine!"

The phone buzzed again, this time with a text. I glanced down, and the words sent a chill down my spine:

> I'm watching you, Serena. Meet me now, or this gets messy. It doesn't have to be. No more ignoring my calls, sugar.

I felt a jolt of unease. Watching me? Here? My eyes darted around the room.

The phone buzzed again, and this time, a photo appeared on the screen—a snapshot of me from just moments ago, sitting exactly where I was now. The angle was off, as if taken from the upper balcony overlooking the auction floor.

My gaze immediately went up. The balcony was dim, almost too dark to make out details.

Another buzz. Shit. Another photo.

This time, it was from the exit of the auction room, the back of my head facing down at my phone.

The message beneath it read:

> Time's running out. Follow, or everyone finds out who you really are.

My eyes flicked back to the auctioneer. I couldn't afford to lose the property—not now, not when I was this close.

The auctioneer's voice droned on, and I raised my hand, my voice steady despite the turmoil raging inside. "Forty million."

Another buzz.

"Forty-two," another bidder called out.

Focus, Serena. I gritted my teeth and lifted my hand again. "Fifty million."

Another buzz. The next photo was even more damning—a shot of me in the auction room, my face a mask of stress and anxiety.

The text was short, just three words:

> Last chance, Serena.

"Fifty-one million," Miles said.

I shot him a sharp look. My heart raced as I raised my paddle again. "Fifty-three million."

I could feel my composure slipping like sand through my fingers, but I forced a smile, as if I were still in control.

Another buzz.

> Your sisters like to hang out at Café L'Amour, right? Do they know about me?

The sound of bidders around me faded, drowned out by the

pounding in my ears. I shot to my feet so fast my chair scraped against the floor. "Sixty million."

Gasps rippled through the room. Miles's smirk faltered for a fraction of a second, his brows lifting in disbelief.

The auctioneer hesitated, his gavel poised midair. "Uh… Sixty million from Ms. King. Going once…"

My vision tunneled on the auctioneer, willing him to bring the gavel down.

"Going twice… Sold!"

Without waiting for the crowd's reaction, I grabbed my bag and stormed out, my heels clicking hard against the polished floor, I was nearly running out the building. My phone buzzed again, and I nearly crushed it in my grip.

I shoved through the doors, my mind racing. I needed to figure out what the hell I was going to do next.

"Sunny!" Miles's voice sliced through the hallway, startling me. I turned.

I can't with this shit. Not now.

"Don't call me that!" I snapped. "I don't have time for this right now."

"Sunny—"

"Goodbye, Miles." My voice was cold. "Let's not meet again."

I pushed through the front doors of the auction hall, into the bright daylight.

I took a deep breath, trying to steady myself, but then I saw her—Jenese.

She was leaning against a sleek black car at the curb.

People walking by slowed, staring at her curiously in her burgundy leather trench coat that hugged her frame, the hem just brushing the tops of her knee-high snakeskin boots. Her Afro was an impressive halo, the salt-and-pepper curls catching the sunlight. A gold chain glinted against her collarbone, and a cigar rested between her fingers.

I tried to steady myself as I descended down the steps. "Jenese."

"Serena." Her voice was smooth, and she tilted her head. "You look nice, sugar. Love what you're doing with the short hair."

"Why are you here?"

Jenese took a slow drag of her cigar. "Can't I drop by to see my number-one prodigy?"

I took a deep breath. *Stay in control. Calm.*

"Mm, whew, chile, that's a handsome man right there. What's his name?"

I glanced over my shoulder and froze. Miles had followed me. He stood at the top of the stairs, his expression unreadable. *No.* He shouldn't see her.

"Nobody."

She shrugged. "Get in."

The smoke burned my eyes, but I turned to follow her lead but paused midstep, my eyes betraying me as they flicked back to Miles.

Remember what he did to you. Remember why you're in this position now.

"You don't think I'm too old for him, do you?" Jenese slipped into the driver's seat with practiced ease, adjusting the rearview mirror as if she had all the time in the world.

"You're old as dirt. Now drive."

The engine roared to life, the rumble grounding me as I scrambled to push past the chaos in my head.

"Oh, Serena," she said with a laugh. "Wait till you get to my age. Now, buckle up."

CHAPTER 6

Miles

SIX YEARS AGO...

BAM! *Bang! Boom!*

I jolted awake, heart racing, reliving the night's events. Pops hit Vincent. Out of nowhere, he attacked him, and I didn't get it.

I frantically searched for my ringing phone. It buzzed incessantly with texts from Serena, Erik, and countless unknowns.

"Miles!" Ma called from downstairs.

Without a second thought, I ripped the blankets off, ignoring the chill as I bolted out the door barefoot and shirtless. I sprinted down the long hall.

"Ma!"

A cacophony of sound—the urgent blare of sirens and a sea of shouting voices—suddenly surrounded me. I pushed myself faster, the marble cool beneath my feet as I spun to the top of the grand stairs.

My eyes fell upon the overwhelming number of police officers in our entryway, their faces grim and serious.

They had a grip on Pops. Dragging him out of the mansion.

"Lemme go! You don't know what the hell you're doing. This is my house!"

Spit flew from his mouth. His eyes were wild, bloodshot as he twisted and turned like a rabid animal in a cage. They were pulling him out the front door while Ma was screaming, trying to pull him back before more cops stepped between them to break them up.

Frozen on the stairs, I gripped the banister. My heart jackhammered. A metallic taste filled my mouth.

"This is a goddamn setup!" Pops bellowed. "It is!"

He thrashed once, hard enough to knock a vase from the entry table—it shattered like gunfire. I jumped into action.

"Wait!" I said.

Pops fought as they took him out of the front door, I pushed through the cops who were holding Ma back.

Outside, I wasn't prepared. The morning sun was brutal, blinding. And standing just past the property gates—the press.

They were everywhere. Clustered just outside the wrought-iron gates, holding mics through the bars. Some had climbed onto car hoods for a better shot. Others hoisted mics on long poles, aiming them like spears toward the front steps.

"Omar! Is it true you're doing drugs with the mayor?"

"Do you deny the possession charges?"

"Miles, did you know your father was using?"

I ignored them, and ran down the steps toward Pops. "Let him go!"

A cop stepped in my path, pressing a firm hand to my chest.

"Get off me—he didn't do anything!"

That was a lie, and we all knew it.

Still, I surged forward. Another officer blocked me. My shoulder slammed into his, a searing pain shooting through my arm, and suddenly there were arms on me—strong arms that held me back, pinning me against him.

"Sir, stand down!"

"Back up—now!"

I pushed back at them. "I don't give a fuck, let him go!"

Pops twisted in the officers' grip, trying to look back at me. His robe had slipped entirely off one arm now, exposing the ink along his ribs and a welt blooming on his side from where they'd pinned him.

"Miles!" he barked. "Don't you let them do this to me—don't you fucking let them win!"

"Damn it, Serena."

I stared at the mess of papers sprawled across my coffee table.

I tried not to think about the day when the cops came and dragged Pops out. That had been only the beginning of a long, long battle.

Legacy.

I didn't know how I felt about the word. No. That was a lie. I knew how I felt about it.

I didn't view it how the Kings did. To them, legacy was fixed and rigid: you inherit it, you uphold it, you don't question it. My grandfather used to think that way before he died. Pops maybe felt that way at some point.

To me, it all felt like old, bittersweet memories and pain.

But underneath it, the burning sense of hope and reinvention. Legacy was both this giant to be slayed but as fragile as the falling snow.

But still in my thoughts of our legacy being up for debate…I couldn't get Serena out of my mind.

I was distracted by her at the baby shower. I wasn't thinking straight. It had always been like that with her.

Those same damn brown eyes, like pools of dark honey, looked right through me, and despite any walls I put up, it didn't matter to her. She saw through the bullshit, and that terrified and excited me at the same time.

The Harrington estate, my only way out, was lost.

Fuck.

She must've been smiling when she signed that contract. Smug. Laughing all the way to the fucking bank.

I could have planned this better.

Despite the sting of my loss, I should have sat in my seat, but I couldn't resist the pull to follow her. I was always trailing after Serena. I shouldn't have watched her walk away, her curvy round ass in those slacks. Who made slacks sexy?

It was the way she carried herself, that effortless glide in her step, like she wasn't walking but cutting through space, making room for herself whether people wanted to give it or not.

Serena King didn't do soft. She didn't do approachable.

It used to be a game to me, to see if I could break through her tough exterior—a dangerous game to play with my best friend's little sister.

She wasn't like the other girls in Lush. Hell, she wasn't like anyone. You couldn't charm her. Couldn't flirt your way into her world. Never in my life in Lush did I have to...*work.*

It'd been easy being Erik King's best friend.

He was the King. I was the Prince. Not too much expectation, just girls trying to get close to me or Erik, parties and bullshit. I could coast on my name, my face, the Whitmore legacy.

Serena was sharp, steel-edged, and disdainful looks. The opposite of me.

Every time she cut me down with one of those icy one-liners, it felt like a dare.

And I was never good at walking away from a dare.

But it wasn't just her fire that got me. It was what she *demanded* of me—without ever saying it outright. She made me want to come correct. Every conversation was a test I didn't know I was taking.

She'd ask things no one else did. Real questions. *Why do you want the company? Where do you see yourself in ten years? What would you do with it if you weren't trying to prove something to this town? What do you really want?*

No one ever cared what I thought—just what I *inherited.*

And for the first time, I realized I wasn't sure I knew either.

I told myself it was harmless. I was just teasing. Just flirting.

But it wasn't harmless.

My fists curled as I leaned back, my eyes fixed on the ceiling. The Sunny I remembered would've been in a pair of old jeans and a baggy Cranberries tee, hair sticking out in every direction because she didn't care. She used to push those too-big glasses up her nose and laugh at me for not knowing something simple.

"Damn it, Serena," I muttered again, and I swiped the glass off the table, sending it shattering to the floor.

I needed to get my shit together. I was being too dramatic.

The estate was lost. Reggie was still in the hospital, his wife calling every other hour for updates Carlus and I didn't have. I was back, scrambling for…what?

Is this the life you want to live, Miles?

Every day, fight after fight. It felt like going a hundred rounds with Mike Tyson, Floyd Mayweather, and Muhammad Ali back to back.

I kept telling myself that restoring Whitmore Ventures was the goal. The *only* goal. That if I could rebuild what my father broke, I could scrub the family name clean. That if I won, I'd finally be enough.

Maybe I wanted out after that.

But what the hell would I be without the Whitmore name? Without the fight?

No.

I couldn't run. I couldn't walk away. My legacy was *here*.

I was just a smooth-talking rich kid with a broken family and no real plan.

I leaned forward, elbows on my knees, rubbing at the tension clawing its way up my spine.

I should've stayed at the auction. I should've held my tongue. I should've been smarter.

I still had that number.

Wasn't your life fucking ruined when you called before? The last time I'd called, our lives had already been destroyed, and it hadn't been easy sweeping that under the rug. No. I wouldn't call.

A knock at the front door startled me. I froze when I saw who was on the other side.

"Surprise, surprise." Mayor Dante Castillo was leaning against my door frame.

What shit have I gotten into now?

"Look who left the marble throne for the slums. Whatever you think I did, I had a good reason for it."

His expression didn't budge.

"Unless," I added, "you're here to donate. In which case, I'm thrilled to accept money, favors, or women."

"Evening, Miles. I hope I'm not catching you at a bad time," Dante said, looking over my shoulder.

"What you want?" I narrowed my gaze on him, blocking him from entering as he stood straight. "We ain't friends."

"Aren't you gonna let me in?"

We stared at each other before I stepped back, and Dante strolled in like he owned the place.

"Quite the mess you've got here," he noted as glass crunched under his foot and he looked at me. "Thought you could afford a maid again."

"I know about them wild-ass orgies you be throwing. Don't let me start talking to folks. Wouldn't look too good with reelection creeping up."

Dante's smile thinned. "I need humor like that on my team. You should come around city hall more."

"My bad, homie, I don't do politics," I said with a smirk. "You want tea? Sparkling water? Maybe a lil' foot rub?"

He grunted, looking around my house before making himself comfortable on the couch.

"Have you turned on the news yet?"

"You interrupted my evening to come over here to watch the news?"

"Turn on the damn TV, Miles," Dante said, all the charm drained from his voice.

I flipped through a few channels before landing on a news station.

"Whitmore Ventures under fire with allegations of unsafe work conditions," the news anchor announced.

My stomach fucking dropped.

The camera panned to my office building, a group of my

guys standing out front. The anchor walked over to one of them and shoved the microphone in his face. "Can you describe the conditions at the site?"

"It's dangerous. You don't come home the same after a day on those sites. I saw people hurt—bad. But they told us to keep working anyway. There's nothing they care about more than profit."

"That's fucking bullshit!" I growled.

Dante didn't even blink. He shifted in the chair, lazily adjusting the cuffs of his shirt, his expression unreadable. "Is it?"

"Where the fuck is Carlus?" I turned sharply toward him, reaching for my phone to call him.

"Employees have been risking their lives every day, and Whitmore Ventures has turned a blind eye to it all," the worker continued. "We're not asking for much, just basic safety measures, but they've refused to listen. Currently we have a coworker in the hospital, and Miles Whitmore and his construction manager are hiding it."

Of course, name *me.*

The screen cut back to the anchor. "The worker's claims are now being investigated by authorities, and his lawyer is preparing a lawsuit against Whitmore Ventures for negligence. We've reached out to the company for comment but received no response."

My phone rang. Ma.

"Serena," I said, the name slicing out like a blade. "It must be her fault."

"Ah." Dante nodded slowly. "How could I forget the petty fighting you and the Kings have been doing for years? Haven't decided on a winner yet?"

I ran a hand across my face, trying to prevent myself from blowing up.

"Let's change the channel, shall we?"

He grabbed the remote and pressed a button. The screen showed a protest outside King Developments office. It was intense: tons of banners and signs protesting pollution, and massive crowds chanting and holding signs saying things like "Protect Our Planet."

"Our top story tonight is an environmental protest is underway outside King Developments' headquarters. Activists are rallying against the company, alleging its role in environmental degradation linked to several recent projects."

The anchor continued while putting a photo of Serena on the screen.

"Activists have recently mobilized in response to leaked documents that suggest the company has been engaged in shady practices for the last several years," the anchor continued.

"Funny how these things play out, huh?" Dante tilted his head before sucking his teeth. "You're both having a bad day."

The screen showed images of polluted waterways, deforested areas, and the leaked documents.

"These revelations have sparked a wave of scrutiny and backlash against the company, highlighting their disregard for environmental protection."

"I didn't, but should have," I said. Dante clicked his tongue. "Thanks for letting me know, but you gotta go. I obviously have shit I need to handle."

"People have told me they saw you and Serena fighting at the auction hall this afternoon. And at Laurene's baby shower a week ago. And before this at a dozen of other places around town." Dante's eyes widened. "You're not happy about this?"

I stood up, and Dante did the same, his gaze darkening.

"She's the one who's been sabotaging *me*. Don't I get to be the victim?"

"And what've you done in return?" Dante cut in. "You've been fighting so long you forgot the town's watching."

"That's bullshit." I waved him off. "Did you have this conversation with her too? Or you didn't 'cause you on they payroll? You're here as their lackey?"

He stepped closer, slow, calculated. "You two got more

power than you know, Miles. And you're wasting it. Burning down the empire your families built for what? Pettiness? She hurt your feelings? You can't take rejection?"

I laughed bitterly. "Don't act like you care now. Where were you when all this shit started?"

Dante's smile faded.

"I care about the wreckage. The donors. The headlines. The way your drama's making *me* look like I don't have control over my city anymore. Now was not the time to fuck up."

His voice dropped a notch.

"Now I'm taking control."

I looked at him, confused. "What the hell does that mean? You mean Yvonne King is *actually* going to let you do your job?"

"I have plans, Miles. *Big plans.*" Dante waved his hands like he was pushing back a curtain. "Because of you two, who I suspect planted these stories on each other—"

"I didn't do—"

Dante shook his head. "I don't give a fuck who did what. I've just lost a deal that was going to bring a huge festival to Lush. A multimillion-dollar, three-day extravaganza. So much money was coming here." Dante's faced balled up into anger. "And now they're pulling out. Why? Because no one wants to be tied to a town in the middle of a public war with two prominent families. They looked into our history, and guess what was the first thing they saw?"

I swallowed and looked down at the floor.

"Yeah, you know. Your father's fucking face. Conrad Ashbourne's death. Nobody wants to be tied to companies destroying the environment. Or workers getting hurt, unfair work conditions. Sabotage between founding families. We look like a fucking daytime soap opera."

"Then, buddy, you need to put on your big-boy draws," I said. "Go talk to Yvonne. We all know she pulls your puppet strings."

Dante looked like he wanted to strangle me. There was a knock at the door.

"You should answer that."

I glared at him, then slowly headed for the door.

"Ma?"

She rolled my pops in, both looking grim—but that wasn't even the worst of it. Yvonne and Vincent King were right behind them.

"Why are you here?" I asked them. It was only the grace of respecting my elders that I didn't snap on Miss Yvonne's ass like I wanted to.

Yvonne glared at me. I shut the door and turned around to face my parents and the Kings standing awkwardly, with Dante in the middle like a ringmaster.

"Now that we're all here, let's really get down to business." He nodded. "I'm giving you all forty-eight hours."

"To do what?" Yvonne snapped, looking around my place like it was a trap house.

"Get my money and the festival back."

"We can just as easily cut a check," Ma said.

Dante shook his head. "That's not enough for me."

"What do you mean, it's not enough?" I said.

"I need security that this petty little feud is not going to affect Lush or the business I'm conducting as your leader. Excuse me for not trust either of your words."

"You have a lot of nerve!" Yvonne glared at him. "I'm the reason you're in this position, don't forget that."

"Never, Mrs. King, but don't *you* forget that nobody in this room's position is secured forever. Legacy or not," Dante stated bluntly, and he looked over at us. "We all can fall from grace, which I'm sure individuals in this room understand."

"Stop the games. What do you want from us?" Vincent said.

Dante gave a short, humorless laugh. "I need the Kings and the Whitmores to bury the hatchet."

Yvonne snorted. "That'll never happen. They know what they did."

"We have nothing to say to them." Pops nodded.

"That's not going to work for me." Dante adjusted his cuffs like he was bored. "See, if you don't do what I ask, I'll start talking. And trust me, when I talk, people *listen*. Journalists, prosecutors, board members."

He leaned forward slightly, voice dropping into something colder than a threat.

"Both families have blood under their nails. You've been here for generations, and I've got access to archives. Land stolen, contracts forged, bribes paid, witnesses vanished. I don't even need it to stick—all I need is to get people questioning."

He looked at Yvonne. "Or I could shut it all down. State audits. IRS. Code enforcement. Environmental violations. Things you didn't even know were violations." He chuckled. "One phone call, and the Kings and Whitmores will be too busy putting out fires to notice they're already burning."

"I'm a *King*," Yvonne snapped and glaring at Dante. "My ancestors built this damn town. Who the hell do you think you are? You getting too fucking comfortable in office, Dante."

"Your ancestors are dead, Yvonne," Dante's voice was a whip. "They're not coming back. And if they were smart, they'd tell you to sit down and *listen*. Because this isn't about what your family *built*. It's about what *I* can destroy."

"You're bluffing," Yvonne said, though her voice wavered ever so slightly.

"Am I?" Dante shot back, not even flinching. "I just want to make Lush a better place. That's why I was elected."

Yvonne fell silent.

Dante took a deep breath and looked around the room. "I'm talking about an arrangement. A merger. Permanent. So you both can't fuck the other over."

I blinked. "A merger?"

"You end this goddamn feud right now. And I'm not talking

about some fake handshake and a smile. What's something in this town that can ensure that between both of you?"

We all looked up at each other, and it was like the air got sucked from the room.

"A marriage," Vincent said reluctantly.

But then, all eyes turned to me.

"Fuck no." I shook my head, the anger rising in my chest. "You think I'm just going to marry into their family like nothing happened?"

"You will, *son*. For all our sakes," Pops spoke up.

"Then who will I marry? Gigi?" *Please don't say it. Don't say it.*

Yvonne looked at me. "Serena."

CHAPTER 7

Serena

A FEW HOURS EARLIER...

THE BARTENDER HANDED Jenese her French Blonde, and she took a sip. "Perfect." She smirked at me.

"Why are you here?" I forced my fingers to loosen their grip around my glass, but my heart was another story. It hammered against my ribs, panic coiling tight beneath my skin.

"Don't be like that, sugar. It's me."

I hadn't seen her in years.

I made sure of that.

Yet *here* she was.

The woman who pulled me out of my shell and shoved me into fire. The one who taught me how to read a room—and how to tear it apart if it didn't bend for me. The first person who ever saw past the nervousness and timidness and told me, *You could be more.*

"I don't do ghosts," I said, taking a sip of a whiskey that scorched all the way down.

We'd met at a party years ago. Mama had just torn me down in front of two board members. Said I wasn't ready. Said I needed polish. Said I was "too emotional."

That same night, Jenese put a glass in my hand and said, *"Fuck what they think. Wanna know how to run shit?"*

I did.

Jenese tapped her long acrylic nails on the table. "I missed you. And I think you missed me too. We're just two friends having drinks—"

"We're not *anything*."

Jenese thrived on the chase. If I let her know I was nervous, she would be on me like a fly on shit.

"You used to consider me the mother you never had." Jenese pouted.

"You were never that to me."

"Don't tell me you and Mommy Dearest are on good terms now? You showing her all the tricks I taught you?"

The truth was, she lived in every sharp line I drew, every choice I made to finally get Mama's attention. Every time I cut someone off at the knees in a boardroom, it was her voice in my head whispering, *Faster next time, sugar.*

That version of me—the one Mama finally approved of—was Jenese's blueprint.

I frowned, gathering my bag to stand. "Goodbye."

"Don't rush out of this conversation, Serena. We got shit to discuss. I like the new confidence, but pipe down."

Confidence.

I was twenty-three. Miles was gone. Laurene's engagement party had ended in disaster, and Mama and Daddy were scrambling to get things in order. The whole town was freaking out over Conrad Ashbourne's accident, then Lu's disappearance.

I think Mama threw King Developments at me just to get me out her face.

I was so hyped, but clueless. Then I met Jenese.

I couldn't make Mama see me beyond her backup plan. Jenese knew all the ways women like us were dismissed. She promised to teach me a different approach. She gave me short-cuts. Secrets. Power.

She taught me how to carry myself. How to command attention. She gave me armor.

And then I walked from her before she could pin our last disagreement on me. And we never spoke again.

Until now.

"Didn't you just spend sixty million dollars on a property? That's more money than I recall you having six years ago." Jenese tapped her chin.

"And?"

"I did my homework. It's a good property. So fascinating. Old money. Pool. I bet the walk-in closet is amazing."

I stared at her.

"Don't act like you don't know what I'm saying." She leaned in, her voice low and smooth. "You owe me. I think this is a good makeup for what happened between us before."

"You mean the time you tried to sell me to a married man in exchange for shares in a company?" I was still angry. I felt so stupid walking into that meeting, only to realize I was just a pawn.

Her lashes fluttered. "Don't be dramatic."

"I said no then, and I'm saying no now."

"Oh, honey." Jenese tsked like I was a child. "I don't like to hear that answer."

She slipped her phone from her clutch and slid it across the table. A photo glowed on the screen.

Me, six years younger. In a black dress I hadn't worn since. Sitting too close to an *old* man who wasn't my type.

"Where did you get this?" I asked, though I already knew.

"Oh, sugar," she said, voice like satin over a knife. "If I send this to the right people with just a hint of context, you might just have a scandal on your hands."

My nails dug into my palm, sharp enough to draw blood, but I didn't let her see me flinch.

"You need more convincing? Fine." Jenese sniffed, and she sat up in her seat. I noticed the concealer not quite covering the puff beneath her eyes. The faint stiffness in the way she held her jaw.

"I'm writing a tell-all book. And guess what? You're my main character."

My heart stopped. "What?"

"It's all about *me*, of course." She swirled her drink like she had all the time in the world. "My life. My journey. My regrets. And of course, the people who fucked me over." She shot me a look that made my skin crawl. "It's a beautiful piece, really. Raw. Honest. I couldn't write it and not have you in it, obviously. You're one of my masterpieces."

I calmly exhaled. "You're lying. Half the shit you've done, you'd go to jail."

"Don't worry, I talked to a lawyer. Just changed some name, dates, details. It won't come back on me. But we need action in this book, or it'll just be some boring-ass diary. I added it all!" She grinned at me, giddy like a kid. "I...exaggerated on some details, but who cares? People like the messiness. Espionage! Embezzlement! And oooh—the *thefts*."

I must have died. Died at my desk in the office, and now I was in hell.

"That's not what we did," I protested weakly.

"Oh, please," Jenese said. "I covered your ass more times than I can count. Who do you think made those permits go through when you couldn't because they wanted your brother instead?"

"You're lying."

Jenese shrugged. "Your word against mine."

Breathe, breathe.

"This is *our* story, Serena." Her voice sharpened. "Yet you cut me out like I was trash. But when you needed leverage back then, help, compassion, was I not there? I kept your hands clean. Now I'm telling *my* side."

I couldn't lose my temper. I should have expected this.

King Developments was climbing, and nothing—nothing— could slow us down. This was just a curve in the road. A deer in the headlights. You swerved in time…or you hit it head-on and keep driving.

From her bag, she retrieved a black flash drive, idly twirling it.

"A little draft. The early stuff. You wouldn't believe the reception it's gotten in certain circles already."

My pulse knocked against my ribs. I didn't let it show.

"I'm hoping now you'll take me seriously. I want that Harrington estate."

"You should know me too," I said slowly, trying to work moisture back into my mouth. "You think you're going to paint me as some kind of villain? I'll sue you, your publisher, and anyone involved for defamation."

"Now, I'm not a callous woman. I know you've made a life without me," Jenese continued as if I hadn't spoken at all, "and I wouldn't want to mess with that. Truly. I'm rooting for you. I've come to make a deal."

"You're offering a lot of deals today."

"You're not someone I can easily intimidate." Jenese grinned. "So, let's keep it simple: you give me the estate. I don't release the photo. And if you're cooperative, I'll give you a chapter of the manuscript. You do a few small things for me, I might even give you editorial input. How's that for generosity?"

I glared at her. "You're blackmailing me with a book and want to collaborate on it?"

"Beta reading," she said, amused. "Very modern."

Jenese stood up, her chair scraping loudly against the floor. I watched as she slid her sunglasses on and tossed me the flash drive.

"A sample chapter from my book. I think you'll find it…*enlightening*. Do give me critique, okay?"

Before I could say anything, Jenese turned to leave, pausing just long enough to glance over her shoulder.

"The estate. Or the photo is going out right now."

"Fine," I said. "You'll get the estate. Two weeks."

Her eyes gleamed.

"But it won't be in your name—not directly," I added coolly. "I'll move it through a holding company. Clean. Quiet. You'll get full control, just not…ownership. Not yet."

She studied me, narrowing her eyes.

"Just a formality," I said. "You taught me to cover every angle. Can't have people at my company flagging it, right?" I was already spinning with a thousand ideas on how to delay the transfer. Every day I delayed would give me more space to work.

Jenese smiled, satisfied. "There's my girl.

"Don't take too long, Serena, to tell me what you think. I'm not one for waiting—and oh, is that your company on the news?"

I glanced at the TV behind me.

People protesting at King Developments.

Jenese let out a loud laugh, heading for the door, as my phone began to ring and Mama's name flashed across my screen.

Fuck.

CHAPTER 8

Serena

SIX YEARS AGO...

"YOU FUCKED UP, *Laurene. You were supposed to marry Conrad, and the boy is in a fucking coma! What if he dies?"* Mama yelled at Laurene from upstairs.

The voices bounced off the marble floors, sharp and echoing like broken glass. I stood rigid, heart racing. The words weren't aimed at me, but somehow they still felt like they were.

Keep still. Be quiet. Don't make it worse.

I wished Miles was here right now. He would've pulled me out of the room. No questions. Just grabbed my hand and gone.

Mama's voice was sharp—it always was when she was mad. And Laurene... Laurene was fighting back.

"I didn't ask him to fight his brother!"

"I know you had something to do with it," Mama hissed. "Was that your plan all along? Make these brothers fight and you got out of this deal? Even when you know what it means—"

"You mean what it means for you! *For the company!" Laurene screamed back.*

I started to go upstairs, but a firm hand landed on my shoulder, and I jumped, looking behind me to see Erik.

"Stay here," he said.

"But they—"

"Stay." Erik rushed up the stairs, leaving me there alone.

My hands were clenched into fists in the sleeves of my sweater. My stomach hurt. There was this buzzing in my ears, like the room was too loud and too bright and too much.

"You need to see this through," Mama spat. "You leave now and there's no coming back. Do you hear me, Laurene? If I gotta fix this, you get nothing!"

"Then clean it up," Laurene said.

I heard a door slam and quick footsteps. Laurene was coming down the stairs, clutching a bag and her dress. Despite tears, she defiantly lifted her chin.

She stopped next to me and squeezed me tightly.

"Don't let her turn you into something you're not," Laurene told me.

Before I could speak, before I could even process what the hell was happening, she was gone.

My life was falling apart. Miles was long gone.

It was pathetic. Even now. He could've made a joke. Something stupid. Something that would've made me feel like I wasn't suffocating.

I could fix things. We weren't that badly damaged. Nope, not yet. We were the Kings, we would survive—

Out of nowhere, Mama yelled, "Serena!"

I immediately bolted up the stairs. She was in her office, the door open. I started to head that way, but I could hear the sniffles of Gigi down the hall and Daddy's voice muttering to her.

My feet didn't want to move, but I forced myself anyway.

Step.

Step.

Pause.

As I leaned against the wall, my hand was hand was on my chest. I was terrified; my heart leaped into my throat, and I stumbled back.

"Serena, don't make me call you again."

My gut said run, but I made myself go into Mama's office. She was sitting at her desk, a bottle of alcohol in front of her. For the first time,

Mama looked…old. Way beyond her fifty-something years, like time and responsibility had collapsed onto her.

She drank straight from the bottle. I closed the doors to her office softly.

"Yes, ma'am?"

"Who is that?" Mama pointed above her, to the back wall where our great-great-great-grandfather Augustus King's portrait was. He'd lived on the space of the wall for years, looming, watching us to see if we'd made a mistake.

"Augustus King."

Mama nodded. "Lush wouldn't exist without him. Without us."

I'd memorized the story. He founded it after the Tulsa Massacre, then made it flourish.

"We owe it to him. To what he sacrificed. We cannot have it end now. Not because your sister wants to be selfish—" Mama stopped, angry, then drank again. "I can't. That's not what I promised my father. And I'll be damned if we fail."

Her eyes flicked to me.

"I've always said you were the smart one, Serena. You see the cracks before anyone else does." She stood and came around the desk, her voice softening. "You think I don't notice, but I do. You've always wanted to help. And now I need you. I need someone who won't run away when things get hard. Someone I can trust not to disappoint me."

Her fingers curled around my wrist, and I froze. "You can be that. I know you can."

I swallowed, and nodded slowly.

"Make me proud then. Step up for me, for the family, for Augustus. You don't want to let him down, do you?"

The mansion was creepily quiet. No staff bustling about, no distant hum of chatter from the other wings. Only the old clock ticking softly in the corner.

I approached the door to Mama's office. The muffled sound of her irate tone carried through the heavy oak. Even without seeing her, I knew she was pacing, her sharp heels leaving tiny scuffs on the Persian rug.

"This is a disaster," Mama's voice cut through the door. I couldn't hear Daddy's low response before something crashed.

I reached to knock on the door, but stopped.

"Come in here, Serena." Mama declared came through the door.

No failures. Only strength.

I opened the door to Mama's office.

Daddy sat across from her desk. He looked exhausted. Mama stood, harshly lit by her desk lamp. She glared sharply at me. I steeled myself.

Don' t let her words get to you, offer solutions.

"I know, Mama, I'm handling it—" I took a deep breath, trying to steady my nerves.

"Handling it?" she scoffed. "You're *handling* it? Is that why this has been on the news for the last few hours? Erik is taking shit from all sides! He's in an emergency meeting right now with the board. Did you know they've made shanty towns on the goddamn sidewalk outside the office? That's you *handling it?*"

I knew this tone. Knew it better than my own heartbeat. Mama was angry, but not just angry—*disappointed*. And that? That was worse.

Because anger I could fix. Anger meant there was still room to prove myself. Disappointment was a closed door. A verdict.

Mama turned to the TV mounted on the far wall, the muted screen replaying the breaking news. "They're saying *our* company destroyed habitats, poisoned water sources, displaced families. Did you sign off on any of this?"

Yes.

"No. It's staged," I said, cool and flat. "The protestors were hired. Paid to create buzz for a competing firm trying to tank our deal."

Mama stared at me. Not shocked. Not impressed. Just…still. Measuring. I hated when she got like this. Silent judgment was worse than shouting.

She walked to the bar, poured herself a drink, and said nothing.

"We'll get this cleared up," I told her. "Immediately."

"See, Yvonne, I told you something like this wouldn't happen under Rena's watch," Daddy said.

"Mama—"

"You're telling me, with all our connections, all the people *you* know, you didn't hear anything about this *before* the news got hold of it?" Mama narrowed her gaze on me.

Lie.

"Of course I did," I said, lifting my chin. "But it wasn't credible intel. Protest threats come in with every project—and a couple of our competitors always send some. This wasn't anything new. They just actually decided to be bold this time."

Her eyes flicked toward Daddy, but she didn't look convinced.

"Yvonne, Serena's never had an issue before running the company. Let her fix this instead of stressing ourselves out," Daddy said.

Finally, Mama's shoulders lowered, and she nodded slowly.

"We need to shift the focus. Establish it's a lie, but prove that we're committed to the environment and the people. Create a new narrative that overshadows the protests." I took a deep breath, trying to project confidence. *Don't crumble now.*

"And what do you suggest?" Mama finally said after several moments of silence.

I wanted to tell Mama everything, about Jenese's blackmail, about the impossible situation I was in. But she would never understand. She would never forgive me.

"We could announce a new initiative, or highlight some of our past work. Something that shows we're proactive and committed to positive change."

Her eyes narrowed, calculating. "Go on."

She's counting on you. That sick, familiar panic crept up my spine.

"That's not the only thing you're gonna do to fix this."

"Yvonne!" Daddy looked pissed as he pushed himself from his seat. "Let's not tell her like this."

"Tell me what?"

"You will be getting married."

It felt like you could hear a pin drop.

"Married? To whom?"

Daddy exhaled loudly, wiping a hand over his face, and he looked every bit of his sixty-plus years.

"I know this is a lot to ask, Serena, but I believe you can handle it. You've always been strong."

She was doing it again—pushing, manipulating, pretending like this was just another thing I could *handle*.

"You're the one who always figures things out," she continued, her tone dripping with false warmth. "You keep it all together for this family. You're the only one who can do this."

"*Who* am I marrying?" This was my first time raising my voice at her, and I clenched my fists.

Daddy sighed. "Look, Rena—"

"Miles."

I blinked, doubting what I'd heard.

"Miles? As in Miles *Whitmore*? Don't make me laugh."

Mama and Daddy showed no emotion.

"W-wait, you cannot be serious."

"It's not our first choice, and believe me, baby, we don't make this decision lightly," Daddy finally said, looking at Mama. "But this arrangement is necessary. We should…find peace with the Whitmores."

"Necessary for *who*? Did you forget what Omar did to you? You've got to be fucking kidding me."

"Watch your language," Mama shouted.

"Why?" I demanded.

"Dante," Daddy said. "We all know that the only thing more important than this family is ensuring this town's survival."

I frowned and shook my head. I was *not* hearing this. "That doesn't even make sense! What did Dante really say—"

"You messed up, Serena. All the fighting with Miles put us in this position."

I frowned at her, my eyes growing wide. "You said to destroy them! I was following your directions."

"What's done is done," Mama snapped. "Dante's threat was more than enough, and it might be the best thing for all of us. After all, Laurene and Reese were able to repair things for us with the Ashbournes."

I narrowed my gaze. "You still hate Harold Ashbourne."

"Doesn't matter. We need more allies than enemies." Mama waved away my objection. "We can't trust Dante."

I wanted to tell her how *wrong* this was. I wanted to scream that I would *never* marry Miles, that she couldn't make me do something like this. But the words wouldn't come. Because deep down, I knew I had no choice. Not really. Not when she'd already made the decision for me.

"We've already talked to him," Mama continued. "Miles is willing. He knows what's at stake."

"Mama, please." The room seemed to spin around me. "How? After everything that happened? Miles hates me—hates *Erik*. Audrey hates you. Daddy hates Omar. How will marrying Miles even help us—"

"It's done."

"No, it's not done." My voice sharpened with desperation. "I want to know: what are the pros and cons of this arrangement? When was this decided? How? Why?"

Mama's eyes narrowed, her patience clearly wearing thin. "If you refuse, you'll lose everything," she said, her voice flat and emotionless. "Your position in the company. I'll strip it all from you without hesitation. And don't think for one second that I won't."

My pulse pounded in my ears as she continued. "None of it matters? After all the work I've done?"

"Look at this as another assignment." Mama sighed as she sat in her chair. "You both follow the rules laid out for you, and two years will pass before you know it."

I blinked. "Two years?"

Daddy cleared his throat and turned to me. "We did a risk analysis. That's the time our investors think it will take to shake off this bad press and really get an investment out of the new partnership—"

"What do you mean, *get an investment out*?"

Daddy and Mama glanced at each other.

"We've decided to merge King Developments and Whitmore Ventures. By Monday, both companies will be one. I know this feud has been going on between you and Miles for a while, out of loyalty to your father, but our companies are greater together."

I shook my head as I began to pace. "You're serious?"

"There's a mandatory two-year term before any annulment or divorce can be considered. In that time, you'll maintain appearances. Joint interviews, business conferences, holiday gatherings—you'll fulfill every family obligation as a united front. You will help restore both companies' images and finances with the help of Miles."

I shook my head, not believing what I was hearing.

"And if you try to sabotage this marriage or make a mockery of it," she said, her tone deceptively calm, "you won't just lose your position in the company. Your position in this family is at stake. Don't forget what happened to your sister."

I stood frozen, the weight of her words pressing down on my chest. There was no way out.

Her smile returned, a predator satisfied with its prey. "Now go. Your father and I will finalize the details."

There was no escape. Not from this.

She had already sealed my fate.

CHAPTER 9
Miles

WEDDING DAY

HOLY SHIT, *I'm doing this.*

I stood in the hallway of city hall just outside the mayor's office. A whirlwind of arrangements and hurried decisions, and fuck, here I was.

Getting ready to marry Sun—*Serena* in order to save my family and my company.

Dante had us by the balls, and we'd have to play his way. For now.

Both families agreed not to delay. With the current protest against the Kings and the threats Whitmore Ventures was facing, it was decided to just get the ceremony done.

But all I could think about was the woman I was about to marry—the one I used to love. She *ruined* me. And I was supposed to vow forever to her?

Was Whitmore Ventures really worth it?

It was. *Legacy.*

And all the bullshit that came with it…

I shook my head, instead thinking of the other pressing thought.

Erik.

Don't have a choice now, huh? He's your brother-in-law.

My phone began to ring in my pocket, and I dug in, lifting it to see a number I didn't recognize.

"Miles," a man's voice rasped, low and oily, slick with familiarity. "Long time."

I stiffened; I knew that voice.

"Victor."

Then a soft laugh. "I was wondering if you'd answer. You always were a polite boy. Even when you were desperate."

"We have nothing to talk about. I paid you back. Every damn cent. With interest."

"Which I'm glad you did. I would hate for it to have to get ugly between us. You know I don't like that."

I swallowed and clenched my fists. Over the years since my last dealings with the "businessman"—and I used that word extremely lightly—I'd heard through the grapevine what happened to those that didn't pay him back promptly which I did. So why was he calling now?

"Touched as I am by this random-ass call," I said tightly, "I'm busy. So maybe get to the part where you tell me what the hell you want."

"You're valuable again, Miles," Victor said slowly. "I always knew you had it in you, son."

"You did, huh?" I couldn't help but puff my chest out. "Glad the streets are talking. I'm hanging up—"

"I'm coming back to town for a visit. When I get there, I want you available."

"That's not poss—"

"It is," he cut in. "See you soon."

The line went dead.

I sighed and pocketed my phone, rubbing my face. Well. Shit could have gone *worse*.

That was fucking terrifying in itself.

You just had *to take the money.*

I heard footsteps. I saw Laurene walking toward me with a veil.

"Miles?" Lu waddled closer. "How are you feeling?"

"Like shit."

She just nodded knowingly, then looked down and touched the veil. "I hear you. This kind of thing…it's not easy. But you'll be surprised over time it gets easier."

I remembered the abrupt wedding between her and Reese. She was probably the only one truly who understood my predicament and all the challenges that came with it.

"This wasn't supposed to happen. But her? Of all people, Lu?"

Laurene looked at me closely. "It's not just about what happened with your dad, is it? It's from before."

"Huh?" I squinted at her.

"*I know*, Miles."

That made me blink, and Laurene gave me a look.

"I saw you sneak out her bedroom the day before the summer soirée."

Well, shit.

I shifted awkwardly. Laurene looked after her sisters. She was second oldest, but like Erik, she was super protective, so I needed to tread lightly.

"Lu…" I started. "You don't understand—"

"Don't worry, I didn't say anything to Erik or our parents."

She reached forward, placing a hand on my shoulder.

"Listen, I get it," she said, her tone softening as she leaned in a little. "I've been there, Miles. With Reese, I—" She paused, as if the words were hard to say. "We were together before everything happened. Before my engagement to his brother. Before everything went to hell."

What she said made my throat close up.

"It wasn't easy coming back home, Miles. And it sure as hell wasn't easy when my family decided to set me up in an arranged marriage with the one person I tried to forget. I know it's hard for you because you stayed. I couldn't have done that."

I watched as a myriad of emotions crossed her face, and she placed her hand on her swollen belly.

"I thought I was over it. Over him," Laurene continued softly. "Our marriage was supposed to be a duty. I thought I could just show up, smile, survive. But the feeling that…you've been ripped apart by your own choices and the what-ifs keep you up at night? You can't ignore that. And when I was standing across from the man who knew me better than anyone else—who still *saw* me—I couldn't just let all my feelings die."

For a second, it felt like she forgot I was even there.

"Serena is different. We've always loved her, but it was clear she never moved through the world the same way as us. She doesn't do mess. Chaos overwhelms her. Feelings overwhelm her. She likes structure. Predictability. Control. It's how she protects herself."

I nodded.

"It takes someone brave, open-minded, patient, and extremely compassionate to be with her," Laurene said. "And I think that person has always been you."

I whistled low, scratching my neck. "Damn, Lu. Brave, open-minded, patient, compassionate? You got me sounding like a therapy dog or some shit."

She rolled her eyes. "If you're standing here, trying to act like you don't feel any of that with Serena, maybe you should ask yourself if you're lying to her, or just to yourself."

I sighed. "My situation is not the same as yours."

"I know it's not the same, but there's this…tension, right? Between you two? The kind that doesn't go away just because you're forced to stand next to each other or you pretend to hate one another. It doesn't *have* to be about what our families expect from you. It's about what you both choose to face—and what you're willing to fight for together."

My heart was pounding in my chest.

"I think you both could be happy together. It you want to be."

That word hit harder than it should've.

Happy.

I didn't know what to say.

Because deep down, I remembered her smile too.

"Thanks," I said, my voice rough. "I'll…think about it."

Laurene smiled, patting me on my shoulder she brushed by. "We'll be in there soon."

The veil in Laurene's hand was still a reminder of everything I had to lose—and everything I didn't know how to fix.

I walked toward the mayor's office and stepped inside with no hesitation.

Standing by the window, looking out, was Erik.

Of fucking course.

"Erik," I said.

He turned to face me, his eyes filled with a mix of emotions—anger, sadness, and something else I couldn't quite place.

"Miles," he said, his tone flat.

"I didn't think you would come." I closed the door, taking a few steps inside.

"I had to see if you still had the fucking balls to go along with this."

I gritted my teeth, my back stiffening. "It's not like I had a choice."

Erik turned, eyes blazing. His brown skin flushed; his fists clenched. "You have a choice. But you did back then too, and you made the wrong one with the whole Victor thing."

"Don't try me," I snapped, stepping forward. "You wanna talk about leaving shit in shambles? Let's talk about what *you* did to my family. You wrecked us, man. That's why I made that deal."

"That was after! I warned you about those guys and their sketchy deals." Erik's voice cracked, his tone cutting deeper. "I didn't *want* to tell, Miles. Omar was family to me too, but he was outta control. Somebody had to do something. You were obviously too pussy to do it. Don't make excuses because you stooped fucking low to make deals with criminals."

"You weren't funding us!" I had to keep my voice steady. "Who was making sure my family was fed, hmm? You and the rest of your family turned your fucking backs on us. If anything, you should've kept your damn mouth shut."

"You caused all this!" Erik yelled, closing the distance between us. "You always thought all this shit was a game, Miles."

We bumped chests, and I lost it, shoving him hard. Years of anger finally blew. "Say that shit again, Erik. I dare you."

He stumbled but caught himself, his face twisting into something feral as he came right back, shoving me with both hands. "You caused all this by pussyfooting. You ruined the town. You ruined our friendship."

My blood was boiling as I stepped forward again, this time grabbing his shirt. "You got a lotta nerve, acting like you're the victim. You destroyed my family, and now you wanna act all high and mighty? Fuck that!"

Erik didn't flinch, his hands coming up to shove me off him. I stumbled back this time, but came right back at him, but before I could swing, the door opened and a voice broke through the haze of rage.

"Hey! Break it up." Dante suddenly entered the room and stepped between us. "Please try not to destroy anything in here. My aunt would kill me if you cracked that statue."

Erik and I froze, our breathing heavy, faces inches apart.

He took a step back. Then he reached into his jacket pocket and pulled out a manila envelope. He held it out to me, a silence stretching as I stared at the envelope.

"The fuck is that?"

Erik's expression was grim. "A way out."

I opened the envelope and found a stack of money.

"What is this?" I asked again, though I had a sinking feeling I knew.

"You're smart enough to figure it out," Erik said, his tone sharp. "Let's end this marriage before it starts. Name your price if you need to, but don't marry Serena. I can figure out how to fix this for both of us."

Dante raised a brow. "Interesting decision, Erik, knowing the stakes."

"Mind your business," he snapped at Dante.

I looked at Erik, stunned. "You're trying to *bribe* me?"

"This is about keeping my sister away from you before you drag her into your fucking mess of a show."

"Fuck your offer, Erik. And fuck you."

Before either of us could throw the first punch, our parents walked in, Yvonne's eyes narrowing as she took in the scene. "What the hell is going on here?"

"Nothing like a good ol' fight before a wedding to get everyone in the mood," Dante drawled.

CHAPTER 10
Serena

"YOU LOOK BEAUTIFUL, SERENA," Laurene said, putting the veil on me.

A veil. Symbolic. Decorative. Pointless.

I'd never thought my wedding would be this way. Scratch that. I never imagined a wedding at all.

Don't lie, you wanted a wedding, but this is all that you're getting.

Not because I didn't believe in them. Logically, they had utility—merging estates, aligning power structures, consolidating influence. I just always thought that Mama would have enough use for me that she wouldn't marry me off.

But no. I was serving a purpose.

This wedding was *not* like Laurene's.

No dramatic announcements or parties, no fancy location. No pomp. No string quartet. No flashbulbs. No dress. Just a city hall wedding in my best pantsuit and expensive heels.

Laurene came around to face me. "Are you okay?"

My first instinct was to say yes. *Yes* was tidy. *Yes* didn't open the door to a conversation I didn't know how to have.

What was I supposed to feel right now? Nerves? Resentment? Relief?

I'm marrying Miles.

I wanted someone to tell me what the right emotion was, so I could feel that one and move on.

"You can talk to me. Be honest. This is a lot to take in," Laurene said.

I straightened my ivory pantsuit and fixed my cuff. This calmed me down. Details. Always the details. They were easier to handle than my nervous stomach and racing heart.

"I'm *fine*," I said, sharper than I meant to. "I'm not falling apart. I'm not scared. I don't *need* to cry to process this like you do. I'm doing what's required of me. I don't have the luxury of running away to Paris, screwing everything up, and coming back to open arms and applause. That's not my function."

It might have been wrong the way to say it, but Laurene didn't understand.

I'm not her. No matter what I did or tried, I could never amount to Laurene. The one people made room for, bent over backward to protect, praise, *love*. It never happened for me.

But it still fucking hurt.

Laurene's face fell. I regretted what I said, but couldn't undo it.

Gigi rushed into the bathroom with a bouquet in her hands.

"What's taking so long? We're on a schedule here," she snapped as she gave me a once-over. "Nice suit. Very you. *Bland*."

I flipped her off.

Gigi looked between us. "What happened?"

"Nothing," I said quickly.

"You did something, what did you do? You got that look on your face."

"G, it's fine—" Laurene started.

"Let's just go." I took one last look in the mirror and turned, ready to walk out, and Gigi shook her head, stopping me with one hand and pushing me back.

"This is more than you just being mean and surly." Gigi

narrowed her gaze on me. "We're gonna air this shit out before we go. So, who wanna talk first? I got all day."

Sighing loudly, I glanced at Laurene, who just shrugged and looked away.

Great. I hurt her feelings.

But that was life. I only got praise when I *produced*. Good grades. Flawless plans. Keeping it together.

Love was *usefulness*.

So where was my love when I was being useful to the entire fucking family right now?

Gigi snapped, "Don't be a bitch to Lu. Nobody is telling you that you gotta act all gangster about this! All of us would be pissing our pants, you damn robot. If you can't be real with your sisters, who you gonna be real with?"

Her words hung in the air, and for a moment, I almost let my guard down. Almost.

Would they even understand? I was going to have to look at and *live* with my mistake each and every day.

"I'm doing what I have to," I insisted. "What more do you want from me? I'm not going to cause a scene. It's bad enough I'm playing along with the veil and bouquet. That's what we do in this family, isn't it? We show up. We get it done."

Laurene and Gigi shared a look. I *hated* that look. It was one they'd had since childhood when they were in on the joke and I wasn't.

"No one's asking you to fall apart, Serena. But you're allowed to feel *something*. Even about Miles," Laurene said.

"God, give poor Miles strength if he's dealing with her," Gigi muttered. "You got shit easy, at least you know Miles. Lu didn't even know Reese like that, imagine going through that."

Laurene pursed her lips but didn't say anything.

"I'll make sure to say the same to whoever gets stuck with your ass," I snapped at her.

"It's obvious you've had a crush on Miles since we were kids.

You ain't even happy you gonna get to have him in your place? Shirtless. Naked..." Gigi grinned evilly at me.

I do not need more thoughts about naked Miles.

"He's my arranged husband, not a gigolo," I responded stiffly.

"Don't knock the profession. I've dabbled with the escorts."

Laurene made a face. "You have?"

I turned back to the mirror, inspecting my makeup. There were no flaws.

Gigi ignored her. "You think he's not gonna be walking around in *just* a towel sometimes?"

Laurene mulled over that. "I mean...she's not wrong."

"I'm just saying. Miles might be willing to put you through the mattress even if it's in the name of revenge against Erik or if he just needs to get a load off. If I were him, I'd do it to be petty. I'm pretty sure you're still a virgin."

Laurene and I shared a glance, and I hated that my skin flushed and I looked away.

"Ah!" Gigi pointed. "You *are* a virgin."

"Georgiana, please," Laurene told her. "We have a wedding to go to—"

"What's the rush? We are all *grown-ass women*. We can talk about sex. Hell, we are the physical manifestation of the consequences of it! Look at you! Hunching." Gigi pointed at Laurene's baby bump.

"Look, no!" I snapped and shook my head. "I don't need any lessons. I don't want advice. Can we just get out of here, so we can all go home and I can start to forget that this is happening?"

"Welp, I tried. I'm just gonna let God handle you. Here." She tossed the bouquet at me, and it hit my arm before falling to the floor.

Laurene shook her head. "Damn, G."

I picked the bouquet off the floor. Gigi looked like she could spit, and Laurene just looked sad.

"Let's go."

I pretended to be calm, but I was terrified the closer I got to the mayor's office. What were my priorities? My goals? If I ran through those again, I would feel centered, calmer. Not like I was hurtling off a skyscraper at this very moment.

Emails. Had to send emails. Final financial snapshots. Get rid of Jenese and get my life back on track.

Erik exploded out of the mayor's office. He bowled us over, ignoring us completely.

"Erik, where the hell you going?" Gigi called after him. "You're my ride!"

He didn't even look back as he marched down the hall and disappeared around the corner.

"Well damn, I guess he objects," Gigi muttered.

"You gotta joke about everything?" Laurene frowned at her.

My heart hammered, and I gaped at Miles, standing in the doorway frozen, jaw clenched tight, a fist balled so hard his arm trembled.

My eyes just drank him in, from his chest to his waist, to his legs all ready to rumble. My skin prickled with heat, low and treacherous.

My husband.

Miles quickly spun on his heel, storming inside.

"Not a good sign necessarily, but maybe the after-party will be better? We are gonna eat after this, right?" Gigi asked.

I ignored them and tightened my grip on the bouquet, walking slowly into the office. Fine. He wanted to be an asshole. I could match that energy as well. I'd be the biggest bitch he ever saw coming.

The temperature of the room dropped the moment I stepped inside. The room was split cleanly in two, like a courtroom. My family on one side, Miles's family on the other.

Half the room hated this moment; the other half hated each other.

There were no happy faces.

Only grim. Sad. Angry. Depressed. No one could even bother to pretend and fake it for me.

Then came the chirp of a breathy voice that didn't match the tension. "I'm sorry I'm late! I had an emergency at work…"

Every head turned.

Noelle, Laurene's best friend since childhood, flew in, wide-eyed. "I saw Erik…" She stopped talking when she saw our faces, and grimaced when she glanced at Miles.

"Oh," she squeaked, blinking rapidly. She scurried over to sit on my side next to Reese, who was the only one who seemed unfazed.

"Shall we get started?" Dante said.

My gaze lingered on Miles for a last moment, a silent question hanging in the air between us.

I clutched the bouquet tightly in my hand, its stiff stems digging into my palms. Laurene kindly offered to take it, freeing my hand to accept Miles's outstretched one.

"Grab his hand," Gigi whispered loudly, pulling Walter out of her purse to sit on her lap. The dog barked at me, and I glared at him.

This isn't justice. This isn't healing. This is PR.

This was two broken legacies being stitched together in public view, as if slapping our last names into a headline would somehow fix the rot beneath it all.

But then I looked up.

And in Miles's eyes, I saw it—that flicker of old memories coming back to haunt.

I'd liked how he saw things—tilted, funny, unsanitized. I liked that he noticed details, the same way I did. That he made chaos seem charming. I liked how he saw me.

Until he didn't.

My hand trembled as I held Miles's.

His palm was warm. Solid. Familiar in a way that made my stomach knot.

I wanted to hate the way his touch felt solid when everything inside me felt like it was fracturing.

But I couldn't. Because I remembered what it felt like to be held together by him.

Do not cry. Do not shake. Do not run.

Mayor Castillo cleared his throat. "Ladies and gentlemen, we are gathered here today to witness the union of Serena Colette King and Miles Donovan Whitmore in marriage."

My name didn't feel like mine.

But I nodded anyway. I could nod. I could recite the script. I could survive this.

King Developments was all that mattered. That company was *mine.* I couldn't lose it. What would I be without it?

"Marriage is a commitment to life together," Mayor Castillo continued. "It offers opportunities for sharing and growth that no other human relationship can equal, a physical and emotional joining that is promised for a lifetime."

I would have felt better if the mayor just gave the cheap, generic vows and let us get the hell on with this sham.

I made myself look Miles in the eye. I hope he knew I'd never be his, I needed to remind myself to not let those pesky emotions come back. But his eyes…they were still impossibly kind, impossibly open, full of wonder. He'd been through hell, and now he was marrying someone who didn't deserve him.

"Do you, Miles, take Serena to be your lawfully wedded wife, to have and to hold, in sickness and in health, for richer or poorer, for better or worse, as long as you both shall live?"

"I do," he said.

"And do you, Serena, take Miles to be your lawfully wedded husband, to have and to hold, in sickness and in health, for richer or poorer, for better or worse, as long as you both shall live or this business arrangement runs its course?"

I wasn't about to lose it.

This was a game I had to win. I had to prove I was a champion.

To my mother. To Jenese.

The silence was deafening, and I felt everyone staring. Mama's glare, Daddy's frown, Laurene's thinned lips, and Gigi's arched brow.

"I do," I said, resolute.

Nothing was going to stop me from making King Developments the number one real estate company in this town *and* state.

"I officially declare you husband and wife."

Miles and I stared at each other, my heartbeat pounding in my ears. I hated that I still felt something standing this close to him.

I hated I couldn't name what it was.

"You can kiss your bride," Dante said, but gave us a very strange look.

Miles hesitated before finally cupping my face—if you could even call it that. His fingers barely grazed my skin, more like a doctor assessing a patient rather than a man about to kiss his wife.

I remembered the first time he kissed me, under the magnolia tree behind the tennis courts at his parents' home.

"You know I'd fight the world for you, right?" he'd whispered, low and raw.

I remembered thinking I could fall in love with him right there.

His mouth met mine, and the heat of it—the familiarity— shook something loose inside me. It was something between hunger and heartbreak, like he didn't know if he wanted to like it or destroy me. I told myself to be still. I hated the instinctive way my hands shot up, my fingers digging into the rough wool of his jacket lapels to keep myself from falling.

The scent of him—oakmoss, citrus, and something distinctly *him*—pulled me under.

His palm against my spine, dragging me closer like he didn't care who saw. Like he had never stopped wanting this.

When he pulled back, the loss was immediate.

Dante smirked. "Congratulations. A new heavenly match for this town."

"You have the weekend to get acclimated to one another before your sister's art exhibit, which you will attend together," Mama told us. "I say we get the shock over with and announce this union immediately."

"We need more time than that," Miles said.

Audrey's face was a mask of diplomacy. "Miles, we don't have much time."

Omar nodded curtly. "Yvonne is…right."

"A weekend isn't enough time to really adjust to…this." Miles looked at me. "We don't get a honeymoon? Hell, a chance to say goodbye to our old normal?"

"Honeymoon?" Mama laughed cruelly. "There won't be a honeymoon. What we need is to fix our companies, which is all hands on deck starting now."

"We need more time," he insisted.

"*Make* the weekend enough," Mama said to us. "You need to decide where you'll live. Your place or Serena's?"

Miles's shoulders slumped slightly, his frustration giving way to resignation. "Serena can decide."

The room fell silent, all eyes turning to me.

"We'll stay at my place," I said finally, my voice steady despite the turmoil inside me. "It's more practical."

What?

"And you." Mama looked at me, ignoring Miles entirely. "I assume you've sorted out the Harrington estate."

I inhaled, Jenese flashing in my mind.

"Yes."

Mama smiled. "That can be the first property King Developments and Whitmore Ventures partner on to show everyone that our companies are fine. No unsafe work conditions, no environmental disasters." She glared at Dante. "That satisfy you?"

"Immensely," he said.

Mama nodded and turned back to me and Miles. "First, there will be no personal discussions regarding your marriage outside of this room. Whatever you feel or have felt, it stays between you two. Be at the gallery with big fucking smiles on. *Everyone else* here will keep the nature of this marriage to themselves."

I felt my chest tighten.

"Second," my mother continued, "you'll need to start thinking about your future together—not just as a couple, but as business partners. You need to have a plan by Monday. We're merging the companies whether you're ready or not. Miles, with your failing track record, I'm sure you can learn a lot from Serena."

He glared at Mama but didn't say anything.

"Good," Mama said, her voice clipped but satisfied. "Now, let's move forward, and have some lunch."

The room began to clear, the air heavy with the weight of decisions made and the unspoken tension between us as Miles and I looked at each other.

"I need to grab my things from my apartment. You're in the condo downtown, right?" he asked, his voice surprisingly soft.

I nodded.

"I'll be there in an hour."

"Seems you've got quite a bit on your plate," Dante said. "Can I give you some advice?"

I'd forgotten he was still in the room. I turned to him, and I wondered how much of what he said was genuine and how much was merely another layer of the game we were all playing.

"In your world, appearances are just as important as reality. It's about what's *perceived*. Use it to your advantage."

That sounded strangely similar to something Jenese would say.

"Thank you for the advice," I said, unsure what to make of it.

Dante gave a small, enigmatic smile. "Anytime. I'm sure we'll be seeing more of each other, Mrs. Whitmore."

CHAPTER 11

Miles

"NO ESCAPE, DOUGHBOY," I told my cat.

I looked up at Serena's condo. I was way later than I was supposed to be, but I found it hard to pack my stuff up and actually leave my home to come to…hell?

That was too dramatic.

Her place was too quiet. No protesters, no paparazzi, not even some angry old man with a picket sign and a bad comb-over.

I stood outside, suitcase in one hand, and the rest of my damn life in the other.

I'd hated her for six years. And now I'd have to hear her laughing in the next room? Smell her damn perfume down the hall? See her in pajamas at night and act like I don't remember how she used to love me?

"Mrow," Doughboy said, purring and rubbing against my face from his spot on my shoulder.

At least one of us wasn't freaking out.

I finally exhaled deeply and knocked on her door. Seconds felt like centuries, and Doughboy shifted on my shoulder when I heard footsteps approaching and then they stopped.

"You gonna open the door?" I asked, staring at the peephole that I knew she was staring through.

Silence.

The door finally creaked open, and there she was, her face composed as ever, a mask I knew all too well. But then her gaze landed on Doughboy.

"What is *that*?"

I glanced at him. "Doughboy."

"It's a *cat*. Why is it here?"

"I'm not leaving him in my place alone." Like I didn't know she was stalling. "Where should I put my things?"

"Wait—" Serena stopped me from entering. "We didn't talk about pets. They're dirty and have fur. When did you get a cat?"

"You know I like cats. Where I go, he goes. Would it make you happier for me to call your mama and tell her we can't do this marriage thing?"

Serena narrowed her eyes on me and then Doughboy. Like she was really considering banning us from coming in.

"Mrow," he said to her.

"It's huge."

"*He's* a Maine coon. Respect his breed."

She stepped back, holding the door wide enough for me to slip through, and glared at Doughboy.

"Keep him away from me."

The inside was all slick lines and sharp corners. Muted tones dominated the space, with floor-to-ceiling windows offering panoramic views of the town down to the marina and the Pacific Ocean beyond. The furniture was clean and angular, every piece looking like it belonged in some fancy design magazine.

"Doughboy is a free spirit. He goes where he pleases," I said. "If he graces you with his company, be glad."

"You will abide by my rules," Serena snapped.

"Your rules, huh?" I said, slipping into the condo like I wasn't seconds from combusting in annoyance. "Damn, déjà vu.

Just missing the chore wheel and being grounded if I forgot to take out the trash."

Serena sent me another glare, but I felt like it was losing its threat.

My rules. My rules. My rules.

I remembered how she used to say that when we were kids. Whenever Yvonne put Serena in charge of stuff, like cleaning the attic or garage, Serena bossed us around like a drill sergeant.

"Open blinds and dim the lights," Serena commanded.

The condo sprang to life instantly. The blinds whooshed open, and a warm glow filled the room from the setting sun. Smooth jazz started playing from hidden speakers.

"Wow." I whistled low. "So this is how the other half lives. Must've cost a fortune."

"Noelle." Serena's tone was flat. "She wants me to test her new software. We're thinking of partnering on a few smart houses."

"Tell Noelle I'm impressed. I only have that basic shit that comes on the phone, and it judged me every time I ordered pizza at two a.m."

Still nothing.

I finally noticed that Serena had changed out of the pantsuit from earlier.

Loose, comfortable jeans. I felt like I was twenty-seven again, peeling them off her body, listening to her breath hitch as my hands mapped skin I had no business touching.

I dragged my gaze up, past the wild strands of hair slipping free from her short ponytail, past the delicate line of her throat. Her bare feet tapped against the floor, an absent, restless habit.

She looked so fucking touchable. And I wanted to.

Which only pissed me off more.

"I have a pullout couch." Serena crossed her arms. "It's in my office. You can put everything there."

"All I get is a pullout couch? Damn, no guest room with a little mint on the pillow?"

"I don't like people in my space," she said. "A guest room encourages...lingering. And I've worked very hard to ensure that Gigi and Walter never get the idea to sleep over unannounced again."

I smirked. "I'm being punished because your sister's a bad houseguest?"

"Exactly," Serena said, turning toward the hallway. "This is not the Motel 6. You'll be on your way soon too."

"This is a marriage," I pushed. "Couples share beds. Isn't that in our marriage clause?"

"Don't play with me, Miles."

I raised a brow. "I'm being serious."

"You and your cat will be on the street if you keep pushing me."

I held up my hands in surrender. "Fine, fine, I'll let it go for now."

"You'll let it go *period*."

"You wouldn't kick me out. I'm good company."

She rolled her eyes. "You're exhausting."

"Yeah, but you love it."

Why the fuck did you say that?

Her lips curled, but she didn't meet my eyes. Instead, she took another step, brushing past me, close enough that I could feel the warmth of her body, the whisper of fabric against my arm.

"Follow me," she said roughly. "The rules are Doughboy stays out of my room. And he better not scratch up my couch, which you *will* replace if he does. No touching my Italian imported coffee. Don't touch my stereo—"

I couldn't help but let my gaze drop back to the roundness of her ass as she rattled off rules and pointed out closets and bathrooms.

When we finally reached the office door, she pushed it open and stepped aside, motioning for me to enter.

"Here you go," she said, her tone brisk, professional. "It's not much, but it should be comfortable enough."

I was expecting the same cold, curated minimalism—but this space felt warmer. Lived-in. *Her.* It was smaller, cozier, the faint scent of eucalyptus in the air. A soft overstuffed chair sat by the large window, the couch on the left wall. A deep blue rug covered most of the polished floor. The desk was still precise—papers aligned, pens grouped by color in a matte ceramic mug—but it was less…defensive.

"Well, it's better than the cellar I thought you'd put me in."

Serena side-eyed me. "Don't tempt me."

I set my bags down and gently placed Doughboy on the floor. He sniffed around cautiously, his nose twitching as he explored.

"My room is right next door."

Next door.

Just a thin wall separating us. Dough jumped onto the pullout bed that had already been made up, curling into the sheets like he owned the place. Why was I now imaging Serena in bed, in a T-shirt and panties only? Her hand trailing down her legs and into her—

"Clean sheets?" I asked, though my chest felt tight. "Or did you get them out the trash?"

"I washed them this morning. On hot. Dried with lavender sheets." She paused. "I don't use trash linens even if I don't want guests."

If I piss her off enough, maybe we could get it down to a year.

"Would you like a drink?" she asked abruptly.

"Got something strong?"

Without another word, she spun on her heel and practically ran toward the kitchen.

I followed her, turning the corner into the kitchen. It was sleek and modern, but I saw the small stack of cookbooks lined up on the counter, and one was open.

Serena stood at the counter. Her movements were practiced, almost rehearsed. She reached for the bottle of whiskey, then paused. Her fingers flexed around its neck—once, twice, again—like she was remembering how much pressure to use. Then she poured.

She handed me my glass without looking up.

"Here," she said, forcing the cup to me. "From Reese's new Rebel Spirits line."

I took a sip, letting the rich taste settle on my tongue.

"Cinnamon? Honey?" I finally said as the flavors sat on my tongue.

Serena nodded, but she didn't look at me as she set her glass down. The jazz music drifted from the living room, soft and seductive, but it did little to ease the tightness in the room.

"Guess this is how dinner is gonna be every night, huh?" I joked.

"We're two people fulfilling an obligation. Let's not pretend it's anything more than that."

"But we don't have to treat each other like you just picked me off a random curb outside. Damn, you can be chill, you know? It's me."

"*Precisely.* It's you." She looked away, her fingers tightening around her glass. "I think it's better if we set the ground rules and expectations."

"Rules, expectations, order—"

Serena raised her voice. "It's better to go through this—"

"For you or for me?" I asked.

She went silent, and a puzzled look crossed her face. Frustrated, I ran a hand over my face and muttered, "Lay them on me."

"Rule number one: No bringing up...what happened. The past."

"What happened to the rules before? Aren't we on fifteen by now?" I let out a short, humorless laugh, and she frowned. "The past, huh? That's the first thing you want off the table?"

"Yes. It's in the past for a reason, Miles. We don't bring it up."

Her eyes flickered to mine, sharp, like a warning. "It's not helping either of us, or our situation."

Just forget one of the nights that changed my life? Okay. *Simple.*

"We can't erase what happened, no matter what you do to sleep at night."

Her jaw tightened. "I don't—"

"Don't what?" I stepped closer still, until the heat between us was thick enough to choke on. "Don't think about it? Don't remember? Because I do, Serena. Our past is *here.*"

She sucked in a breath.

I leaned in. "I remember how you felt that night. How you looked at me. Like you wanted me more than you wanted to be careful. Then the next night, it was like I didn't matter."

"We were kids," she said, her voice softer now, but no less sharp. "It was a mistake. Grow up. Move on."

"Hmm, how can we move on from something we never fully addressed?"

"I'm not changing my mind."

I leaned back, crossing my arms. "And what's rule number two?"

"Rule number two." She frowned at me. "We keep things professional. We go to work. We come home. You live your life. I live mine. I'm not making you dinner, cleaning your clothes, vacuuming your room. Take care of yourself like the adult you have been."

"Professional?" I echoed, the word like a stone dropping between us. "You are really focused on eliminating the past, huh? Fine," I said, rolling my shoulders like none of it mattered. "We'll keep it professional. Like strangers in an elevator." I knocked back the rest of my whiskey.

She looked away, her grip on the glass tightening.

"And what's the third rule, Serena?"

"Rule number three: No touching. No hugs or kissing. No

pretending to fall in love in front of others. If it's not for photos, we shouldn't touch. That'll make things easier."

I took the bottle from her, pouring myself another glass. Whatever she needed to erase her guilty conscience, I'd let her. I didn't regret our night. Only what happened after.

"What's the first thing for us on the Harrington renovation? I can have Carlus inspect the property, get us some estimates. Maybe we can do some damage control there, and show people our companies are ethical and sustainable."

She didn't respond for so long I thought she somehow hadn't heard me. "We…we need to figure something else out," she said finally. "We don't have it."

"What do you mean, 'we don't have it'?" The disbelief sat heavy on my tongue. "You won the damn auction, Serena. It was yours."

"The family decided to sell it privately. Another buyer came in with a better offer."

Something about the way she said it made my jaw tighten. "Bullshit."

Her brows lifted. "Excuse me?"

"You don't just *lose* deals like this." My voice was steady, but I could feel the heat rising under my skin. "You're telling me someone just swooped in last minute and took it from you?"

"We don't have it," she said flatly, her voice colder than I ever imagined it could be. "You're getting upset and there's nothing we can do about it."

"So, what now?" I asked, voice low. "We were banking on that property. There's nothing else as good."

"We'll pivot," she said, as if it were that simple. "Find another high-profile estate, something to solidify our standing."

I turned back to her, arms crossing over my chest. "And who's picking this time? Because if you're the one negotiating, I'd like to make sure we don't get blindsided *again*."

Her nostrils flared slightly. "You think you could've done better?"

"Yeah," I said without hesitation.

We were too close now, the energy between us shifting.

"I have a lead on a townhouse by the wharf, so you know we can sell it for ten times the price." Serena pulled away from me, heading back to her side of the kitchen. "It's not on the market yet. I found out Mrs. Fontaine is gonna do a direct sell to Rhodes Realty. We intercept that and get the property instead. We'll meet with the owner tomorrow."

"I need a game plan for how we're moving forward on it."

"I don't need a game plan," she said, her voice cool, almost dismissive. "You just come in and look pretty. Let me handle the strategy."

"I'm not in the business of just showing up to look good. I've got more to offer than that, Serena. I did steal the yacht club from you."

She glared at me.

"Be ready at eight in the morning."

"Eight?" I raised an eyebrow. "You know I'm not a morning person."

"You'll survive."

CHAPTER 12

Serena

PEOPLE BARGAINED IN THE FARMERS' market like the world would end without a tomato. I needed to focus. I wasn't here for fruit or honey, even though the honey stand was already catching my eye. They had those hexagonal jars I liked.

I don't know why, but when Miles was staring at me last night, I wanted to confess. Say everything out loud. Maybe not everything. But something.

Did you forget the main threat? Worry about Miles and petty feelings later.

Jenese's threat echoed in my head, over and over.

If she actually wrote that book, everything I'd worked for would crumble. Everything I'd hidden would be exposed. At one point I thought that was the way to get ahead. But I was wrong, and I was glad I'd woken up from her spell when I did.

I was smart enough to not be recorded. So how did she do it?

Why did I even fall for her scheme?

Miles. He was to blame. If I hadn't slept with him, if he had taken control of his father that night, my parents wouldn't have fought. Laurene's engagement would have gone well instead of the disaster that happened. She wouldn't have fought with Mama, and I wouldn't have been sent to that networking dinner.

I'd never have met Jenese. I'd never have fallen for her lies. I'd never have done everything I did with her.

So really… He was the one to blame for the mess of my life.

"We're not here to really shop," I told him when he finally decided to pull himself from the deep debate with the man selling avocados.

"You literally have nothing in your fridge but baking soda, whiskey, and those sad-ass-looking paleo meals. I need protein. You think I keep this gorgeous body right and tight off of rice cakes?" Miles looked at me with a frown before he finally settled on a deal for five insanely priced avocados.

"Those meals are prepared by a Michelin star chef."

"They look like those meals Eddie Murphy was eating as Sherman in *The Nutty Professor*. I will not be putting it into my temple." He placed a hand on his pecs, and I tried not to get distracted by that at all.

Fine. I wouldn't argue with him about having more food in the fridge.

Miles finished talking to the guy, and we kept walking through the crowd. We passed a small wooden fruit stand stacked with peaches and strawberries.

"You still hate peaches?" he asked.

"Absolutely. They're slimy. The texture freaks me out."

That earned me a side glance. A flicker of a smile tugged at his lips. "I remember you pretending to eat them then spitting them in a napkin and throwing it away when your grandpa wasn't looking."

A warm feeling spread through me, and I couldn't help but smile.

"Grandpa Ben liked them. I tried to like them for him but…" I shrugged. "And you used to eat them like they were gold."

"Because they *are*, Miss Rice Cakes."

Only two years. We could do this for two years, right? I slowed my steps, and Miles walked ahead of me, a canvas tote slung over his shoulder, brimming with fresh herbs and vegetables like some kind of domestic fantasy we didn't earn.

With an easy confidence, he moved through the dense crowd; his broad shoulders carved a path, the sounds of chatter and laughter fading as people instinctively made way.

I bit my lip, watching as he smiled at people walking by.

Even with the entire mess that happened with his father, Miles was still smiling. *Happy.*

And not pretend-happy. Not the tight, professional smile I'd spent years perfecting. His happiness was unbothered. Loose. Real.

I tried to remember the last time I felt anything close to that.

Had I ever?

No. I'd trained myself out of joy. Joy wasn't productive.

Miles never measured his worth in quarterly reports or proximity to perfection. He laughed at dumb jokes. He made room for chaos. I still remembered when he convinced me to sneak out of the house for the first time when we were kids.

Shit. Miles was a bad influence on my life. He'd always been a bad influence.

He looked back at me suddenly—just a glance over his shoulder. Caught me staring. A slow, knowing smirk curled on his lips.

"You good?"

"I'm fine," I said quickly, too quickly.

His lips twitched like he didn't believe me, but he didn't press. Instead, he gestured to a stall up ahead, and without thinking, I assumed, he grabbed my hand. "C'mon. I got something to change your mind."

The warmth of his hand in mine felt like a strange, potent drug, leaving me weak and vulnerable.

Was I that desperate that holding hands sent me in a spiral?

He turned away, but not before I caught the subtle flex of his biceps as he shifted the tote bag higher on his shoulder. I felt the heat rise in my chest, that damn familiar pull. His body had always been a weapon.

My gaze drifted down involuntarily, trailing over the taut fabric of his shirt, the subtle bulge of muscle beneath it, the way his jeans fit just a little too perfectly.

God, Serena, stop it.

We reached the next stall, the one with the vivid display of peaches and plums, and Miles handed me a peach. "These are actually imported from Colombia. They taste like cotton candy."

"I don't try things."

Miles rolled his eyes. "Today you're going to have a new experience."

I bit into the peach. Juice slid down to my chin, the fruit almost melting against my tongue, sticky-sweet and ripe. Our eyes met, and the intensity of the moment sent shivers down my spine. The sweetness clashed with the bitterness in my chest. Miles didn't move, not at first. He just *watched*, his gaze dragging down to my mouth.

Without warning, Miles took the peach from my hand, his fingers grazing mine. He held another piece of fruit to my lips, not asking this time.

"Here." His eyes locked on my mouth. "You're not done."

My lips parted before I realized what I was doing. He fed me slowly, watching the way my mouth closed around the soft flesh. I bit down, and his fingers lingered on the stem, like he wasn't ready to let go.

"See?" he said, softer now. "Sweet. Like I told you."

His thumb brushed against my lower lip, wiping away some of the juices.

I pulled away, my chest rising and falling sharply as if I'd just run a mile.

"Stop doing that," I whispered, my voice unsteady, but the words felt hollow.

He tilted his head, his lips curling into a knowing grin, as if he saw right through me. "Doing what, Serena?"

I didn't answer. I couldn't.

"Can we look for Mrs. Fontaine, please? And get out of here?"

Miles's head snapped to the right, and he frowned. "That guy owes me brie!"

My brows furrowed. "What?"

Miles dragged me across the aisle, nearly running over others.

"Miles, we don't have time—"

Then I saw her—Mrs. Fontaine. Standing near a stall just a few feet ahead, sorting through fresh flowers.

"That's her."

Miles frowned. "That's the lead? Mrs. Fontaine? Serena, I—"

"Just follow my lead, and I'll handle it."

I left Miles, rushing over.

"Mrs. Fontaine?"

She turned, her eyes narrowing slightly as she tried to place me. "Yes?"

I offered a friendly smile. "Serena King. We met briefly at the charity gala last month. I couldn't help but notice your exquisite taste in flowers."

"Ah, yes, Serena. How lovely to see you again. How is your sister Laurene? Has she had the baby yet?"

"Not yet. I wanted to speak to you about—"

Miles caught up to us. His hand slid to the small of my back, the heat of his palm burning through the thin cotton of my dress. He began a slow massage, a wave of agonizing heat surging up my spine.

"Oh, Miles. Good to see you!"

Her wrinkled hands reached out, gripping his arms, before she leaned in to place a kiss on his cheek, her eyes crinkling with affection. I frowned, looking between them.

"You two know each other?"

Miles grinned smugly. "Mrs. Fontaine and I both go to a care-givers' support group."

"Miles was a great support during a very difficult time with my husband. How's your father? Did he like my soup?"

"He loved it. Did you try that shrimp étouffée recipe I gave you?"

Mrs. Fontaine shook her head. "Too spicy for me."

Miles laughed, and I felt my irritation growing. "A little cayenne pepper ain't gonna hurt you."

"You are a devil! Are you coming to our meeting next week?"

My stomach twisted slightly.

"Actually, Mrs. Fontaine," I said, subtly shifting closer to her and moving him back, "Miles and I were hoping to speak with you about something. We recently got married—"

"What? Congratulations! How haven't I heard this through the grapevine yet?"

"Thanks," Miles said with a strained smile. "I think the gossip mill is just running a little slow."

I sighed. "We're looking to make a deal—"

"Oh, really? How...interesting." She looked over at Miles, then back at me. "And when did your families start speaking again? I'm sure that would have made headlines."

Before I could respond, Miles casually shrugged. "All things come to an end, don't they?"

"I guess you're right. Your families' reconciliation will be an example for everyone." Mrs. Fontaine just laughed like it was the most hilarious shit she'd ever heard.

"Would you be willing to sell your home? For a reasonable price?" I asked her bluntly.

Mrs. Fontaine's eyes narrowed slightly.

"We're ready to make an offer," I continued, trying to clarify. "We've done our projections, and your property is a strategic cornerstone. It's ideal."

She frowned. "You think that's how you ask someone for their home? Like it's just...nothing?"

I paused. My mouth went dry. That hadn't gone how I expected. I thought—

"I didn't mean to sound—" I started, but she cut me off.

"I've heard about your reputation, Miss King," she said coolly. "Bulldozing over families who've been here for generations."

My brain scrambled for a proper response, but all I could think about was how fast everything had shifted. I replayed the words I said. Was I too direct? Did I miss something?

"That's not who she is anymore," he said, voice warm and practiced. "Our companies are merging now, and we're approaching things differently. More responsibly."

He pulled me close, smiling at Mrs. Fontaine.

"We understand the heart of this place matters," he added. "And we'd love the chance to prove we'll honor it."

Mrs. Fontaine blinked.

"Your company hasn't done well either, Miles. I would hate for it to get foreclosed on or sold for scraps."

Disaster. This is a disaster!

"Did I not mention this isn't for business?" I looked at Miles, who was giving me a *what the fuck are you doing* look. "This is… personal. For us. We want to live there."

The lie slid out before I could stop myself, and I felt Miles staring at me.

Lie. That's what I learned from Jenese and from Mama. Lie to get what you want.

I needed this property. I wouldn't let it go. Did it matter if I lied to the little old lady? We needed to restore our companies. After selling it, it was no longer her concern.

"Is that so?"

I nodded and forced a smile.

"How lovely." Her tone was pleasant, but her eyes were sharp. "What was it about the house that caught your eye, then? The stained-glass windows? The garden in the back? The hand-carved staircase? I imagine you've done your research."

Miles cut in, giving me a look, "I told Serena all about the sunroom you have out back overlooking the bay. I think it would be a great place for an office for her. She loves looking out to the hills."

He remembered.

"Yeah, sounds lovely," I agreed.

Mrs. Fontaine seemed mollified. "Okay. For you, Miles. I'll let you look at the house. Since my husband, you know I've been wanting something smaller."

"Of course. Quincy meant a lot to you," Miles said.

Mrs. Fontaine wasn't even giving me another look.

"How about you both to come over and tour the house? If you're serious about keeping it as is, we'll talk more about me selling it to you first before anyone else gets a look."

"I would like—"

Miles cut me off. "We would love that."

"It's a date. Miles, good to see you again and looking forward to our next meeting."

Mrs. Fontaine gave us another glance before walking off. I waited a safe distance before I turned on Miles.

"What the hell was that, Miles?" My voice was low but seething. "You didn't think it was important to tell me you *knew* her? You could have mentioned that, right? Could've—I don't know—given me a heads-up before I stood there like a damn fool?"

"Did you even make small talk before you stormed in and asked for her house? I don't see how you've been in business for so long with no damn tact."

"Oh, so now it's my fault?" I ground out, my voice trembling with barely contained fury.

Miles glared at me. "Yes. You need to treat people like they're fucking humans and not robots. Just because you want something out of them doesn't mean you can't give a little respect."

"Our parents gave us orders—"

"*Fuck* what our parents want. We are the ones working, and if we're gonna work, we need to get on the same page on how we conduct business. Compromise."

"I don't compromise," I said flatly.

He rolled his eyes. "Of course you don't."

"My way has worked time and time again."

"For *you*," he snapped. "But this isn't just about you. You want to bulldoze your way through everything, but news flash, Serena—you're not the only person in this partnership. My way works too."

"Your way is slow. We don't have time to ass-kiss."

"And your way is reckless."

We glared at each other, neither one willing to bend. The air between us was thick, electric, the tension thrumming like a wire about to snap.

Finally, Miles exhaled sharply, shaking his head. "You know what? Fuck it. Do whatever you want. Clearly, you think you know everything. I'm going to get some shallots."

He turned on his heel and walked off, shoving through the crowd of the farmers' market without looking back. I stood there, my jaw tight, my hands clenched at my sides, furious at him—at myself—at this entire situation. I felt my phone vibrating in my purse, and I exhaled loudly, reaching in for it.

It was a text from Mama.

Be at the gallery tomorrow for your sister's exhibit. Wear something appropriate. And bring Erik and me your updated business plan. I want both companies forecasted through Q4.

No greeting. No asking how I was after marrying our mortal enemy. Just the usual: be present, be polished, and produce results.

CHAPTER 13

Serena

"YOU COULD TRY TO SMILE," Miles muttered as the limo slowed in front of the Lush Art Gallery.

"Now you're talking to me?" I glanced at him.

"Yes, *wife.*"

If he keeps tapping that ring against the door, I swear I'll snap his fingers off.

"Pettiness is beneath you, Miles. Grow up."

The limo was too small for this conversation. Or maybe it was just too small for *him.* Miles was too big, too broad, too imposing in the worst kind of way.

And right now, he was close.

His thigh brushed mine, the heat of him seeping through my dress. I smoothed my palm over my knee, pretending I wasn't affected. Miles exhaled a laugh, low and sharp, the sound of a man who wasn't amused in the slightest.

I kept my gaze forward, refusing to look at him.

The limo turned a tight corner, forcing him to press his thigh more firmly against mine. He didn't move. Neither did I.

Miles made a noise in the back of his throat. "You don't get tired of this, do you?"

"I don't get tired of winning."

"Funny. Neither do I." His smile didn't reach his eyes. "I can make your life hell, Sunny. It's better to play nice with me."

His fingers found the hem of my dress and slipped beneath it. His fingertips grazed the bare skin of my thigh—light, teasing, maddening.

Something passed between us then, something slow-burning and dangerous, tangled up in old wounds and new grudges. "What are you doing, Miles?"

"You don't get tired of playing games," he murmured, his lips near my ear, "but you haven't realized"—his fingers slid higher—"I play dirtier than you now. I'm not the same."

I swallowed hard. My pulse was in my throat, my thighs, everywhere.

"Then play," I whispered.

His palm flattened against my thigh, warm and possessive. His thumb dragged slow, lazy circles into my skin, inching dangerously close to where I was aching.

"Careful, Serena," he murmured. "Say that again and I might forget this is supposed to be a business merger."

The limo slowed, the muffled sound of cameras and voices filtering in from outside.

Showtime.

I pushed his hand away, and I smoothed down my dress, forcing my pulse to steady.

Don't let him get to you. Keep it controlled.

"Try not to embarrass me."

Don't look at his hands. Don't look at his jaw. Don't look at his goddamn mouth—

"Don't tempt me, wife."

The door opened. I stepped out without another word, the cool air hitting my skin like a warning.

It was like a hush fell over the crowd when they saw the two of us together.

"Serena! Miles! Over here!"

I smiled. Or I thought I smiled; my brain was focused on

placing one foot in front of the other. What were they saying about me? My posture? My dress? The lie I was living?

Miles's hand slid into mine, and I almost flinched. His grip was firm, almost possessive, but his touch was ice-cold. He raised our hands slightly as if to say, *Look, we're in love. We're just fine.*

I barely had a second to react before he was waving stiffly at the paparazzi, nodding along to whatever they were shouting at us. And then, finally, finally, we were inside.

The moment the doors shut behind us, he all but flung my hand away like I was contagious. I watched, half-stunned, as he wiped his palm against his slacks, his jaw tightening like he had touched something foul.

I scoffed, crossing my arms. "Seriously?"

"What?" Miles didn't look at me.

I frowned at him and brushed past him, letting my shoulder knock into his as I entered the party.

The gallery was packed, no doubt thanks to Laurene's talent for reinvention. When she returned to town, she'd taken the gallery and turned it into the hottest spot in town.

Now, being *seen* here was just as important as the art itself.

Most Lush social gatherings boiled down to three objectives: networking, social climbing, and the art of thinly veiled sabotage.

I felt the weight of their gazes. Some subtle, just a flick of the eyes before turning away. Others were bold stares, murmured whispers behind champagne glasses.

"Serena!" Mama's voice snapped suddenly.

I glanced to my right. Mama was strutting over in a gold flowing gown, her hair pinned back.

"Where's that husband of yours?"

"He's…getting us champagne, ma'am," I lied.

She glanced at the ring on my hand. Not warmly. Just… observant. Like she was checking a box.

"I heard some people muttering how they saw you both get

out of the limo with frowns on your faces. You know that won't do."

No *How are you feeling?* No *Is he being kind to you?* Just the optics.

"We'll fix it," I said quietly.

"Good." Her voice was clipped. "Because we can't have this falling apart. At least until I can figure out how I want to take Dante's conniving ass down. The worse mistake of my life, if I'm being honest."

I nodded, letting my eyes drift over to the party. It would be nice to be asked how I was feeling about this, or even for her to *pretend* to care.

"This stress has not been good on me, Serena. My blood pressure, you know," Mama continued. "I might need you to pick up my prescription when you're back in town. I have meetings all day next week. I can't get away."

Prescription?

"Are you okay?" I asked.

Mama waved me off. "Nothing for you to worry about."

I sighed before nodding, and looked back around the room.

"Where are Omar and Audrey?" I suddenly asked.

Mama made a face. "Not here."

"The point of all of this is to *show* people our families are friends again. They should be here too," I said.

"Are you questioning my decisions?"

"No, ma'am, but I want this to work for all of us too. No failures, remember?"

God, she's looking at me like I've ruined everything.

"Then perhaps don't point out problems in public," she said coolly, lips barely moving. "I got this. You just do as I say."

I felt my throat tighten.

"Your posture's slipping," she added, already turning her head toward a passing guest.

I straightened.

"Everything okay here?" Miles stepped in, his presence solid and disarming all at once.

Mama's eyes immediately went to his empty hands. "Where's the champagne?"

"They ran out," Miles said smoothly.

"Don't embarrass me" was Mama's finally warning before she disappeared into the crowd.

We stood there in silence for a few more seconds. My brain was trying to come up with an appropriate response to this situation. But I felt…stuck. I didn't like feeling this way. I could fix everything else, but not when it came to my own heart and feelings.

Miles, however, wasn't as composed. I could see it in the set of his shoulders, the way his fingers twitched at his sides.

"Crowds like this can be overwhelming," he said suddenly.

I saw the way he balled and released his fist. Everything told me to be petty and ignore him, but my damn mouth opened. "Really? I thought you loved being the center of attention."

"Not anymore."

He grabbed two flutes of champagne from a passing server and handed one to me.

"Since my dad's incident, I don't get invites anymore. I mostly bully my way into places."

I blinked. "Really?"

"I *am* the hottest shit, but…" Miles shrugged. "People stay away. Or they always want to bring up the old shit."

He shrugged, downing half the flute.

I tightened my grip around my flute, debating. "I didn't realize it was that bad."

Just like the rest of the town, I could only watch in shock when Omar's trial and arrest went public. There had been a whistleblower who'd said former Mayor Johnson and Omar had been caught selling and consuming illegal drugs.

Substances that he'd been on when he attacked Daddy.

I remembered seeing Miles on the news in dark shades,

supporting his dad. But I never picked up the phone. Never asked him if he was doing okay. I told myself it wasn't my business. That whatever happened to Miles and his family had nothing to do with me anymore.

I thought they would just…leave. But Lush was their home, and they stayed.

I could have called. I could have defied Mama and reached out.

"Yeah," he muttered finally. "People stay away from us now. It's easier that way, you know? But I'm changing it. That's why I've been working hard to get the company back to a reputable place so people can respect us again."

I took a long sip of champagne, trying to swallow down whatever emotion I didn't want to face.

"Really?" I said, my tone sharp, a little more biting than I meant it to be. "You think that's what people care about? Respect?" I scoffed. "It's not about legacy, Miles. It's about *leverage*. Everything in Lush is a transaction. They'll never respect you—at least not like they respected your grandfather."

His lips pressed together, and I could see the flicker of doubt in his eyes.

"Then what? I should let it go?" he asked, his voice cold now. "Let the past bury me? Not try to redeem what's fucked up about my family or my life?"

I tilted my head. "If you could fix Whitmore Ventures tomorrow, would that make you happy? Give you peace?"

Why are you engaging, Serena?

"You're a hypocrite," he said.

A young man with a camera approached us. "Um, excuse me, could I get a photo for the *Lush Chronicles*?" His eyes flickered back and forth, unsure, with equal amounts of curiosity. "If that's not a problem."

Public appearances were part of our rules. If I appeased Mama and really embraced this, maybe I could get my sentence with him cut down to a year and a half.

"Sure."

Miles didn't say anything, but he did step closer. My ass brushed against his leg, and his chest pressed against my back, sending a thrill down my spine. His hand flattened just above my hip. Not lewd. Not sweet. Just there. Like a claim. I tried to breathe like it didn't affect me. Like his touch didn't burn through the silk of my suit and thread heat through my bloodstream.

The flash went off, and I felt the phony smile fall from my lips.

"Ah, you made it!" Laurene made her way toward us, Reese close behind.

I pulled myself away from him, trying to place the coldness back into my veins. Laurene, with surprising strength, pulled me into a tight hug.

"You look amazing, Lu," Miles told her.

Laurene sucked her teeth. "Don't lie to me, Miles. I'm huge, I'm wearing flats, and this dress is working harder than you ever have in life. But I appreciate the compliment."

"Can't lie to a pretty lady." Miles grinned.

"Flats?" I added my two cents, raising an eyebrow and crossing my arms. "Don't let Gigi see. You know what she did to your closet when she found corduroy in it."

"Oh, trust me, she's already cursed me out," Laurene replied, her grin spreading wider. "But when your ankles are the size of cantaloupes, the Gianvito Rossis get a well-deserved vacation."

Reese raised a brow, glancing between us with a weird look in his eye. "So…both of you. Here. *Alive.* How's it going?"

Laurene hit him on the shoulder, giving him a look.

"What?"

We did that sitcom thing where we looked at each other, then away, and I crossed my arms and shook my head.

Reese coughed awkwardly. "Okay… Come on, baby, I see someone we need to talk to."

He dragged Laurene off, and I turned to Miles, but then I froze.

Jenese.

My worst fear had come to life. Jenese was with Gigi, laughing at something she said.

No.

She had no business being around my sister. Gigi didn't know. She didn't understand what kind of game she'd just stepped into.

What the fuck do I do?

I reached them just as Jenese was leaning in, tugging at the fabric of Gigi's gown.

"Gigi." I not so subtly snatched her by the arm, pulling her away from Jenese. The older woman raised a brow, and Gigi took her arm from me, looking at me like I was crazy.

"Who is this?" I said, not letting my eyes leave Jenese.

"Rena! This is Jenese," Gigi chimed in, completely oblivious like she always was. "Did you know she's wearing a Pam Grier gown from the '70s? It's vintage—*iconic*." Jenese was draped in an emerald green silk dress with her wild Afro swept up into a high ponytail.

Jenese's smile widened, her eyes glinting with satisfaction as Gigi fawned over her before she glared at me. "Oh, darling, it's nothing. A little gem from the *past*, just like me."

"Gigi, this isn't someone you need to be getting close to."

"Why?" Gigi looked at me like I was crazy. "You know her or something?"

Shit. No, no, no, I cursed in my mind. I'd slipped. I could feel Jenese's eyes on me, that smug, knowing look creeping across her face.

"I don't think we've met," Jenese said, playing dumb.

"No, I just wanted to say—" I was scrambling for an answer, and Jenese just laughed.

"I'm new in town, just soaking up the atmosphere. I'm glad I ran into *Gigi* here. Apparently, she's opening up a boutique? I know quite a few designers, and they're always looking for a store with the right clothing and accessories—"

"Boutique?" I glanced at Gigi.

"Yes! I got the idea last night. I'm opening up my own boutique."

"You're playing," I said.

"Who said I'm playing?" She frowned at me. "Y'all always talkin' about me not having a job. Not finishing college. I like clothes. I like shopping. I like money. It's perfect for me."

"Yes, why can't she have a boutique?" Jenese asked. "She seems like a capable young woman."

"Yeah, you right," Gigi said, smiling at her and then glaring at me. "You never back me up."

"I support everything you do," I said.

"When?" She damn near snapped her neck as she looked at me sideways.

"It's a shame, though, when family doesn't support you, huh? Especially when you're trying to make something of yourself." Jenese looked pointedly at me. "Gigi's got big plans, Serena. You should be proud of her."

"I love how you're all business, Jenese. You're such a pro! *Some* people can learn from your professionalism." She turned to me. "Can you imagine, Rena? Me? Taking over Rodeo Drive?"

I forced a smile, stepping forward taking Gigi by her arm, and yanking her over to me. I didn't care to be subtle. "Let's go. Mama wants us."

"Let me give you my card, Gigi, and you reach out when you're ready—"

I snatched it before either of them could respond.

"Okay, weirdo." Gigi gave me a disappointed look before smiling at Jenese. "You should come to Café L'Amour. We all hang out there. What do you think?"

"*No,*" I said, and they both looked at me, surprised. "That's *our* tradition. Jenese is… I'm sure she'll find herself in the right circles soon enough."

"But—" Gigi started to protest.

"Mama is looking for you."

Gigi made a face but looked at Jenese and shrugged. "Excuse me. Duty calls."

I waited briefly, checking for family. "What the hell do you think you're doing, Jenese?"

"What do you mean, sugar?" she cooed, playing dumb with effortless ease. "I'm just getting to know Gigi. I'm new here, after all. And she's so full of energy. A real breath of fresh air."

"Cut the bullshit," I snapped, my voice low but sharp. "You stay the fuck away from my family."

She looked at me like I was being ridiculous. "Serena, you came to me because no one else took you seriously. Not even your own mother. Now you want to be mean?"

How did Jenese ever convince me to see her as a mentor?

It definitely wasn't the row of cars in her driveway or the clothes or the fancy homes she had. I was used to that. It was just *her*. She was an outsider too. She told me how she'd fought for every inch of ground she stood on. How no one handed her a damn thing. How she had to watch from the outside until she learned how to break the doors down herself.

"Where's my property, Serena?"

"I told you. Paperwork."

"Hmph. Did you read the manuscript?" Jenese waved me off. "You're ignoring me. I don't like to be ignored, sugar."

Yes. And it was awful. Both in the writing and the truth.

But people wouldn't care. They'd see my name, attach it to my family, and bam. Another King scandal.

"I was going to respond."

She sucked her teeth. "Not fast enough. So now I'm here. And I'm going to need you to do a job for me."

I needed time to clean this up. I needed to figure out what she actually wanted—because this wasn't just about leverage. Jenese never played short-term. If I could stall, keep her close, I'd find a way to flip it.

I glanced around again. "Fine. What's the job?"

"There's a guy in the next town over who's been a pain in my side for a while now. Alan Price. Runs a consultancy firm. Thinks he's untouchable." She smiled, but there was a bite to it. "Get some documents from him."

"What kind of documents?" I asked, suspicious.

Jenese's grin widened. "Oh, nothing too fancy. I just need to make him eager to negotiate with me."

"How?"

She shook her head. "All you need to do it put a USB drive into his laptop. It'll do the rest."

That was too damn simple.

"I'll do it. Send me the details," I said, the words tasting like ash in my mouth. "Now get out."

Her smile widened, the satisfaction in her eyes unmistakable.

"Good girl," she purred.

Suddenly, the gallery doors flew open, and a bunch of environmental protesters began yelling and waving signs. Chaos erupted.

She started to walk toward the exit. "I wonder how they got in."

Around us, guests recoiled in shock, their faces masks of confusion and fear as chants filled the air.

"Stop the destruction! Save our homes!" one of the protesters shouted, waving a sign that read "Stop the greenwashing!"

My mind started cataloging threats, exits, faces I didn't recognize. My feet moved before I could stop them, heading straight for the protestors.

Another protester with a megaphone yelled, "Your company is ruining our environment! We won't stand for it!"

A hand wrapped around my arm, firm but not rough, pulling me to a stop. "Serena." Miles's voice cut through the noise like velvet over steel—low, commanding, dangerously close.

"We need to do something," I said firmly, my eyes scanning the scene. "I can't let them ruin Laurene's event."

His breath grazed my ear, and despite the chaos around us, my pulse tripped for an entirely different reason.

"You need to stay out of this," Miles said. "Let security do their damn job."

"I can't." I tugged at my wrist, the rough fabric of his shirt scratching against my skin as I tried to escape his firm grip. "I can't ruin this for Laurene."

"Stop. I'm serious."

He stepped in close, face inches from mine, his hand curling around my arm with quiet authority. Not enough to hurt. Just enough to remind me he was there. That he wasn't going to let me go barreling into chaos without him.

"You're not going over there. Don't draw attention to yourself." His gaze flicked to the protestors, then back to me. "We don't need to make this worse."

"Watch me," I bit out.

I pulled myself away and headed into the fire.

"Excuse me!" I called out, my voice cutting through the noise. "If you have concerns, we can discuss them calmly. This is an event meant to celebrate art, not to turn into a battleground of opinions on false facts."

One of the protesters shouted back, "You should be ashamed of yourself!"

"This is a misunderstanding," I said coolly, stepping even closer. "Our goal has always been to bring progress, not destruction."

"You think we're just going to take your word for it?"

My jaw tightened. "I understand your frustration, but you're misinformed. I have the reports to back it up."

"Reports can be bought!" the protester retorted, his voice rising. "We've seen it happen before. Corporations like yours always find a way to twist the truth."

"I'm not here to debate corporate ethics. You need to leave."

The protestors were closing in, so I braced myself, but Miles stepped up and glared them down. "For fuck's sake, Serena. Let security handle this."

One of the protestors, his face twisted with fury, clutched a container of bright, vivid paint. I tried to pull Miles back, but he stood firm as a brick wall. The liquid splashed across his chest. Miles didn't flinch. He remained motionless, the red paint dripping down from his face to his shoes.

Gasping, I recoiled with trembling hands as the crowd's chants grew frenzied.

"Security! Get these people out of here!" Laurene suddenly came forward, her voice sharp and piercing.

The security team surged forward, their boots pounding on the floor, pushing a wedge between us and the protesters. But that didn't stop the chaos entirely. Some of the protesters were still fighting back, trying to make their point, while others were tackled to the ground as security closed in.

All of that was insignificant.

Not while Miles was still standing there drenched in paint.

I dragged my thumb slowly along the line of his cheekbone, and he tilted his head just slightly—like he wasn't sure if I was touching him to clean him off or to memorize the shape of his face.

"Are you alright?" I asked. My voice was steady, even if everything else in me was not.

Miles nodded, and he let me tug him toward the back of the room. Security guided us toward another exit, but when I looked up, I saw Mama standing there.

Her chin high, arms folded, and eyes burning straight through me.

She didn't speak. She didn't have to. The slow shake of her head said it all.

CHAPTER 14

Miles

THE WORDS "ART GALLERY CHAOS: Serena King & Miles Whitmore" flashed across my phone screen in neon.

At least they got a good photo of me.

I waited for Serena, stretching my cramped legs in the car, the smell of freshly cut grass drifting from Mrs. Fontaine's yard.

That picture made me jump. Serena's knuckles were white as she gripped my arm, her eyes wide with terror. I was covered in paint.

Serena King's new hubby, Miles Whitmore, rescues her during gallery protest

The *Lush Chronicles* didn't waste any time.

"Power couple or already breaking up?" I mumbled, rereading the article. "I figured we'd get a month before the divorce rumors started."

They didn't stop with the gallery mess.

"When did the Whitmores and Kings bury the hatchet? Or, more importantly, why? The two families spent years at each other's throats, their once-close ties shattered by scandal. Now, out of nowhere, Serena King and Miles Whitmore are rumored to have had a secret wedding? Either love moves at lightning speed, or this 'surprise' wedding was in

response to the controversial recent drama concerning King Developments and Whitmore Ventures."

I clenched my jaw as I kept reading.

"Omar Whitmore's scandal with former mayor Robert Johnson was the kind that rewrote history. Caught indulging in a drug-fueled night of 'business negotiations,' he didn't just lose his reputation, he took down an entire administration with him. While Johnson disappeared into obscurity, Omar took a light sentence and stint in rehab after his car wreck. But rumors still swirl that the elder Whitmore never really got clean, making his son's uphill battle for redemption that much steeper."

Another article. Another podcast. Another backhanded think piece from people who didn't know shit.

Can Miles Whitmore really revive the empire his father buried?

Like I haven't heard that shit a thousand times before, remixed, sampled, played over and over till I wanted to fucking scream.

And the worst part?

I couldn't even blame them.

For years, my grandfather led Whitmore Ventures solo. Pops and I were cool to just chill and go along with whatever came with the last name. The private schools, the golf clubs, the easy respect.

When Gramps got diagnosed with stage-four brain cancer, it was a punch to the chest. He didn't last long after that.

Pops stepped in, but he didn't have a fucking clue.

We thought the legacy alone made us qualified. That we'd just somehow inherit power and know-how by osmosis. I never studied the details. I never asked the hard questions. I was too busy being the fun one. The one who charmed, cracked jokes, made people like me.

Then Pops got dragged out the house in cuffs, and boom—twenty-four hours later, I was CEO. Family provider. Public face.

I kept trying to figure out if I was fixing what they broke or just stalling until I could build something that's actually mine.

What would that even look like?

The Kings had skyscrapers, university wings, whole city blocks with their name carved in stone. They were the legacy. The gold standard.

We were one of the founding families too. Whitmores helped shape this town, just like they did. But somewhere along the line, they kept climbing and we started coasting. Got comfortable.

And now? I was cleaning up the mess. Trying to prove we're still worth something.

Did I want the company to survive? Of course I did. It was all I had left of my grandfather. Of the version of my family that didn't fall apart.

But I was starting to think survival wasn't the goal.

Reinvention was.

And then there was Serena.

I was batting a thousand—married to a woman who hated me, partnering with a family that would rather bury me, and living in a condo that smelled like eucalyptus, espresso, and her skin.

It hadn't even been a week, and I'd caught her walking around in a silk thigh-length robe, loose at the chest, no bra. A sliver of lace panties peeking when she turned too fast for the oat milk in the fridge. Hair slicked back from the shower. No makeup.

She was doing that shit on purpose. I knew it.

People loved to act like Serena King was all brains and boardrooms. All logic and silence.

But I knew better.

She was a fucking temptress when she wanted to be.

I turned my car toward the gates of Mrs. Fontaine's place and shot up in my seat.

Victor stood at the edge of the driveway, cigarette dangling, head tilted in thought. He hadn't changed much—still wore those tailored suits with large-ass handkerchiefs in his pocket.

Stepping out of my car, I looked over my shoulder, hoping

none of Mrs. Fontaine's gardeners were paying attention as I made my way down the driveway. The gravel crunched underfoot, and I tried to steel my beating heart as I drew closer to him.

Fuck, why did I take the money?

"You've grown up," Victor mused. "Last time I saw you, you still had hope in your eyes."

"Life beats the shit out of you," I said.

Victor laughed.

"What are you doing here?" I asked, voice low.

"Is that the warm reception I was looking forward to?"

"I didn't realize we were still on speaking terms," I said, checking over my shoulder again. Serena was supposed to be here fifteen minutes ago.

Victor blew out smoke, slow and smug. "We were never *off* speaking terms. You just stopped answering my calls."

"Must've been bad reception," I said, forcing a smirk. My hands were still in my pockets, but I curled my fingers into fists. "Or maybe I figured we were square."

I hadn't known what I was walking into back then. I was twenty-seven, Pops had just been arrested, the accounts were frozen, and no one in Lush would touch the Whitmores with a ten-foot pole.

Victor was the only one who said yes. No paperwork. Just numbers and a handshake. And I was too desperate to ask the right questions.

"You're not here just to be a blast from the past. What do you want?" I asked.

"There was an…incident with a business of mine," he said. "It was ruled an accident, but you know how people talk."

"So sorry for you." I crossed my arms. "What do you need from me?"

"Well," he said, glancing around like someone might be listening, "I started hearing your name again. Some merger talk. A little press. You're getting invited back to the table, yeah?"

I gritted my teeth.

"Figured it couldn't hurt to stop by, see how the golden boy's doing. Maybe ask for a little help, the kind that makes the right questions go away."

"Help," I echoed. "From me."

"I just need a place to sit some money—"

"You want to launder your shit through *my* company?" I asked, my voice sharp now.

He chuckled. "That's such an ugly word. I'm offering a partnership, Miles. You hold some money from me while I have a few deals go through. I get a little cover. I cut you a check in the end."

"And when the Feds come knocking, should I play dumb?"

Victor's smile didn't falter. "You're smarter than that."

"I can't do that, Victor."

"You can." Victor shrugged. "Emails. Texts. A few creative ledgers. It's not hard to make it look like you were deeper in than you were when you took my money. If someone starts digging…well. You'd be surprised how convincing a paper trail can be." He smiled, slow and oily. "People might even think you're a real criminal."

"You're threatening me now?"

He stepped in, close enough for me to smell the smoke on his breath.

"Do what the fuck I say," he said. "Or I make sure your pretty new wife and her family find out exactly who you are. Who you've *always* been."

I didn't blink. "What am I, Victor?"

He laughed. Not loud—low and cruel.

"You're your father's son."

That landed like a slap.

Fuck, fuck, fuck, fuck—

"Let's meet at that new office of yours? The one with the protestors? How about ten o'clock tonight? I'll bring the champagne for this new partnership." Victor grinned at me. A car I hadn't noticed creeping up behind us stopped, and he opened the passenger side door. "Tell your wife I said congratulations."

Then he turned and got in the car. I didn't breathe until he was gone.

A car honked loudly, and I jumped. I turned to find Serena in her Range Rover giving me a look.

"Why are you standing out here? Are you coming in?"

I turned to glance back down the road Victor had just been.

"Miles?"

I schooled my face into something that wouldn't raise questions and motioned toward the mansion.

"Let's go."

CHAPTER 15
Serena

"I DON'T GET what you're upset about. She sold us the house." I stormed into the condo and deleted the text message.

Miles slammed the door shut, and I checked my watch. I had to get out of here, but Miles was making it difficult.

"Don't you think she sold it way too fast?"

Mrs. Fontaine was all set to sign after we checked out the house, and all I saw was an opportunity to make money. Another shot at success. The chance to make Mama happy for a bit.

Miles had been sulking since. I wanted to know what his problem was, but I had enough on my plate right now.

"She's a lonely, rich old lady with no family close by, and she hated being alone in that big house."

Walking into the living room, I tossed my bag on the couch, waking up Doughboy, who was sleeping there.

"What did I say? Off! Off my couch." I shooed at the cat, but he just lifted his head and blinked slowly at me before lowering it back down.

"You didn't ask about the shady-looking electric setup that was on the first floor, or the water damage in the attic. Why the hell are you acting so desperate over this place?" Miles glared, hands on hips.

I wasn't going to explain myself, even if he was furious.

"You're just looking for issues. This place is our only viable option. Unless you've got a magic wand and another estate tucked up your ass, we're buying it." I crossed my arms. "I've got this, Miles."

With the merger announcement, board meetings, and Mama and Jenese drama, I needed a quick, easy win.

"Yeah, no shit." He stepped closer, until I could practically taste the musky, expensive cologne on his skin. "But why? You won't say why you don't have the Harrington estate."

"I told you, they sold to someone else."

"Bullshit. I deserve to know the truth."

Deserve? Everyone thought I owed them something. My time. Energy. Patience. But what was I getting out of it? More requests, *more requests,* and damn complaints.

"You deserve the truth?" I taunted. "That's rich, coming from you."

Miles frowned at me. "What the hell is that supposed to mean?"

I knew what I'd been getting myself into with Miles. I knew he was charming, a bit of a player. But he'd been my *friend*. One of my few friends.

I knew it was a bad idea. Not because our families were enemies then—they weren't. They were long-time friends. And *that* was why we kept it quiet.

"I told you when we started this…whatever it was…that my work came first. That I wasn't built for distractions. And you said you understood, Miles. You looked me in the eye and said you got it."

My voice broke, just slightly.

"But the moment it got hard, the moment I didn't prioritize us the way you wanted, you acted like I'd betrayed you."

If anyone found out, it would've become a thing. A headline. A strategic alliance. A legacy union. And we weren't ready for all that. We were just two people trying to figure out what the hell we were feeling.

"Because you didn't prioritize us at all, Serena." He stepped closer, jaw tight, voice quiet. I flinched.

"You talk like I gave up," he said. "But you never gave me anything to hold on to. Soon as shit got messy, you chose your family over me. How the hell do I compete with that?"

"It wasn't that simple—"

"It was for you." His voice hardened. "You picked a side. Own it."

A bitter breath escaped my lips, the memory still causing a painful clenching in my chest.

I whirled around, a sudden rush of determination propelling me toward my bedroom.

"Serena!"

I didn't stop. I had to get dressed and go. I was already late, and I didn't like being late.

"This conversation is over," I said.

I felt his hand wrap around my arm and spin me back.

"You keep talking to me like that, Serena…" His tone sent a chill straight down my spine. "One day, you're gonna find out I'll do it."

"Do what?"

I could feel the tension in his chest as it rose and fell sharply, each breath brushing the space between us. My eyes flicked down—traitorously—to his mouth. Full, pink, parted like he was about to say something else, or maybe just bite back whatever he was thinking.

"I'm late." I snatched my hand away from him and slammed my bedroom door in his face.

"Late for what, exactly?" Miles's voice came through the door.

I leaned against the cool wooden door, taking a breath. I touched my chest—pressure always helped me calm down. I pressed down. Inhaled. Counted to four. Exhaled. Again.

King Developments couldn't have any mistakes. That was all that mattered.

I shed my jacket, tossing it on the bed. What was I supposed to wear tonight?

"We're not done talking, Serena. I can stand out here all night."

The truth was, I *had* walked away from us. I hadn't just chosen my career—I'd chosen control. Stability. A future I could plan, execute, dominate. Love didn't fit in that structure. Not his kind, anyway.

I told myself I was being smart. That Miles would be fine. He always bounced back.

But the way he looked at me tonight…

I heard a soft meow and turned to see Doughboy was in my room.

"How the hell…" I mumbled and shook my head at the orange cat giving me that sideways look. I quickly changed into a dress, but couldn't find the shoes that went with it.

"Where are my shoes?" I asked the cat.

Doughboy stretched out more, his body spread across the comforter in a way that screamed, *This is mine now. You may leave.*

I narrowed my gaze. "You know you're not supposed to be up there."

It had always been Miles. Even when I told myself it was casual, even when I told him I couldn't afford to be distracted. He'd wormed his way under my skin. And I'd let him. I liked how easy he made things feel.

I wasn't good at this. At feelings. At regret. At admitting I might've chosen wrong.

Doughboy yawned, showing off tiny sharp teeth, then flopped over. He couldn't have cared less about me or my rules.

"You're a menace," I muttered, walking over to shoo him off.

He stayed put, a furry ball of defiance.

I gave him a little nudge. "Off. Get off, Doughboy."

He let out a grunt, glared, and hopped down with that superior cat attitude. As he landed, a black thing slid out from under him onto the floor.

My black stiletto. How the hell did it get on my bed? I saw little teeth marks in it. Damn cat.

You can do this. Do the job. Give Jenese whatever she wants. Get her out of your life.

My dress was still half-zipped, the cool air hitting my exposed back. I yanked at the stubborn zipper, the teeth catching and snagging on the fabric, refusing to cooperate.

"Shit," I whispered, tugging harder. With a resigned sigh, I cracked the door open just enough to peek through. Miles raised an eyebrow.

"Miles…" I rubbed my temples, feeling a headache come on. "Let's just end this for tonight, okay? We can argue in the morning."

I still awkwardly clutched the neckline of my dress to keep it from slipping.

"I can't get it," I muttered. "The zipper, I mean."

"Turn around."

I hesitated, but the command in his tone left no room for argument. I slowly turned away, gripping my dress as he came closer. His fingers, cool and smooth, grazed my back as he reached for the zipper, a fleeting touch that sparked an electric jolt.

The zipper moved smoothly under his hand, the soft *zzzip* loud in the quiet of the room.

"There," he said, and I suddenly felt coldness on my back.

Miles had stepped back, his hands in his pockets.

"I'll be back later," I said.

"You're my *wife*, and that means I care to know where you're running off to at night in a short dress."

"Miles, don't make this more than what it is, we're not that same couple from before." I gave him a look, and he shrugged.

"Don't wait up." I grabbed my jacket and brushed past him, slamming the door behind me before he could say another word.

CHAPTER 16
Serena

MY PHONE BUZZED with another text from Jenese right as I pulled up to the party. Like she knew I was already there.

I just had to get into his office. Plug the USB into the laptop. Hand her the USB back.

Be smarter than her, Serena.

"Victimless crime," I mumbled, stuffing my purse with the little pouch I got from the back of my closet. I stepped out of my car, and a memory hit me like a brick:

I can do this, I repeated to myself. My first time out on my own. No Mama. No Daddy. Just me. Crystal chandeliers dripped from the ceiling, casting golden light over the sea of socialites in front of me. Voices hummed—the low, pretentious laughter, the clinking of champagne glasses, the undercurrent of whispered deals being made.

And me, standing in the middle of it, utterly out of place. I shifted my weight in my heels, smoothing my dress with sweaty palms.

Mama had chosen it for me—sleek, elegant, and just a touch too tight. A dress meant to be noticed. A dress meant to tell the world I belonged here.

But I didn't.

Laurene was gone, though, so I had to do it.

Six months, two weeks, and four days—no calls, no postcards. Just

Erik's update that she was in Paris and apparently preferred strangers to us. Fine.

Grandpa Ben was gone. Gigi was a wreck. Erik was stoic. Mama and Daddy were fighting.

The King family was crumbling from the inside.

"It's time you stop hiding in the shadows," Mama said before I arrived, her tone clipped, assessing. "Your last name isn't just for decoration. Show them you can be a King."

I almost fell onto the bar, I was buzzing with so much nervous energy. The bartender gave me a curious look. "What'll it be?"

"Something strong."

The bartender raised a brow. Was that the wrong thing to say? A voice said, "Give her a Manhattan."

I turned to my right, and there was an older Black woman watching me.

She was striking. Not just beautiful, but arranged—like she had chosen each element of herself with intention.

I hadn't noticed her before, which bothered me. I always noticed people. I could remember the face of a contractor I'd passed once in a hallway when I was eight.

She looked to be in her fifties. Her posture was impeccable—shoulders relaxed but back straight, legs crossed just so, her fingers cradling a glass of red wine like it had always belonged there. Her dress was deep red satin. Not burgundy. Not maroon. Red.

Her jewelry matched—real stones, real gold. Expensive, but not flashy. No labels, but everything about her screamed money.

She smiled back. Not warm. Not cold. Just amused.

"Let me guess—you'd rather be anywhere but here?"

My throat felt tight. "Is it that obvious?"

"Parties like these are a drag. Just big dick investors showing off their money and the women scrambling for it."

I blinked. That was...blunt.

She reached her hand out. "I'm Jenese."

I shook it. Firm grip. Polished nails. Diamond ring, right hand. No wedding band.

"Serena."

The bartender came back with the drink, leaving us alone once again.

"I think you might the most interesting thing here, Serena." Jenese smiled again, tilting her glass toward me. "Do you have time to chat, or should I let you go about your business?"

I looked over my shoulder. I didn't even see the investor Mama wanted me to talk to. And maybe talking to this woman would help me loosen up.

"Sure. I have time."

I didn't realize I was standing in the grand lobby of the home till someone bumped into my shoulder.

The inside of the building was a big, lively space with people chatting quietly, glasses clinking, and bursts of laughter. Crystal chandeliers dripped light onto the polished marble and gilded bits.

I strolled up to the bar. A few people glanced my way, their eyes skimming over me, curiosity piqued but fleeting. That was the trick—blend in just enough to be forgettable, yet carry your-self like you owned the place.

Jenese always said, *"Blend in until you don't."*

Smiling slightly, I leaned against the bar. "Manhattan, neat."

I scanned the room, my gaze lingering on clusters of people, their conversations animated yet contained. I didn't see him yet.

But I didn't need to *see* him. I knew the rhythm now. I knew what to listen for. What to say. What to withhold.

The first couple of lessons had felt like power. Control. Like I was finally being let in on secrets no one in my family thought I could handle.

I didn't realize they were hooks.

I'd been so eager to impress her. So starved to be told I was doing something right for *once.*

Mommy issues could make a naïve, inexperienced rich girl do strange things. Like follow a woman with a prettier smile and sharper claws. I just wanted to go back to Mama and show her what I knew.

I grabbed the cocktail from the bar, the chilled glass cool against my fingertips.

My lips touched the rim, but I didn't drink—just held it as a prop. My attention swept the room again as I tried to make my brain work like it did before in times like this, taking in every detail: the rooms, the exits, the security cameras discreetly tucked into corners.

And then I saw him.

Alan Price was leaning casually against a table near the far corner, a drink in one hand and his phone in the other. He was taller than I'd expected, his sharp suit impeccably tailored. His dark hair was slicked back, and he looked exactly like Jenese's type.

Rich. Married. Emotionally unavailable.

Alan had definitely fucked her, and now she was using me to get back at him.

The ex-lovers who'd crossed Jenese before had been my first examples of how to manipulate and how to get revenge. She was definitely taking me back to the basics.

I told myself I wanted to be better at business. Smarter. Tougher. But the truth was uglier. My mother was too busy running an empire to teach me how to build one.

My grip on the glass tightened as another thought surfaced.

Miles wouldn't recognize this version of me.

That's the point.

It was why I hid Jenese, this life, from my family. They could only know me as Serena. The one who already knew how to do everything. Not the one stumbling through this life.

I took my drink and made my way across the room, weaving through clusters of people while keeping Alan in my peripheral vision.

I had to shake off the cobwebs. This wasn't me being someone else. This was me remembering who the hell I was.

There was an empty spot at the high-top table just a few feet away from him. Maybe I could catch some of his conversation.

I perched on the edge of a barstool, crossing my legs. I pretended to be interested in my drink, my expression neutral but my senses tuned to him like a wire stretched tight.

Before I could decide my next move, a voice cut through the air.

"Well, well. Serena King."

I froze for half a beat. *No. Nobody can know me here.* Turning slowly, I plastered on a faint smile, bracing myself. "Do I know you?"

"You should," he said. "Bryan Royce. We met at the King Foundation's fundraising dinner last fall. How's your sister doing?"

"Bryan," I said smoothly, offering my hand. His grip was firm, lingering just a fraction too long. I didn't like the clammy feeling of his hands. "It's good to see you again."

"And here I thought I'd have to survive this night without a single interesting conversation," he said, leaning in. "What brings you to Elysian Bluff? I didn't take your family from straying too far from Lush."

I laughed lightly, the kind of practiced sound that didn't betray anything real. "I'm here for the ambiance. And you?"

Deflect. Get him the hell out of my face.

"Oh, you know," he said, gesturing vaguely with his drink. "Networking. The usual."

Bryan continued to talk, but I tuned him out, my gaze drifting back to Alan. He'd moved slightly, now angled in my direction as he scanned the room.

"…but enough about me. Your sister said you're busy these days. I had a property I wanted to get your…*expertise* on. Is your schedule only filled with business?"

I smiled tightly, the edges of my patience fraying. "Just business. You know how it is."

"You're wasted on that stuff, you know. A woman like you should be the center of every room."

Men like him always thought flattery was currency.

I gave him a bland expression. "Then let's not waste either of our time pretending this is going somewhere."

His smile faltered.

"Enjoy the party, Bryan."

Alan finished his drink, setting the glass down on a passing tray with a casual flick of his wrist. Then, without a word to the people around him, he stepped away from the crowd. I waited a beat, then followed, leaving Bryan standing there gawking.

Alan turned down a hallway. It was quieter here, the low hum of voices from the main room fading into a muffled backdrop.

Once it was safe, I noticed the lighting was dimmer, and the air seemed thicker. Or was I just nervous?

But that feeling bloomed low in my gut, dark and familiar again. I hadn't felt it in years—the quiet, electric rush of doing something I shouldn't. The slippery kind of thrill that came from walking a razor-thin edge and knowing I could fall, but still choosing to balance there anyway.

That was the feeling I hated the most. I knew it was bad. But why did it feel good?

I inhaled shakily, flexing my hands and rolling my shoulders back.

It felt like going up to the top of a rollercoaster and waiting for the drop.

Alan stopped in front of a door that I presumed led to another hallway. Then he pushed inside.

I counted to five before following. The door swung open easily under my hand, but as soon as I stepped inside, I realized my mistake.

The room wasn't empty.

Six men stood in a semicircle, their conversation cutting off the moment I entered. Alan was among them, his posture shifting from relaxed to guarded as he turned toward me. Another man, broader and older, took a step forward.

"Lost?" the older man asked.

My stomach dipped. Still, I summoned a look of mild embarrassment—chin slightly tilted, brows drawn together, just enough to look harmless.

"Oh my God yes," I said, laughing softly. "I was looking for the bathroom. Must've taken a wrong turn."

Too breathy. Too casual.

I used to be better than this.

The man didn't move, his eyes narrowing as he assessed me. "The bathrooms are back by the main hall."

Get the fuck out of here and pray they don't recognize or remember my face.

I nodded, stepped back, slow and easy like I wasn't dying to bolt. The door shut behind me.

And then it hit me—*hard*.

What the hell was that? I used to be smooth. Lethal. Jenese had taught me better than this.

But now? I was offbeat. Sloppy. Rusty.

I heard the door open up behind me, and I knew the man was watching me.

I pretended to look into a few open doors before I found a restroom and stepped inside and closed the door.

I was fucking up.

Mistakes. Mistakes. Mistakes.

Once inside the bathroom, I locked the door and leaned against it, exhaling slowly. My pulse was racing. Reaching into my clutch, I slipped my gloves on, each finger fitting snugly. The sensation was strangely comforting, but there was no time to savor it.

I glanced once more at the door. Silence—no one outside. I moved quickly. The hallway was quiet, but I could hear faint murmurs in the room.

Alan's office wasn't far away.

I had maybe two minutes.

I quickly but quietly checked each door down the hall's right side. The first opened to a supply closet, rows of neatly stacked linens and catering supplies. Then a mailroom, a mess of boxes and cubbies.

Locked. Locked. Another locked door.

I let out a sharp breath. Time was running out.

Then, finally, one handle gave way.

I went in quietly and closed the door, on high alert.

Alan's office. The desk was super clean, just a stack of papers and a few photos.

I quickly scanned the room for anything useful. A filing cabinet was on the left, locked up tight, no surprise there. The desk was the most important thing. I stepped closer, fingers hovering over the top drawer, and started opening drawers, hoping he left a laptop somewhere in here.

Bingo.

I pulled out the laptop, opening it.

I looked at the sign-in screen. Jenese didn't tell me a password or anything, just to put the USB in. I reached into my clutch and slipped it into the laptop's port.

Immediately, the screen lit up. The screen went blue before white text started to form across the screen. This…

Whoa. What the hell was Jenese into now?

We didn't have this technology before. It was mostly just talking, manipulating people out of their money or deals. Viruses? When the hell did she learn this? I tried to track the lines of code, but they were moving too fast.

Finally, the laptop lockscreen opened, revealing his homepage.

Jenese was definitely holding out on me.

Then things began to move on the screen. It started to open things up. Files, folders, an open email inbox, and…*shit.* Another window popped up that showed something I hadn't expected. Financial transactions, personal details, passwords.

This was bad. This was *felony* bad. And I didn't know if I was the accomplice…or the bait.

Think. Compartmentalize. Control.

The files kept pulling up, one after another, too fast for me to process. Whatever Jenese had set up, it was working on its own, scanning, collecting, taking.

Then—*footsteps*.

I froze, my pulse hammering in my throat. Quickly, I grabbed the laptop, fingers hovering over the USB. Could I pull it out now? Would that screw up whatever Jenese had running?

The screen stopped, and I yanked the USB out of the laptop.

A shadow passed under the crack of light at the threshold. Someone was standing there.

I slipped the laptop back into the drawer.

I scanned the room. The desk was too obvious. The closet was too far. Then, I spotted it. A narrow gap between a tall filing cabinet and the built-in bookshelf in the dark corner of the room.

Heart pounding, I moved fast, pressing myself into the tight space just as the door creaked open. The smell of old paper and wood polish filled my nose as I wedged myself as far back as I could.

Alan stepped inside, his shoes clicking against the floor.

A pause. Then the scrape of a chair.

A drawer opened. The same one I'd just closed.

My breath felt trapped in my lungs as I watched through the tiny sliver of space.

Alan's fingers hovered over the keyboard. The screen glowed as he typed something, then stilled. His brow furrowed. The cursor flickered. A beat of silence.

He exhaled sharply. "What the hell?"

My stomach twisted.

He tapped a few keys. Still nothing. My heart slammed against my ribs as he grabbed his phone and snapped a picture of the screen.

Then, with a frustrated huff, he slammed the laptop shut. Stood. Pocketed his phone.

And walked out.

I waited. Counted the seconds. Ten. Twenty. Thirty.

The hallway outside remained silent.

I slipped out of my hiding spot, my legs stiff, my body wired with adrenaline. I moved carefully—silent steps, no fingerprints, no evidence.

The laptop was closed tight. No getting in. I took a photo of the office. Just one. No flash.

One step into the hallway my heels were hitting the carpet too hard. I needed to get out. Now.

Through the lobby and past clusters of guests still sipping expensive scotch, past waiters balancing silver trays. My breath felt too loud in my own ears, but I kept moving.

What did I just do?

The second I hit the front doors, I didn't stop.

I stepped into the cool night air and kept walking, heels sharp against the stone, every nerve lit like a live wire.

My heart was racing—but not from fear. Not *just* fear.

Something darker. I knew I shouldn't feel this way. It wasn't the right sensation. The kind of sick exhilaration I hadn't experienced in years. I'd forgotten how *alive* this made me. The rush.

I hated it.

I loved it.

And I couldn't stop smiling.

CHAPTER 17
Miles

I WALKED INTO THE GYM, the smell of sweat, mixed with the sharp, almost medicinal tang of disinfectant, hitting me first.

It wasn't the high-stakes poker game I thought it would be.

Slayer's Gym was a total dive compared to my usual spots. Expensive workout equipment gleamed under the bright lights, a stark contrast to the rough texture of the bare brick walls. A couple of fighters were going at it in the ring, their sharp, practiced moves punctuated by the thud of fists and the squeak of shoes.

I saw Reese by the ring. He gave me a sly grin. "You made it!" he shouted above the gym din.

"This ain't poker." I went to give Reese a fist bump. "I didn't know this place was even around."

Growing up, the Ashbournes and the Kings were basically mortal enemies. I didn't hate the guy, but I stayed away from him out of out of respect for loyalty to Erik and the Kings. Now that everything was cool, we would hang out if we ran into each other in town, we both knew what it was like to be an outcast in Lush.

"My buddy Ronin owns the place. I think you'll like him."

Reese gestured toward a burly guy in the ring with dreads down his back engaged in an intense sparring match.

"Ronin, huh?" I scanned the gym, taking in the raw energy and grit of the place. "The heavyweight boxer who killed a guy?"

"He didn't kill him. Those are just false allegations." Reese laughed. "Laurie's been nesting so hard, I'm scared to even breathe wrong in her space, let alone sneak in my poker table. After the wedding, though, well, I thought I'll check in with you. How's it going?"

"Oh, it's going," I muttered, my voice more tired than I intended.

Reese raised an eyebrow, a smirk playing on his lips. "Is it going…well?"

"What did Laurene tell you to find out from me?"

"What?" He had the nerve to try to look innocent. "I'm getting to know my new brother-in-law."

Reese stood up, grabbing a pair of gloves and tossing them to me. "Alright, we can talk later. Let's see if you've still got some fight in you."

I caught the gloves, slipping them on.

He jabbed lightly. "You know," he said between punches, "I can tell you love her. Did you say it yet?"

"Please tell me Laurene put you up to this." I dodged his punch and countered, landing a hit on his arm. "Y'all don't have anything else to do?"

He smirked, but it faded as his gaze sharpened. "Serena, the Kings, your family's company…it's a lot to handle. I had my own shit with my father and brother. At least I had Laurie there with me for most of the mess. Serena… Well, she's interesting, but I think it's great if you both love each other."

"That's a big assumption that I love her at all."

Liar, you did at one point.

Reese stopped and looked at me. "I can tell. You had the same look in your eyes, the way I used to look at Laurie."

That made me a bit uncomfortable. Didn't Laurene say something similar?

I laughed, ducking under his next swing. "Did Erik give you this speech too?"

"Nah. Erik threatened to beat my ass."

"Sounds about right."

We'd been at it for a good twenty minutes, and I was starting to feel the burn in my muscles, the kind that reminded me I was alive. But just as I was about to throw another jab, Reese stopped moving.

He lowered his hands, his grin fading into something unreadable.

"What's up? You getting tired already?" I asked, wiping the sweat off my brow.

Reese didn't answer. He just nodded behind me.

I slowly turned. Erik.

His expression was guarded, his jaw tight.

I wondered if Reese had dragged me to the gym just to arrange this meeting.

"You did this?"

Reese held his hands up. "Laurene insisted I invite him. Thought it might be good for you two to hash things out. You're family now."

Family. That didn't seem to be any fucking help, now did it?

Erik walked closer to us, and his gaze flickered over to Reese. He gave him a quick nod before frowning at me. "Reese. You didn't tell me he was going to be here."

"I'm not exactly doing cartwheels to see you either," I shot back.

"Anything happens to my sister, it's your ass I'm coming after." Erik took a step toward me. "You should have taken the money and left."

"You can't get rid of me." I laughed. "You're the one who ended our friendship. I didn't want to."

"It wasn't an easy choice, Miles. But sometimes you have to make the hard decisions. You should understand that by now."

Erik was the whistleblower. He told everyone and was responsible for the downfall that came after.

Betrayal choked me, my voice trembling. "I thought we were brothers, Erik."

Erik's face hardened again. "And I thought you'd understand why I had to do it. It's not something that I wanted to do."

"You didn't have to do it at all."

"Omar was going to hurt a lot of people, but most of all, you and Audrey. If you weren't going to save yourself, you should have been protecting your mother."

My stomach twisted. "Don't bring her into this."

"You know I'm telling the truth, and that part of you that's ashamed knows it. You bitched out on your own mama."

Reese intervened firmly. "Enough. This isn't helping either of you."

Erik nodded and took a step back, eyeing me up and down. Then he looked at Reese. "Hand over those gloves."

Reese glanced at me and Erik. "I'm not sure that's a good idea."

"Give him the gloves," I said.

He sighed, then passed them over. "Fine."

Erik grabbed them, his eyes blazing into mine. I saw his old rage, a fire waiting to explode. He stepped into the ring, and I followed him. All the gym noise was gone.

We circled each other, feet lightly shuffling. His stance was solid, but I knew the way he fought.

I couldn't forget our hurtful words from all those years ago.

We didn't have to be this way.

My breath was steady, but my mind was spinning. How did we end up here? Best friends once. We were practically like wolves, ready to tear each other apart.

His quick jab caught me off guard. I blocked it, the shock going right through my gloves. I instinctively punched him in the ribs. But instead of backing off, Erik grinned—a piercing, feral thing that made the anger in me surge.

"This didn't need to happen," he mumbled.

"No, it didn't," I said, my fists going wild.

With every heavier blow, the sounds of our fists colliding echoed through the space, an erratic rhythm punctuated by grunts and strained breaths. Erik's hits became harder and his jaw clenched as he sent jabs aimed at my face. I ducked, but his next punch hit my temple, sending a white-hot flash of pain through my skull.

I drove my fist toward his midsection, and this time, he stumbled back, the mat giving a low squeak under his shoes. His chest heaved, a ragged, painful breath catching in his throat, as he wiped the blood from his lip with a gloved hand, never breaking eye contact.

"That all you've got?" he sneered angrily.

That's when I lost it. My vision tunneled, and I closed the distance between us, landing punches wherever I could—his arms, his torso, his jaw. Each strike was filled with all the things I wanted to yell at him. How we'd thrown away years of friendship, how he'd betrayed me, how I'd turned my back on him, how I'd lost the one person I could trust.

Erik's final blow connected hard with my jaw, and I staggered, the world tilting sideways as I fought to stay upright. Blood filled my mouth, the coppery taste on my tongue. But I couldn't fall. Not in front of him.

I steadied myself, eyes locking on Erik.

I took off my gloves, throwing them to the ground. Without a word, Erik did the same. If this was how it was going to end, I wasn't going to hold back.

He lunged first, fists flying. No technique, no rhythm—just raw, unfiltered aggression. My hands were everywhere, my knuckles burning as I landed hit after hit. He shoved me hard, and I crashed into the ropes.

Before I could recover, he was on me again, I shoved him

back, my fist slamming into his gut, and he doubled over, falling to his knees. My legs felt like they were giving out, every muscle burning, but I couldn't stop.

"Miles!" Reese's voice pierced through the haze of violence, but I barely registered it.

Shouts erupted around us, arms wrapped around my chest, pulling me back. Reese was yelling, and others were scrambling into the ring to separate us. Erik was dragged back too, fists still raised, panting heavily, his eyes wild with fury. My chest heaved, every breath burning, my body numb from the adrenaline and pain coursing through me.

"Get him off!" I heard someone shout, their voice distant as I tried to focus. But all I could feel was the sharp throb in my face, a brutal ache blooming around my eye.

Reese stood in front of me, hands gripping my shoulders. "Miles! You good?"

My eyes were still on Erik, who was being held back by two guys, his chest heaving, his face a mess of blood and sweat.

He stared at me, his eyes dark, full of something I couldn't even begin to unravel. He didn't say a word. He just brushed off the guys holding him, and stormed out of the gym without another look.

CHAPTER 18

Serena

THE CONDO LIGHTS WERE ON.

Damn.

That meant he was home.

I stayed parked in my own damn driveway like a visitor, like someone unsure if they were welcome. Which was ridiculous—this was my place. I bought it. Decorated it.

Now it'd been overrun by a man and his cat.

My *husband*.

I hated that word. Not because of what it meant, but because of how easily it fit him. Like the role had always been waiting for him to slip into it. Charming. Carefree. And entirely too comfortable in my space.

I needed a buffer. Which was why it was perfect when Reese called me.

"No offense, Reese, but why are you calling me?" I asked, tone bone-dry. "Don't you have other people to talk to?"

For some reason, Reese talked to me constantly since he became family. I thought Erik and Gigi were better choices, but he picked me. Begrudgingly I allowed it and I ended up talking to him a lot.

The rain had started up again, soft and insistent against my windshield. It blurred the edges of the driveway, made every-thing feel muted and far away.

"No offense taken," he said. "But you're a problem-solver. And I have problems."

"That's not news," I muttered. I already knew what—or *who*—his problem was. "If this is about Laurene, I can assure you she's more than capable of handling herself."

He gave a huff.

"I didn't say it was about Laurene."

"It's always about Laurene."

A beat passed.

"Fine. But listen, I've been researching, and I think she needs to—"

"No."

"What do you mean no?"

I leaned my head back against the seat. "I mean, I am not indulging whatever hyperfixation you've developed this week. Noelle and Gigi will encourage that shit, but not me. Laurene is six months pregnant, not a Fabergé egg. Leave her alone and let her grow your baby."

The silence stretched. A gravel crunch told me he'd pulled up to their house.

"I already caught her sneaking Turtles in the laundry room last night," he said, as if confessing a felony.

I didn't even try to hide my disdain. "Let me get this straight. You are panicking because your wife—who is carrying your child—wanted something sweet?"

"When you say it like that, it sounds bad."

"It *is* bad, Reese. It's deranged."

A flicker of something warm curled in my chest. I didn't like how *human* he sounded. How familiar. How *much like me*. Because deep down, beneath all his neurotic panic, was someone terrified of doing it wrong. Of failing the people he loved.

I *knew* that feeling.

I was sitting in it.

Still parked. Still not ready to go inside and face Miles, who was probably barefoot and comfortable and sipping something expensive, like he hadn't just been forced into a marriage with a woman who was already planning contingency exits.

"I just—" Reese's voice faltered. "I want to make sure she's okay. I want to get this right."

"Want to control the uncontrollable?" I murmured. *The pot calling the kettle black.*

He didn't answer. He didn't need to.

"It's not control," he finally said. "It's…ensuring I get the outcome I want."

"Are you sure I'm the only one you can talk to?" I asked. "What about a therapist?" *Please keep talking, Reese…*

He didn't answer again. I stared up at my condo, at the glowing window upstairs—my office. *Our* office now, because Miles lived in there.

"You could always talk to Laurene," I added, quieter this time. "Have you tried that? Clearly your daddy issues are coming out to play."

"Says the one whose family has mommy issues?"

A pause. Then, begrudgingly, "Touché."

"Did you talk to Miles yet?" Reese asked me.

"Not since this morning, why?"

"Nothing," he said, then immediately started talking about cribs again, cutting me off.

The call with Reese came to an end too soon. It was comical watching him turn into a mother hen and freaking out over this pregnancy more than Lu had. But I knew my niece was in great hands.

I couldn't stay in the car forever, so eventually I dragged myself out, and through the front door. I hadn't lived with anyone since I'd moved out my parents', and this… It was still an adjustment.

"I'm home," I said, and I paused. *I'm announcing I'm home?*

"In here, honey," Miles said, and I headed to living room and called out to him.

"I had some meetings with the finance team. We're good to go on the renovations if we stay under—" I nearly jumped out of my skin when I saw Miles's face.

A deep, angry purple bloomed across the skin around his right eye, mottled with sickly shades of green and yellow at the edges, as if the bruise had already begun its slow, grotesque transformation. The swelling was significantly worse; his eyelid, puffed and drooping, was almost closed, and a thin red line marked where the skin had split beneath his brow.

"It's not as bad as it looks," Miles said.

But it looked *bad*. Raw. Painful. My chest tightened, and for a moment, I couldn't decide if I was furious or worried or wanted to cry.

"Jesus, Miles," I said, circling the couch, rushing up to him. "What the hell happened?"

"It's fine," he said, his tone firm but not unkind. "I've had worse things happen to me."

"Worse than this?" I shot back, gesturing toward his battered face. "People beat the shit outta you often?"

He winced—not at the sarcasm, but from some unseen throb in his face—and I instantly regretted it. Not enough to take it back, but enough to make my chest squeeze tighter.

"Sit," I ordered, already turning on my heel and storming into the kitchen.

I grabbed a baggie, threw some ice in it, and wrapped it in a towel. My hands were shaking a little, so I had to pause before returning. Miles sat on the couch all casual, like it was a normal Tuesday.

I knelt beside him and held the makeshift ice pack up. "Here."

He tried to grab it, but I wouldn't let him. I carefully pressed it against his puffy eye. *You're acting caring, Serena...*

"So, are you going to tell me about the fight or what?"

"Nothing to tell. It's handled."

"Don't lie to me, Miles. *What. Happened?*"

Did Jenese get to him?

With the cold compress on his skin, his eyes fluttered closed, and a thick silence settled between us. Doughboy seemed to have gotten over his aversion to me because he strolled over to us, brushing against me. I stiffened, looking down at him with a perplexed expression.

"I don't like cats," I said absently.

Miles cracked his good eye open. "What?"

"And they don't like me. But Doughboy's been nice to me lately. It's weird."

A smile ghosted across his lips. "You're weird."

I breathed out slowly, still holding the ice on his bruise. Still acting like I didn't freak when I saw him hurt. *I'm such a fucking softie.*

"Miles—"

"Erik."

I stared at Miles, unblinking, my brain trying to process the collision of disbelief and fury rising in my chest.

"Erik?" I repeated, my voice low.

Miles laughed, then winced. "He doesn't look too pretty either. I wore his ass out too."

I grabbed his hand to get the ice, then I was up and ready to go find Erik. Now.

Wait, why are you defending him?

"Whoa, wait, wait, *wait.* Don't, Serena. It's fine." Miles grabbed my arm, bringing me back to the couch.

I glared at him, but Miles shook his head. "Don't be mad at your brother for what we got going on."

"He hit you, and I want to know *why.*" I shook my head. This was bullshit. "Did you forget we're married? We're a team. We have obligations. I can't have my husband walking around beat up!"

"Yes," he said quietly. "But this isn't about you."

"Should I just shut my mouth like a good little wife?"

Miles stared at me with a small hint of a smile. "You? A good little wife?"

I forced him to take the ice pack and proceeded to stand again.

"Whoa, wrong joke. It wasn't funny, I'm sorry. Just sit."

I shook my head. "And Erik is not the type to just *snap*. Which means this wasn't random. Which means you did something or he did something or *both* of you did something that I'm in the dark about."

All we knew was Erik and Miles fell out, soon after, the whistleblower came out about his father and the two never spoke until now.

"You're not going anywhere," he said, his voice low and commanding, his face so close I could see the flecks of gold in his brown eyes.

The shock of his assertiveness froze me, but it was the heat— the undeniable pull between us—that had me forgetting how to breathe. My heart pounded as I stared up at him, his jaw tight, his lips inches from mine.

"Let's celebrate."

I lifted a brow. "Celebrate what?"

"I got a deal on supplies for the renovation. You said the finances are in order. We're gonna fix the company and get the protestors off the front lawn."

I sucked my teeth, looking back at the bruise on his face.

"Miles," I started, softer now. "He's my brother."

"I know," he said. "And he's doing what he thinks is right. That's who Erik is."

His hand slid to my hip, grounding me. "He thinks I'm going to ruin you. Because of what happened with my family."

My breath caught.

"Your brother's just being protective."

I made a face. "Erik has never really *cared* about me. I know he cares about Laurene and Gigi, but he's never shown me love like them."

This time Miles's expression twisted. "That's not true."

"Believe me, it is."

"No," he said. "Erik loves you. Whether you see it or not, I know some of the shit he's gone through with your mother. He's protected all of y'all from a lot of bullshit."

I was surprised to see anger on his face.

"It may look like he has it together, but he don't. Trust me. He may be a horrible fucking friend, but he loves you all."

"But you're my family now. Can't I protect you?"

What are you doing, Serena? Shut up.

"Serena," he murmured, his voice softer now, but no less firm. "Promise me you'll stay out of this."

"He beat you up and now you're defending him? What sense does that make?" I asked.

"Perfect sense. Now promise me."

I gave a slow, reluctant nod.

"Come here," he said gently as he went back to sit down on the couch.

I blinked. "What?"

"Just—come here, Serena."

My eyes narrowed, wary. "Why?"

He didn't answer right away. He sat, legs wide, elbows resting on his knees. The lamp by the window caught the edge of his jaw.

"Come here and stop asking questions."

I sucked my teeth, and did as he said, but the moment I sat, he snatched me till I was sitting in between his legs, and I gasped.

"Miles!"

His fingers found the clasp of my necklace like they'd done a hundred times before, and before I could stop him, it was gone—just a cool absence on my skin where gold had been.

He set it gently on the coffee table, then moved to the

earrings. "You've been wearing these all day. Bet your ears are sore."

"They're fine," I muttered, my voice too soft.

"They're red," he said. And just like that, the second earring came off.

I hated how easily he handled me. Not rough. Not demanding. But with that annoying kind of care that made me want to cry and scream and melt all at once. He knew too much—*still* knew too much about me.

He leaned in, his breath warm against the curve of my neck. "Relax."

My body stayed taut, stiff as concrete.

"This isn't a good idea," I whispered.

"I know," he murmured, pressing his palms against my arms. "But you need to breathe."

I closed my eyes.

His hands slid up, fingers grazing my shoulders, then paused at the base of my neck. He found the first pin in my updo without asking. Slid it out. Then another. Then another.

I swallowed hard. "Miles…why are you doing this?"

He didn't answer right away.

The pins clinked softly on the table beside us as he removed them one by one, until my curls began to fall loose around my face, wild and uncontained.

"I don't know."

"It's not right," I said.

"I know."

My heart squeezed, traitorous and loud. He shifted behind me, drawing me deeper into him, his legs bracketing mine, his chest firm against my back.

Then his fingertips moved to my scalp.

I didn't expect the tenderness—the slow, circular motion, the exact pressure he knew I liked. My eyes fluttered shut before I could stop them.

Damn him.

I used to lie in his lap just like this. Sunday mornings. After board meetings. On days when I hated the world and he refused to let me carry it alone.

Back when it was easy.

"If anything, I should be doing this for you," I told him.

"Shh," he said.

Now it was all secrets and deals and pretending we didn't remember what this used to feel like.

I told myself not to lean into it.

But slowly, stupidly, I did.

My body softened. My spine curved into his chest. And when his lips brushed the top of my head, I didn't flinch.

I just breathed.

CHAPTER 19

Miles

"WASSUP, PEOPLE," I shouted, stepping into my parents' house.

When I'd gotten the money for Victor, this had been the first thing I bought. We had needed somewhere safe. We were now on the other side of town, in a quiet, less flashy neighborhood, away from prying eyes.

"Who's that makin' all that noise?"

I heard the soft shuffle of shoes and smiled—it was Mama Teagues, Pops's caretaker during the day when Ma or I were at work. After everything that happened with Pops, Ma and I both stepped in to keep Whitmore Ventures afloat. She'd walked away from her career in marketing years ago to raise me, but when the company started slipping, she dusted off that corporate hat without hesitation.

Mama Teagues came around the corner. Her gray hair was pulled back into a neat bun, and she wore her usual Sunday best: a floral-print dress, thick gold chains around her neck, and a pair of sensible shoes.

"Boy, you how I feel about noise. Damn, what happened to your face?"

I went over and picked her up, and she squealed like a girl

before hitting my side to be put down. She was the only one willing to take on the case that was Pops after the whole town blacklisted us.

"You should see the other guy. Sorry, Mama Teagues. How you doin' today? I stopped by Café L'Amour and got you those brownie cookies you like."

Mama Teagues's eyes went wide behind her coke-bottle glasses, and she snatched the paper bag from my hand.

"Your father out on the back with lunch. Beware, he's in a mood today."

When wasn't somebody always in a mood?

Victor was still on my mind. Always in the corner, always lurking. He was back—and holding a fucking knife over my throat. Laundering money. The fuck I look like? A white-collar criminal?

I should've been focused. I needed to be. But instead, my head was full of her.

Serena.

The way she'd looked at me when I pulled her in—sharp at first, all warning and fight—but she came anyway. Sat between my legs like muscle memory, like her body remembered mine even if her pride refused to admit it.

She gasped when I unhooked her necklace. That sound…low and surprised, a little breathy. I'd felt it in my chest. And when I removed her earrings, her whole body had gone still, like she didn't trust what was happening but couldn't stop it either.

Now she was my wife and still a stranger. Still walking around like she was built from glass and sharp edges, like softness would kill her.

And I hated how bad I wanted to be the one she could collapse against again.

God, she felt good in my arms. Familiar. Right. Like she belonged there. It felt how it used to be, before all the world fell apart. Damn. Each day I wished things were like how it *used* to be.

I was a damn fool for wanting more.

Because wanting her meant risking it all again. Trust. Control. Love.

And love…love got you gutted.

Should I do what Victor wanted? I tossed it around in my head. But what would that mean for us? My family had suffered enough. I was hesitant to tell them, but needed advice.

I went out back, and the sun cast long shadows on the cracked patio. Pops was sitting with his back to me, eating breakfast. He rhythmically tapped his wheelchair, gazing distantly.

"How you doin', old man?"

He turned, frowning. "Came to check on me, huh? How's the wife? What happened to your eye? She did that?"

"She's fine. I just got into a little fight."

"Little fight?"

Grabbing a piece of toast, its crust giving way with a satisfying crunch, I plopped into the chair opposite him, observing him closely. Pops looked worn and weary. The sun had kissed his bald brown head with a scattering of freckles, and his once-black beard was now largely white. Deep lines and shadows marred his face. He looked older than his fifties.

"You been talking to Vincent? Or Yvonne?" I couldn't look at him when I said it, but I knew he'd catch the weight of it. Vincent. The man who had been more of a brother to him than a business partner. "Dante come back with any other back-door tricks he wants us to turn like we hookers on the street?"

Pops shifted in his seat, his jaw clenching.

"Thank fucking God, *no*," Pops muttered, shaking his head, his voice lowering. "Remember, we're only worried about covering our asses. You not getting sucked too much into the marriage, are you?"

How could I not? I was living with Serena. The only woman outside of my mother I ever loved.

"No." I shook my head. "I know the game."

"Your mom said when she went to the store with Drill Sergeant Teagues, it was better." Pops grunted, reaching for his orange juice.

"Better?"

I remembered when Pops began acting strange. It was a few weeks after Gramps's funeral. He used to be up by 6:30 sharp. After Gramps died, some mornings he didn't come out of his room till noon—or not at all. I thought it was just normal stress. Staying at the office late. Coming in during the early morning. Not eating dinner with us. Phone calls at all hours of the night.

That was business, right?

"They let her into the store?" I asked. Last time she went to the grocery store in town, they "closed early for inventory."

After the Kings' soirée six years ago, things went to a fucked-up place.

At first, when Ma or I would call to hang out with our friends, people just said they were "busy." Then they stopped saying anything at all. The Whitmore name disappeared from charity committee rosters. Then we stopped getting cc'd on event invites—no more ladies' brunches for Ma, no more community real estate mixers for Pops.

"She said they were able to shop, easy as pie."

"So…we're back in?" I said.

Pops shook his head. "Nah. Don't jump the gun. It's tentative. These fuckers will turn on us again like that—" Pops snapped his fingers. "The moment Queen Yvonne says so."

"Yvonne's a lot of things, but she's not gonna risk her family's reputation just to spite you or Dante."

"You don't know her like I do."

Pops's and Yvonne's fathers were best friends so they'd grown up together like siblings. In the photos he hadn't cut up or burned, they were kids with big smiles and skinned knees.

I shook my head. "We just need to focus on us."

"You think rebuilding Whitmore Ventures is gonna fix that? That you can make them respect us again?"

"You're saying I've been wasting my time? That none of it mattered? That I should've let it all rot with you?" Sometimes I wanted to do just fucking that.

His jaw clenched. "Don't start—"

"No. *You* started."

After the accident, he didn't do shit. Ma and I had to drag him out of bed. I remembered sitting outside his room with a tray of food, knocking until my knuckles were raw. He wouldn't bathe. Wouldn't eat. Wouldn't speak.

"You gave up," I said. "You let everything Gramps built slip through your fingers." I felt that familiar anger coming back. "You didn't fight for anything. For us. We talk a lot of shit about the Kings, but one thing they don't play about is their name. Their legacy. Say what you want about them, but they protect their own—no matter how messy it gets."

Again, Miles. Is Whitmore Ventures worth saving? Or do you start something new?

"You were in that courtroom, boy. You watched them pretend we didn't exist. Watched them rip me apart while they walked away clean. Now you wanna be them? You always wanted to be like that damn Erik."

I shook my head. "Erik was my brother. I didn't want to be him, but at least his father poured into him and helped make him a leader. Maybe we'd be a better family if we gave just a *fraction* of a damn the way they do."

What I didn't say—what I was only just starting to admit—was that I didn't want to be them anymore. Not Erik. Not my father. Not any of the men who wore their legacies like chains.

I wasn't just trying to fix what my father broke.

I was trying to figure out what belong to *Miles*.

He didn't yell. He didn't deny it. He just looked away. And maybe that hurt worse than anything he could've said.

"Look at my boys!" Ma's voice rang out as she opened the patio doors and stepped outside.

Her silk blouse was pressed to perfection and paired with

high-waisted cream trousers, and her locs were pinned into a neat updo, twisted high and tight at the crown of her head.

"Uh-oh." Ma's face fell when she realized the tension between us. "Something happened."

"Your *husband* happened." I stood up, ready to go.

"Miles," Ma said, and she held up a hand. "Sit."

I hesitated. "Ma—"

"We're not doing this today," she added.

"He won't listen to you, Audrey. He's always been hard-headed like that," Pops said bitterly.

"Like you?" I countered.

"Miles," Ma warned. "Please. Don't upset your father."

"Sometimes you need to know when to throw in the towel. I think we've come to that point," Pops said. "It's bad enough we forced you into this marriage. It's not right."

"Omar, we discussed—" Ma started.

"I know, but maybe we should just leave town. I think it's best. I won't have my son tied to that bloodsucking family."

"Kinda late for that now that I married into it," I said sarcastically. "Where were you years ago when I didn't want this shit?"

My mind flashed with Victor's voice again. *Emails. Texts. A few creative ledgers. It's not hard to make it look like you were deeper in than you were when you took my money.*

"I—" I started, jaw locking halfway through. I was going to say it. I *wanted* to say it. Tell them what was really coming for us. That it wasn't Serena. It wasn't the Kings. It was something way dirtier. Older. Mine.

But what would it change?

She turned to Pops. "Omar, he's trying. And whether or not you agree with *how,* you owe him the space to try not to just give up what your father built for us."

Then to me. "And Miles… He's not the man he used to be. You may never get the father you wanted back. But don't let his silence convince you that he doesn't care."

Pops's eyes shifted, his hands gripping the arms of the chair, knuckles pale. "I never wanted this for you," he muttered. "I'm going inside."

With a push of the joystick, his chair rolled backward with a quiet mechanical hum. He didn't meet my eyes. The screen door creaked, then clicked shut behind him.

"You were going to say something," Ma said quietly.

I didn't answer at first. The words were there—Victor's voice, those damn emails, numbers that didn't add up unless you knew what you were looking for.

"It's nothing. I need to handle something," I told her, stepping back. "Don't worry about me."

I would have to deal with Victor on my own. Like I'd been dealing with everything else.

CHAPTER 20
Serena

"HUNGRY?" I asked Doughboy, who I'd reluctantly let sit next to me. He'd been creepily staring at me for four hours while I researched Jenese.

Of course it wasn't easy.

She'd covered her tracks pretty well. Jenese knew how to stay in the spotlight just enough. A party photo here. A foundation gala there. Always with someone who had money. Jenese gave Zsa Zsa Gabor and Liz Taylor a run for their money when it came to marriages.

I didn't know her. Not really. Not the way I thought I had.

She told me she grew up with a single mom who often couldn't afford both food and electricity. But had that really happened? Apparently, she went to an all-girls college that was now closed. Highly doubt it.

"Meow."

I frowned at Doughboy. "Are you super hungry or just a bit hungry?"

Why the hell was I talking to a cat? I didn't even like Walter, Gigi's decrepit dog.

I dragged myself off the couch; I knew I could find something to blackmail Jenese with if I just kept looking. I walked to the kitchen, and heard Doughboy jump off the couch and follow me.

I sucked my teeth and looked at the clock.

It was close to one in the morning.

Where on earth was Miles?

"You know where your owner is?" I asked Doughboy as he came strutting in, his tail high before he launched himself up onto the counter.

"No way, get off the counter! It's not sanitary!" I swatted him away with a dish towel. He had the *audacity* to hiss at me. "Oh, don't you *dare*. I *will* call animal control."

Doughboy blinked slowly. After that, he licked his paw, flashed his butt at me, and leaped back to the kitchen floor, going to the edge of the kitchen.

"That's right, you ain't crazy," I muttered.

Eyeing the menace just a bit longer, I opened the fridge and was quickly disappointed.

I had forgotten to order more of my premade meals, and there was nothing left. The quinoa bowls, the grilled salmon, even the sad-ass kale wraps—all gone.

I had to do the unthinkable. *Cook.*

I glanced at the stack of cookbooks on the counter, perfectly color-coded and absolutely untouched.

"Okay…" I picked up one with the title *Simple, Sexy, Soulful Suppers* in gold lettering. The edges of the page were still crisp.

I didn't want a recipe with a million steps. I definitely wasn't using a bunch of pots and pans and bowls. I didn't want to experiment either.

What was easy?

Pasta.

It couldn't be that hard, right? Boil water. Stir. Maybe throw something green on top. I could do this. The staff at my parents' mansion made it for me all the time.

I found a spaghetti recipe, but we were missing half the

ingredients. I grabbed the only pasta I could find—some expensive linguine Miles got at that farmers' market.

"First step, boil water," I muttered.

I set a pot on the stove like I was preparing for battle.

"Done. Easy." I turned to my little enemy, who was staring at me with those big green eyes. "Watch, you can't have none when I'm done."

Again, why are you talking to a cat? You can't be this damn lonely.

Well. I guess I was. I couldn't go to my sisters or Noelle about Jenese. I couldn't confess to Mama or Daddy—that would be pointless. I definitely wasn't confessing to Erik.

"What's the best way to chop garlic?" I muttered. "Up and down? Or sideways?"

The recipe needed tomato sauce and garlic. We didn't have sauce but I had tomato juice, ketchup, and a real tomato.

I picked up the heavy knife. My grip was all wrong, I could tell. But I was tired and hungry and wired on too much caffeine and not enough sleep, and Jenese's name was echoing in the back of my skull like a song I couldn't turn off.

The blade hit the cutting board with a loud *thunk*.

I forced myself to keep cutting, each slice a small victory against the overwhelming task. I aggressively chopped the garlic.

When I was done, I looked down at the massacre. The garlic was mangled—some pieces slivered too thin, others still nearly whole.

"Goddamn it."

Doughboy meowed once, like he was trying to tell me to just give up.

Nope. Time to move on to the sauce.

When was the last time I'd cooked? Probably with Miles. Why had I had so many of my firsts with him? Miles always loved being in the kitchen, even if he couldn't cook well back then. Now I knew he was a pro. I'd always been perfectly content to just watch and taste his questionable creations after.

Don't go there.

A violent sizzling sound, like bacon in a pan, and the gurgling of boiling water drew my attention to the stove where the pot had bubbled over.

I grabbed the linguine and snapped it in half—poorly. Some slid into the pot. Some scattered across the counter. One piece hit me in the neck.

"Not ideal," I mumbled. "But we move on."

I reached for the saucepan, dumped in my tomato-ketchup-garlic improvisation, and stirred it with a wooden spoon, the scent of garlic filling the kitchen as I pretended to know what I was doing.

After a few minutes, it smelled…weird.

I turned up the heat to hurry it along.

Big mistake.

I really didn't know what happened next. The concoction began popping. A rogue droplet landed on my wrist. I yelped and jumped back, knocking into the pasta pot. With a loud splash, water sloshed onto the stove, sending a plume of steam into the air. The handle tipped. I grabbed it—too late.

With a curious sniff, Doughboy padded back into the kitchen, one paw rising to investigate the heat emanating from the oven. Miles would fucking kill me if something happened to his cat.

"Move, Doughboy!"

A guttural meow escaped the cat's throat before he silently slipped away. I turned, searching for a sponge or cloth to wipe away the mess.

The sauce boiled over, splattering thick, sticky droplets onto the burner with a loud hiss. The smell changed instantly—a sharp, acrid scent filled the air. I reached for a paper towel—

"Shit—shitshitshit—" The paper towel slipped from my grasp as I reached over the furiously boiling pot of water, the heat radiating up toward my face. A small flame licked the edge of a paper towel.

From the hallway, a long, slow, rumbling mrowl, like a self-satisfied sigh, echoed from Doughboy—a clear *told you so.*

"Oh my God," I cried, a searing pain shooting through my fingers as I frantically grabbed the scalding paper towel and tossed it into the sink. I turned on the faucet. Nothing. I jiggled the handle. A sputtering, metallic shriek and then a geyser of frigid water erupted from the faucet, soaking my shirt and the counter.

The smoke detector started screeching.

I was going to burn down my condo.

Then the front door opened.

"What the hell?"

Miles stood there, his dark eyes assessing the wreckage—scattered ingredients, sticky countertops, and the bitter tang of failure hanging heavy in the air. His mouth parted, but no words came out.

The smoke detector finally gave one last pity *beep* and went silent.

"Why are you about to burn down the damn house?" He looked up at Doughboy. "You cool, D?"

"You're asking the cat if he's alright?" I frowned at him. "Where were you?"

Why do you want to know, Serena? You don't care what he does, right?

His eyes, dark and intense, slid to mine, and his smirk curled with that lazy, infuriating charm, the corners of his mouth twitching with a cruel amusement. "Why? You worried about me?"

I placed my hands on my hips.

"Did I ask you that when you came home late the other night?" Miles said. "I'm a grown-ass man."

"It's not the same," I said stubbornly.

"Oh?" His voice dipped lower, silkier. "Because when *you* disappear, it's no questions asked."

"We're starting renovations on Mrs. Fontaine's property

tomorrow. I thought we could have gone over the site plan together."

"Now you want to collaborate?"

I ignored the bite in his voice. "I waited for you for hours."

"You could have texted."

"You could have told me you weren't coming home."

He took a step closer, looking over the mess once again, and sighed before shaking his head.

"Go change," he said quietly.

"What?"

"You heard me." His gaze dropped, lingering at the curve of my waist. "You're a mess and the kitchen is a mess, and the scent of garlic is about to make me fucking throw up. I'll clean while you change."

When I came back, barefoot, hair loose and twisted into a messy knot, the kitchen was spotless.

Miles was at the stove, one hand on a pan, the other braced on the counter. Sleeves pushed up. Veins visible in his forearms.

"You actually cleaned," I said, my voice softer than I expected. "And you're cooking now?"

"Don't pass out. It's grilled cheese and soup," he said, finally glancing over his shoulder. His eyes dropped to my bare legs and lingered, just long enough for me to feel it. "I don't feel like having to evacuate a burning place. My back is fucking killing me as it is, we started moving some stuff out Mrs. Fontaine left behind."

Before I even thought it through, my hand slid to the small of his back, right where I remembered the pain always settled. I pressed gently. "Still the same place?"

His body went still.

"Yeah," he said after a second, voice rougher now. "How'd you—"

"I remember," I said. "That game sophomore year. You got hit so hard I thought you were dead."

He let out a dry laugh, but it was low, almost breathless. "You and half the school."

"You didn't move for a minute," I murmured. "You always played like you were invincible. That was the first time I realized you weren't. I still don't like thinking about it."

Miles and Erik played football together from middle school through college. I never liked the sport; it was too aggressive, but Miles wanted to be like his dad, who also played.

His shoulders relaxed under my touch—just a little—but the tension still simmered beneath the surface, coiled and ready to spring. "Serena King, nervous over *me*?"

I didn't answer. I didn't have to.

I just kept my hand there, warm on his back, letting my thumb move in slow, deliberate circles. The kitchen was quiet, save for the soft bubble of soup on the stove and the static of unspoken things between us.

His hand reached back blindly, found my hip, and rested there like it belonged.

"Can you grab us two bowls?"

Why did I feel dismissed? I removed my hand, putting it back to my side as I went to the cabinet. I moved slowly, reached for the silverware. He still didn't answer my question.

"I don't remember you being able to make anything other than instant ramen. And even that was questionable."

A laugh burst out of him. "That's because I couldn't. Ramen and toaster waffles were about the extent of my skills back then."

"When did you learn? Did the support group teach you like you said before to Mrs. Fontaine?"

"Partially, yeah," he admitted. "One of the guys in the group was a chef before his wife got sick. He ran these meal-prep sessions to help us out."

"That's...thoughtful." I didn't think about the day-to-day living going through what he experienced back then. To have to worry about meals on top of your life falling apart?

"Yeah," Miles said. I hated that he still had that ugly bruise on his face. Then, after a beat, quieter: "He was the one who told me I had to stop feeding my dad frozen lasagna and burritos."

My chest pinched. "Miles…"

"Shit. That sounded way sadder out loud."

Doughboy meowed at that, and Miles winked at him.

"No," I said. "It sounded honest."

He leaned his hands on the edge of the counter, head down, jaw tight. "I didn't know what the hell I was doing. Mama was going through a lot—hell, even she wasn't eating. We couldn't afford a chef anymore. I also had to keep the business going. Somebody had to do it, you know?"

I nodded. I never thought about the quiet humiliations. Grocery store stares. Empty cabinets. I'd only watched the trial, but never in my head did I allow myself to feel what he could possibly feel. I felt too much regret about him, and I knew I was protected with my family's name.

Miles didn't have that protection.

"One day my dad was the one running things, yelling across boardrooms and hosting cigar nights with the guys. Next thing I know he's got this blank look in his eye and he's calling me 'buddy' because he doesn't remember my name."

I stepped closer, and he looked back at the grilled cheese in the pan.

"I used to get mad at him," he admitted, almost in a whisper. "For forgetting. For slurring his words. For needing me. It wasn't fair, but I did."

"That makes you human."

"It made me an asshole." His throat worked. "He got diagnosed with diabetes not too long before the car wreck and all the other shit. So I had to learn how to inject insulin, clean wounds, fight with insurance, and bathe a grown man who used to scare me into silence with one look."

I gripped the counter tighter.

"Your sandwich is ready," he said abruptly.

He busied himself with pulling it out, and then looked at me. "Can I ask you a question?"

I nodded.

"It hasn't been easy for you either these last few years, has it? With the company? Your mom?"

No. It wasn't easy. I'd been so hellbent on proving myself. Trying to compete with Erik and Laurene when I knew I would never have their positions in the family. I knew I couldn't change how King Enterprises would run.

"I got what I wanted, that's all that matters." I crossed my arms, watching as he stirred the tomato soup. "I knew the cost I had to pay."

Miles paused. "Which was us."

"I—"

"It's the truth. You can't lie about it," Miles said. "I just can't help but think maybe we've been running parallel lives. Trying to save companies, help family, make sure we don't fucking go under and never come out."

"You think about it a lot?" I asked, barely above a whisper.

He didn't flinch. "Every time something good happens, I'd think about telling you. Every time something goes to shit...I wonder if you'd care. We were more similar than we thought growing up."

That cracked something in me. Something I didn't even know was still holding on.

"I wasn't popular."

He made a face. "That has nothing to do with it. I meant I enjoyed kicking your ass in every competition."

"Oh no you didn't." I couldn't help but laugh and shake my head.

We competed over everything. If I finished a book, he'd start two. If I made honor roll, he'd aim for valedictorian—just to get under my skin. Spelling bees, student council elections, debate tournaments, even damn volunteer hours.

Growing up as a King, we weren't challenged much. He brought that for me. And I loved it back then.

"I'm still better," I sniffed, tilting my head up.

"Really?" Miles pursed his lips. "I was student of the year throughout high school."

"You rigged that." I leaned against the counter, and I realized I was smiling big at him.

"Sometimes I wonder," he said, "what would've happened if we just…stayed. If we didn't let all of it tear us apart."

He handed me the steaming bowl of tomato soup, its rich aroma filling the air. Our fingers brushed.

"Open," he commanded.

I did it without thinking, and he fed me the soup, rich and tangy, bursting with flavor. My throat tightened as I swallowed, and his eyes followed my every move. He fed me again, and I ate slowly.

"You shouldn't be doing this," I said at last, the weight of my words heavy in the silent room.

"I know," Miles said simply, his eyes downcast.

"If you could do anything else, what would it be?" I finally asked, my voice trembling slightly.

With a satisfying crunch, he bit into his sandwich, his eyes drifting away before he broke off a piece and tossed it to Doughboy.

"A chef. I like when people enjoy something I make."

A small smile came across my face. "It's really good."

"What about you?"

I was silent, taking the bowl from him. I fed myself slowly, even dipping the grilled cheese into the soup. I hopped up to sit on the counter, taking in his full glory.

"I don't know… I never imagined myself doing something else."

I blinked hard. It was true. I never thought to be anything else than a King. This was my life here.

Don't cry. Not in front of him.

He took a step toward me, the warmth of the soup bowl forgotten, my knees brushing the front of his shirt.

"You know you can do something else," he said.

"What would that be?"

He didn't respond. "The world's our oyster, right? You have time to figure it out."

"What are you trying to ask me, Miles?"

He shook his head. But I knew him.

And I remembered.

The late nights we used to sneak down to the kitchen after everyone was asleep.

The arguments that turned into debates, then laughter.

The first time he called me *brilliant*.

When I looked at him as more than my older brother's best friend, and as a man who saw me as a woman he wanted. He never wanted to fix me or use me. He just wanted me to *want* more. And maybe that's what scared me the most.

That he always believed I could be someone else. Someone free.

His hands didn't ask permission.

One cupped the back of my neck, fingers sliding into my hair. The other pushed past the open edge of my robe, finding the curve of my breast beneath the silk slip I wore.

He squeezed like he had every right—because he did once.

My gasp hit his mouth just as he kissed me. Hard. Devouring. Like he needed to taste what he'd been deprived of for years. It wasn't sweet. It wasn't careful. It was six years of heartbreak, resentment, and *want* finally detonating.

I didn't pull away.

I let it happen. Let him take. Let myself need.

The robe slipped down my shoulders like it understood it didn't matter anymore. That there was no point in pretending.

I pulled him closer with both hands, fisting the front of his shirt, my mouth opening under his. The kiss deepened—messy, hot, reckless. His hand slid lower, across my thigh, then under, fingers skating up until he found the lace between my legs.

His mouth was still on mine, but his breath stilled.

"You're wet," he muttered into my mouth. "Still want me, even now?"

He didn't wait for an answer.

His fingers pushed the lace aside, teased, pressed. I shuddered, legs tightening around him, my head falling back with a breathless moan.

He kissed down my throat, biting gently at my collarbone. "You miss this?"

God, yes.

I'd spent six years pretending I didn't.

He slipped a finger inside me. Then another. Slow. Deep. My body clenched around him.

I moaned, low and shaking. I hated him. I wanted him. I needed—

Then he stopped.

Pulled away.

I made a sound I couldn't control—half whimper, half protest—and reached for him before I realized what I was doing.

But he was already backing up.

He didn't look smug. Or proud. Or even satisfied.

He looked…ruined.

"I shouldn't have done that," he said, voice hoarse. "You make me forget this is a bad idea."

I swallowed hard, my chest heaving.

"Miles—"

"Good night, Serena." And with that he left, leaving me panting with a half-eaten grilled cheese and stirred-up feelings.

CHAPTER 21

Miles

THE SHARP SOUND *of tires crunching on gravel cut through the ocean's roar, jolting me from my reverie. I leaned against my car, the salty tang of the sea air filling my nostrils and the vast Pacific stretching before me.*

He actually came.

It'd been a few days after the summer soirée and the whole town had found out what had gone down between Pops and Vincent.

I'd noticed Pops had been off his mark for a little while now, but for him to do what he did at the party? I was hoping I could either fix things or find some reasonable explanation.

Serena wasn't answering my calls. At first the phone would ring and ring and ring, but now it was straight to voicemail.

That fucking stung.

Erik exited his G-Wagon, looking as exhausted as I was, a baseball cap pulled low over his eyes, obscuring his expression, his hands shoved deep in his sweatpants.

"I can't believe you did it," I told him. I could barely look at him.

Erik shook his head. "Miles—"

"You knew what it would do to my family. You knew what it would do to me." I couldn't believe he did it. Betrayed me like this.

"I also knew what it was doing to my family. To this city." His voice cracked just enough to make me flinch.

I shoved off the car. "So you just decided you were judge, jury, executioner now? Huh? You decided you knew better than me?"

"I went back to Whitmore Ventures last night because you left your jacket in my car," he said quietly. "I walked in and saw Omar."

I was breathing hard as I watched him, and he had the nerve to look upset.

"He was with Mayor Johnson. Doing lines in your father's damn office. Didn't even lock the fucking door. You didn't see it, man. But I did. And in that moment, everything made sense."

"No." I shook my head. "You—no. You're twisting this."

"I'm not." Erik stepped forward. "He was coked out of his mind, Miles. With the mayor. You wanna pretend it was one mistake, one bad night? Fine. But I've been watching him spiral since Woody died... And so have you."

"I haven't—"

"You have." His voice rose. "You just didn't want to admit it because then you'd have to stop playing the loyal son."

"He's still my dad, man."

I didn't come here to fight with Erik. I wanted to apologize. Maybe even come clean about Serena and me. That was the plan. Not this.

But Erik was right.

I didn't want to admit this. Admit that my father was weak.

Pops wasn't Pops anymore. He'd stopped showing up to meetings. Stopped shaving. Was staying out late and stumbling home smelling like liquor and smoke. Some nights, I heard him arguing with Ma so loud I thought the neighbors would call the cops.

"You're standing there defending the man who nearly killed my father, and you expect me to what—nod along? You got more fucking balls than that, Miles."

"I'm not defending—"

"You are!" he roared. "Every excuse, every 'he didn't mean it'— that's defending, Miles! You know I love you, man, but if it was me in your position, I would want you to keep it real."

"Keep it real? That meant telling Lush Chronicles? *People are already blacklisting us, man—our phones are ringing off the hook, Ma can't even go to the fucking store."*

Erik's head dropped.

"He's not some monster. He's my father," I said, desperate now, but then anger filled me. "Is this that 'King tough love' you trying to show? That perfect family bullshit you always hide behind? My family doesn't roll that way."

Erik's eyes narrowed.

"My family's having issues, and all you do is judge. Like your dad isn't cold as fuck at times. You think your mama's love means shit when you have to earn it every second of your life? Nah. That's not a family, that's a fucking brand. My family might be messy, but at least we give a damn about each other behind closed doors. So don't sit here looking fucking down on me like your life ain't fucked up too."

Something shifted in Erik's face—something small, but real. That one landed.

"That's your whole family. Just one big, shiny lie wrapped in designer clothes and fake-ass smiles. Maybe if y'all were real, more fucking people would like you and not just tolerate you."

"So that's what you do? Tolerate me?"

"Yeah. I guess I do."

"So that's what we on?" Erik finally said.

I nodded. "That's it."

"Then what the fuck am I here for?"

I'd been hoping that after over twenty years of friendship with Erik, of growing up next door, of him being my boy that he would offer some type of kindness for this situation. I believed we could figure this out.

"You're my best fucking friend, man."

"I didn't want to be the one," Erik whispered. "But someone had to."

I looked away, jaw tight, tears pressing behind my eyes. I refused to let them fall.

"I slept with Serena. Right before the party."

For a second, Erik froze, every muscle tense, his breath held in his chest.

Then his whole body jerked violently, as if the words were blows landing on him, each one a painful jolt.

"The fuck did you just say to me?" His voice dropped, quiet and dangerous.

I held his stare. If I backed down now, I'd lose whatever dignity I had left. "You heard me."

He moved so quickly, I barely had time to react before his chest knocked into mine. His hands were already balled into fists, knuckles white and tense.

"You touched my sister?" he hissed, his voice a low, dangerous growl.

I didn't even get the chance to explain, to tell him I loved her, that it wasn't just some random shit. His fist connected with my jaw with a sickening thud, a sharp, shocking pain that made my eyes water.

I stumbled backward, the metallic tang of blood filling my mouth.

"I love her," I whispered, as I dabbed at my lip.

"Don't you fucking come near Serena. She's not like those other hoes you sleep with, and I'll be damned if you ruin her."

"You don't care. All you care is that you get the company. Admit that shit, Erik."

Erik shook his head.

"I can't fuck with you, Miles. Not like this." He turned around and walked off, snatching open the door of his truck.

"I didn't hurt her!" I shouted back. "I care about her! More than you or your family! Y'all don't even fucking know her!"

"I'll always love you like a brother, man. But I can't... I can't."

Erik didn't respond. He spun the car around, tires screaming, and fishtailed back onto the road.

A few hours later, my phone rang, the harsh buzz cutting through the silence of my apartment like a gunshot. I stared at the screen, the name "Unknown" flashing in front of me. I hesitated, then picked up.

"What?"

"Miles Whitmore?"

"Yeah?"

"This is Officer Lawson," he continued, his tone dropping into something darker. "We're calling about your father."

The air in my lungs seemed to vanish.

The rest of what he said was a blur, drowned by the thundering rush of blood in my ears. "Accident" was the first word I caught. My stomach dropped like a stone. "Car wreck."

"I thought I was going to have to come find you," Victor said as he stepped into my makeshift office that was now in the King Developments headquarters. "This is your office? Not the nicest view."

While Serena had the biggest office in the building, I'd been relegated off to an old side room they'd been using for storage. I knew Serena did that shit on purpose.

I shut the door behind him and double-checked the blinds.

"Let's get this over with," I said.

He chuckled. "It's been a while. We should catch up."

"We're not friends," I said flatly.

I wanted Victor out of here as quickly as possible. Erik had been right all those years ago. Victor wasn't a good man. He was a fucking criminal. But sometimes to survive, you had to do things. It wasn't like the Kings gave a fuck if the Whitmores lived or starved.

I just walked around the desk—if you could call a scratched-up table a desk—and sat down.

"I got the money. I just need you to do your thing." Victor sat in the chair across from me, and pointed at the computer.

Despite what Erik and others thought of me, I wasn't going to be fucking stupid this time. If I let Victor come back and tell me what the fuck to do with my own business, what had I worked for all these years?

"There's a problem."

Victor raised a brow. "There always is."

"The consolidation of King Developments and Whitmore Ventures isn't done yet. If I pull in outside capital now—especially silent capital—it'll trigger questions. Paper trails, audit flags. Serena will sniff it out before it clears."

Victor stared at me. "So? Aren't you the man in the relationship?"

Don't let him piss you off.

I needed to stall. For as long as fucking possible till I could get out of this mess.

"Tell me why you actually need me here," I said.

Victor frowned. "I already fucking—"

"I want to know the truth. Front and back, Victor. That's the least you can do."

His lips thinned, and he narrowed his eyes at me, staring hard enough to burn a hole between my eyes. Then finally the man sighed.

"It was one of my sites down in LA. The poor piece of shit's name was Luis Calderón." Victor worked his jaw. "It was an accident. Next thing you know, cameras, people asking questions, private investigators—"

"Private investigators?" I asked.

"Listen, all you need to know and do is hold my money so these blood-sucking ticks and the court systems don't get what I rightfully earned for myself. Just like I helped you when your daddy pissed away all your money. It's quid pro quo."

I just needed him to say more.

"Victor—"

"I'm done talking."

I frowned at him. "I'm not moving a cent until I know people won't be paying attention. If I move too fast, I burn all of us. We need to take it slow."

Victor's face darkened. "I made things clear to you, Miles."

"I understood perfectly." I sat up straighter in my seat.

"I heard about what happened at the gallery. We don't want to add me into the mix as well. If I go down, you don't think they won't look into me? I keep records, Miles, my boy. Good-ass records. Audio. I'm sure your wife wouldn't want to be blind-sided by this terrible news."

I gritted my teeth. "Stay away from my wife."

"Your pretty wife won't get touched if you do what I say." He slammed his hand on the desk in front of me. "You think I trust anyone? You think I walked into this town without an insurance policy?"

I leaned back in my chair, forcing myself to breathe. Victor was a desperate man—but even desperate men slipped.

"Audio, huh?" I asked, keeping my voice flat. "That new?"

"Gotta keep up with the times."

"I'm not backing out of our deal. Just give me some time. Can you do that?"

Silence.

"Or," I added, "you can move now and risk all the bullshit coming down on you."

Victor leaned forward. "You think you're clever?"

"No." I smiled. "I've learned running a business you gotta do the hard stuff."

"You've got one week." Victor stood, fixing the front of his suit. "And if all this shit goes up in flames? It'll be *you* who did it. Remember that."

The door shut behind him.

My smile dropped.

One week.

I could do a lot in a week. Burn a business to the ground, resurrect another from the ashes, lie through my fucking teeth if I had to.

But I was going to need someone to help with Victor. The question was just who?

I left the office, the door slamming behind me. The elevator was too slow, so I took the stairs, two at a time, my brain already spinning through names, favors, old debts.

Stepping onto the street, I saw Victor a few feet from his car, his hand on the door handle. He paused, sensing me. With a mocking wave, he slid into the driver's seat, and then the blacked-out Mercedes pulled off smoothly.

I scanned my surroundings, and a cold dread washed over me.

Across the street, Erik sat in a parked G-Wagon, the streetlights glinting off the polished surface of the SUV.

Fuck.

CHAPTER 22

Serena

"C'MON ON, PLEASE!" Gigi said through the phone.

"I barely like you, why would I want your geriatric ass dog over here?"

I stared at the front of Mrs. Fontaine's property. Workers were already moving in and out, hauling materials and shouting over the noise.

"Walter is a distinguished senior citizen, and I have a date tonight."

"Haven't you dated every man in the state already? This sounds like a *you* problem."

"Don't be a bitch," Gigi said.

My thighs ached. A dull, traitorous throb. I shifted in my seat, as if that would erase the memory of him. Of his fingers. Of my shameful gasp.

God. Focus.

But why did I like it? Why couldn't I sleep for hours after that, listening for every creak in the house to think he might come back to finish what he started? It had been a while since I'd been with anyone, and that wasn't anything long-term. But nobody was better than him. The feeling of his hands on my skin was uniquely intense, a sensation no one else could ever match.

"Helllloo?" Gigi yelled into the phone. "Do you hear me talkin' to you, heifer?"

I snapped. "I don't want your dog in my condo! It's bad enough Miles got a freaking mammoth of a cat—"

Gigi gasped indignantly. "You let Miles bring his cat? A stranger? But you can't let your own nephew come over?"

I pinched the bridge of my nose. "Walter is *not* my nephew."

I opened my Notes app and typed as Gigi yapped about bullshit:

Inspect renovation budget.

Confirm permits pulled for electrical.

Do NOT think about Miles.

Three actionable tasks. Two professional. One impossible.

I told myself it was a lapse. A biological event. Like hiccups. Meaningless.

"He is my *child*," she shot back, offended, like I'd just disrespected a blood relative. "I carried that dog in my purse for years! You *will* show some respect."

"He's half-blind, deaf, and has more arthritis than a nursing home. No. If anything, he's a liability I don't have homeowner's insurance for."

"You know Laurene won't watch him since he made her fall down that ditch, and she's pregnant now so she can't stand his smell anyway. Erik's had a ban on him for years since he peed on his Star Wars figurine collection. I'm running out of options."

"Too bad for you."

I spent all morning buried in paperwork and meetings. Anything to stay busy.

"I can't leave my baby unattended," Gigi whined.

"Why not ask Mama or Daddy?"

Her voice got huffy like always when she got an attitude. "Mama and I aren't speaking."

"Again? Why?"

"I told her I wanted to start my own boutique, and she all but laughed in my face."

I rubbed my temple. "You're still on this?"

Gigi gasped. "Excuse me? I was serious. I'm starting my own business."

"G, you change career paths more than you change your wigs. Last month, it was candle making. Before that, you were gonna be a model. And let's not forget the infamous 'I'm moving to LA to be a celebrity stylist' phase."

"That was a valid career path until I got blackballed."

"But how long before you quit? Three weeks? A month?"

Silence.

"You're such a bitch sometimes, you know that?"

I blinked. "I'm trying to help you have realistic expectations—"

"You and Mama," she snapped. "Y'all sit up on your damn high horses, acting like I'm some *failure* because I don't wanna work myself to death in a damn office or force myself to kiss ass. We're the top of the motherfuckin' food chain here! Why am I a second-class citizen?"

"This isn't about—"

"Yes, it is." Her voice crackled with anger. "Y'all respect Laurene because she was the graceful, elegant one. Y'all respect Erik because he's the leader, and you, Miss Perfect Serena, are the businesswoman. Me? I'm the joke, huh? The mistake 'cause Daddy forgot to wear a condom?"

"You are doing too much. It's not that serious," I told her.

"Keep your negativity. I'm gonna do this, whether y'all support me or not. I'm gonna open my boutique, and when I do, don't even bother stepping your uptight ass through my doors."

"Gigi—"

"Oh, by the way, Mama is summoning you and Miles to dinner tomorrow."

"Wait—"

She hung up on me. I stared at my phone, then I closed my eyes. I'd deal with Gigi and her drama later. I had to focus on work.

Stepping out of my truck, I was happy to see some progress was starting to be made. Several of the workers turned to look at me as I approached.

An older man stepped in front of me. "So this is the wife?" he said in a Haitian accent.

"Excuse me, who are you and why are you on my property?" I asked, my voice clipped and cool. I didn't recognize him. And I didn't like not recognizing him. Not here. Not on my site.

The front door opened, and Miles stepped out.

And just for a second, I forgot how to breathe.

He wasn't in a suit. No pressed collar. No shiny cuff links catching the light.

Just a worn black T-shirt clinging to his chest, the fabric damp at the collar and stretching over muscle like it belonged there. His jeans hung low on his hips, faded in all the right places, and his boots were scuffed and dirty like he'd just stepped out of trouble.

His forearms flexed as he wiped his hands on a grease-stained rag—slow and deliberate.

He looked like sin.

Like sweat and sex and the kind of mistake you don't regret until your legs are shaking and your heart's in your throat.

The heat between us curled low in my stomach, and I hated how easily he still did this to me—just by standing there, all golden skin and grit and that mouth that drove me up the fucking wall.

"This man was not approved in hiring," I told Miles as I glared at the man.

"Carlus has been with *my* company for almost ten years. He ain't going nowhere, and I trust him more than anyone here. Do I need to remind you we're both the bosses here?"

"Renovations are supposed to have a *full* crew. Where is everyone?"

Miles looked annoyed, and didn't bother hiding it.

"We're still in a middle of scandal, remember? We gotta work with what we got."

I had to count back from five. I was used to people doing what I wanted when I demanded. This partnership… It was gonna take some getting used to.

"Besides, I think we have more important things to worry about," he continued. Miles and Carlus looked at one another before Miles swept his hands toward the house. "After you."

I stepped inside. The place looked exactly how it did when we walked through with Mrs. Fontaine.

"Looks okay."

"Walk with me." Miles motioned for me to follow.

I trailed behind him through a set of wide French doors into the formal living room. The moment I crossed the threshold, I was hit with a smell. Damp. Musty. Almost metallic. I wrinkled my nose.

"Was that smell here before?" I asked tightly.

"Nope."

"We've got wood rot in the walls," Carlus added, voice calm, like he was reading me a bedtime story. "Water damage too. Roof's leaking in at least three places."

"I don't—" I blinked, trying to smooth over the confusion cracking through my mask.

"You bypassed the inspection. An inspector would have caught this." The disappointment on his face actually had me feeling a *tiny* bit bad.

"Fontaine gave you a curated tour," Carlus told me. "Didn't think the old woman had it in her to be a snake."

I stared at the bubbling paint on the corner of the ceiling. My throat tightened. "It shouldn't be too hard to fix." I was determined to make this work. Jenese couldn't take this from me too.

But Miles was watching me. "Serena, how the hell have you been in business making wild decisions like this?"

I flinched at his scolding tone.

Carlus motioned with his head, subtle but tight. "Follow me."

We ducked around a stack of drywall and stepped into the dining room. The space had been gutted down to the studs, one whole wall stripped open. Light spilled in through the broken windows, casting stripes over the dusty floors.

He pointed to the far wall. The wiring snaking through the beams looked like it hadn't been touched since the fifties. Old cloth-covered wires, frayed at the edges. Burn marks traced a jagged scar up one of the studs.

"Old wiring," Carlus said. "Almost sparked a fire. We shut it off before anything caught."

I stepped toward the scorched stud—heels crunching on loose debris—and reached out to it.

"Don't—" Miles caught my wrist.

A sudden whooshing sound filled the air, like a gust of wind. The sound of a sharp crack, like flint striking steel, reverberated through the room, making the old wood tremble.

The exposed panel was suddenly illuminated by a violent arc of searing blue light, the intense heat making the metal sing with a high-pitched whine. A snake-like hiss preceded a blinding flash of white-hot light from the wires, showering the air with glowing embers.

Miles yanked me back from the exposed wall, just as another shower of fiery sparks, sizzling and spitting, filled the air. I stumbled into him, and he wrapped both arms around me, shielding me.

"Shit!" Carlus cursed, already rushing toward the panel. "Thought it was off—guess we missed a breaker and someone plugged something up. Y'all okay?"

All I could hear was the blood pounding in my ears and Miles's breath, fast and shaky, brushing the collar of my shirt.

His arms were still locked around me, his body flush against mine.

"I'm not dumb," I said quietly.

"No one said you were."

"I'm not going to stand here and let you talk down to me like I'm some rookie."

His eyes narrowed. "Then don't act like one."

That cut, because he wasn't wrong. And I hated that he wasn't wrong.

My jaw tensed, but the silence between us stretched—too long, too loud. I could feel it building in my throat, a confession I didn't want to say out loud, but it was already there.

"I didn't vet it properly," I admitted finally, the words tight and bitter. "Not the way I usually would."

Miles blinked, surprised, maybe, that I admitted it. Or maybe that I sounded like I hated myself more than he ever could.

"I was rushed," I continued. "Pushed into making a move before I was ready. I needed something—*anything*—to replace the Harrington estate. You were right, I lost it."

I didn't say Jenese's name. I didn't tell him *how* I'd truly lost that bid. How I'd been blackmailed and boxed in. How desperate I'd been to cover the loss before anyone noticed the crown jewel of King Developments was gone.

"So you panicked," he said.

"No," I snapped, but then sighed. "Yes. Maybe. I don't panic, I just—" I exhaled sharply. "I don't sit and cry about what I've lost—I replace it. I win something else."

He tilted his head. "Even if it's the wrong thing?"

I hated how that question hit. I hated that he asked it so softly. I hated how much it made me *feel*.

"Go ahead—gloat. You want to rub my face in it? Say it."

He was quiet for a beat.

"We're partners, Serena. I don't know how many times I have to say that. When you win, I win. When you hurt, so do I. We might not like our arrangement, but I'm not gonna sit here and bask in the fact that you made a mistake. I know it's going to take some getting used to, but you can trust and depend on me."

He stepped closer. "You're brilliant. You're cutthroat. I

admire the hell out of that. But you don't get to treat me like I'm an employee. Like I don't matter."

My gaze slipped from his, landing on the cracked floorboards.

"I don't treat you like an employee," I murmured.

Miles chuckled. "You're gonna fight me to the end?"

"No. I…agree. With everything you've said."

Miles nodded. "I think we need to make a decision right here, right now how we're gonna work."

"You hate meetings."

He blinked. "I do."

"And I hate sweating in jeans."

That made him smile, just a little. "So?"

"So I'll handle the logistics. Permits, paperwork, scheduling, meetings with city officials, supply tracking—all of it."

"And I'll run the crew," he said. "Keep construction moving. I'll bring you in when we hit milestones."

"You'll give me progress reports?"

He stepped even closer, eyes dipping to my mouth. "Only if you say please."

I hated that he made me smile.

"Fine… I guess we can work together."

"That's my girl," Miles murmured.

We finished the rest of the walkthrough in near silence, save for the creaking floors and my internal monologue screaming bloody murder.

Mrs. Fontaine really had played me.

By the time we stepped back outside, I was vibrating with rage. The kind that made me dangerous. A table had been set up outside, and we walked over and spread out the floor plan.

"Well, let's make it worth it," Miles said, and I watched as he looked over the blueprints in front of us. He seemed…excited.

He pointed at the current kitchen layout. "We knock this wall out, expand the space, add an island. Flow matters. If it's gonna be used for events, we need functionality over fluff."

I narrowed my eyes. "Fluff? You mean style. Aesthetics. Charm. The things people remember."

"No one remembers a backsplash. They remember if there was nowhere to put their wine." He rolled his eyes.

"Shows what kind of parties you throw."

"Shows what kind of kitchens you build."

We leaned in at the same time, reaching for the same section of the layout. My fingers brushed his. I didn't move them.

He didn't either.

"Okay," I murmured, "we compromise. We open up the space, but we do custom cabinetry—white oak, something elegant. And the wine station stays."

He arched a brow. "You need a whole station for that?"

"It's Lush. People drink like it's a competitive sport."

His gaze dropped to my lips. Briefly. Barely. But I saw it.

I swallowed. "We also move the powder room. Right now, it's too close to the dining room. No one wants to hear someone pee while they're eating."

He smirked. "Speak for yourself. I love ambiance."

I elbowed him. "You play too damn much."

His hand slid forward on the table, palm brushing mine.

"I still think you're wrong about the backsplash," I murmured, because I had to say *something* or I was going to lose the last of my resolve.

The sudden, insistent ringing of my phone jolted me, and my body froze. I dug my phone out of my purse.

UNKNOWN NUMBER

I stepped away from the table, turning away from Miles as I pressed the phone to my ear. "Hello?"

"I need you at the cigar lounge," Jenese's voice snapped, cold and sharp as ever. "Thirty minutes. Don't be late."

The line went dead.

When I turned back around, Miles was watching me.

"I've got to go," I said, trying to keep my tone neutral.

"You heading back to the office?"

"Yes," I lied, already grabbing my purse. "I'll be home late."

CHAPTER 23

Serena

I SNUCK into the booth opposite Jenese, hoping nobody would notice me in the dim light. It worked out well that she chose the darkest corner. I rummaged through my purse until I found the USB drive and flung it onto the metal table.

"It's done. Now give me the manuscript."

She let out a sigh, gently putting her drink down. A half-smoked cigar dangled from her lips, the scent of rich tobacco filling the air. "Whoa, whoa, now. Tell me, how was it? Like getting back onto a bike…or a dick after a long time?"

"Cut the bullshit, Jenese. We had a deal." I set my purse on the table, the charm attached to it jingling.

"Cute charm," Jenese said.

Yes, it had been thrilling.

Exciting.

I had felt truly alive for the first time in years.

But it was *wrong*. That's why I walked away from it. Her. She'd been a great mentor for a time, but the lying, the stealing, all that got old. I wanted everything I owned to be because I worked for it. Not because I did something underhanded to get it.

"Where is the Harrington estate? You said two weeks. It's been four." Jenese glared at me.

"Legalities take time."

"Don't insult me." Her voice cut sharper now. "I trained you better than that. You've been stalling. You're not slick, sugar."

"Jenese—"

She leaned forward, eyes glinting.

"But here's the thing, baby girl: I don't bluff. I sent a little something off to the *Lush Chronicles*. Just a teaser. Names omitted. For now."

My heart skipped, but my face didn't move. I couldn't let her see it.

"You couldn't."

She slid this week's paper over to me, with a section circled for me to read.

DEAR DAHLIA,
WHAT'S A WOMAN TO DO WHEN THE GIRL SHE
MOLDED AND RAISED STARTS PLAYING QUEEN?
WHEN THE PROTÉGÉE BECOMES A
BACKSTABBING LITTLE HEIRESS WITH A TASTE
FOR DIRTY MONEY AND EVEN DIRTIER MEN?
ASKING FOR A FRIEND. MAYBE TWO.
—RETIRED, NOT FINISHED

"It's one of those *Dear Abby* sections, but I love the name Dahlia. I knew a girl named that twenty years ago. Skanky hoe. But I know the old ladies in society are gonna be talking about this column for a while." Jenese leaned back, crossing her legs, entirely too pleased with herself.

I crushed the paper in my hand. I needed to buy every copy of that magazine in town. Right now. Burn them if I had to. Call in favors, cash in leverage. Whatever it took to bury this before it bloomed into something I couldn't control.

She smirked. "All roads lead to you eventually."

"You spiteful bitch."

Jenese didn't even flinch. "Takes one to know one."

"How's your food?" Jenese cut into her veal without looking up.

She promised to teach me how to be like her. Demand respect.

Now I felt like I'd been used.

For months we'd just been doing this. Dinners and watching people. I'd messed up again yesterday, and Mama's put-downs were still echoing in my head. Weak. Naïve. Mistake.

"Okay, what's happening? Aren't you going to teach me?"

Jenese didn't even look up. "I told you, wait and see."

I sighed in frustration. That's all she said. Wait and see. Patience. *I was beginning to think I got scammed. I'd been too desperate. She'd taken the easy mark I'd been.*

"I'm just going to go—"

I pushed back my chair, the legs scraping against the hardwood floor, ready to cut my losses, but Jenese's hand shot out and caught my wrist, her fingers surprisingly strong.

"See?"

I followed her gaze across the room.

A woman had just walked in—tall, polished, in a simple beige wrap dress. She wore oversized sunglasses despite the low light.

Jenese's smile curled sharp. "There she is."

"Who?"

"Kaitlin Halstrom," Jenese spat.

I blinked.

"She slept with my ex-boyfriend," Jenese said calmly, spearing another bite of food. "I slept with hers. But that's not why we're here."

I narrowed my eyes. "Then why?"

"Because two years ago, Kaitlin tried to have me blacklisted from every boardroom in the city." Jenese finally turned to look at me, her gaze cool and unreadable.

My brows lifted. "What?"

"She was supposed to partner with me. We'd drafted a proposal. Shared confidential info. Then she pulled out last minute and went public with an 'anonymous' story about me." Jenese leaned back in her chair, lifting her wineglass. "It almost worked. I didn't forget that."

"So what do you want me to do?" I asked, throat tightening.

"You'll befriend her. Get close. Make her trust you. I'll take care of the rest."

I tilted my head at her. She wanted me to pretend to be someone's friend? "You said you'd teach me to be like you."

Jenese raised an eyebrow. "You want power, or pity?"

I looked back at Camille again.

"I don't see how befriending her is going to make me a CEO."

Jenese smirked like I'd said something adorably naive. "You think CEOs are chosen? They're built. And before that? They're underestimated."

She set down her fork with care.

"You need to understand that there are two types of people in our world. Those that are for us, and those against. Those against? Well..." She tilted her head, gaze sharp. "We get rid of them. Or we make it impossible for them to move without stepping through us. Your mother wants somebody like that."

I sat with that. Let it settle in the pit of my stomach. I thought she'd give me books to read. Tools. Strategy. A blueprint.

But if I wanted Mama's respect, I had to prove I could be like her.

I picked up my water glass, hand steady. "So how close do you want me to get?"

Mama would be proud of me. I just knew it.

"I bet you felt it. That fire. That hunger. Lush is too small for you, Serena. You can pretend you don't miss *us*, but I know better." Jenese leaned in, eyes gleaming like a cat that had cornered its prey.

I clenched my jaw. "I'm not like you."

"Oh, honey. You are exactly like me. That's why I picked you."

I hated her. I hated that she was right. But most of all, I hated the part of me that still wanted more.

Jenese tapped her fingers on the table before she flicked her cigar into the ashtray. "There are some things we need to discuss concerning our original deal."

"You said I do the job, you give me the chapters."

"Why, yes. In theory."

I shook my head. "We had a deal."

"Which you still haven't fulfilled."

"I just need another week—"

Jenese held up her hand. "Save the excuses. You're not done until *I* say you're done."

"I don't owe you forever."

"You owe me as long as I have this manuscript," she said, tapping the side of her bag. "Unless you'd like me to share it with someone? Maybe your charming husband? Or better yet, the press? How about your mama?"

She never intended to let me go.

Of course.

"I've got another opportunity. A small thing. You'll be doing what you're good at—blending in, observing, smiling when needed."

A pause.

"It'll be fun. And once it's done, we can revisit the topic of the manuscript."

I could walk away. Say to hell with the manuscript, the secrets, the leverage. But what would that make me? Powerless. Exposed. Predictable.

We had screwed over too many names and faces. Could I really handle that fallout?

Miles.

I couldn't handle him seeing me as someone else, different than how he saw me now. If I said yes, I'd give her one more inch of rope. If I said no, she'd strangle me with it anyway.

Jenese wanted to play? Fine. "What do you want now?"

"I just need you to place a small little item on someone's property."

"Who is it this time?"

"A fella named Jasper Crowe."

"Two men? Exes you're trying to get back at? I thought you were the love 'em and leave 'em type, Jenese."

She kept a straight face, but a little amusement flickered in her eyes.

"Are you going to give me any more information?" I asked.

Jenese rolled her eyes. "Jasper Crowe is a former polo player still holdin' on to the glory days. *Sad.* But he does like to host these matches where he is miraculously the winner. During the match, get inside his house and leave my gift somewhere personal." She reached into her bag and slid a small velvet box toward me.

"What's in it?"

"Don't worry. It's not explosive," she said with a sly grin. "Now run along."

I sighed, taking the velvet box and putting it in my purse. "I'm serious, Jenese. This needs to be over."

"Whatever you say to make yourself feel better."

I stood, and Jenese cleared her throat.

"Remember this feeling, Serena."

I paused for half a second.

"The rush. The fear. The stakes." Her smile curled like smoke. "That's what power tastes like—when you know just how fast it can all fall apart."

I spun around, the plush carpet yielding softly beneath my feet as I hurried from the lounge. I wanted to get back home. Back to Miles.

Hell, I'd take Doughboy over this.

Down the hall, I could hear the low hum of voices coming from the front door. I turned the corner and froze.

Mama.

My first thought was to run, but I couldn't. I saw her talking to the receptionist, and the receptionist pointed back toward me, her eyes still on Mama.

I stumbled backward in a panic. I had to hide.

My heart pounded in my chest as I hurried down the long, dimly lit hallway, each echoing footstep amplifying the feeling that I was losing my mind. Mama couldn't find me here.

What the hell was she doing here?

Mama didn't smoke. She'd have a drink now and then, but after her checkup, she cut back to just two glasses of wine weekly. The lounge was full of either really young people or really old people.

I turned sharply and ducked into a doorway on my left, slipping inside before I could second-guess it. The space was small —just a private room, dimly lit, empty except for a few leather chairs and a cigar tray on the side table.

My breath hitched as I eased the door almost shut, leaving just a sliver of space to see through.

"Right this way, ma'am," I heard a voice say.

"You have private rooms?" Mama said.

No, no, no.

I pressed myself against the wall, my breath caught in my throat. If they picked this room—if she walked through that door—

I gripped my purse so tight my knuckles ached, my mind racing for an escape. But there was nowhere to go. No back exit, no furniture big enough to hide behind. Just me, a few chairs, and the suffocating weight of bad luck pressing down on my chest.

The floor outside creaked. I bit down on my lip so hard I tasted blood.

Please, not this room.

"Yes, ma'am. Our private lounges offer more discretion. Would you like to see one?"

Mama made a sound, a thoughtful hum.

"No need," Mama said. "I'm already late." Her heels picked up again, moving away.

My shoulders sagged, my legs so weak I had to brace myself against the doorframe. I stayed still for several more seconds, my body locked in place, waiting until I was sure she was gone. Only when the sound of her voice faded completely did I let out the breath I had been holding.

Then I eased the door open a bit more and looked down the hallway.

The coast was clear.

I slipped back into the hall and made my way toward the front door, my pulse still racing.

That was too close.

Too damn close. But I reached for the little charm on my purse. I flipped it over to where there was a light blinking.

Yes.

It had recorded our entire conversation, and I was one step closer to getting rid of Jenese.

CHAPTER 24

Miles

"YOU'RE LATE," Serena said as she opened the Kings' front door. "Dinner is being served."

Fuck, back here again.

This place was practically my second home. I knew where everything was. I'd slept here as a kid after video game marathons with Erik and as an adult after one too many drinks at a party. I knew where Serena's room was on the first floor on the other side of the mansion, and how to get in without being seen.

"I had to handle some things at the site," I muttered as she shut the door behind me.

"Why? Is something wrong?"

I looked down at her, noticing the way the sunlight caught the strands of her hair. She bit her bottom lip, her hands twisting nervously as she looked at me with a forlorn expression.

"We can go if we need to. That property is an investment for us, and we cannot—"

"You're overthinking again," I said quietly, with the smallest tug at my mouth. "You get that crease in your brow when you're doing it."

I pressed my finger to her skin, gently smoothing away the

frown lines, feeling her softness beneath my touch. As much as I didn't want to be here, at the least I could do was push down what I was feeling and be here to support her.

I remembered dinners at the Kings'. Sometimes I would nudge Serena under the table with my foot, just to make her look at me. Sometimes she'd play back, brushing her leg against mine like she wasn't doing a damn thing, like she didn't know exactly what that did to me.

I leaned down before I could stop myself, moving a strand of hair behind her ear. *Just for comfort,* I told myself.

Then I kissed her.

It started soft—just my lips to hers. But when she didn't pull away, I pressed a little deeper, and she opened to me like she'd been waiting. Her mouth was warm, and she tasted like wine and everything I hadn't let myself want.

"The faster we eat, the faster we can go home."

Her head tilted just slightly—barely a shift—but I caught it.

And I felt it too, the quiet weight of that word. *Home.* Not my place. Not hers. *Ours.*

Serena extended her hand, her fingers intertwining with mine, her skin soft and warm.

The scent of old books and polished wood filled the air as Serena guided me down the hall, though I knew where to go. In the dining room, a massive crystal chandelier cast a glittering light onto the highly polished mahogany table. Deep, plush velvet clothed the high-backed wooden chairs, gold trim glinting softly in the dim light.

Yvonne King was at the head of the table when we entered.

"There's the man of the hour," Vincent said next to her, and he offered a tight smile as he glanced back warily at Yvonne. "Didn't think you were going to show. Good to see you, Miles."

I forced a jovial tone. "Vince. I wouldn't miss it."

To my relief, Laurene and Reese were seated at the table as well. They would definitely make tonight more tolerable. I gave Laurene a hug, her belly protruding even more since I last saw her a few weeks ago, and before she released me, she murmured, "Try not to start a war at dinner, hmm?"

I stepped back and gave her a grin.

Giving Reese a quick dap, I was surprised to spot Noelle, Laurene's best friend, at the table too. "Wassup, Short Stack!"

Noelle rolled her eyes at me, but she was another little sister, and she hugged me anyway. "I told you to get a better nickname to call me."

Serena nudged me to sit, her gaze pinned on Miss Yvonne.

"Gigi won't be here tonight." Yvonne hadn't taken her eyes off me. "Apparently some rapper is more important than family."

Miss Yvonne used to be…warmer.

I remembered once she called me *baby*, just offhand. I think I was fifteen. But I still remembered her pulling a blanket over me when I'd crash on their couch. The way she told Erik and me to watch each other's backs like we were blood.

She used to smile more, I remembered that. Not often—but when she did, you felt like you'd won something.

"He's not a rapper, he's an entrepreneur," Laurene said as a server placed a plate of braised short ribs and truffle grits in front of her. "He's worked with all the celebrities and stylists down in Hollywood. He's going to give her advice to start her boutique."

Miss Yvonne rolled her eyes. "Where did I go wrong?"

"I think it's great," Noelle chimed in, all bright-eyed and sugar-sweet. "It'll give her some focus. A project of her own."

Yvonne cut her a look so sharp it could've sliced through the beef. "We've handed that girl every opportunity money could buy, and what does she do? Half-asses it and runs the other way. Let's move on before I lose my appetite."

"Gigi's resourceful. She can do it if she wants it." Vincent shot Yvonne a look.

"Agreed," Reese said.

I looked around the room. "Where's Erik?"

Right on cue, the antique double doors creaked open, their aged wood protesting with a mournful groan. "I'll call you back," Erik muttered into his phone, slipping it into his pocket.

Then we locked eyes.

I felt myself sit up in my seat, a jolt running through my spine. The memory of seeing him outside King Developments with Victor that night, the streetlights blurring around us, had kept me on edge, waiting for him to tell Serena and for her to confront me. But when it didn't happen, I knew Erik well enough to know he was up to something.

Nothing in his face shifted. No smile. No sneer. Just that blank, heavy stare. He took his seat across from me, next to Noelle, and looked to Miss Yvonne.

"Sorry about that," he said. "Jose was able to secure that deal for us."

Miss Yvonne just nodded. "Good." She sliced into her short ribs. "So, you two," she began, "let's talk about your progress. How is the Harrington estate?"

Serena glanced at me and reached for her wine.

I cleared my throat, slow. "We've had some delays."

"Delays?"

"Permits," Serena added quickly. "We're working through it."

"Is that so?" Erik said slowly as he stared at the both of us. "Nothing else? No outside *investors*?"

I played dumb and shrugged. "Not any that I know of."

Erik's gaze narrowed.

"We're right on track," Serena said firmly.

"Bullshit," Erik muttered.

I frowned at him. "You got something you wanna get off your chest?"

"A lot actually," he said.

"Boys," Vincent said.

"You just letting him do it?" Erik turned to Serena.

"What are you talking about?"

Don't say shit, Erik.

"Aren't you running King Enterprises? Serena and I got our businesses handled. Nobody needs your opinion on how we do things."

He sat back. Noelle, who was sitting next to him, reached out to place a hand on his arm. "Oh, so you big shit? Just come into my company and take over?"

"*My* company," Serena emphasized. "*I* run it."

Erik shook his head. "Relax. No one's taking your sandbox away."

I saw Laurene's and Noelle's heads whip to Erik, and Serena grabbed her knife, giving him a look of disgust. "My sandbox?"

"All due respect," I said, leaning forward, voice calm but cutting, "but King Developments *is* the only part of your family's empire actually innovating right now. So maybe instead of talking down to her, you should be taking notes and not banking on the rest of our hard-ass work."

"What work? You're company's been piss-poor for years and you haven't even been able to get it back on track until us," Erik shot back.

"How you mad at me? My family was ruined, yours is sitting up here eating braised rib and lobster," I snapped.

"Don't do this at the table," Vincent told Erik.

"This was a mistake," he said, looking at his parents. "We should have done things my way."

"I'm the head of this family," Yvonne said calmly. "Your input isn't needed, Erik."

He scoffed, leaning back in his chair like he was too exhausted to hold his tongue any longer. "It is. Serena's sitting here like she has *no idea* what's actually going on—and from the looks of it, she can't handle it or him anyway."

"You that much of a pussy you want to insult your sister? You? The one who needs Mommy's approval for everything? Do you even know all the hard fucking work she's been putting in? Day in and day out."

"Miles…" Serena placed her hand on mine. "It's fine."

"It's not."

Erik pushed his chair back with a loud scrape and immediately I matched him.

Vincent cleared his throat. "That's enough."

"Don't insult my wife."

I ignored Laurene's and Noelle's squeals, watching him. I still wanted to see a brother somewhere in him but it was hard as fuck to find any semblance of it.

"No," Yvonne said, voice like a whip crack. "Let them finish since apparently dinner is now a street brawl."

"I'm not the one starting shit," I said, voice calm but tight. "I came here out of respect."

"Respect?" Yvonne arched a brow, slicing her rib again like she was imagining it was my neck. "I think your family lost that when your father was doing crack."

"Mama!" Serena said.

Reese cleared his throat and pointed to a server. "More wine, please."

"Reese!" Laurene hissed and I saw her pinch him.

"My father served his time," I said, looking her straight in the eye. "And I'm not him. It would be nice if we can stop bring up old issues that have been resolved."

"Well, I've yet to see the difference," Miss Yvonne replied.

"Mama, please," Laurene said. "We didn't invite them over for this."

"Exactly," Vincent said.

"Can I get some more bread?" Laurene called to a servant. "Quickly!"

"It's never going to work between them," Erik said.

"You don't have to like him," Serena said, her voice almost too even, "but you don't get to talk to him like he's beneath us. Especially not in front of me."

Yvonne blinked, slow. "Excuse me?"

"I said what I said," she murmured. "You heard me the first

time. Miles is a part of this family, he deserves just as much respect as the rest of us. What his father did is done. For the sake of all of us, it's better we get along."

The table went still. Even the servers froze in the background like they'd felt a shift in air pressure.

Miss Yvonne looked shocked at Serena's words. "You think you're grown enough to talk back now?"

"You know what makes you nervous?" I said, calm as hell. "It's not my father. It's not the past. It's the fact that I lost everything, and I'm still here. Still at your same fucking level. What if I tell your family what you really did?"

Everyone turned to him. Erik opened his mouth—maybe to speak, maybe to spit—Yvonne's chair scraped back, loud against the marble.

"Well," she said crisply, rising, "dinner's over."

No one argued. Then it was just the servers collecting dishes like they wanted to be invisible, and me. Still at the table. I didn't move until I felt Serena's hand in mine again.

"You knew Erik would say something. You knew exactly how he'd react."

"I'm not like you. I don't sweep shit under the rug. I address things."

Her fingers twitched in mine but didn't pull away.

"You didn't deserve that," she said. "You never did."

That made my hackles lower, and I squinted at her. "Are you being…comforting?"

Serena didn't say anything. She placed her hand on my cheek and then kissed me. Leaning back, she blinked at me before her mouth brushed mine again, slower this time—like she was tasting something familiar but long lost.

I didn't move at first. I was too stunned.

Then I sank into it, cupping her waist like I'd been waiting for this moment since we fell apart.

And maybe I had.

CHAPTER 25
Serena

TONIGHT WAS A DISASTER.

I couldn't sleep, staring out the window.

Erik. Mama. Jenese. *Lush.* The weight of all those judging eyes and opinions felt crushing, like a physical force bearing down on me. Dealing with their expectations, criticisms, and need to control me was draining.

I was tired of trying to be what everyone wanted.

After threatening the Lush Chronicles with Mama's wrath and a threat to town funding, I managed to get them to pull that *Dear Dahlia* section from the newspaper, with a vow to keep quiet about it.

Tossing back the sheets, I jumped out of bed and padded across the room, and I counted back from five before opening the door and peering out.

It was a dark hallway, and it had been for hours since we got home.

I held my breath as I tiptoed out, and to my office door. Should I knock? But what if I woke him up? What if he wasn't asleep?

Do it.

I turned the knob—luckily he hadn't locked it—and peered inside.

Miles was actually up, sitting. Staring out the window, and in his lap was a copy of a thriller I had started to read but abandoned. He didn't say anything at first. Just looked up from the book, our eyes locking.

"You're awake," I breathed.

He wore nothing but a pair of black shorts slung low on his hips. His chest was bare—cut and golden in the moonlight, his skin smooth except for the faint scar slicing across his collarbone. A silver chain glinted at his throat. His braids were hidden under a black durag, tied clean and tight.

He tilted his head. "Couldn't sleep."

I stepped inside, trying not to stare, but my gaze dropped to his chest anyway, the slow rise and fall of it pulling heat through my body.

Behind him, on the pullout bed, Doughboy was stretched out on his back, all four paws in the air, snoring like he owned the place.

Miles's gaze stayed on me, slow and steady, like he could see right through the thin night slip I'd thrown on without thinking.

I cleared my throat, folding my arms. "I—uh…I thought I heard something in my closet."

"In your closet."

"Yeah." I nodded, too fast. "Like scratching. Or…movement."

He glanced over at Doughboy then back to me. "You sure it wasn't him or his toy?"

I shook my head. "No I just heard it now." *Why the hell are you lying?*

A smile pulled at his mouth, slow and dangerous. "You want me to come check your closet at"—he glanced at the time on his phone—"two forty-six in the morning?"

"Can you do it?" I snapped.

"Be nice," he said, standing up and stretching like he had all the time in the world.

My eyes dropped, involuntarily, to the way his abs flexed when his arms went up. The stretch revealed even more of that deep cut along his hips, the waistband of his shorts hanging criminally low.

"Show me," he said.

I turned before he could catch the flush creeping up my neck and led him to my bedroom.

Pointing toward the closet—casually, like my heart wasn't thudding against my ribs. "It was coming from there."

He gave me a look like *Really?* but said nothing. Just moved toward the door. I crawled back onto the bed, sitting cross-legged near the pillows, pretending not to stare while his broad back stretched and shifted. My eyes had adjusted to the dark and the light from the moon shining through the window gave me a lot to see.

I tried not to squeeze my thighs together.

He bent slightly to open the closet door and peered inside, muttering something under his breath as he leaned forward—tattoos flexing, abs tightening. Miles had to be one the finest men I'd ever laid eyes on.

Serena. Get it together.

After a moment, he straightened. "Nothing here. Closet's clear." He turned back toward me, brushing his hands together like the job was done. "No ghosts. No monsters. Just clothes and expensive shoes."

He walked toward the door, and started to open it.

"Wait," I said suddenly, sharper than I meant to.

He paused. Looked over his shoulder.

I swallowed. My fingers curled in the sheets.

"Can you…stay?"

He didn't move at first, just stared at me—those eyes unreadable, like he was trying to figure out what game I was playing.

Then his voice came low and warm, a little teasing, but softer than before.

"You scared again?"

I shrugged.

He stood there for a beat longer, then pushed the door shut and turned. "Make room."

I scooched to the side, and Miles pulled the sheets back, lying down on his back. I watched him for a few seconds longer before I did the same, staring up at the ceiling.

"I'm pretty easy, if you wanted me in your bed, all you had to do was say so," Miles finally broke the silence.

I let out a breath of a laugh. "Don't flatter yourself."

But the warmth in my chest betrayed me.

He didn't say anything, just shifted slightly—his body was so much bigger than mine, his heat radiated like a low-burning fire beside me. The mattress dipped more on his side, and I could feel the brush of his arm against mine.

"When you proposed…six years ago. Did you mean it?"

He turned his head slowly. "You really gotta ask me that?"

Everyone said we made sense. Serena King and Miles Whitmore. Two legacies. Two names. But if you looked closer, if you really looked, we weren't built the same.

He lived out loud—messy, charming, bold. I lived in silence and strategy. I thrived on control, while he trusted instinct and chaos and that reckless gut of his that always somehow worked.

But we weren't opposites, not really.

We were mirrors. Just…cracked in different places.

We both carried too much on our backs and smiled like it didn't weigh anything. Both so desperate to prove we weren't our parents' shadows that we didn't see how much we were already replicating them.

I stared up at the ceiling. "I didn't know. Back then, everything between us happened so fast. One minute we were sneaking around, the next…you were asking me to be your girlfriend, and I thought—" I stopped. My voice dropped to almost nothing. "I thought it was a joke."

He shifted again, facing me now. "A joke?"

"You're Miles Whitmore. You flirted with anything that had legs and a smile. I didn't think you were serious at first."

"I was."

"I know that now," I said quickly, like I owed him that. "But back then? I was so used to people not choosing me. Or wanting me for the wrong reasons. And then you showed up at my house, looking like that"—I gestured vaguely to him—"and talking about forever like we even had a shot."

"You said yes."

"I panicked." My laugh was bitter. "I was scared not to. Because a part of me thought, *What if this is it? What if this is the only time someone ever sees me like that?*"

His voice was quieter now. "And then my father's scandal hit."

I nodded. "And suddenly I had to choose between the only man who ever really looked at me…and the family I'd spent my whole life trying to prove myself to."

"And you didn't choose me."

"I couldn't." My throat tightened. "But it didn't mean I didn't love you."

He was quiet. The silence was so long, I almost wished I'd kept quiet.

"I wasn't ready either," he admitted. "I think part of me proposed just to keep you. Lock it down before you changed your mind."

It was my turn to look at him.

"You can do a lot better than me, in fact, you can do it now. I… You didn't just treat me like the ditzy best friend to the most popular guy in town. You saw something in me that no one else ever has. You pushed me. Why you think I kept stealing all those clients from you over the years? I wanted to be your equal. But being with you back then—it felt like the first thing I got right," Miles said.

I turned fully toward him, the sheets rustling between us. His face was half-shadowed in the dark, but I could still see the tension in his jaw.

"You inspire the hell out of me, Sunny. You always have."

"I'm sorry I didn't choose us," I said quietly. "I was scared. Of losing my family. Of choosing wrong. Of how much I loved you and how fast it all happened. I thought if I held on, every-thing I'd imagined for myself would fall apart, but when I got it… It really wasn't what I needed."

His gaze flicked to mine, something raw in it now. "You did what you had to."

"No," I whispered. "I did what was easiest. You were right."

He stared at me for a long, loaded moment. Then his hand reached across the space between us, his palm brushing the side of my neck.

"You still taste like pomegranate," he murmured, the memory flickering behind his eyes. "Sweet, a little sharp…"

I let out a breath, and he forced me to meet his eyes.

Then he kissed me.

His mouth moved slow at first, patient, but hungry. His tongue teased along the seam of my lips until I opened for him, and then there was no patience left. Just heat. Pressure. Memory. His tongue slid against mine. I moaned into his mouth, and let myself melt into the mattress.

I kissed him like I'd never stopped. Like I'd always meant to come back.

His hands found my hips, drawing me closer till I was flush against with him. Miles let his lips fall from mine, across my jaw and cheek, and down my neck, where I knew he would feel my pulse beating out of control, and I gripped his shoulders.

"Miles," I gasped.

He didn't stop. One hand slid beneath the hem of my slip,

dragging it up slowly—inch by inch—until the fabric pooled at my waist.

Then he shifted, lowering himself between my thighs, guiding one of my legs over his shoulder.

His breath grazed the inside of my knee.

"I missed this," he murmured, voice husky. "Missed you."

I felt him pull my panties to the side, and kiss once at my clit, making me jolt. His eyes locking on to mine from between my thighs, then his fingers slid inside, slow and sure, working me open like he was tracing the map back to myself. I couldn't even remember the last time I'd been in a position like this— with someone who saw all my broken edges and still wanted me.

He scissored his fingers inside, curling them upward to hit my G-spot. I arched off the mattress, breath catching in a way that made my chest ache.

"If I do this, you gon' behave?" he cooed, and before I could answer, another smack to my pussy caused me to squeal. "Huh… I can't hear you."

That first lick from his tongue sent a shock straight to my core. My toes curled involuntarily as heat pooled, spreading faster than I expected. I pushed his head lightly, nails digging into his scalp. Miles blinked, slightly taken aback, then smiled against me, his nose bumping the hood of my sensitive mound, before slipping his tongue inside and curling deep.

The sensation was electric—intense and overwhelming—and I gripped the headboard, fingers clawing the wood as if it could anchor me against the wave crashing through my body.

I wanted to run. To hide. To shut it all down.

But I didn't.

Because with every stroke of his tongue, every flick against the places I'd buried deep inside myself, I felt something else breaking through.

The walls I'd built, the cold armor I'd worn to survive—it started to crumble.

Here, in the heat and quiet, I wasn't the calculated Serena King.

I was just me.

Messy.

Flawed.

Wanting.

And for the first time in years, that scared me more than anything else.

Miles released a deep groan. I felt the vibrations of it run through me, deep and low, as his lips wrapped around my clit and sucked, slow and intentional. He ate my pussy like a man starved, like he'd been dreaming of this moment, memorizing me in my absence. My legs started to twitch helplessly, my body chasing the high even as my mind tried to catch up.

I gripped Miles's head, desperate for something to hold on to, and one of his hands slid up my body, disappearing beneath the hem of my slip—still clinging to me like some last bit of armor. But even that didn't last. He shoved the fabric up, over my hips, until it was bunched under my arms and out of the way. His palm cupped my breast, his thumb brushing over my nipple before he rolled it between his fingers.

The combination of his tongue circling my clit, his fingers curling deep inside me, and the sweet ache of his hand gripping and twisting my nipple—it was too much.

Too much heat.

Too much feeling.

Too much of him.

My body convulsed, surrendering before I could even think to stop it.

"Oh my God!" I screamed, voice breaking apart like glass.

I squeezed my eyes shut, sobbing in relief—relief I didn't even know I needed—when he hummed against my clit in encouragement. Like he wanted me to let go. Like he needed it too.

Blinking slowly, Miles was suddenly bringing me into

another kiss, and I could taste myself on his tongue, then he released me. "You sure?"

"Yeah," I whispered, breath catching. "I want you. In the nightstand."

He shifted off the bed just long enough to reach in my nightstand. I used this break as a chance to gather my breath as I watched as he tore the foil packet open with his teeth, rolled the condom on, and came back to me.

I opened my legs without thinking. My body already knew him.

But my heart...my heart was still catching up.

He lined himself up, running the head of his cock through my folds, slow, teasing, letting my slickness coat him as his mouth found mine again.

"Fuck me," I said.

When he finally pushed inside me, stretching me open inch by inch, I let out a broken sound in the back of my throat.

"Still feels like mine," he murmured, voice low, reverent as he pressed deeper. "Pussy still mine, hmm, Sunny?"

"Fuuuck... Miles," I choked out, my voice unraveling as my head fell back against the pillow.

He had one hand gripping the back of my thigh, pushing my knee up toward my chest while the other braced near my head. The headboard slammed with each thrust, jarring, relentless —*perfect*. He was deep. Too deep. The angle had my spine bowing and my body trembling, pinned beneath his like I was something to be claimed.

My hand pushed at his chest, not because I wanted him to stop—but because it was too much.

He didn't stop.

His eyes dropped to where our bodies were joined— watching the way he stretched me open around him, wet and pulsing and full.

I shook my head, even as my hips lifted into his, greedy for more.

"I hate you," I whispered.

"No, you don't."

He kissed the inside of my knee. Then my thigh. Then dragged my leg up and over his shoulder, pressing in so deep I could feel him in my chest.

The headboard slammed again, louder this time, the obscene rhythm of it making my face flush and my body clench.

"Miles—" I gasped, but it came out as a moan.

"Look at me, baby," he ordered, voice rough and steady.

And God help me—I obeyed. My big, teary eyes locked on to his, wide and overwhelmed and glassy. He grinned when he saw the bliss painting my face, pure and unfiltered. That smug bastard. That beautiful, ruined man between my thighs.

He twitched inside me like crazy, cursed under his breath, and then started fucking me harder—deeper.

"Fuck, thaaaat's it, baby," he praised. "Feels good, hmm?"

"Please...I'm going—" I mumbled, eyebrows knitting together as I felt something bubbling up inside of me.

"Perfect size jus' for you too," he purred against my ear, his tongue flicking at the sensitive skin there, making me shiver even as my nails dug into his back. "Ain't nobody else make you feel like this."

How long had I been convincing myself that strength meant solitude? That power meant pushing everyone away before they had the chance to leave?

But now...with him all over me, inside me, whispering things he should never say but somehow meant every word— now, I wasn't sure.

Maybe it wasn't weak to need someone. Maybe it was brave.

Maybe it was brave to let him see me like this—raw and open and wrecked. Maybe I didn't have to do this life alone.

"I can't!" I cried out.

Miles was hitting me *deep*, and with a sloppy pivot of his hips, the angle got even deeper—obscene, dangerous. My mouth fell open, a silent cry scraping up my throat. I could see the sheen of sweat on his golden-brown skin, could feel how his body trembled as he pushed through it—through me.

"I know," he murmured, out of breath, forehead pressed to mine. His strokes slowed, hips still grinding steady, so intentional I could barely take it. I was coming undone, unraveling like thread in his hands, and he was *right there* with me.

"You feel that?" he panted.

His mouth found my temple, pressed a kiss there so soft, so reverent it shattered me.

"That's it," he whispered. "Let go."

My nails bit into his back. My thighs shook.

And then I shattered.

It tore through me, blinding and hot. My eyes squeezed shut as a scream punched out of my throat—half moan, half sob. My pussy clenched so tight around him I felt him *jerk*, and then he was groaning into my ear, stuttering inside me with a long, drawn-out curse.

I felt the condom throb with his release, heat pulsing into the latex as he rode it out, hips twitching, breath hitching. His body collapsed on top of mine for just a moment, his weight anchoring me. Grounding me.

And still, I held him there.

Chest to chest. Heart to heart.

I should've pushed him off. Should've let the moment end. But I didn't.

Because in that silence—his breath mingling with mine, his lips brushing my cheek like he couldn't *not* touch me—I realized the truth.

I still loved him.

Even after everything, through all the hate, all the pain, all the years… I still fucking loved Miles Whitmore.

CHAPTER 26
Miles

"YOU GOTTA BE KIDDING ME," I muttered.

"No, that's what we're looking at," Carlus said, his flashlight beam highlighting the warped seam along the ceiling joint, the beam catching dust motes dancing in the air.

Even though I'd struggled the last few years with what to do with Whitmore Ventures, I did love getting my hands dirty. Getting into a place, building, shaping it till it was something someone else would call home for years to come.

I leaned the ladder against the wall.

"Easy, man, that looks like it's gonna come down."

"I got it."

I climbed up and ripped a piece off. The plaster crumbled with a soft sigh, releasing a cloud of fine white dust that looked like powdered sugar. Then, with a groaning crack, the whole ceiling gave way. A torrent of cold sludge, gray muck, and broken drywall slammed into me, the smell of dust and decay thick in the air.

I hit the floor, coughing violently, dust and memory filling my mouth.

Serena.

The sound she made when I told her to look at me. The way

her body clenched around me like she couldn't help it. How she whispered she hated me right before coming so hard she damn near blacked out.

That face—eyes glassy, lips parted, hands grabbing at anything she could find to anchor herself. That was mine. That was *real*.

I'd seen her wrecked. And she let me see her like that.

No armor. No claws.

Just her.

And now here I was, face-down in drywall and rot, thinking about the woman who's both the sharpest weapon I've ever held and the only softness I've ever really wanted.

She'd never admit it, but something shifted between us last night.

And I felt it.

"Goddamn!"

Carlus cursed. "You good?"

"Peachy," I spat, the word tasting like ash as I pushed plaster dust from my braids.

I wasn't stupid enough to believe she trusted me again. But maybe…maybe for the first time in a long time, she didn't hate me either.

Maybe she needed me.

And fuck—maybe I needed her too.

"Mr. Whitmore." I turned to see one of our workers enter the living room, nervously glancing over his shoulder. "There's a guy here for you. Not sure how he got past the gate."

I frowned. "Send him away—"

"Hmm, didn't think you got your hands dirty here, son," Victor said as he entered the living room.

I didn't say anything at first. Couldn't. The shame hit me in two waves—first, that Victor was here, now, in front of my people. Second, that he'd found me like this.

"What are you doing here?"

He looked around the room like he was taking inventory. "Nice spot. A little busted up, but I see the potential."

"Do you know who this man is?" Carlus asked.

Victor gave a lazy grin. "Just a man with an opportunity." Victor offered a seemingly innocent smile, and I glared at him as Carlus did the same. "I don't want to cause any problems for you, Miles."

"Let's talk outside. Carlus, you mind fixing this?" I pointed to the ceiling. I didn't wait for his response, as I motioned for Victor to follow me. I led him through the back and onto the patio, away from the main area people were working.

"What the fuck are you doing here?"

"Some new developments have happened," Victor said, and I didn't even notice the black bag he had in his other hand that he tossed on the floor. "I can't keep the money. It has to go to you."

Victor bent to unzip the bag. "Five million. In cash."

My stomach dropped. "Wait. Wait, wait—"

Victor reached into the bag again—not for a gun, but something that felt just as dangerous. A folder. Slim, manila, with a thick gold paperclip across the top.

He offered it.

"I can't take it."

This wasn't part of the plan. I was supposed to drag this out —nod, smile, let him talk himself into a corner. Wait for Victor to get too comfortable, say something that could burn him. Then *bam*. Flip the script. Use it.

But if he was already moving money, already trying to get it off his hands, then I was too late.

"A dummy company," he said. "LLC. Looks like landscaping. Clean books, clean payroll, even a little website in case someone gets curious at your company. You slip it into your subcontractor list. You pay it out, no questions. But let me tell you when to pay me."

I stared at the folder like it might catch fire in my hands.

"I told you I'm merging. Anything new on the books—"

"I *heard* you." His voice stayed soft, but there was steel behind it now. "And I understood. But here's the thing, Miles. You already took money from me years ago. You remember that?"

I swallowed hard, eyes narrowing, but I held his stare. That's when I saw his hand—slow, unbothered—slip inside his jacket. This time, he pulled out a gun.

Then, with a deliberate movement, he brought the gun down, pressing the cold, hard barrel right into my stomach.

"It was me that saved you. *When nobody gave a damn.*"

"Giving me money doesn't constitute you forcing me to commit a crime," I said, not looking away even when he pressed the gun harder.

"You *owe* me this favor, Miles," he snapped. His voice cracked. "I don't have anyone else. You hear me? No one."

I shook my head, eyes dropping to the dirty duffel bag at our feet.

"Some people think I'm a very bad man. I can show you why some people fear me. If you're caught with me? Hmm, I don't think people here will like that. Or that wife of yours?"

I stiffened.

"It would be a shame if something happened in the parking lot. Dark nights, bad lighting. A mugging gone wrong. Or maybe her car goes off one of these pretty little cliffs Lush is so proud of. Terrible accident."

"You fucking touch her, and you'll have much worse problems on your hands," I growled at him.

"Or maybe someone leaks some emails. Hacks her laptop. Finds something private. Some explicit photos. Or—hell—fabricates them. Who do you think the media will blame first? Her? Or the husband with dirty money on his hands?"

I clenched my jaw. My fists. Everything.

"You're a smart man, Miles. I don't need to spoon-feed you what I'm selling here." He gestured to the bag at my feet, the folder on top. "Make the right choice."

CHAPTER 27

Miles

I LEFT the money in the trunk of my car.

The whole ride home, it felt like I had a bomb that was ticking away, ready to explode at a moment's notice. It was like after Victor left, a curse fell over the site.

Equipment kept malfunctioning. Materials went missing. I almost fell off the fucking ledge inside the mansion.

I had a plan—clean, simple. Get him talking. Get evidence. Pass it off to somebody. Maybe even Dante could help with something like this, even though I didn't fucking trust the guy. I heard that last year, when Reese's mom's assistant freaked out and almost killed Laurene and Reese, Dante and the Kings covered it up.

You need help.

I was hurt everywhere—plaster stuck to my skin, aches in every damn muscle. I needed a good shower, a drink, and sleep.

Now I had a duffel bag full of dirty money in my possession like a bomb and a sick feeling crawling up the back of my neck. That bastard had flipped the script.

And if I went down? I took Serena with me.

I needed to end this. Fast. Permanently.

Opening the front door, I shouted, "Honey, I'm home."

Kicking off my boats, I drug myself down the hall, and I could smell food.

"Oh lord, please don't tell me you cooked."

"Haha, jerk," Serena's voice rang out.

I did some more research on just what was going on with Victor.

Victor was sloppy.

The dude had three companies under review, two permit violations, and a sex-trafficking rumor tied to one of his warehouses. Bad shit. Just bad.

You could have prevented this years ago.

And that was the part I couldn't stomach.

Because I knew what King Developments meant to her. Knew how hard she worked, how deep her loyalty ran—even when it didn't serve her. Yvonne. Erik. The entire King legacy. She'd burn herself alive to keep it intact.

Victor wasn't just a liability. He was a shadow, dragging Whitmore Ventures back into the same gutter my father had drowned us in before.

And maybe…I'd been too stubborn to admit it, but—

This company wasn't a legacy. It was an anchor tied to my ankle.

I kept trying to save it like it was some life raft. A way to prove I wasn't Omar Whitmore. That I was different. Better.

It was clear to me now.

I had to let it go.

Not just the name. The guilt. The story I'd been telling myself —that holding on meant I was winning. I wasn't winning. I was just stuck.

"What's smelling so good in here?" My stomach did growl but part of me was also alarmed if Serena had cooked.

When I rounded the corner, I stopped.

Serena was curled up on the couch in one of my shirts— sleeves too big, collar slipping off one shoulder, her bare legs tucked under her. Doughboy was beside her, head on her thigh like he belonged to her now.

"What happened to you?" she gasped. "You look like a ceiling fell on you."

"Part of the ceiling and roof," I muttered.

She sucked in a sharp breath. "You're not kidding. Please tell me the roof did not cave in."

"Just part of it, don't worry. Now, food, woman?"

She narrowed her eyes but licked the spoon and I felt my dick twitch. "Jennie called—Reese's sister, remember? She said a wedding at their resort had a ton of leftover food. She asked if we wanted any, so I picked it up on the way back."

She gave me a small smile.

"I didn't want to subject us to my cooking again, and I felt like being a good wife. So… Hope you like chicken marsala and truffle potatoes."

I rubbed my hands together. "Yummy."

"Uh, no!"

Footsteps padded behind me, fast and full of judgment. I turned just as Serena rushed over, eyes sweeping me head to toe.

"You're filthy."

"Thank you." I grinned, winking at her, and she rolled her eyes.

"I'm serious, you're not touching food looking like the way you are. It's not sanitary."

"Thank you, Mrs. Germophobe."

Her gaze tracked over my shoulder, then up—zeroing in on my head. "Is that plaster in your hair?"

I ran a hand through it. Flakes dusted onto the counter.

"I'll wash it out later," I said, brushing some of the mess onto the floor with my sleeve.

"Miles Whitmore, did you just dust my floors with your crusty-ass scalp?"

"Technically, it's not *my* scalp—"

She stepped closer. Her fingers reached up, brushing lightly through my hair with more focus than I expected. She plucked a small clump of dried plaster out, inspecting it like it personally offended her.

"You need to take these braids down and wash it properly," she said quietly.

"I'll do it in the morning."

She shook her head. "You're going to do it tonight. Take a seat, and let me get a comb, I'll take down your braids."

"When did you start doing hair?"

She shot me a look like I was slow. "I'm Black, Miles. Who did you think Laurene taught?"

I chuckled. "I need to call my stylist and get an appointment with her to rebraid it anyway."

"*Her?*" Serena sniffed.

"She's sixty. Old enough to be my grandmama." I frowned.

"You don't think I can take down your hair, wash it, and rebraid it? I did it all the time when we were kids."

"You had my parts looking crooked too."

Serena playfully punched me in the arm and I laughed but sighed, running a hand over my face. "You've been at work too, Serena. We'll be up all night doing this. You know my hair is too thick."

"I'll fix you a plate." Serena shook her head. "Sit your ass down. I won't tell you again."

"Yes, ma'am." I grinned.

Heading to the living room, I slowly lowered myself to the floor, letting out a groan as I leaned back on the couch. Doughboy jumped down, stepping into my lap and looking up at me with a curious expression.

"Wassup, man?" I murmured, giving him a few slow scratches under the chin. "You looking after my woman?"

He let out a little sound, half purr, half judgment, like *barely.*

"Yeah, I feel you."

I leaned my head back with a sigh, just trying to breathe for a minute—but then I heard it. The soft but unmistakable theme music coming from the TV.

I cracked one eye open.

"Oh, *hell* no." I groaned louder this time.

I heard Serena coming from the kitchen, and then I felt a nudge.

"Here you go."

I took the plate from her, and then she surprised me with a beer.

"Look at you being domestic, taking care of you man."

"You lucky I can't divorce you without ramifications," she said, deadpan. "Don't get used to this treatment."

She disappeared again briefly, and then I felt the cushion behind me shift. Serena dropped down on the couch, a small container of hair products and a comb nestled in her lap. She eased herself behind me, her thighs brushing my shoulders, warm and bare and smooth.

Her scent wrapped around me—clean linen, soft musk, and something sweet. My body sank deeper into the floor, jaw unclenching, spine relaxing just from being near her.

"You're not seriously gonna make me watch this, are you?" I asked, eyeing the screen.

"*13 Going on 30*." Her voice was light, teasing. "You know you like it."

A slow grin curved my mouth. "You used to make me watch it every summer."

"It was my guilty pleasure after Gigi made me watch it… And you liked it."

"I tolerated it."

"Liar." I let my head fall back, resting against her belly.

She ran her fingers through my hair, comb teasing gently at the edges. My eyes fluttered shut before I meant them to. Between the warmth of her body, the softness of her hands, and the familiar sound of her voice—damn. I could've stayed there forever.

Her fingers were slow. Careful. She undid each braid with a patient rhythm, her nails scratching lightly at my scalp, and I had to stop myself from moaning at the pleasant sensation. Each tug felt like tension being pulled out from my body, from the day, from my past.

The feel of her unraveling my braids, the soft scrape of her nails against my scalp, my head dropped forward.

"You okay?" she asked, pausing, looking down at me.

"Yeah," I said, trying to wake up. "Just tired."

I felt her hand caress my cheek. "If you want, we can switch places. I can stay on site; you go into the office?"

I never liked the office. I hated staring at spreadsheets and zoning forms and permit requests. I'd do it when I had to, but that part of the job had always felt like dragging a dead weight behind me.

And…truth was, it was nice having Serena out there with me.

For the first time in a long time, I wasn't trying to do everything. I wasn't running around like a one-man crew trying to keep a sinking ship afloat. With her around, I could breathe. Focus on what I enjoyed. Actually building.

"Nah, I like things the way they are."

Her fingers kept moving. "Your scalp's dry."

"You gonna shame me while you do my hair?" I teased.

"I might." Her nails scraped gently over my temple.

A long silence passed.

Then I said, "You smell good."

Her hands paused, just for a second. I felt her breath catch, then exhale like she hadn't meant to hold it.

"You taste good too."

"Miles…" Her voice sounded strained. "All done. Take a shower. Wash it. I'll finish it off."

I leaned in close, just to be an ass. "You gonna join me, or just supervise from the doorway?"

"Miles."

"Yes, *wife*?"

She pointed toward the bathroom like it was exile. "Wash your ass."

I nodded, and with tired legs, I went to the bathroom. The hot water hit my back, loosening the plaster from my skin, the sweat from my scalp. I took my time, part of me hoping she'd be join me in the shower.

She didn't.

I stepped out, dried off, pulled on some sweats. When I came back out, Serena was waiting—fresh oil and a comb ready on the table beside her. No Doughboy on the couch, and luckily she'd changed the channel to ambiance music.

"Come on," she said, patting the spot in front of her.

She poured a little oil into her palms, rubbed them together, and started working it through my hair.

"You're good at this," I murmured, eyes closed, relaxing into her touch.

"I watched a few videos," she said, a small smile in her voice.

She parted a section, smoothed it, started a new braid.

A few more minutes passed in the quiet before I asked, "Do you think I'm fighting something hopeless?"

She paused, her fingers going still at the top of my scalp.

"What do you mean?"

"With Whitmore Ventures. With trying to bring it back. Sometimes it feels like I'm just rebuilding something that's meant to stay broken."

Serena didn't answer right away. She finished the braid she was working on, sealed the end, and leaned forward just enough that I could feel the heat of her chest brush my back.

"What do you want?"

"That's not what I asked you."

Serena parted another section. "You know the answer, Miles. You don't need to ask me. What does your gut say?"

Leave.

The silence stretched, and she finished my hair quickly.

She completed the last braid and let her fingers rest against my scalp.

"There," she murmured. "All done."

I didn't want to move—didn't want to lose that weight, that warmth.

But eventually, I sat up slow, rolling my shoulders as I stretched. I ate a bit of my food. She gathered the comb and product, but instead of walking away, she placed them aside and slid onto the couch next to me.

I turned to look at her.

And damn.

She was watching the screen, pretending she didn't feel my eyes on her—but I saw the soft curve of her lip, the way she sat with one leg tucked under the other, her thigh brushing mine.

I was tired, sore, full—and still, I wanted her.

Bad.

She glanced over, and her brow lifted just slightly.

I didn't hide it. I let her see exactly what I was thinking.

Then she surprised me.

Without a word, Serena stood, and slowly sank down onto the rug between my legs. The move was fluid, deliberate, and when she looked up at me, I saw the heat in her eyes...but also something else—curiosity, maybe even nerves.

My breath hitched.

"Serena," I said low, a warning and a prayer.

She placed her palms gently on my thighs, her thumbs moving in slow, absent circles over the fabric of my sweatpants.

"I wanted to try something," she said softly, her gaze flicking up to meet mine. "Just to see if I could still do it."

I stared at her, heart pounding, completely still—like if I moved too fast, the moment might disappear.

Her fingers found the waistband of my sweats, and she tugged—slow, unhurried, like she had all the time in the world. My body lifted for her on instinct. I couldn't look away.

She dragged the fabric down my hips, past my thighs, until I was bare beneath her gaze. My chest rose as I exhaled, tension tightening across my shoulders.

When she wrapped her hand around my dick, I hissed between my teeth. I was already leaking, and she didn't waste a drop of it—slapping the head on her tongue, her eyes fluttering closed like she'd missed the taste of me.

"Baby—damn," I groaned, my stomach caving in when I hit the back of her throat.

But what undid me wasn't just her mouth. It was the feeling underneath it.

Her hands on my thighs, grounding me. Her rhythm—slow, savoring—like I wasn't a man to just take, but something to be remembered. She knew me. Knew how I liked it, knew where I tensed, what made me crumble.

"Sunny... Shit, take your time with it, Ma. It ain't goin' nowhere." My voice was a rasp, my hips pumping steadily. My breath stuttered as my head dropped back against the couch, vision blurring for a second.

One hand cupped my balls, working them with slow, gentle rolls that had my spine tightening. My chest rose and plummeted, breath shallow, heart thudding.

By now, her nose was smashed into my pubic hair, taking every inch like she was starving for it. My dick was drenched in her mouth, slick and noisy with every wet plunge into her throat. The sounds—those *fucking* sounds—were sinful, like she didn't care how messy or deep it got, only that I felt *everything*.

My hands fisted the couch cushions as a warning crept up my spine—tight, hot, impossible to ignore. Her cheeks hollowed as she took me deeper and sucked hard just like I loved. Focusing mostly on the tip because she knew what that would do to me.

"Ma... baby, I'm—" My words dissolved into a groan, deep and broken, as my hips bucked and my release hit fast and hard.

I spilled down her throat, my whole body bowing, locked in the heat of it. My muscles jerked, trembling from the pressure, and she didn't flinch—not once. She took it, all of it, swallowing like she *wanted* it, her hands still firm on me, like she was anchoring me in the storm she'd created.

And fuck, if that didn't undo me all over again.

I blinked hard, breath jagged, vision blurry with the aftermath—but even through the haze, I couldn't take my eyes off her. Her lips were swollen, glistening, eyes flicking up to meet mine with a quiet defiance, like *Yeah, I still got it.*

I reached for her without thinking.

Got her off the floor, hands firm beneath her arms as I pulled her up into a kiss—deep and messy, tasting myself on her tongue, not caring. I turned her, pressing her into the couch face-first, her knees hitting the cushions, her spine arching just the way I liked it.

"You know what you do to me, Serena?" I rasped, voice low, rough as gravel against her skin. "You *fucking know*?"

My hands gripped her hips, dragging her ass back against me. She gasped—half challenge, half surrender. I was still hard, still pulsing, already aching to be inside her again.

"You take me apart," I muttered, guiding my length between her thighs, pulling down her panties and sliding against that slick heat. "And I *love* it."

I didn't wait. I pushed into her slow but deep, watching her crumble as I filled her. Her fingers clawed at the cushions, her breath hitched.

I braced my weight in my palms, pinning her hips where I needed them, grinding into her with a roll so deep it dragged a sob from her throat. I moved like I owned her—but fuck, she owned me just as much. My hips clapped against her ass, each stroke deliberate, dragging out her moans, feeding mine.

"Fuck, Serena," I gritted through clenched teeth, sweat dripping down my back. "You feel so good... Always—always so fuckin' good to me."

I bent lower, my chest over her back, lips against her spine.

"I don't want this to be a deal anymore," I whispered, the

words catching in my throat. "Not just a fuckin' arrangement. Not when I feel like this. Not when it's *you*."

Her body trembled, but I didn't stop. I couldn't.

"I want you to want me back, Serena," I murmured, dragging my hand up her belly to palm her breast, holding her to me while I drove into her slow and deep. "Not because you have to. Because you *want to*. Because we could make this real."

My rhythm stuttered, hips faltering as the weight of it hit me full force. *I love her.* Not just the way her body felt—*her*. All her sharp edges, her fire, her silence, her ambition. The way she's still here, letting me in.

And for the first time in a long fucking time, I didn't feel alone.

"Fuck! Fuck, fu—*Miles*!" Serena gripped one of the pillows close as she gasped and I saw her eyes flicker white like the damn exorcist. Her body quaked beneath me, skin flushed and slick, and that sweet little pussy kept sucking me in, like it never wanted to let go.

But I wasn't done.

Not when this meant something. Not when she meant something.

Her arms went limp, but I wasn't letting her go. I folded her wrists behind her back, locking her in, my fingers wrapped tight so she had no choice but to take every pounding inch of me.

"You said you could handle me," I growled against her shoulder. "So take it, baby. Take all of me."

I gripped her hair and yanked her head up, turning her face toward mine.

And fuck, she was wrecked.

Eyes half-lidded, mouth swollen and open, breath stuttering like she didn't even know where she was anymore. But her body? Her body knew exactly where it wanted to be—*with me*.

I kissed her hard, no finesse left. Just need. Just truth.

Teeth clashing, tongues sliding, lips bruising. I kissed her like I was trying to brand her, to make her *feel* what I couldn't say.

I couldn't say the words, but I poured them into her mouth. *I love you. I want you. I need this.*

All of it.

Her ass bounced with every thrust, slapping against my thighs, and her pussy? God—*melting.* Dripping. Sucking me in like I belonged there.

"Fuck, Serena," I hissed, jaw clenched, breath ragged as I watched us move. My dick slid in and out of her slick heat, covered in the creamy mess she left behind. "You creamin' all over me, baby. Fuck—look at that. You want me to cum inside you? I'll get you a pill."

She whimpered, nodding, pleading, "Please, Miles. Please, please, please—"

That was all I needed.

My hands locked around her waist, holding her up, keeping her where I needed her as my hips slammed into her, hard, desperate, possessive. I grunted her name as I came, spilling deep inside, grinding through it like I could give her more. Like I could make her *feel* everything I couldn't say.

We just stayed there, sinking into the couch. Both of us breathless, her ass still pressed to my stomach, my hands smoothing over her skin, gripping her thighs, then her back, needing to *touch* something real—*her.*

I gave her one more smack—slow this time—then pressed a soft kiss to her temple, my voice a low rumble, "Good shit, baby. So good."

I stayed inside her for a moment longer, like I was afraid if I pulled out, I'd forget how this felt. She shifted just slightly, like she was going to speak. I held my breath, but nothing came.

"I love you, Sunny."

CHAPTER 28

Serena

"WHATCHA THINK OF THIS?" Gigi asked, showing off a feathery mini-dress totally Vegas showgirl style as we stood in one of my favorite boutiques in town.

"I don't want you here," I said, crossing my arms. I was desperate to get home to Miles. Standing here, it felt too distracting and a waste of time. Being near him was the best feeling. I felt all wrong when I wasn't with him.

What is happening to me?

"You're happy to have us here," Laurene said, sitting on the chair and flipping through her baby book. "Did you know some babies are born with hair, while others may not develop hair until later? I hope my baby comes out with hair. All of us did."

I was losing my strength. I didn't care for that. I was becoming like my sisters. Ew.

"Go home, Gigi," I said sharply. "I only needed a dress. This was not supposed to be a big deal."

"You're in a *mood*," she said, wrinkling her nose at the dress and tossing it back onto the rack like it offended her. "Let me guess. Miles?"

Laurene looked up from the book. "Have y'all been fighting this whole time?"

Far from it.

We'd been fucking almost every night and morning. On desks. Against walls. Bent over my damn bathroom sink while the shower still ran.

And yet, somehow, it never felt like enough.

I couldn't get enough of him.

"Oh my God, it *is* Miles," Gigi gasped, delighted. "*Ooooh,* y'all get nasty? He blow your back out? I was betting with Reese and Laurene on how long it would take you to give in. I'm sorry, sis, but you so damn uptight, just enjoy the dick. I mean, I do with my guys. They're like a bus or train line—ride them to the end of the line, then get off, get a new one."

I scrunched my face up at her.

"If you're having fun with him, that's not bad." Laurene shrugged and relaxed back in the seat, placing a hand on her belly. "Just use protection. Pregnancy sucks."

Gigi nodded. "Take it from the queen of busting it wide open."

"I know you not talking. Wasn't you just busting it open on a yacht?" Laurene glared at her.

"My coochie only gets wet when his bank account has several zeros and commas in it. Nothing less. I'm highly expensive." Gigi blew her a kiss.

"We're talking about me." I pointed to myself.

"Rude, but y'all in there hunching, don't lie." Gigi shot me a look.

I sighed and nodded. Laurene and Gigi screamed their heads off.

"Yes!" Gigi said. "Tell Reese to run me my money."

"I swear, I told G you were glowing," Laurene gushed.

"Get a life," I said, shaking my head.

I rolled my eyes up to the ceiling, and Gigi went back to the rack and searched again. I didn't realize the polo match had a strict dress code, and I needed to shop for something new.

"You're almost thirty, Serena. Should you really be dressing like Hillary Clinton and Kamala Harris with all those pantsuits?" She plucked a dress off the rack—a sleek yellow number with a plunging neckline—and held it up against me. "Show some ass."

"She is showing ass." Laurene gave a devilish smirk.

I shouldn't have told them anything.

"You gotta use them repressed feminine wiles. You have amazing legs, Rena, don't hide them."

This was not what I came here for.

My mind was on Jenese. That manuscript still sat like a ticking bomb—coded names, thinly veiled stories, and just enough truth to set fire to everything I'd built. I'd gotten distracted by Miles but I had to get it together.

There were gaps in her story.

The last time I saw Jenese was in New York. Right after our failed sting. I knew she'd been hanging out with a man, but she wouldn't tell me his name. A reverse image search got me the name Roman Tolland. Hedge fund billionaire.

Gigi waved a short orange dress in my face.

"What about this? Too obvious?"

I blinked. "Huh?"

"You didn't hear a word I said."

What was the shocker last night was I found an old photo of Roman with Jenese on his arm. It was at some charity gala. Next to them was a couple. A lovely younger woman.

And Dante Castillo.

Jenese fucking knew Dante. *He knew her.*

"And you need to give me your perspective on what went down at the family dinner. Lu said shit went left. Was Erik about to fight Miles?" Gigi looked at me with wide eyes.

"Erik didn't fight Miles. They just had…a disagreement." I shook my head. "Again, not your business."

She plucked another dress off the rack, this one a bold red, and held it up with a critical eye. "Ooh, this one might actually make you look like a woman instead of a walking corporate PowerPoint presentation."

The second job for Jenese, the damn blackmail, I'd been hoping to forget it. But I couldn't. The suffocating weight of it all—it was eating me alive. And I knew I couldn't let this continue. If I let her goad me into this, what else would she want?

"Talk to me, Rena. I mean I know y'all just think I'm here for fun and my looks, but I can be deep," Gigi said.

Laurene finally put her book down. "We all wanna know how you're handling being married to Miles."

"I'm serious, talk to me," Gigi said again.

I stared at the row of silk blouses in front of me. My mind should've been focused on work, on damage control with Jenese, on keeping the King legacy intact—but all I could think about was *him*.

"I don't do this," I said finally. "I don't spiral. I don't *feel* this much. It's inefficient."

Gigi blinked. "Girl, what?"

"It's like—there's a framework for everything. I know how to win a negotiation, secure a deal, destroy a competitor if I need to. That makes sense to me. But this?" I shook my head, my voice dipping. "He makes me feel things I don't know how to categorize."

"So what's the problem? That y'all fucked and you caught feelings?"

"I love him."

It was comical the way Gigi's and Laurene's expressions went blank, and they stared at me like I had grown a second head.

"And he told me he loves me."

Laurene clasped her hands together. "Serena! That's amazing."

"Wait, wait, wait. What? How the hell did this happen so quick?" Gigi looked between us. "What Lu said before was correct? You were sleeping around with Miles years ago."

I hesitated, then looked at Laurene.

She nodded gently, like she was telling me it was okay. That I could say it.

"We weren't just messing around," I said quietly. "We were in a relationship. He proposed to me."

Gigi's mouth fell open. "Bitch, what?"

Laurene's jaw dropped. "He—what?!"

Gigi damn near collapsed onto the floor, flailing like someone just told her the world was ending. "Y'all been sneaky as hell! And I *knew* something was off!"

She sank onto the edge of the chaise, clutching her chest like she was genuinely winded. "Nah. Nope. Uh-uh. This is too much."

Laurene leaned forward, still dazed. "Serena…why didn't you tell us?"

"Because I didn't want anyone to know," I said, quieter now. "I didn't want anyone to see how much it meant. And when it ended, I—I couldn't even talk about it."

It was kinda weird telling my sisters all that. I liked figuring things out myself, but…maybe Miles had a point. It helped having them understand, it made things easier. "I don't like being seen," I admitted after a long pause. "Not like that. Not when I haven't controlled what's being shown. There's too much I haven't figured out yet. Too much that could go wrong."

Gigi softened. "You mean like getting hurt?"

"Or being vulnerable?" Laurene said.

"I mean like losing," I said sharply. "You don't understand what that feels like for me. It's not just emotional—it's personal. Strategic. If I slip, even once, it's not just me that falls. It's our name. Our legacy. Everything I've spent years building could unravel."

Gigi studied me, and then her voice lowered, unusually gentle. "Rena…that sounds exhausting."

It *was* exhausting. But I couldn't say that. Not out loud.

Instead, I glanced away. "I don't know what I want from him. I only know that I can't stop wanting."

"I mean, I know I give you shit about being Mama's little solider, but you've been serious since we were kids, Rena." Gigi smiled at me.

I turned to look at her, brows pulling together. "What does that even mean?"

"You've always been *on*. Class president. Valedictorian. If there was a team captain, you were it. Every time. You like…seek out the weight. Like if no one else is carrying it, you'll do it just so it doesn't get dropped."

"That's not true," I said, but it came out a little too quickly.

"Isn't it?" She tilted her head, gold hoops catching the light. "You're always worrying about somebody or something. I think you *like* to be anxious."

I scoffed. "That's ridiculous."

"No, it's control," Gigi said, picking up momentum. "You can't control feelings. You can't predict people. You can't make love fit in a spreadsheet or a ten-year plan. So instead, you fill your life with things you *can* control. Titles. Wins. Legacies."

I stared at her. She was usually the chaos tornado, the glitter bomb. But now she was peeling me back like she'd been watching all along.

"So what are you saying?" I asked, quieter.

"I'm saying maybe this time, you don't have to *lead* the moment, Rena. Maybe you just let yourself be in it. Let him love you, or mess up, or surprise you. Let yourself want him without needing to control the outcome. You can't stop bad things from happening in life, and the way you're always holding on too tight? You won't let the good happen."

Gigi paused, then grinned.

"Let the bus take *you* for a ride for once, sis. Stop tryin' to be the damn driver all the time."

I blinked at her, stunned into silence for a beat too long.

Gigi. Of all people. Making sense.

"Okay, Dr. Phil," I said finally, rolling my eyes. "Did you rehearse that in the mirror before you came?"

She smirked, pleased with herself. "Nope. It's all natural, baby. Wisdom from the baddest."

I shook my head, lips twitching despite myself. "I'm actually embarrassed that was helpful."

"Don't be," she said, flipping her curls over one shoulder. "I got layers like lasagna. You just gotta dig past the hot girl aesthetic."

"I do want to add onto the *sage* wisdom of Gigi." Laurene pushed herself up and waddled over to us, and she stood in front of me, her brown eyes wide. "Remember what we talked about at my baby shower?"

I did. I hadn't wanted to. I'd brushed it off at the time, called her hormonal, too soft since she got pregnant. But the words stuck with me.

"Yeah," I said slowly.

"You know what I realized once I left the house?" she continued, tone quiet but steady. "I didn't know how to make a single decision that didn't sound like Mama's voice in my head." She touched her stomach. "Not one."

I stayed silent.

"You don't have to be her." Laurene met my eyes fully now. "We love Mama. I'm not saying not to, but she's got things she's fighting on her own, and that means she may not show up the way you need. But I'm letting you know *I'm* here for you."

Maybe you should leave, Serena. You've made King Developments the best. What do you want?

Laurene reached her hand out and grabbed mine, giving it a squeeze.

"You're allowed to want something just because you want it, Rena," she said. "It's okay to not have a plan either. That's the beauty of life. But *lean* on us. Even Erik. We know the pressures better than anybody, and while we might not have been good at supporting each other before, we're better now."

Gigi snorted. "Yeah, even with your mean ass, I love you."

Why were my eyes feeling prickly? It was a weird feeling.

"Group hug, bitches!" Gigi grinned, and the two of them rushed me, all lavender and citrus and the faint burn of expensive perfume.

I stood stiff in the middle, arms hovering awkwardly at my sides like someone being restrained at a checkpoint.

"I—okay—this is happening," I muttered.

Laurene's cheek brushed mine. Gigi wrapped herself around us like a human boa constrictor. Somewhere in the pressure of the embrace, my hand twitched, then slowly, I let my fingers curl into the back of Laurene's blouse.

"We love you, Serena."

CHAPTER 29

Serena

THE AIR WAS thick with the smell of old money—a blend of leather and pipe tobacco, tempered by the sharp, clean scent of recently mown grass.

One foot in front of the other. Smile. Nod. Don't trip.

The breeze, warm and gentle as silk, rolled off the hills, whispering through the tented canopies and rustling the crisp white uniforms of the valet attendants, carrying with it the faint sounds of distant music and laughter. The sound of hooves across turf pounded like a heartbeat.

I could feel the tension in my calves from walking too precisely in heels that were *just* a little too high for the turf. Stupid. I should've gone with the thicker heel. But Gigi said I'd need to look polished and sexy, and the stilettos went best with the dress.

My palms were sweating. My throat was tight.

I shouldn't be nervous. This was like any other job, right? And this was the last time. I promised myself that. No matter what.

Three violins played by the main tent, their music carrying on the wind. Beneath the linen of my dress, my purse pressed against my hip, the weight of the velvet box inside a silent reminder.

I took a deep breath through my nose. Held it. Released.

You're Serena fucking King. You've walked into worse rooms with a bigger target on your back. You know how to finish.

The grass crunched softly beneath my heels as I moved toward the VIP tent, spine straight, hips relaxed, mouth curved in that calculated, unreadable smile.

But a very familiar laugh made me pause.

No.

I turned and made eye contact with Mayor Dante Castillo.

Fuck.

He stood in the center of a small circle, an entourage around him. He tipped back his drink, his dark hair glinting in the sunlight, and I saw a woman place a hand on his shoulder.

"Serena?" I heard Dante say.

I drove almost three hours to get here. What was Dante doing here? Did Jenese do this on purpose?

The laughter in his circle faded as I approached.

"Serena *Whitmore*," he mused, tilting his glass in my direction. "To what do I owe this pleasure? Are you here with your—"

I offered a professional smile. "Mayor Castillo."

"No need to be formal. Not here." He glanced at the men and women around him—people who I assumed were low-tier celebrities, city planners, donors, and one I swore I'd seen in a leaked article about offshore accounts.

"Give me a minute," Dante said to them with that easy charm. "You all go grab another drink. On me."

They peeled off like trained birds, laughing and murmuring as they made their way back to the bar. He didn't look at them. His eyes were on me.

"What are you doing so far south of Lush?" I asked.

"What are *you* doing here?"

"I don't think my mama would like this. You know she prefers the mayors that keep it professional."

A dark look flashed across his face, his jaw tightening as his eyes lost their warmth. "Yvonne doesn't agree with a lot of my methods. I'm guessing as her favorite daughter you share the same opinion."

Her favorite daughter? Hmph.

"I think for myself, Dante," I told him.

His lips curled. "You have potential, then."

Maybe Dante being was a good opportunity to get another perspective on my current situation. "Dante," I began, watching him sip from his glass. "You ever have someone in your circle who…outlived their usefulness?"

He lifted an eyebrow. "You mean a problem? Don't tell me you want to get rid of Miles already."

"I mean someone who doesn't know when to quit. Someone who thinks they're smarter than they are."

He chuckled, smooth and amused. "Darlin', that's most of the people I know."

"Can you tell me what you know about Jenese Delacroix?"

Dante's face dropped. "Jenese? How do you know her?"

"I found a picture of you two online. And I asked you the question first."

"That's not how we're going to do things, Serena," he said, shaking his head. "That's a very specific name to ask about, and you don't seem like the type that should know a person like her. So I'll ask again, and be honest. How do you know her?"

"She was my…mentor."

"Mentor?" Dante repeated like he didn't believe me. "Your mother is Yvonne King."

"I know who my mother is," I said. "I met Jenese six years ago after Laurene first left. She taught me things about business. But now she's back and threatening me."

"I thought I saw her at the cigar lounge, but I hoped my eyes were deceiving me," Dante murmured, and I watched his face flicker with emotions.

"Don't tell anyone this." I lowered my voice. "She's writing a book. I'm in it. With some incriminating evidence."

Dante looked more intrigued.

"I need a favor," I said finally.

Dante's smile was immediate. Hungry. "Now we're speaking the same language."

"I need to get rid of Jenese *and* evidence," I told him.

"And what happens after I give you what you want? What do you plan to do with the address?"

"That's not your concern."

"See," he said, wagging a finger, "that's the part that makes me nervous. My term is ending soon. That means reelection. I can't jeopardize that, you understand."

A ripple of cheers rolled through the crowd, followed by the thundering of hooves thundering across manicured grass.

Despite the helmet and dark sunglasses, I recognized Jasper Crewe instantly from Jenese's picture. The sun glanced off his polished boots, his frame bent low as he urged his mare into a gallop, rumbling toward the ball.

A collective gasp swept through the crowd as his bat connected with the ball, sending it flying in a clean, sharp arc across the grass; his teammates surged forward as one.

"You think I'd come to you if I had options?"

He didn't answer right away. Just took a long sip of his drink.

I rolled my eyes. "If I can find out some more dirt on Jenese, what she's been doing these last few years, maybe she'll be willing to scrap the book and leave me alone."

"Oh, I've heard about her. She's definitely dirty. I've got stories from my interactions with her and some…close friends of mine."

That was both helpful and alarming.

"You basically are going all *Dog the Bounty Hunter* on her, hmm? What will you give me in exchange?"

"I'll owe you a favor," I said.

"A King, offering favors? What's the world coming to?" He studied me again, his amusement dimming into something more dangerous. "You wouldn't be the first King to bite off more than they could chew."

"What's that supposed to mean?"

Dante just grinned.

"Can you do it or not?"

"Alright," he said, stepping back, that slick smile stretching across his face. "I'll think about it."

My brow arched. "That's not a yes."

"It's not a no either." He leaned in just enough that only I could hear. "We'll talk again. Soon."

I watched Dante disappear into the crowd when a deafening roar erupted as Jasper's winning shot swished through the net. His horse kicked up turf, nostrils flaring, and the referee's whistle cut through the air like a blade.

Jasper slid off his horse with ease, handing the reins off to a waiting staff.

His helmet came off, and his smile flickered wide and easy as a crowd started to gather. Men slapped him on the back. Women leaned in a little too close. He said something that made them laugh.

A tall, willowy woman appeared at his side, her caramel-blond hair twisted in a silk scarf that matched her pale blue dress. She kissed his cheek, possessive but poised.

I wove through a manicured garden toward the side of the house. Jasper's estate was a well-oiled machine—event staff stationed at every entry, servers ferrying champagne and charcu-terie, private security lingering at the perimeter.

Two bored security guards, more interested in chatting than work, stood by the side doors. I kept walking as if returning inside from the terrace like I had a right to be here.

"Ma'am?"

I didn't blink. "Sorry, just needed a break. My shoes are *killing* me." I gestured to my heels.

"Stick to this area only."

"Appreciate it." I slid through before they could say anything else.

The hall was cooler, quieter. Still opulent, of course. Cream paneling, gilt trim, a massive painting of someone's ancestor glaring disapprovingly from the wall. I kept my pace calm. The adrenaline was there, buzzing under my skin, but I didn't let it show.

I moved down the hall, looking for any opportunity.

An office. Bedroom. Closet. *Something.*

When staff rushed by, I dropped my head and turned away, pretending to find the paintings interesting before continuing my search.

Then I saw it: a discreet sign beside a narrow hallway. *Private Suite—Riders Only.*

The farther I got from the main corridor, the quieter it got.

The hallway forked—one direction led to a lounge still echoing with laughter, the other to a closed door marked with Jasper's monogram. I went with the second.

Locked.

Of course.

I pressed my ear against it. Nothing. No voices.

Reaching into my clutch, I found the small lock pick. I worked the lock. One soft click.

Inside, the suite was surprisingly clean, all sleek and masculine. Leather chairs. A rack of uniforms pressed and waiting. A wall of gleaming trophies.

I crossed the room fast, already pulling the velvet box from my bag.

Somewhere obvious, but not sloppy.

I tucked the box on the shelf that looked to be his regular streetwear clothes.

Done.

Now Jenese was out of my life. I'd get the manuscript. I'd move on with my life. Rushing out of the room, I retraced my steps and turned the corner, and almost ran into somebody.

"I'm sorry—"

I sucked in a breath, and I froze.

"Daddy?"

He stood there, shocked, but even worse—Audrey Whitmore was coming out of a room behind him.

CHAPTER 30

Serena

THE SUNSET GAVE the road ahead an orange glow, only lit up by my headlights and the occasional green-blue signs. I didn't turn the music on. I didn't need to drown anything out.

Daddy was with Audrey.

If I started assuming the worst, I'd just be Gigi. I didn't even want to *think* that of him. Mama was a handful, but we all knew Daddy loved her. He'll never do anything wrong like that. To destroy us. To destroy our legacy.

My phone buzzed beside me on the passenger seat.

I jumped. *Please… Don't let it be Jenese.*

Reaching for it, I gave it a quick glance. It was Miles.

Come meet me. Trust me.

There was a pin with his location, but I didn't reply. Just clicked it. Let the GPS guide me.

The farther I drove, the heavier the silence became.

It was clear to me what I had to do. About Jenese. About my family. I couldn't keep living the way I had before. It was impossible to return to that life, when now I had Miles with me.

I had to let the old Serena go. The girl who let herself be used by someone like Jenese.

The girl who believed survival meant domination. That the only way to be strong was to win. At any cost.

I had been angry—so fucking angry. At my family. At men like my father. At the world that made me feel like I was nothing unless I took everything.

I let Jenese feed that anger. Shape it into something shiny and dangerous. Something that looked like control but was really just fear dressed up. What I had was what I needed. Yes, I'd always want King Enterprises, but the more I sat with it, the more I didn't want that. I just wanted what I thought would get me that approval.

The only approval I needed was from myself.

I had Miles. I had Laurene. Gigi. Noelle. Maybe even Erik.

I had myself.

Turning off the exit, I looked at the blinking arrow on my GPS. *Really?*

I pulled into the small gravel lot. It was nothing like the King parties or the rooftop lounges. It was a small brick building with fogged windows and soft light seeping through. A jazz club.

It'd been one of Dante's economic development ideas these past few months to bring in new business to Lush.

When was Miles hanging out at jazz clubs?

I stepped out of the car, the wind cool against my arms, and walked in.

The sound hit first—slow jazz, sultry and rich, melting into the air like honey. The room was dim but golden, like something paused in time.

And then I saw him.

Miles.

"A jazz club?"

"Surprised?" He looked down at me. "How did your meeting go?"

Right… My meeting.

"Uneventful. We don't have to worry about the protestors anymore," I said quickly, looking around.

"We are almost at our two-month anniversary, and we haven't had a date night, so I thought this would be the perfect place."

I raised a brow. "You're planning dates? Who's gotten domestic?"

"We can go," he said, and I rolled my eyes at him, pushing him. "But I wanted to take my wife out for a special night, just us and no work."

"Or your cat."

"You love Doughboy, don't deny it."

Hmm... The cat wasn't the *worst* thing in my life. He provided some company, but not much.

"Dance with me."

"Miles—"

"Just one song," he said.

I hesitated, but then slipped my fingers into his.

He smiled, that soft kind of smile that always made me want to believe him. He led me toward the dance floor, weaving us past small round tables dressed in white linen and gold candles. The club was low-lit and warm, every surface bathed in amber and burgundy. Exposed brick, wood-beamed ceilings, and a jazz band tucked into the corner, their music curling into the air like a secret.

The saxophone wailed a rich, aching solo that melted right into my chest. Around us, couples swayed—slow, effortless movements, like the world outside didn't exist.

I swallowed as he turned to me. His hands found my waist, and mine slid up over his shoulders on instinct. Being this close still disarmed me. Still made everything feel softer, hazier.

He pulled me gently into the music, guiding us through the rhythm like he already knew where we were going.

We moved in slow circles, his touch steady, grounding.

And then I did what I always did—I tried to take control, shifting our pace just slightly.

Miles leaned in, mouth brushing my ear. "You need to let me lead."

The heat from his breath scattered down my spine. I looked up at him.

"Then lead me," I said.

Miles chuckled, and I relaxed.

His hand slid down my back, guiding me closer, and I let myself breathe in the moment—the music, the flicker of candlelight, the way his touch steadied me even when everything inside still felt unmoored.

But my mind wasn't quiet.

I'd seen her—Miles's mother—talking to my father at the polo match. A match no one I knew was supposed to be attending. What secrets was Daddy hiding? Hell, my whole family was hiding secrets.

And then, Dante. I made a deal with the devil because he was my only hope.

Miles turned us again, and I exhaled.

"I was thinking," I murmured, my voice barely audible over the saxophone. "About what you said back at home a few nights ago."

He tilted his head, eyes flicking to mine. "Yeah?"

"You asked if you should still run your family's company." I nodded, my throat tight. "I've been thinking about that a lot."

His gaze softened, but he didn't interrupt.

"I love what I do. I'm good at it." I swallowed. "But I'm tired, Miles. I'm always tired. I don't know who I am outside of King Developments. I don't know what I like. I haven't had a real hobby since I was seventeen."

He held me a little closer, like he could feel the weight of what I was admitting.

"I was reading about sabbaticals," I said with a dry laugh. "You know, the kind where people take time off to...I don't know. Find themselves? Travel. Take pottery classes. Whatever the hell people do when they're not working themselves into the ground."

Miles grinned. "You'd look cute with clay on your nose."

"Shut up," I muttered, but I smiled.

He spun us slowly, one hand catching mine again, and I let him. Let him hold me steady.

"I just...I've built everything on the idea that I had to prove I was stronger. Smarter. Untouchable," I said. "But I think it's time I step back. I'd been fighting giving Erik my company, but...he can have it for now. I just wanna relax."

Shock clouded Miles's features, and I felt fearful of what I said aloud. This was scary. Unnerving. Nerve-racking.

His thumb brushed over my knuckles. "You deserve more. All I ask is that you don't start collecting chickens and ugly statues."

I rolled my eyes, but the laugh escaped before I could stop it.

He smirked, then without warning, dipped me.

My breath caught. The saxophone wailed behind us, and the room blurred into soft candlelight and clinking glasses. His hand held me securely, and I clung to his shoulder, startled but smiling wide.

"You're ridiculous," I whispered, heart still racing from the drop.

He leaned in, eyes molten. "You're radiant."

And then he kissed me.

But even as my eyes fluttered closed, even as warmth bloomed in my chest like jazz on the speakers... I couldn't ignore the thought pressing at the back of my mind.

I still had to face my father.

CHAPTER 31

Miles

"YOU DIDN'T WAKE ME UP," I grumbled, getting in the shower.

Sunny had her back to me. The steam billowed around us, hot and fragrant, as her head tilted back, the shower cap clinging to her hair.

"It's Saturday," she said, looking over her shoulder at me. "I let you sleep because you deserved a break after a long week."

"I don't need a break, I need you." Bringing her body close to mine, I could feel the heat rising between us as she was flush against me, placing a kiss on her shoulder.

"You need to rest," she said.

She wasn't wrong—but it wasn't just sleep that had kept me going. It was her.

We weren't a bad team.

That thought hit me somewhere deep in my chest as the steam curled around us and the water beat down like warm rain.

But last night, hearing her say she was thinking about stepping away from King Developments, it shocked me. Not because she couldn't do it. Serena could run that company blindfolded with a broken hand and still outdo us all in Lush. But because she was finally asking herself if she *wanted* to.

And that…that made me feel closer to her than I ever had before.

"What you said last night…" I pressed a kiss to her damp shoulder, letting my lips linger there. "You meant it?"

"Yeah. I did."

I nodded slowly, forehead brushing her temple.

"I've been thinking the same thing," I admitted, my voice barely audible above the hum of the water. "I'm gonna go tell my parents today, I'm resigning as CEO."

For a second, Serena stilled in my arms, and then she turned around to face me.

"You're…what?" she asked, blinking up at me.

I nodded again, slower this time. "I've been thinking about it for a while. I kept telling myself I had to fix what my father broke. Rebuild the name. But…I don't want to anymore. I never asked myself if I even liked what I was rebuilding."

She studied me for a beat, eyes searching, like she was trying to see if I really meant it.

"I thought you loved the business," she said.

"I do. I'm just leaving Whitmore Ventures. I'm starting my own company."

Serena let out a quiet breath.

"You sure?" she asked.

"Yeah." I nodded. "I want to build something else. Something mine. Not his."

She touched my face, thumb brushing under my jaw. "Then we're both about to be very disappointing children."

She leaned up on her toes and kissed me. I accepted her invitation gladly.

The glass of the shower seemed to fogged up quickly as I pressed closer until her back hit wall, steam coiling around us. My hands trailed over her naked body, and I felt enraptured looking at her dark brown skin gleaming like bronze in the light.

I bent slightly, gripping the backs of her thighs and lifting her. Her legs hooked over the crease of my arms, just above the elbow, and I held her there and I felt her hand slide down between us, gripping my dick. Slowly she tugged, and I groaned when I felt her rub the head of my dick against her slick folds.

"Fuck." I slowly pushed into her, but the second I feel the plush, wet heat, I pressed deep within her.

The wet slap of skin echoed in the tight space, mixed with the low thud of her body hitting the glass wall over and over again.

Thump. Thump. Thump.

It vibrated with every thrust, a soundtrack to how desperately I wanted her.

Her arms looped around my neck, her mouth parted in silent moans. I felt her nails dig into the back of my head as I drove into her harder, as if I could lose myself in the rhythm of our bodies colliding. "Yeah… Fuck me just like that, baby," I rasped, my voice rough against her ear, hands roaming over her slick, trembling body.

She bit at my neck—sinful and greedy—and I nearly lost it.

"Say my name," I growled.

"Miles," she gasped.

Her tits pressed hard against my chest, ass grinding tight against my thighs. My hands tangled in her hair, ridding her of her shower cap. I knew she was gonna be pissed, but my fingers clutched like I needed to hold on for dear life as the rough stubble on my jaw rubbed against her face.

I was fucking her fierce and fast, my forehead pressed to hers, breath ragged and heavy.

She clawed at the back of my neck, and her squeaks and screams tore through me, making me lose every damn bit of control.

"That's it, baby," I whispered. "Come for me."

And when she did, she came hard—back arching, her walls squeezing me like she never wanted to let me go. I followed with a guttural groan, pulling out of her, and spilling onto her stomach, holding her through every wave, every twitch, every aftershock.

I held her closer, going over what I was about to do today.

I was afraid of wasting my life trying to rebuild something that no longer fit who I was. I'd been running on ego, guilt, and family legacy for so long, I forgot what it felt like to make a choice just because I wanted to.

I wanted *this*.

I wanted *her*.

I wanted peace.

A few hours and a half-assed attempt at looking presentable later, I was stepping through the back door of my parents' house.

"There's my favorite ladies," I said, stepping into Ma's kitchen, the smell of frying bacon and coffee filling the air.

Mama Teagues and Ma stood at the kitchen island, their voices rising as they argued over the colorful array of fresh produce. They both looked up when I stepped in, and Ma grinned at me, outstretching her arms.

"There's my baby!"

Mama Teagues snorted. "That's a grown man."

"Hush, Rosetta. He's my baby."

Ma came around the island, her locs swishing in her ponytail, and I scooped her in a hug. I pressed my head into her shoulder, inhaling her sweet vanilla perfume, a scent that instantly transported me back to my childhood days.

"You spoil him too much," Mama Teagues sniffed, her wrinkled face a picture of disapproval, before shuffling to the stove.

"What are you doing here?"

"Just came over." I shrugged, sitting at the bar stool while I looked around. "What's going on here?"

"Your father won't eat." Ma grimaced. "You know the medicine sometimes messes with his system."

Was it the medicine? Or was he being stubborn?

Ma suffered more than she ever told anyone.

Living in that house with him—managing his moods, his silence, his sudden flashes of temper—it was like walking through a field of landmines. The medication helped sometimes, but not enough. There were days he'd sit for hours, eyes fixed on a spot on the wall like he was still doing time. Other days, he'd lash out over the smallest things—burnt toast, a news segment, a car door slamming too hard outside.

"You want me to talk with him?"

Ma reached over. "No. I can handle him. Now you want something, so tell me." Ma grabbed my hands and squeezed.

I looked over at Mama Teagues and then back to her, slowly deciding what was the best way to confess what happened.

"I may have made a mistake."

Ma raised a brow. "What you do?"

I licked my lips, and dropped my head.

"Miles Donovan. You tell me what happened. It's not going to affect our families, is it?"

Yes. Regret was a helluva bitter pill to swallow, and it felt like I was trying to force my emotion down but I couldn't.

"It might."

Ma looked over at Mama Teagues, who was clearly eavesdropping, and she cleared her throat.

"Rosetta? Can you take that to Omar? Make sure he eats and gets his insulin after."

Mama Teagues looked disappointed at the dismissal, but turned off the stove and plated the food before slowly walking out of the kitchen, hoping she could get another piece of the conversation.

"I've been…feeling some things for a while now," I forced myself to say. "I love you guys. I love the company. I loved Gramps. But some days it's so fucking hard, Ma."

She squeezed my hands, her face turning downward.

"Then, when I come around here, Pops just wants us to drop everything and throw it away. Did I just waste six years of my life when I could be doing something else?"

"You volunteered for this, Miles—"

"Could I really let you take over the company? *And* take care of Pops at his worst?" My voice cracked. "What kind of son—what kind of *man* would I have been if I had?"

Her lips pressed together, eyes turning away from me.

"Do you wish we were more like them?" I asked quietly. "The Kings."

She was still for a long moment.

"No."

I blinked. "Really? Even with everything that happened? Miss Yvonne was your best friend, Ma, and she just dumped you quicker than trash."

"Yes, Yvonne was my best friend. Our relationship wasn't perfect, but I can't get mad at the reaction she had. Especially after dealing with her own father. I wasn't there for her like I should have been."

"Don't make excuses for her."

"I'm not. I'm just telling the truth." She looked at me, really looked. "The Kings hold tight to legacy, but they weaponize it too. That's one thing Yvonne and I used to argue over. I may view it differently since I married into the Whitmores, but to me, legacy isn't just about continuing a name. It's about *family*. The bonds between one another. Compassion. Empathy. What's the point of having a legacy if everyone in the family hates it and each other?"

I stared at her, the weight of it all settling in my chest.

"I'll admit, we haven't been on top of our legacy like we should. We might have been in the shadow of the Kings, but I think what we have is better. Resilience. We survived. How many people can say that? Look at the Sterlings—no one has heard from or about them since they left."

I thought about to the other prominent family here in town. When Blair and Tobias's secret came out, things were never the same for them.

"You could have left. Started a new life. But you care, Miles. You care even on the days where you feel like you've hit a brick wall. The Whitmore legacy isn't just real estate development. It's you. It's the way you stayed. The way you fought. I'm so proud of you for that, baby."

"I… After we're done with renovations on this property, I want to step down as CEO for a while. Will you take over?"

Her eyebrows lifted. "You sure?"

"Yeah. I think it's time," I said. "You've been doing most of the heavy lifting anyway. I want you to take over. For real this time. Full title, full control."

"Okay. What's your plan?"

"I want to start something new. Build something from the ground up—with my name on it. It'll still be a part of the family's portfolio, but it's mine."

There was a pause. Then she smiled, soft and proud and a little sad.

"Then that's what you're gonna do."

I looked down at our joined hands.

"Your father's in the living room."

I knew what she was saying. Bite the bullet. Do it. *Finally*.

Squeezing her hand, I turned to head into the living room.

"Hey, old man, how's it going?"

"Mama Teagues got me watching this garbage," he grumbled, his eyes glued to the screen as he nodded along to the plaintiff's testimony.

"Do you have a second to spare?"

He nodded, the silence of the room amplifying the sound of his neck cracking slightly as he turned to look at me.

"Did he apologize for what he did to your face?" Pops said.

"I'm not here to talk about Erik," I said. "It's about Serena."

"Don't tell me she set you up."

I shook my head. "I love her."

Pops blinked at that.

"I've loved her for a while. Years now. I just didn't tell you and Ma."

Pops turned fully in his seat to give me his undivided attention.

"For the last six years, you've sat around this house sulking. Not doing anything. Leaving it all for me to fix. Your name's still on the company's deeds, but it's me out there trying to clean up your mess. Trying to rebuild something people laugh at now."

Pops frowned at me.

"I'm tired, man," I told him. "I don't want to keep doing this. I'm tired of trying to fix something I didn't break and then dealing with the bullshit that follows. I want to just be with Serena. I just wanna do something that's me."

"I didn't ask you to do anything."

"You also didn't stop me. You haven't for six years. You've been sulking. You've been a victim."

He flinched at the words.

"No one made you do what you did, Pops, but it's Ma and me who been dealing with shit. What have you done? You haven't protected us. Nor have you stood up for us, and I don't know why you even did it in the first place."

I blinked, feeling a surge of emotion hit me.

"I always thought you would tell me why. We had every-thing we could have possibly wanted. Why do the drugs? Why hide it? Why bring down everything without so much as a goddamn sorry?"

Pops looked back at the screen. The judge on TV was frown-ing, and I saw Pops's hand curl around the remote control.

"I didn't think you'd understand."

"Understand *what*, exactly?" I asked.

He pressed mute on the television.

"I was drowning," he said quietly. "I didn't even realize it until I was halfway to the bottom. After your grandpa died… I never really worked before, Miles. He handled all that. And then suddenly I had to deal with watching him die, taking care of you all. You know what people called me when I first took over? Lazy. Stupid. Irresponsible. I wanted to prove them all wrong."

He had never told me any of this. I'd never heard about this at all.

"I tried. So damn hard." He blinked rapidly. "I needed to stay awake. That's…that's how it started. I wanted to be awake and alert. First it was pills. Then powder. Then pretending it was all under control and that I could stop at any time."

He flinched. It was small, but I saw it.

"It spun outta control too quickly. How could I tell you and your mother that their father became an addict? So I needed to solve it on my own. I really thought I could."

I exhaled hard, throat tight.

"I did something, Pops," I told him, and this time I looked away. "Back when things got bad. Right after the scandal, right after everyone pulled out. We needed capital. No one would touch us. I was desperate."

He stayed quiet.

"I took money from someone I shouldn't have. A man named Victor Raines. On paper, it was a private loan. Off the record, it was…dirtier. He's got ties. You know the kind and he's back in all kinds of shit. Bad shit that can ruin all of us."

Pops's jaw flexed.

"But I'm handling it," I added quickly.

Pops leaned forward slowly, elbows on his knees.

"I'm leaving the company."

He looked up at me, brows furrowed. "Miles—"

"My mind is made up. Ma knows what to do."

Standing, I patted Pops on the shoulder before I headed out of their place. I was halfway down the steps when I got a call from an unknown number.

"Miles Whitmore?"

"Who's asking?"

"This is Burke Hale. I'm a private investigator. I think you might be an associate of Victor Raines?"

I stopped walking.

"You might be able to help me."

CHAPTER 32

Serena

DONE.

The last of the protestors had either lost interest or we paid off or were gone. No more shanty towns in front of the office, no more bad publicity. Everything at the office was going back to normal. What was more important was telling my parents my decision.

If Miles could do it, so could I.

I could tell them I was stepping down. Leaving King Developments.

My stomach flipped, but I forced a steady breath through my nose. I could do this. I *would* do this.

That's when I felt it—a slight weight, a cautious movement—and I looked down just in time to see Doughboy, Miles's smug, lazy furball of a cat, leap into my lap like it was his rightful throne.

I froze.

He…had never done that before. He might have lain next to me, placed his head, but fully laid in my lap?

My heart did a skip.

"You little demon," I muttered, stunned.

Doughboy purred and curled himself into a ball, content as ever, and I held my breath looking down at him. Slowly I lowered my hand, threading it through his orange fur.

My lips twitched. I hated this cat. I had *said* I hated this cat. But right now, I couldn't bring myself to move him.

I took a sip of my coffee, trying—and failing—not to smile.

"Don't think this makes us cool," I whispered, scratching behind his ears anyway.

Someone knocked on my front door. I sucked my teeth, leaning forward to place my coffee on the table, but when I tried to move Doughboy, the massive cat wouldn't budge.

"Ugh," I groaned, and taking a dare, I started to lift him off me, expecting claws or protest.

But to my amazement…he stayed.

His green eyes blinked up at me, and he made a low purring sound, like he approved.

"Well, this is new," I muttered, rising to my feet with a Maine coon draped in my arms like some ridiculous accessory. "You've got maybe ten seconds before I remember I'm allergic to love."

I crossed to the front door, hugging the cat close, and I peeked through the glass. And froze.

Daddy was standing there.

Straight-backed. Hands in his coat pockets.

My stomach dropped.

"Serena," he said, his voice just clear enough to carry through the door.

"What are you doing here?" I asked.

I didn't open the door.

"Open the door."

I dropped my head forward, and inhaled deeply, before maneuvering Doughboy enough to open the front door.

"I'm busy," I said.

Daddy lifted a brow before walking in anyway. "It's been a while since I've been over."

I closed the door behind him, holding Doughboy tighter as if he could give some kinda of comfort.

"I see you like pets now." Daddy pointed at the cat.

"I don't. He just wouldn't get off my lap." I crossed the room quickly, going to sit on the couch. Placing Doughboy back into my lap, I petted him slowly, and I heard him begin to purr.

"So—"

"What do we need to talk about?" I said in a clipped voice. "I meant what I said, I'm busy."

"I know you, Serena. We need to talk about what you saw."

I looked away, and Daddy took a seat in the chair across from me. His face was drawn, and he even leaned forward, picked up my coffee cup, and took a sip.

He raised a brow. "Is this…Kopi Luwak?"

"Yes." I didn't even blink. "You can get your own cup in the kitchen."

"This is fine with me," he said.

I watched him finish my coffee before he set the cup down, and sighed.

"It wasn't what you think."

"Then what was it?"

This time, Daddy rubbed his face, scratching his beard, and his brown eyes met mine. "I wanted to talk to her about your mother. About maybe…helping. Maybe rekindling their friendship again."

"Helping? You needed to talk to her three hours away for that?"

He let out a long breath. "Your mama's been off lately. More than usual."

"What do you mean off?" My stomach tightened.

"She's having some health issues," he said slowly, his gaze dropping to the floor like he was searching for the right way to lie gently. "She won't admit it, but she's tired, Serena. Bone-tired."

I didn't say anything.

"I don't know how long she's gonna last running all of this. It's like…" He paused, scrubbing a hand over his face. "It's like she's trying to deny reality. We're getting older, not younger, sweetie. Time is wearing all of us down."

"She should see someone—"

"She won't. You know your mother. Pride before anything. But between the press, the protestors, losing Ben, everything with Laurene and Gigi…" His eyes met mine. "And you—she's stretched thin."

I swallowed, the weight of it hitting deeper than I wanted to admit.

"She's not invincible, Serena. None of us are."

My jaw tightened.

"So now it's my fault?"

He shook his head. "Never. But when I look at you, I see more of your mama in you than I'd like."

I ran a hand down Doughboy's back, needing something to do with my hands. "That supposed to be a compliment?"

Daddy gave a small smile. "It's supposed to mean I worry. You inherited her ambition, her grit, but you also inherited that tendency to carry everything like the world would fall apart if you dropped even one thing. I thought you would grow out of it when you were a kid… You never did, you've always been high strung."

I stayed quiet, still petting the cat.

"But lately," he added, "I've seen you smile more. You've been spending time with your sisters again. You're not breathing and bleeding this business twenty-four seven like you used to. I thought we'd never see the day."

I blinked, unsure what to say.

"I'm proud of you, Rena. I know it probably doesn't sound like it coming from me, but I am."

I frowned. "Now you're proud of me? After almost thirty

years, you're proud? That's all I ever wanted from you and Mama, but now I'm with Miles and you're proud?"

"Don't take it that way—"

"The reality is, you and Mama were not good parents to me."

Daddy went silent and you could hear a pin drop in the room.

"You sat back, passive, Daddy. Like your family didn't have just as much money as Mama. You let her push us, you let her run Laurene away. You let her push Gigi away. You watched her burn me out, and you didn't do a damn thing."

He bowed his head. Quiet. Not arguing. Just listening.

"Only Erik got to be his own person. Was it because he's a boy? Because he's the firstborn?"

His eyes flicked up at that. But I wasn't done.

"I've spent my whole life chasing your approval. Sacrificing my joy for a nod, a pat on the back. I never got to make a choice that was just *mine.*" I swallowed. "But now I have. I chose Miles. I chose me. And for once, I don't care if you or Mama approve."

His face was unreadable. And I hated how much I still looked for the flicker of emotion in it.

"I'm tired," I said at last. "And I'm done pretending that all this didn't hurt."

Daddy made a face but nodded. "I'm going to tell you, like I told your sister Laurene on her wedding day. You are right."

I glared at him.

"We were not good parents to you."

That hit me like a ton of bricks; the force of it left me breathless and stunned.

"We haven't been good to all of you," he said, voice lower now. "We watched you shape yourself around this family. Around your mother. Around what people expected. And we let you."

He didn't look at me when he said it. He stared off like he was ashamed. Like he couldn't bear to see what it did to me.

"You learned to survive in two worlds—one for us, one for

everyone else. You didn't complain, and we took that as permission. We thought your silence meant you were okay with how things were."

Then slowly, he rose from his chair. I stiffened as he stepped around the coffee table and knelt down beside me.

He reached for my hand first, then pulled me into a hug. Not the kind I was used to—stiff, short, impersonal. This one stayed. Doughboy meowed between us.

I didn't hug him back at first. My hands were still curled in my lap.

"So I had to break for you to notice?" I asked, bitter and small.

His voice cracked. "I think you've been breaking for a long time. We just chose not to see it."

That hit deep. Too deep.

"You've done enough," he said into my hair. "You are enough, Serena. You always have been."

I swallowed, emotion hitting me harder than I wanted. I didn't like this feeling.

"I'm gonna go on a sabbatical, once we finish renovations. I… need to be away for a while."

His hand stilled on my back.

For a moment, he didn't say anything. I could feel the hesitation in him—the way his breath caught, the way his fingers gently curled into the fabric of my shirt like he didn't want to let go just yet.

"A sabbatical," he repeated.

Then he pulled back enough to look at me. His eyes were glassy.

"You deserve that. You do."

He straightened his spine but didn't stand, like part of him was bracing for something heavier. I tangled my fingers in Doughboy's hair deeper.

"Just…prepare yourself."

My brow furrowed.

"For what?"

He gave me that look I remembered from childhood—the one he gave before he handed out consequences he didn't agree with, but stood by anyway.

"You know your mother," he said gently. "She doesn't take change lightly."

He paused, then added, "But you need to tell her. Not me."

"Why not you?" I asked.

He shook his head. "You need to step into your power. Finish what you've started."

Finally, Daddy released me, standing up to his full height.

"I'll let you get back to it," he said, voice low. "But I meant what I said. I'm proud of you, Serena. I always have been. I just didn't say it enough."

He turned, heading toward the door. I stood frozen, Doughboy still curled in my lap like a warm weight. I shook my head, placed Doughboy on the couch, and shot up.

"Daddy—wait."

He paused in the doorway.

I rushed toward him before I could second-guess myself and wrapped my arms around him. He stilled for a moment. Then his arms came around me, strong and sure. A real hug. I couldn't remember the last time I'd gotten.

"I love you, Rena," he.

I swallowed hard. "I love you too."

Releasing me, he took a step back, and started to leave but paused, and turned.

"Wait, why were you at the polo match?"

My chest tightened, but I forced a small shrug.

"I was tracking a potential acquisition," I lied. "Someone said some of my leads might be looking to offload a few properties."

He squinted slightly, not fully convinced.

"Spur of the moment."

"Hmm." He didn't press further.

"But I am late," I said, ushering him out the door.

He nodded, before turning and saying, "Listen to your heart."

"That didn't take you long," I said, stepping back into Dante's office.

"I admit, I was very, *very* curious about your situation." Dante leaned back in his seat. "I just had to know what happened. It's like a soap opera."

I pressed my lips together, taking the seat across from him. "You watch soap operas?"

"I grew up with telenovelas."

Asking for help was still strangely uncomfortable for me. I was so used to doing things by myself. But Jenese wasn't someone who I could defeat on my own. I recognize my limitations now.

"Start from the beginning." Dante said. "Tell me everything."

I released a deep breath, looking to the right outside the window to our coastal town.

"It started like any other partnership." I kept my voice even, but my fingers curled slightly against the edge of the seat. "You know how Laurene left after the Ashbourne incident. Mama needed help running King Developments at the beginning. Erik didn't have time to get the company off the ground. So I volunteered. I wanted it. Wanted to show my mother what I could do."

I sucked my teeth, thinking back to the moment.

"But I was in way over my head. I don't need to tell you who my mother is. But she didn't have the patience to really teach me. All of that went to Erik. When I met Jenese, I guess..." *What was I then? Dumb? Desperate? Lonely?* "I was easily influenced by what she could teach me. I thought I could impress Mama. Jenese had all this money, accomplishments, and seemed like a successful businesswoman. So I went along."

"Hmm." He leaned forward, lacing his fingers on the desk between us. "You said you found a photo of us?"

I nodded. "With someone named Roman Tolland?"

"Roman…" Dante sighed. "Yeah, he was a good friend of mine."

A sad look crossed his expression.

"Was?"

"He's dead," Dante said plainly. "Killed himself a few years ago."

I inhaled sharply, leaning back in the seat. "Jesus."

"Yeah. I never believed his death was a suicide." Dante's voice was quieter now. "Roman had enemies. And secrets. I can't prove it wasn't but…Roman ran blackmail networks. Staged bankruptcies. Managed offshore accounts."

"Why would you call someone like that a friend?" I asked, narrowing my gaze on him.

"You never know who you're going to need help from."

I rolled my eyes. Criminals were not allies. But it wasn't like I could talk.

"He was turning things around, if you want to believe it, then he met Jenese and everything unraveled."

"When was this?"

"About two or three years ago." Dante tapped his finger on the desk. "I had seen her before with some other wealthy guys. Didn't think anything of it—who am I to judge who's in somebody's bed? I thought she was too old for him. I just…had an uneasy feeling about her. She gets with one of these men, then suddenly everything goes wrong."

"You think she's a black widow?"

Has Jenese just been causing chaos everywhere she went? Was she killing men now?

"When Roman died, he left her everything. I heard recently

she's with some guy who runs cons down in LA, but we'll see how long that lasts."

Fuck, how did I get here? I couldn't let her harm anyone in my family. I had to protect them.

"Alright," he said, switching gears, "let's stop talking in circles. What do you have, Serena? Evidence."

I nodded. "She had me place a USB in Alan Price's laptop. I took a picture. I also have another photo of the box she had me leave for Jasper. I recorded my last conversation with her."

Dante whistled under his breath. "You've been sitting on gold."

"Is it? It's not enough to intimidate her, I show someone *two things* when she has years of dirt on me."

"It's about how you spin it, Serena. You're going to have to get over that black-and-white morality thing you got going on."

I made a face at him.

"Now my methods are...not as stringent as yours, but they get results. If she's blackmailing you, we need to threaten her entire system and how she operates," Dante said. "If we cut off her source, she'll be willing to bargain."

"What source?" I said. "And what exactly are you suggesting?"

Dante stood, walked over to the window, and stared out for a moment like he was already playing it out in his head.

"We bait her," he said. "With me."

I blinked. "You want to get involved?"

He turned back, eyes gleaming. "She knows me. Knows my name carries weight here. If I reach out and say I've got an interest in her—want to talk business, maybe something more—it'll stroke that ego of hers just enough to make her reckless."

My stomach twisted. "You're going to *flirt* with her?"

"Please." He smirked. "I don't have to try. I have a private property just outside of town, a nice bottle of wine, and an invitation to 'talk discreetly.' She won't be able to resist. We'll be alone, which is perfect for what you need to do."

"Which is?"

"She'll find you there instead. You'll be wearing a wire. Plus the evidence you have collected already is more than enough, just put the nail in her coffin. Get her to talk. I'll get her off your back and get that manuscript."

I exhaled, chest tight. "You really think this will work?"

Dante smiled. But it wasn't comforting. It was razor-sharp.

"It will."

CHAPTER 33
Serena

I WAS IN CONTROL.

Miles was under me, his body stretched out, eyes dark and dazed, lips parted as I rode him like I owned him. His hands gripped my thighs and his brown skin gleamed with sweat beneath me, his chest rising fast.

His mouth had been everywhere—my breasts still tingled, nipples swollen and aching where he'd sucked me earlier.

Miles usually took the lead, and I let him. I liked letting him take care of me.

I rubbed his shoulders, kissed his temple, whispered soft against his skin, "Let me take care of you."

He didn't say no.

Now he was under me, and I was moving slow, rolling my hips in deep, steady circles. And I could feel it—how close he was, how much he needed this.

"You awake now?" I teased, sweet and low, letting the rhythm slow just enough to make him whimper. His eyes fluttered like he couldn't handle it.

He let out this deep, wrecked groan that made my pussy clench around him tighter. His voice rasped against my skin,

"Hell yeah… Goddamn, baby. Pussy grippin' me like she don't want me goin' nowhere."

His hands locked around my ass, pulling me down harder, and I mewled—soft, desperate, needy. God, I needed this too.

"I just wanna make you feel good…" I whispered against his lips, kissing him slow, deep, tasting every inch like I was claiming him all over again. Then I picked up the pace, grinding down on him with purpose.

His dick curved just right, hitting that perfect spot deep inside me, again and again, until my whole body buzzed. And when his palm cracked against my ass, sharp and hot, I moaned loud, grinding deeper like it fed me.

I broke the kiss and trailed down his jaw, brushing soft kisses over his skin before I whispered, low and breathy, "Am I makin' you feel good, Miles?"

My tongue flicked over his earlobe, then I nipped it lightly with my teeth—and that sound he made? Broke me open.

A whimper. A real, broken, raw sound.

"F-fuck, baby…yeah," he panted. "You doin' so good. So fuckin' good."

I felt it in my core—tight, hot, surging. My hips moved faster, chasing it. The pressure building until I couldn't hold it anymore. Until my thighs were shaking, my fingers digging into his chest. "Miles—"

And then I shattered.

Clenching around him, pulsing, crying out as the pleasure tore through me.

He groaned deep in his chest, thrusting up into me once, twice—and then he was gone too, head thrown back, body jerking beneath me as he came hard into the condom.

I collapsed on top of him, breath tangled with his, heart racing.

He didn't say anything for a moment. Just wrapped his arms around me, holding me tight. "If you want…I'll come with you."

I lifted my head, blinked down at him, still catching my breath.

But I shook my head slowly, brushing my thumb over his cheek. "You need to finish the renovations. You're already behind."

He studied me like he wanted to argue, but I pressed a kiss to his lips—soft and sweet—and that was enough.

My phone started buzzing on the nightstand.

I sighed, rolled off him, and reached over to grab it.

Mama.

I answered, trying to catch my voice. "Hello?"

"I'm at the office," she said, curt and clipped. "Get here."

The line went dead.

I stared at the screen for a beat before tossing the phone aside and slipping out of bed. I made it to the office in record time, and as I stepped into my office I said, "Mama, I—"

I froze.

Erik was standing with his back to the door, staring outside the window. He turned slowly around, and he gave me a half smile. "Wassup, Rena."

"Where's Mama?"

"She's here," Erik said.

My knuckles went white as I gripped the strap of my purse tighter, the weight of its contents pressing into my side. Before he could speak, before I could think better of it, I walked up to him and my hand flew. The slap rang out, a sound like a gunshot that filled the room.

Erik's head jerked sideways, spit flying from his mouth as he stumbled a step back.

"How dare you?" I asked Erik. "Why? Miles was your best friend and you brutalize him in that way? What? Is he an easy target for you? Like everyone else in this town thinks?" I glared at Erik.

"Don't you *ever* put your hands on my husband again."

Erik's jaw flexed, but he didn't respond.

"Oh, I get it." I laughed, bitter and cold. "You didn't do it for *me*. You did it for you. For your little ego. For the messed-up sense of brotherly affection you *finally* decide to have after twenty years because you have a vendetta."

"He didn't tell you?" he asked.

"Tell me what?"

"I have *always* loved you," Erik said defensively.

"Miles makes me feel like a woman. Not like some toss-away in this family. It's always been *you*. Then Laurene. And Gigi. *Then* me. I won't let any of you run him away, and you need to get over yourself and whatever problem you have with him. Is it that bad you can't get over it?"

I swallowed hard, blinking through the burn.

"You get everything! Let me have Miles. Treat him with respect. Did you even consider how that would make me feel? To always come last?"

"I didn't ask for this, Rena," Erik said quietly.

"Of course you didn't ask for it!" I snapped. "But you took it. And Mama gave. Everyone *gave and gave*."

"All the shit I do is for you, Laurene, and Gigi to not have to deal with the bullshit. So you all can live your lives. You think I didn't notice? I saw the way Mama treated you. I hated it."

He dragged a hand down his face, like it burned to say this.

"You know who told Mama to start King Developments?" He stepped closer. "Me. 'Cause I saw you reading them architecture books all the time. You ain't even know I was paying attention, huh?"

His voice dropped. "I didn't want the company. She offered it to me, and I told her I was too busy. But I knew you'd kill it."

I sucked in a sharp breath.

"You think I wanted to inherit all of this? I wake up every day wondering if I'm fuckin' it all up. You know what it's like to carry this family and have nobody ask if you tired? If you scared? If you *can't* do it one more goddamn day?"

I looked away.

"I kept it together for all of us. I hold the line so you don't have to," he said, softer now, eyes rimmed red. "You don't even know the things we've kept from you all. But some days, I don't even know who the hell I am outside of holding this shit down."

He exhaled like he'd been holding that in for years.

"When Laurene wanted to run off, who booked her flight?" He kept going. "When Gigi got picked up in LA for drinking, I bailed her out before anybody in the family knew. You think Miles the only one out here protecting you?"

He beat a hand against his chest. "Have you asked how I was doing? Just once in the last six years? I lost my best friend too."

For so many years, I'd had this one-sided competition with Erik, and now for him to say he created King Developments for me?

"You really think this is about me being petty toward Miles?" Erik said. "It's not. It's because he's hiding things from you, Serena. Big things."

I crossed my arms, and gave him a sour look.

"Miles is doing business with a known criminal. Victor Raines." Erik's voice was clipped. "He took money from him years ago. And a few weeks ago, I saw the bastard leaving Miles's office." I stared at Erik like he'd grown a second head. "No. No, that's—no, you must've seen someone else. Miles wouldn't—he's not—"

Erik's expression didn't change.

"He is. I know what I saw. And I *know* what I'm talkin' about."

I shook my head. "How do you even know this?"

"Miles told me years ago when he first got the money from Victor. I didn't trust the man, so I looked into him. I told Miles, but he didn't care."

His eyes searched mine. "That's one of the reason he and I fell out. I didn't want his shit to affect us."

My chest squeezed tight. Miles *never* told me. Not once. Not even when we were—

"Victor's name been tied to an open Fed investigation. An employee died under mysterious circumstances and other bad shit. I came to your office one night to talk to him about it, maybe put our shit to the side. I found them together… We don't really know Miles. What if all this has been a big 'get back' at us because of what I did—"

"What did you do?" I said darkly.

"You remember the whistleblower from back when Omar got exposed? The one who tipped off the press?"

His jaw flexed.

"It was me."

"Erik!" I exclaimed, and I turned away from him, running a hand through my hair as I paced.

For years, I remembered the night it came on the news about Omar being arrested. They'd only said a whistleblower. Mama and Daddy were shocked. Everyone was.

No one ever said it was us.

That we did it.

That it was my family who took them down.

"That's why he hated me?" I asked him. "That's why you've both been at each other's throats?"

Erik looked away and nodded.

"I did it," he said. "I told them everything. I didn't do it to hurt you or Miles—I did it because it was right. Omar needed help. I have a responsibility to this town and what it looks like. And no one else was going to step up."

I stood there, reeling, my heart cracking wide open. I didn't even know who I was mad at more—Miles for keeping secrets, or Erik for doing the same.

I remembered the way Miles looked after the scandal— hollowed out, humiliated. I remembered what people said about the Whitmores, how their name got dragged through every gutter in Lush. And all that time…it was *us*.

Erik.

My own damn brother.

My hands trembled, rage and betrayal coiling tight inside me like a snake about to strike.

"You never thought I deserved to know? Either of you?"

My voice cracked at the end, and I hated it. Hated how small I sounded.

The door opened, and Mama finally came in.

"Oh, you're both here," she said. "Let's talk about your disrespectful behavior, Serena."

I blinked. "Excuse me?"

I glanced at Erik, and he didn't even look at me.

"You defending that boy at our dinner when you need to be on your family's side first and foremost. Or has living with him corrupted your brain?"

"I just think we should move on," I said.

"Move on?"

Erik inhaled deeply.

"Move on?" Mama repeated. "I should just…*move on*." Her hands flexed at her sides. "You want to *forgive* the same family that almost ruined ours? That trial nearly ruined us like it did them. People were questioning *us*. We *are* this town. You think because you're playing house with Miles Whitmore I'm supposed to *pretend*?"

"Mama—"

"No. You listen." Her voice cracked like a whip. "I carried this family's name on my back when your grandfather died. I rebuilt this company from nothing while people whispered that King women couldn't lead. I fought for respect from men who wanted to pat me on the head and make me disappear. And now you want to *move on*?"

Her chest heaved once, and then she narrowed her eyes at me.

"You are not obligated to protect *him*, Serena. You are obligated to protect *this family*."

The silence that followed was deafening.

"Do you think he'd choose *you* if his company wasn't in

flames?"

Erik shifted uncomfortably. "Mama—"

"Tell me, Serena. Do you have feelings for him?"

I froze.

"Yes or no?" she snapped.

My fingers curled into my palm. My first instinct was to say no. To lie. To fold.

But I didn't.

"Yes, I love him."

Mama's lips thinned. "You just can't do what's right, can you?"

She looked between us and shook her head.

"Erik, you're taking over King Developments. Serena, you will step down."

"What!"

Erik looked just as shocked.

"You're compromised. Emotionally. Professionally."

"Compromised?" I echoed. "I'm compromised?"

"I put you in that marriage to keep this family alive, not so you could get swept up playing house."

That hit like a slap.

"You forced me into that marriage," I hissed. "Did you know all of this is really just our fault?"

"Watch your tone," she warned.

"Why? Afraid I'll finally say what everyone else is too scared to?"

"Miles didn't put his family in this position. Erik did. *You* did. Chasing legacies, pretending we're above people who *bled* for this town just like we did."

Mama's lips curled. "You've forgotten who you are."

"That may be true," I said, stepping forward, "but you forgot who *we* were first. You forgot we were human."

"You didn't need to get sucked into his pity party."

"Did you say the same thing to Laurene?" My voice sharpened like a blade. "Or was the goalpost different for her than it's always been for me?"

Her expression didn't flicker, but I saw the way her fingers clenched at her sides.

"You really do have feelings for this boy?" she said with disdain.

"Miles," I corrected her, chin lifting. "His name is Miles. And he wasn't just some boy. He was our *friend*. His family was our *family*. Their blood, their roots—*they're in this soil too.*"

She opened her mouth, but I cut her off, the words pouring out like a dam breaking.

"You can rewrite history all you want, but you *know* the truth. We built this town with the Whitmores. You used to smile in their faces. Let their checks fund your galas. Now you wanna pretend like we were always better than them?"

Mama stiffened. "I built you for better than this, Serena. *Better.*"

"No," I said, the word like iron in my throat. "You built a version of me that served *you*. That kept quiet. That smiled and nodded and outperformed and outmaneuvered, because God forbid I *fail* or *feel* or be anything less than perfect."

She tried to cut in, but I wasn't done.

"Did you teach me anything, Mama?" I kept going. "Or were you too busy putting a crown on Laurene's head? Taking Erik to board meetings? Only looking at Gigi when she became a liability?"

I stepped closer, the heat rising in my chest.

"And me? I've been your cleanup crew. Your strategist. Your buffer. I've been everything for *everybody*—and you didn't even notice or have the fucking decency to care about me. *Your daughter.*"

Mama's face was unreadable. "You wanna throw this fit now?"

My laugh came sharp and humorless. "This isn't a fit. This is me finally waking the hell up."

"I gave you *everything*," she hissed.

"Maybe, but not everything!" I shouted. "I shouldn't have had to *fight* for my own mother's love!"

For a moment, we just stood there, breathing hard, locked in a war a decade in the making.

"Love and attention, that's all I wanted," I said. "For you to take the time, between all your power moves and your damn obsession with controlling everything, to look at me. *See* what my strengths were. Just like you invested into Erik and Laurene. It's that simple, Mama.

"Don't worry about taking the company from me, I came here to tell you I quit."

"Rena—" Erik said.

"No, Erik. I've spent too many years pouring into this family, I didn't give anything to myself. I'm leaving, I'm taking my work with me and spending time with my man."

Mama's eyebrows lifted.

"I won't be used. I won't be treated like a bargaining chip. Or the backup daughter. Until you can pull your own head out of your ass and treat me with the same reverence you give Erik and Laurene, Mama...we're done. Don't call me. Don't ask for me. Don't look for me until you can look me in the eye and take accountability for what you've done."

Then I turned and walked away. Not a stumble. Not a look back. And for the first time in my life, I didn't feel like I was breaking apart.

I felt like I was finally whole.

CHAPTER 34

Miles

I PARKED FAR from the bar, finding the cool night air refreshing as I leaned against my car.

You're doing the right thing, Miles.

Protecting Serena was my priority. After that, my family. I needed Victor's real story.

A car pulled in, its lights blinding before it crawled toward me, and the door opened.

"You're Whitmore?" he asked.

My mouth was dry. "It depends."

The man stepped forward.

Late middle-aged, unremarkable face. Average height and build. Worn jacket, scuffed boots, weary eyes.

"I'm Burke," he stated.

It had to be ironic or pure fucking luck that somebody looking into Victor found me.

Who else would be able to find me and put two and two together? But…this could also work with my plan. I could do what I couldn't before, and get ahead of the scandal before it all went down.

"Mind if I ask how you found me?"

Burke gave a small shrug. "Wasn't easy. I've been tracking

Victor down for months—turns out he's slippery. But he kept showing up in Lush. Odd little town for a guy like him."

My brows lifted. "And?"

"And one day, I caught him talking to you."

I paused. "Interesting. You tell anyone else that?"

"Do you want me talking about it?"

"What do you need from me, exactly?" I asked.

"I was hired by one of the families suing Victor—he conned them out of a lot of money and justice. I just need something that will stick on Victor and make the cops do a double take."

"And you think I'm the missing piece to solve this?"

"I think you're the only person he's stupid enough to keep orbiting. He doesn't trust anyone, but he keeps showing up near you. That means something. I need to know what he wants from you. What he's planning."

I inhaled deeply, and nodded.

"I'm not asking you to go public. I'm not asking you to wear a wire. I'm just asking you to give me what you know about him. Paperwork. Notes. Evidence. Anything to prove he's into some shady shit."

"What if I can get you a live confession?"

To move forward with Serena, we needed to leave the past behind. We had to put a stop to it, finally.

I leaned in. "I have an idea, if you're game."

The loud squeak of the condo door made me wince. The living room suddenly burst into light.

"You're home," Serena said in a flat voice. Doughboy lay beside her on the couch. Sitting up, she looked tense, her face all pinched.

"Where were you?" she asked, her eyes searching my face for an answer.

"At Mrs. Fontaine's place."

Serena tsked. "That's lie number one."

"What?"

"I went by the property. They told me you weren't there." she said calmly.

I shifted my weight, trying to keep my voice casual. "I had to step away for a bit. Handle a few things. How did it go with Miss Yvonne?"

"Don't." Her eyes narrowed. "Answer my question."

Just tell her. Confess. It'll be better that way. "Erik told me about Victor."

My breath stalled, heart hammering once—hard—before the panic settled in.

"You—what?"

Her jaw clenched. "You lied to me."

"No, I—" I ran a hand down my face. "I didn't lie. I just didn't…tell you."

"Which is a lie, Miles."

He told her. He fucking told her.

I opened my mouth, but the words felt like shards in my throat. Because she was right.

I'd been hiding Victor from her since the beginning. Not out of malice—at least, that's what I told myself—but because if she knew the truth, everything would crumble.

"Serena," I started. "I was trying to protect you."

Her laugh was bitter and quiet. "Don't insult me."

"It's not what you think—"

"No, just…let me finish." Her tone wavered for a split second, but the steel was still there. "I get it, Miles. I do. I know you've had to make choices—do things you probably hated just to survive. To protect your company. I'm not blind to that."

She took a breath, jaw tense.

"But you should've told me. I'm your wife. You don't get to make decisions that could wreck both of us and then keep me in the dark. That's also why you should have told me the real reason you and Erik aren't friends."

"He told you that too?"

"Yeah. He told me everything. That he was the one who blew the whistle on your dad."

Silence pressed down, thick and heavy.

So it was out. Finally out.

"He said he didn't want to," she added quietly. "But after what happened at that party, after what your father did to my dad, Erik said he couldn't stay quiet."

My throat burned. "He didn't have to do it."

"Come on, Miles. You know Erik. He's always had a bigger sense of loyalty than you—especially when it comes to family. It was only a matter of time. And deep down…you knew that."

Serena watched me closely, taking a step. "Unless that was your plan."

"What?"

"You didn't want to deal with your father. You didn't want the responsibility of turning him in or confronting what he did. Erik knew. You kept stalling and let him do it."

I looked away. The air was suddenly too thick.

"You didn't have to betray your father," she said, voice low, "because Erik did it for you. And you've hated him ever since for taking the choice out of your hands when you should have owned it."

"That's my father, Serena."

She shook her head. "And now I'm your wife. What if that was going on today? Would you choose him or me?"

I turned from her, pacing the living room. "I kept hoping he'd stop. That he'd fix it before it got worse. That if I just held the line, kept the gossip off us, kept the company from crumbling, he'd wake up and fight for it too."

Her silence was brutal.

"How do you deal with that? Watching the man you spent

your whole life looking up to…crumble right in front of you? How do you reconcile that?"

"You don't." Her voice was calm. "You adjust. You grieve what you thought he was. And then you face what he really is."

I shook my head, and this time, she was in front of me and reached out.

"Tell me the truth. Was all of this…what we have now…just your plan to get back at us? At me?"

That hit harder than it should've. I staggered back like she'd slapped me.

"Don't fucking do that," I hissed. "Don't act like this was all some scheme. I didn't fake what we had. I love you."

She inhaled sharply, then closed her eyes, pressing her fingers to the bridge of her nose. When she looked at me again, the heat in her expression had cooled—but it wasn't forgiveness. Just fatigue.

"I just need a break, Miles." Her voice was quieter now. "To think. To breathe. We can talk in the morning."

"Serena—"

"I'm not saying I'm done. I'm saying I'm tired." She stepped around me and headed down the hall, her shoulders square, her spine straight.

Doughboy didn't even stay.

The traitor trailed after her, tail flicking as he passed me.

She paused at the end of the hall. Glanced over her shoulder.

"I love you too," she said softly. "But right now, that's not the only thing that matters."

Then she disappeared into the bedroom, the door closing behind her with a soft click that felt louder than any scream.

CHAPTER 35

Serena

I LAY on the bed all day. I heard Miles moving through the apartment, but I didn't make a move to talk. I wasn't as upset with him anymore.

I felt stupid.

Miles had his own secrets, and I still had mine.

But more, I had confronted Mama.

I told her how I felt. I tried not to feel some kind of way when she didn't call. I expected that. If I was going to start putting myself first, I couldn't worry about her feelings anymore.

Eventually, I managed to get up, but when I walked into the kitchen, Miles was nowhere to be found. Doughboy followed, hopping onto the kitchen island, and meowing at me.

The cat hadn't left me all night.

"I don't know about our friendship," I told the cat. "Don't get used to it."

My phone vibrated in my pocket and I pulled it out. A text from Dante lit the screen.

Jenese is making a move. Told her I'd take her out tonight. My place outside town. 9PM. You need to be ready.

My heart caught in my throat. He sent the address a second

later, and a cold rush of nerves slithered through me, sharp and electric.

This was it—the moment I'd been waiting for and dreading all at once.

I stepped out of the car, my breath visible in the cool night air.

I pulled up at Dante's property, following his instructions to take the back entrance so Jenese wouldn't spot me.

We were about an hour out of town, up in the windy hills.

All mayors traditionally lived in the mayor's mansion in town, so why did Dante have property out here in the middle of nowhere? I was clueless. You couldn't really see the house from the road; it was hidden by the pines. I snuck along the back path, my boots crunching on the gravel. I could hear the waves below, a reminder of how close we were to the cliff edge.

The door opened in front of me, and a shadow of a person forced me back onto the wall of the house. "Wait!" Dante hissed.

The suit, shoes, and politician's mask were gone. He wore a black henley, dark jeans, and scuffed boots. His jaw, unshaven, was tight.

Not my type, but Gigi's. I could see why she was flirting with him.

"You ready?" he asked.

I nodded.

"I convinced her to bring her laptop. She's tipsy. Use that to your advantage."

I half expected her to be behind him.

"I told her I was getting more wine. I distracted her with my album collection."

I lifted a brow. "You have an album collection?"

"Not now, King." Dante rolled his eyes. "I know we said wire, but I did something better. I have some cameras hidden.

One in the vase on the table. The other in the mini statue on the mantel. Stand by those, make sure you speak loudly and clearly, and you'll have everything you need."

I made a face. "You handled everything for me?"

"Nothing is ever free, remember that about me." He reached into his coat pocket and pulled out a small envelope.

"If she starts giving you shit, show her this. She's gonna fucking lose it."

I pulled it from his fingers and opened it. My breath hitched.

Inside was a photo. Grainy. But unmistakable.

Jenese. Younger. In a hotel room.

"Where did you get this?"

"I told you. It pays to have friends."

I looked back down at it and nodded, sliding it into my pocket.

Dante stepped in closer, just a breath of space between us now. "You've got ten, maybe fifteen minutes before she gets antsy. Make it count. I'll be around."

"Around?" That didn't sound comforting, and it was almost the middle of nowhere. "What if she tries to bolt?" I asked.

"She won't." He placed a hand on my shoulder, squeezing once before stepping back toward the path where I'd parked. "I'll be watching," he said again.

I stepped inside, the music growing louder. I saw the bottle of Riesling on the counter, and I grabbed it, moving slowly through the kitchen into the front of the house.

Candles were everywhere.

Thick ones, thin ones, tall tapers balanced on brass holders, and fat tealights flickering across shelves and windowsills. Their soft gold glow lit the space in a romantic haze, casting shifting shadows against the walls and ceiling.

I paused just inside the threshold, fingers tightening around the wine bottle. My heartbeat was steady and low, but my nerves buzzed just beneath the surface. This time, I wasn't here to react —I was here to finish it.

You've faced worse. You've outmaneuvered boardrooms, lawsuits, your own damn family. This is just another challenge. You love a challenge.

I forced a breath through my nose, smoothed a hand down my side, and stepped forward.

Her back was turned to me. "Dante, darling...you have exquisite taste," Jenese purred, her tone syrupy and indulgent. Vinyls shuffled gently beneath her hand as she flipped through a crate of records on the floor.

She didn't turn.

"Miles Davis. Etta. A little Donny Hathaway? You've been hiding this side of you."

Then slowly she turned and saw me.

"Well, I suppose I shouldn't be surprised to see you," she said coolly, standing to her full height. "So *that's* what this is."

I held up the bottle of Riesling and offered her a smile. "I figured you were running low."

Behind her, I caught sight of the small marble statue on the mantel—the camera Dante had placed there. I moved toward it with practiced ease, crossing in front of the velvet-draped table set for two.

"Isn't Dante a little *young* for you?" I asked.

Jenese shrugged, pushing up her boobs. "Age is a state of mind. It's a good thing you're here. I wrote another chapter of the manuscript. But before that, I need your help with something else—"

"There was a time," I said softly, "when I craved your approval so badly, I would've done anything for it. Because I thought that's what I needed to succeed."

Jenese's face hardened.

"But I've outgrown you," I said. "Whatever game you were playing—whatever void I was trying to fill with you—it ends tonight."

"*Now* you have self-esteem?" She raised a brow, crossing her arms with a dark expression.

"No. What I have now is clarity."

She gave a bitter laugh. "You're not as sharp as you think, Serena. You really thought I wouldn't keep a copy of everything you've done? You were *pathetic* back then. I cared. I molded you, not even your own mother wanted to. How can a girl with opportunities people would *kill* for be so insecure and jealous? You're still that same little girl, no matter how big you're acting now. It won't ever change, honey, you just aren't the type of person people care about."

"Give me the manuscript. Every copy you have, and we part ways amicably."

Jenese laughed in my face. "You must be doing crack like your father-in-law."

"I'm not here to beg," I said. "I'm offering you a courtesy. But if you want to play—fine." I pulled out the photo Dante gave me.

Her face fell. "A picture is not going to scare me."

"I'll leak it," I said. "That photo, everything we've done—I send it all. Not just to the press. But to every man you've charmed. Every politician you've lied to. Every investor. Every husband."

Her breath caught. She hid it well. But I heard it.

"You're bluffing."

"I don't work for King Developments anymore, so what happens to me is whatever. I can't be your cash cow anymore."

"I'm not leaving without the Harrington estate," she said, eyes glinting. "My partner needs that property. Badly."

I froze.

"Your what?"

"Did you really think I was working alone this whole time? No, sugar. You were never the only one." She shook her head. "Give it to me. Now."

"This photo isn't the only thing I have on you, Jenese. Just bow out gracefully. Don't go out pitiful." I gave her a look of disgust. "You've been played."

Something unhinged in her face. Then she lunged.

I barely had time to brace before she slammed into me, fingers clawing at the photo. We crashed against the dinner table, wineglasses tumbling, the edge of a plate cracking against the floor. My elbow struck the corner hard, and I hissed, but I held on to the photo like it was my last weapon.

"Let me go!" I screamed.

We struggled—hands grappling, knocking over a candelabra as we slammed against the wall. One of the tall candles tumbled to the floor near the velvet drapes.

I didn't see the flame at first. Not until I heard the soft hiss and the sudden whoosh of ignition.

"You ungrateful little bitch," Jenese snarled. "I'm the only one who cared about you. You were like a daughter to me! I taught you how to win!"

I saw a fire starting near the curtain, smoke rising. Jenese knocked me over with the wooden chair; it shattered when I fell.

"I gave you everything. You can give me this. I deserve it. I've worked so hard!"

"You didn't give me shit." I got up and shoved her—hard—but she came right back. She grabbed a fistful of my hair, jerking my head back, and the photo fluttered to the floor between us.

We both looked at it, and she went to dive for it, and that's when I saw it—the Riesling bottle, still standing on the edge of the table.

I grabbed it and swung.

CRACK.

Glass shattered against her shoulder and cheek. Wine sprayed everywhere—onto me, onto her, onto the floor. Jenese shrieked, stumbling back, hand flying to her face as blood ran bright and fast down her cheekbone and she collapsed.

Oh shit, I may have killed her.

The spilled alcohol lit up quickly. With terrifying speed, fire snaked up the corner of the wall. Smoke began to fill the room and I coughed as it filled my lungs.

Jenese, like something out of a horror film, slowly lifted up, and turned to me with bloodshot eyes. "I'll kill you before I let you leave with that photo or my property."

Just as the front door burst open.

MILES

Thirty Minutes before the Fire...

"This is a fucking mistake," I muttered to myself.

Why was I here when I should be back at my home, pleading with Serena? It was over, wasn't it? She wanted to tell me that we were done again. I couldn't...I couldn't let her walk away from me. If she looked me in the eye and said she was done, I still couldn't give up on us. I don't got that in me.

If I had to get on my knees every damn day and beg her not to go, I would.

This marriage? It might've started as some family arrangement—but somewhere along the line, it became mine. Ours. And I'd fight for it. For her. I loved her. Ain't no way was I letting her forget that.

I stepped to Erik's front door. I reached up to knock, but it swung open before I could.

"I told you *no*, Erik! I can do this on my own."

I was surprised to see Noelle rushing out of his house, fury in her face, buttoning up her shirt.

What the hell is going on here?

"Nellie." Erik followed after her, shirt open. "Please, just listen."

"No. Because if I listen, I'll stay," she bit out, spinning around to face him on the porch. "And you know I can't afford to stay."

"You already did," Erik said, voice low, intimate. "You stayed last night."

"That was a mistake. Stay out of my business, Erik."

I cleared my throat, suddenly feeling like a voyeur.

Both heads snapped toward me. Erik blinked in surprise. Noelle's face shuttered in an instant.

"Bad time, Short Stack?" I asked dryly.

Noelle didn't answer. She just pushed past us and got into her car, tires spinning out as she drove away.

"I can come back," I told him.

He stared longingly after Noelle, ignoring me. "What do you want?"

"Don't hook up with Noelle. I told you that *years* ago."

"I know," Erik snapped.

I stood on the porch, and sucked my teeth as I rocked back and forth on my heels. "You gonna let me in or what?"

Erik sent me a look before he turned, stalking back into his house. I followed with a chuckle, closing the door behind me.

"Your place is still dark as hell. You need to add some color," I muttered, following him down the hall. On his walls were pictures of his family. Serena, Laurene, Gigi at various ages in their youth. Some of his old football trophies, college degrees. A big photo of their late grandpa Ben.

Erik entered the kitchen and reached into the fridge. He popped the cap off his beer and slid one across the counter. I caught it, tapped it twice against the edge, and twisted it open. "Serena told you."

It wasn't a question.

"Yeah, it might have slipped out," I said, tanking the bottle. "So are we calling a truce, or just an extended timeout?"

"Truce implies we're on the same side." He shifted his weight, taking a sip of his beer.

"We always made better partners than rivals. Who else is gonna keep you in line, man?" I took a swig of the bottle. "Who else kept your ass from throwing hands at the country club every time some old-ass man looked at your mom sideways?"

Erik gave me a small smile.

"C'mon," I goaded him. "You know I'm right."

His expression furrowed. "You're still fucking around with Victor?"

"I'm trying to get rid of him," I stressed. "I learned my lesson the first time."

"Did you?"

"Maybe we just start over." I nodded.

He leaned back against the counter, arms folded. "Start over? After what happened?"

"We both did what we thought we had to do."

He didn't say anything, just stared into his beer.

"You were right to do it," I said. "About my dad. I hated you for it…but you were right."

He rubbed the back of his neck. "I was angry, man. Your dad was outta control. You knew it. You just didn't want to deal with it."

"I didn't know *how* to deal with it," I admitted. "I was trying to hold the pieces together. Pretend it wasn't that bad."

Erik gave me a long look.

"I appreciate you, Erik. You were the only real friend I had. To actually call things out, to try to help me. I needed that more than ever, just to have someone in my corner."

"You were my brother."

"You're still *my* brother," I corrected him.

Erik nodded slowly.

"I know I don't need your permission," I said, voice steady, "but I'm asking anyway."

He looked at me, puzzled.

"I love Serena," I continued. "And I know I've made mistakes, but I've never used her. I've never lied to her. And I'd never do anything to hurt her. What we have together… It's real.

I'm not trying to get payback on anybody. I'm just trying to live my life."

"For some weird reason, she wants you." Erik's jaw worked for a long time before he nodded. "You ever hurt her, and it won't matter what this conversation was. I'll remind you exactly why we stopped being friends."

I gave a small smile. "Fair."

He stared at me a second longer, then nodded.

"You got my blessing, Whitmore. Don't fuck it up."

Then he stepped forward and pulled me in for one of those one-armed, back-slapping hugs.

"I did beat your ass," he muttered.

"No, you didn't."

I felt my phone ring, and thinking it was Serena, I rushed hastily to answer it.

"Hello—"

"You got thirty minutes. Bring my money. Don't make me wait, Miles."

My stomach turned to stone. "What the hell are you talking about?"

A moment later, I got a text with an address.

Erik stepped closer, reading my face. "Was that…him?"

I slid my phone into my pocket. "Yeah."

"I'm coming with you."

"No," I said quickly. "The less people involved the better. I got this."

He hesitated, then finally nodded. "Don't do anything stupid."

I was already heading for the door when I dialed Burke.

He picked up on the first ring.

"I got something for you," I said. "Victor just called. He wants the bag. He told me where to bring it."

Burke said. "Where?"

I arrived outside at the address sent to me just as Victor was pulling up. He stepped out of the car, coming over to me.

"Miles," Victor said. "You brought my bag?"

I gave a tight nod, popping the trunk but not touching the duffel. "Right there."

Victor reached for it, and I closed the top of the trunk, almost taking his hand off. "Whoa, buddy. Calm down."

He narrowed his eyes at me.

"We have things to discuss."

"You're stalling."

I shrugged. "Maybe."

I needed to delay till Burke could get here and get the pictures he needed. Maybe I could get him to talk, too, and really put the bastard in jail.

"You really think I'm gonna give you back that money just because you *asked*? No contract. No explanation. Just vibes?"

Victor's jaw flexed. "I want the bag, Miles. You either hand it to me like a man"—his hand slid into his coat—"or I take it."

"Don't be fucking stupid," I said, raising my palms.

He pulled the gun anyway. A sleek black 9 mm.

"I'm not giving you shit until you tell me the truth."

Victor cocked his head. "The truth?"

"You're being investigated," I said evenly. "You were trying to hide the money with me because people were coming after you. The family of the man you killed wants justice."

The wind shifted.

A thin thread of smoke curled behind Victor's shoulder.

I glanced past him. Flames licked the corner of the roof.

"Is that house supposed to be on fire?"

Victor turned around, and he lowered his gun. Then he took off toward the house, gun still in hand.

"Are you out of your goddamn mind?" I shouted.

Burke needed his evidence. I couldn't let this man go into a burning house.

The second I stepped inside, heat slammed into me like a brick wall.

Smoke curled in thick ribbons along the ceiling. Flames hissed and danced up the walls, devouring velvet curtains and licking the edge of an overturned ornate dinner table. The air was dense, heavy with heat and the sharp sting of burning wood and wine.

That's when I saw her.

Serena.

Her hair clung to her damp neck, a sheen of sweat glistening across her skin. She was backed against the mantel, her arm raised defensively as she fought off an older woman in heels and smeared red lipstick who I remembered from the auction, one side of her face streaked with blood, rage carved into every line of her expression.

"Serena!" I shouted, voice raw over the roar of the fire.

She turned.

And in that second, the fight left her body. Shock flickered across her face, her lips parting like she'd seen a ghost.

"Miles?" she breathed.

"What the hell are you doing here?" I asked.

But before Serena could answer, a gunshot split the room.

The sound cracked through the smoke, and we all ducked instinctively. A vase shattered behind me, spraying porcelain shards and what looked like camera pieces across the floor.

"Enough!" Victor bellowed, gun pointed to the ceiling, smoke drifting from the barrel. His face was slick with sweat now, his eyes wild.

"You brought the fucking bag, now give it to me," he snarled at me. "Me and Jenese, we need it."

My eyes darted to the bloodied woman Serena had been fighting. She was crumpled against the sideboard, one heel snapped, a fresh flame searing through the hem of her dress. She wiped blood from her mouth and smirked.

Serena's voice cut through the flames.

"So he's your partner?" Her speech was hoarse, but steady. "That's the reason you wanted the Harrington estate?"

"*She's* the reason we don't have the estate?" I asked Serena, coughing. It was getting harder to breathe with the smoke.

I didn't know who this woman was. But Serena did. And that scared me more than anything.

"Serena—" I started, but the house groaned loudly above us. "We need to go," I said, moving toward her.

Victor snapped his arm up, the muzzle of the gun turning— but not on me.

On Serena.

"No!"

"Stay right fucking there!"

"It's a fucking fire, man!" I snapped back, edging closer to Serena.

"She stays," he said. "We're not done."

"She's not part of this," I growled.

"She's always been part of this," Jenese rasped, her voice like sandpaper, cruel and sharp. "She just didn't know it."

Serena's head whipped toward her, eyes blazing. "What are you talking about?"

"You think I found you by chance?" Jenese laughed bitterly. "You think I didn't recognize the King name? Victor and I—we were already here. Already scouting Lush." She nodded toward Victor, who stood stone-faced, the fire casting demonic shadows over his sharp cheekbones.

"We realized we could get more if we worked together," Jenese went on, sweat gleaming at her temples. "He'd shake down the businesses, I'd manipulate the people behind them. You weren't my mentee, Serena. You were my mark."

"You were using me?" she whispered, her voice trembling but dangerous. "From the beginning?"

Jenese smiled—feral, triumphant. "I had to wait things out. I had to set myself up for the big payout in the end, with the manuscript. I taught you how to play the game. But you were never meant to win it."

By now I had inched my way over nearly in front of Serena.

Victor's grip on the gun tightened. "You brought this on yourself. You both did."

The ceiling above us groaned again. Serena's gaze flicked between the gun pointed at her and the burning room closing in.

"Look, whatever the fuck y'all got going on we can deal with it outside." I coughed again.

"Give me the money, Miles," Victor repeated. I tightened my grip on the bag.

Serena's eyes met mine—raw, blazing

"Give it to him," she said.

I blinked at her. "What?"

"Give him the bag," Serena pleaded. "It's not worth dying over!"

Victor smirked, stepping closer, hand outstretched. "Smart girl."

My jaw flexed. I looked down at the duffel.

"You want it?" I said.

Victor gave a sharp nod. "Now."

So I tossed it—hard—straight into the burning corner of the room. Victor went for the bag. I went to grab Serena. The wall behind him gave way, flames roaring through the gap. A heavy beam cracked loose and came crashing down.

Victor tried to lunge out of the way, but it was too late.

It slammed across his back, pinning him with a heavy crunch and a scream that echoed through the burning house.

The gun went off—a deafening shot into the ceiling.

Everyone ducked. My ears rang. Smoke rushed in. I grabbed Serena's hand, tugging her to the exit while we still had one.

"Victor!" Jenese screamed, rushing to him.

He groaned, stuck beneath the flaming wood, the gun knocked somewhere near but out of reach.

"Help me get it off him!" Jenese cried, frantic, shoving at the beam.

Serena gripped my arm. "Miles. Now."

"We're leaving them?"

Flames crawled up the walls, cracking paint and licking the ceiling. Victor coughed violently, smoke curling from his clothes.

Jenese looked at Serena then, eyes shining, lashes wet with sweat and fear.

She let go of my arm—and took a step back.

The front door exploded open.

Dante barreled through in a rush of smoke, his eyes wide.

"Time's up!" he shouted. "We need to move!"

Victor's head lolled, then snapped up. Eyes bloodshot.

"You think saving me's gonna fix shit? I *will* ruin you. You and that cold bitch beside you. I'll finish what I started!"

I froze. "You're talking shit, and you about to die?"

A support beam gave way overhead. I turned just in time to see it fall. It slammed down onto Jenese's legs. She screamed, the sound sharp and animalistic as fire surged up the wall behind her.

She writhed, trying to get free. "Help me!"

Serena staggered, caught between smoke and instinct, one step toward her—

"Don't," Dante said, voice low, firm. "She made her choices."

Serena looked at him, her face pale with smoke, but conflicted.

"She's still a person," she rasped. "Miles is right."

"He dies in here, it all goes away," Dante told her. "No trial. No blackmail. No tapes. No loose ends. It's cleaner. You walk away free."

Serena's face was pale from the smoke, streaked with ash. But her eyes…her eyes were clear.

"Miles," she said softly. "Come with me."

Jenese screamed in fury. "You heartless bitch!"

Serena looked down at her, gaze unflinching. "You taught me well."

The ceiling groaned again.

"Go!" Dante barked. "I'll be right behind you."

We ran. Smoke clung to our clothes, to our skin. I grabbed

Serena's hand as we darted through the hallway, dodging fire, falling ash, and creaking wood.

We burst out the back, stumbling into the night. I collapsed to my knees, chest heaving. Serena stood, her face glowing orange in the firelight. Her expression was unreadable—blank. Not cold, but done.

Dante came out last, coughing.

The roof in the center caved in. We didn't speak. We just stood there in a jagged triangle, watching the house burn. Fire licked out of the windows, roaring like it had teeth. It was over.

Victor was gone. Jenese too.

"Well, there goes my rental property," Dante said with a flick of ash off his shirt.

"This was your place?"

He didn't take his eyes off the fire. "Technically. I inherited it."

"Jesus." I turned to Serena. "Why were you here? Why were you both here?"

"I'll let your wife explain everything to you."

Serena turned to me. "I'll tell you everything, I promise."

"I'll get the fire department up here. Quietly," Dante added. "I've got a guy. Old wiring, faulty box—standard story. You'll have a thirty-minute head start before anyone starts asking questions."

"This is kinda hard to hide," I said to him.

"Don't worry about what I can do." He looked at Serena. "No one will know what happened here," he said. "That's my favor to you."

She narrowed her eyes. "And what will you want later? For this…favor."

"That's for me to decide," he said evenly.

What the fuck?

I glanced between them, confused. Serena didn't press him. Didn't blink. Just gave him a curt nod like…like they'd already made some kind of deal I wasn't privy to.

"Okay," she said simply.

"Wait," I cut in. "What the hell is going on between you two?"

Neither answered. Of course not.

Then Serena's phone rang. Loudly.

Serena flinched slightly and pulled out her phone. She stared at the screen for a second too long. Then answered—on speaker.

"Serena?" Erik's voice cracked through the speaker, rushed and breathless. "Where are you? Laurene's in labor. It's happening. Right now."

CHAPTER 36
Serena

IT DIDN'T TAKE us long to make it to the hospital, after we headed home to clean up and change. In the shower I felt my hands shaking, and every time I closed my eyes, I saw the fire.

Most of the family was already there out front; even Noelle was in deep conversation with Reese's mother, Pauline.

"Is Lu done yet? I wanna see my niece! If they name her after me, it's a bonus." Gigi crossed her legs on the chair.

Daddy didn't look up from his magazine. "No one is naming her after you."

"Why? You named me. Wasn't the name you gave me good enough?"

Reese's family was clustered near the vending machine. His older sister, Jennie, was practically vibrating with excitement, talking a mile a minute to the poor nurse stuck listening.

Erik turned to me.

"Serena," he said quietly. His voice was low, only for me. "You have a second to talk?"

My throat tightened. I nodded, trying to act casual, like my heart wasn't hammering in my chest.

"Yeah," I said. "Yeah, okay."

We walked down the hallway a bit away from the rest, and I cleared my throat. "So..."

Erik shoved his hands in his pockets. His jaw tightened, like he was working out what the hell to say.

"I'm sorry," he said.

I let out a breath. "I should be saying that to you."

He sighed, glancing down before looking back at me. "I shouldn't have put my hands on Miles. That was...that was too far. I should have talked to you about things."

"I shouldn't have slapped you. I—" I swallowed. "I was angry. At you, at Mama, at myself. And maybe I took it out on you because...you've always been the one who had it together."

His brow furrowed, his mouth parting slightly, but I pushed through.

"I was so jealous of you," I whispered. "And I hated myself for it. I should have spoken up, but I thought I could fix things. Then when Lu left, I thought maybe I could take her spot. It would be you and me. But it never happened."

"Rena, you should have told me," Erik said.

"Be real, Erik, we've never been close. I'm used to doing things on my own. You're used to saving Gigi and Laurene."

"You're right," he murmured. "I haven't been there for you the way I should've. And I'm sorry for that."

The apology hit something deep inside me, something I hadn't even realized was waiting. My throat tightened again, but this time it wasn't anger—it was the ache of finally hearing the words I'd needed for so long.

I gave a shaky laugh. "God, I hated myself for wanting her attention so badly."

He gave a small, almost helpless laugh and shook his head. "We're a mess."

"Complete disaster," I agreed, laughing under my breath. "But this is our family."

Erik disagreed. "We'll do better. Not just for us, but the next generation. So they don't have to deal with this."

"I think that's a good thing," I said.

"I'm here for you, Serena. For anything. Whether you want to talk, rant, or have me listening, I'm here and I love you. I hope you can believe and trust me."

I couldn't help but laugh, and wipe a loose tear.

For a second, we just stood there—the space between us tight with all the years we'd let slip by. Then, almost shyly, Erik opened his arms. My heart skipped. And then, without thinking, I stepped forward and wrapped my arms around my brother.

"I missed you, Erik," I whispered into his shoulder.

His arms tightened just slightly. "Missed you too, Rena."

"Can I get a hug?" Miles said behind us.

Erik pulled back just enough to glance at him, brows raised. "After everything?"

Miles shrugged. "I feel like I earned it."

I snorted.

Erik stared for a beat, then sighed and opened his arms. "Come here, dumbass."

A sudden high-pitched screech tore down the hallway, cutting straight through the quiet moment between us.

"What the hell," Erik muttered, already moving.

We hurried back down the corridor, my heels clicking sharp against the tile as my heart pounded in my chest.

As we rounded the corner, Gigi was planted right in front of Reese, her hands flailing.

"Spit it out!" she shouted, clearly unable to contain her excitement. "Are they okay? What's the name? Is now my time to shine as the favorite aunt?"

"Georgiana," Daddy said.

"How's Laurene doing?" Noelle spoke, and Erik was beside her, with a hand on her shoulder.

"She's good," Reese said, looking exhausted but proud. "Tired, obviously. But she's incredible. They're both incredible. Her name is Daisy Ashbourne-King."

A collective gasp filled the room, followed by a round of applause.

Gigi's face lit up like a Christmas tree.

"Daisy!" She clapped her hands together. "Daisy! Oh my God, I'm going to spoil her rotten. Daisy Ashbourne-King, yes! That's such a beautiful name, Reese! You've got taste, man. But you could have named her Gigi."

Heels echoed down the hall before Reese could thank them.

We all turned.

Mama.

Her silhouette moved like a shadow at first, all sleek lines and sharp elegance, her chin lifting as she swept toward us. Her eyes flicked over the group—Erik, Noelle, Daddy, Reese, Jennie, Gigi—and finally, inevitably, me.

Only, when they reached me, they slid past as if I were a stranger standing in the hall.

My chest squeezed, but I lifted my chin. Not today.

"Oh, Mama, you *just* missed it!" Gigi practically launched herself forward, grabbing Mama's hands. "Laurene's perfect, the baby's perfect, and her name is Daisy—Daisy. So feminine and dainty!?"

Mama's lips curved, just slightly.

"Daisy," she repeated, voice soft like she was tasting it. "That's lovely."

She nodded at Gigi, squeezed Erik's arm in passing, murmured something low to Reese. Jennie hovered, practically bouncing in place, and Mama even gave her a gracious nod.

And me?

Nothing.

She didn't so much as glance my way.

"Can we see them?" Jennie said as she came over with her daughter, Faith, on her hip.

"Yes—"

Gigi was the first to dart past me down the hall, followed by

Daddy and Noelle. I stepped back, letting the family steamroll past me into the room.

I was going to follow behind everyone else when Miles said, "Can you stay out here, Serena?"

We were the only ones left in the hallway. I swallowed hard and took a hesitant step forward.

"I don't know how we got here," I whispered, my throat tightening. "But I hate it. I hate not talking to you. Thank you so much for tonight."

"Well, we're gonna be traumatized for a while," Miles tried to joke. His expression turned serious. "We should probably talk about the big ugly thing between us, huh?"

I tensed, the words sinking into the pit of my stomach.

"Who is Jenese?"

Slowly, I exhaled, the truth trembling on my lips.

"She's…someone I worked with. Someone I let get too close." My voice cracked, and I forced myself to hold his gaze. "I met her after things went bad with you. I…lost you, and things with Mama were bad at the time. I thought Jenese could be a surrogate mom or something. But she had me do things that really benefited her more than me.

"At first, it was just about the company. I thought I could control it, play the game. But I was wrong. Jenese got in deeper —she wanted leverage. I thought I had ended things, but then she came back and threatened to ruin everything."

Miles stayed silent for a beat, his eyes dropping to the floor, his chest rising and falling in a slow, controlled breath. "You've been living a double life?"

"I wouldn't say it like that." I sighed. "But it felt like it sometimes. What about you? Who was that man?"

"Someone that was investigating Victor for the family of a man who worked for Victor and got hurt. Hopefully he can still help the family."

I shook my head before the weight of what happened tonight

settled. I let someone die. Someone who was bad… But a life was lost. Two lives.

"I was scared to tell you. To tell anyone," I whispered, my voice barely audible. "That I'd been that desperate and became a mark for a con artist."

He took another step toward me, his hand gently cupping my face, forcing me to meet his eyes. "I've seen the worst parts of you, Serena. And I still love you."

A warmth spread through my chest and I smiled up at him. "I love you too."

Epilogue

MONTHS LATER...

"WHO IS Auntie Gigi's baby? Who? Is it you?" Gigi grinned at Daisy in Laurene's arms, and the baby squealed, her little hands reaching for Gigi's face as though mischief recognized mischief.

It was our tradition, brunch at Café L'Amour out on the patio, and our first in a long time.

"Can I get another martini?" I asked the waiter.

"You? Drinking something other than cappuccinos?" Laurene looked over at me, adjusting her grip on Daisy.

"Damn near had a heart attack," Gigi muttered. "Who would have thought? Married life changed her dramatically."

It had.

Miles and I finished renovating Mrs. Fontaine's property before my official sabbatical from King Developments, just a little bit ahead of schedule and under budget. It was a miracle I couldn't explain.

It felt good to be able to shove it back in Mama's face, even if she hadn't fully wanted to be proud of me. All evidence from Jenese had been burned in the fire. And Dante kept his word— nothing came out of it. No one came looking for Jenese or Victor. Not to speak ill of the dead, but I was glad to be rid of her.

Dante was able to give us some insights into the schemes

Victor and Jenese had been running all across the country. The Harrington estate, if they sold it, would have continued to fund their lifestyle. I didn't know what to do with it; Erik transferred the property into my name and out of King Developments. I think when I was ready to get back to work, it could be a challenge.

Only months into my sabbatical, I didn't want to return to work. Miles was in the midst of opening his own real estate company, and I loved seeing him talk passionately about it. Even when he suggested the unexpected.

"Why don't we start a company? Together?"

It was a little scary to think, especially since we'd both only worked for our family's companies all our lives.

To have a company of our own? Building something with Miles that was all mine would be a different kind of fulfillment.

"I can't have a martini?" I asked Gigi.

"No. You are routine and rhythm, and if you don't stick to that, the world is liable to combust."

Noelle laughed behind her champagne flute filled with mimosa. "Gigi, stop being dramatic. This is a new Serena. We have to get used to it."

It *was* a new me. I'd become hyperfocused on trying hobbies. Apparently, there was a lot you could do when you weren't working twelve-hour days.

I'd tried hiking, which wasn't for me. I didn't have the patience for crochet. I attempted bedazzling at the request of Gigi. My verdict on video games was no to the gore but yes to the cozy farming.

All of it was meaningless, which was hard for me to grasp, but it felt good to do something and not have life-or-death stakes.

"I can't handle it," Gigi said, shaking her head. Walter in her purse next to her barked. "Who will I fight with now?"

"Nothing stays the same," Laurene said, gently rocking Daisy. My niece's eyes were wide open, taking in the world.

"Speaking of that, how's it been?" I asked Laurene, nodding to the baby.

Our relationship had improved greatly. Laurene called more, even if it was about the most mundane stuff. Sometimes I went over to her house just to hang out. Even Gigi and Erik would come along, Daddy, too, when he was feeling up to it.

Only Mama hadn't come.

I hadn't reached out like I said. I got a call from her once, but no phone call since. I wasn't holding my breath.

"Daisy doesn't want to sleep through the night and keeps Mommy and Daddy up, hmm? You like that," Laurene cooed, tickling Daisy's chubby cheek. Daisy cracked up laughing, gums on full display, little fists waving in triumph.

"Well, it's her world, you just livin' in it. You better give her whatever she want," Gigi said, matter-of-fact, leaning back with a smirk. "Or face Auntie Gigi's wrath!"

I could already see it—Daisy and Gigi, hell on wheels, the minute Daisy learned how to talk and walk.

"You're the reason she's spoiled," I told Gigi, shaking my head.

"Ain't no shame in my game." Gigi shot me a grin and reached into her oversized purse, digging with purpose. "I'm not one to gossip, but did y'all hear what happen between Mama and Audrey?"

I glanced at Laurene, who also looked curious. Noelle was the first to lean in.

"What happened?"

Gigi smacked her lips. "Well, I went over there 'cause I was gonna ask Daddy for money. But when I got there, I saw Audrey's car outside. Which is weird. When was the last time Mama talked to Audrey—"

I snapped my fingers. "Get to the point, G."

"Don't rush me." Gigi rolled her eyes at me. "They were out on the patio, just the two of them. *Talking.* I may have even heard a *laugh.* When does Mama laugh?"

I didn't tell them what Daddy told me about getting them together. I guess he was successful.

"That's good, right?" Laurene asked.

"Your mom talking to people and not threatening them is a good thing," Noelle agreed.

Gigi shook her head. "I got the hell up outta there. I'll beg for money later."

Then, with a dramatic flourish, she pulled out a thick stack of papers bound with a clip and slapped them onto the table, right next to the half-eaten croissants and jam. Plates rattled, and Laurene blinked in surprise.

"I meant what I said," Gigi declared proudly, tapping the stack. "Boutique lease, contracts, startup costs—all that. I'm doin' this, y'all. For real."

Laurene's mouth parted in surprise. Noelle's eyes widened. I pursed my lips to stop any questionable remarks from leaving my mouth.

"Hello? Are y'all happy for me?" Gigi looked between the three of us.

"That's big, Gigi," Laurene said slowly, making eye contact with me. "I'm proud of you."

"Awesome, it's gonna be great," Noelle said with a fake enthusiasm.

Gigi tilted her chin, eyes gleaming with a mix of excitement and defiance. "Damn right you proud. Y'all gon' be my first customers too, so don't play."

I cleared my throat. "Well, let's just hope you actually open the doors before you throw the launch party, G."

Gigi's face snapped toward me, eyes narrowing. "Why you always gotta be like that, Serena?"

"I'm just saying." I shrugged, unapologetic. "It's a big deal. A lot of people *say* they gonna do something. Not everybody follows through."

For a second, it was quiet. Laurene's lips pressed together

like she wanted to smooth things over, and Noelle picked at the corner of her napkin, eyes darting between us.

"You're the first person I want eatin' shit when I launch this and it becomes successful. Bigger than Baby Phat! I'll prove you wrong."

I nodded. "For your sake, I hope you do."

Laurene jumped in quickly, steering the conversation before it could tip over. "So, Noelle, how's the search going? For your biological parents?"

Noelle's smile thinned. "Oh. Uh, not much to report, honestly," she said softly. "I've hit some dead ends. Still waiting on some records. It's…a process."

Gigi reached across the table, giving her hand a quick squeeze. "Girl, you gon' find them. You're stubborn like that."

Noelle let out a faint laugh. "Yeah, maybe."

And just like that, the air softened again. I decided to share my news.

"Miles and I are going to have a new addition soon—"

Laurene's jaw dropped. Noelle nearly choked on her mimosa.

"Oh my God, you're pregnant?" Gigi practically shrieked, her eyes going wide. "That poor child. But yay, I get another niece or nephew to spoil."

"Excuse me?" I glared at Gigi. "But relax. I'm *not* pregnant."

"Thank God!" Gigi threw her hands up, falling dramatically back into her chair.

"We're adopting a kitten."

I don't know if I *liked* cats. But I liked Doughboy. Now, it'd gotten to a point where he'd follow me around the house. I made sure he had his food. Took him to the groomers. It was basically like having a human child.

Even when I tried to keep my distance and my hate up for him, the damn cat wouldn't let me go. I had noticed he seemed really depressed whenever Miles and I left the house, and we had a trip planned—I didn't want him all alone.

I guess I understood how Gigi felt about Walter.

For a beat, the table was silent. Then Laurene and Noelle burst into laughter, and Gigi groaned, shaking her head.

"*A cat?* You had me thinkin' you was about to drop somethin' serious!" Gigi huffed, crossing her arms, but the smile tugging at her lips gave her away. "But *you*? With a pet? The ultimate pet hater?"

"Hey, it *is* serious," I shot back. "Doughboy needs a little sister."

"I love this for you, honestly," Laurene said. "Somehow…it fits."

Noelle smiled softly. "Send me pictures when you bring her home."

"Actually…"

They all followed my gaze to find Miles coming through the door, a tiny kitten tucked against his chest in the cutest little harness you've ever seen.

Ew, did I say cute?

"Oh my God!" Laurene gasped, clutching Daisy a little tighter, frightening the baby that had been reaching for her croissant.

But Miles? He only had eyes for me. His grin was lazy, his eyes warm as he strode across the café, the kitten mewing softly in his arms. Without missing a beat, he bent down and pressed a kiss to my lips before sliding into the seat next to me.

"She doing okay?" I murmured, reaching out to scratch the kitten's tiny head.

When I saw her at the shelter, I knew we had to adopt her.

"Did great in the car," Miles said, settling the kitten into my lap. "Didn't cry once."

"She's already better behaved than Gigi," I teased.

"Rude!" Gigi cried, but she was too busy cooing over the kitten to put much fire into it.

"We're trying to harness train her," I explained as the girls leaned in, practically melting over the little ball of fluff. "So we can go places with her and Doughboy."

"And what's her name?" Noelle asked, eyes shining.

I looked down at the tiny gray tabby blinking up at us, then back at the table. "Her name's Elvira, Mistress of the Night. Miles wanted to call her that. I just wanted Kitty." I shrugged.

"You can't call a cat Kitty. It's *basic*." Miles gave me a look of disgust as he snuggled the cat closer.

And just like that, as Miles draped his arm over the back of my chair and the kitten purred in my lap, it hit me. This was our little family.

"Where is Erik? Didn't you invite him, Lu?" Noelle asked.

She shrugged. "He said work."

Noelle's smile faltered, the corners of her mouth tightening just a little. She glanced down at her phone, then abruptly stood, smoothing her dress. "I'm just gonna…bring him something. You know, surprise him."

"Girl, go ahead and chase after your man," Gigi teased with a grin, shaking her head as Noelle waved them off and slipped away before anyone could comment further. "Tell him to give me money for my boutique. I know he got the coins!"

And then, right on cue, Daisy let out an impressive burp, followed by a dribble of spit-up right down Laurene's shoulder.

"Oh, you *would*, baby girl." Laurene sighed with a wry smile, lifting Daisy carefully. "I'm gonna take her inside and clean this up."

"I'll help," Gigi offered, already scooping up napkins and linking an arm through Laurene's as they disappeared inside the café to the restrooms.

Which left just me, Miles, and Elvira at the table.

Dante kept his word, nothing came back to us, but sometimes I got worried about what was to come.

Miles shifted closer, his knee brushing mine, his arm draped lazily over the back of my chair. "Look at us," he murmured.

I let out a laugh, shaking my head. "Who would've thought?"

His thumb brushed along the edge of my jaw, tilting my face

toward his. His gaze softened, the usual mischief giving way to something tender, something that still caught me off guard. "I love you, Sunny."

"I love you too."

He leaned in, pressing his forehead gently to mine. "Can't get rid of me."

"Don't want to."

That's when I felt a buzz from my phone, and I leaned back to read the text.

> Serena… When you have a moment, let's talk. About everything. I owe it to you.

Mama.

A indescribable feeling filled my chest, and I slid my phone back into my pocket.

I closed my eyes, breathing him in, the scent of sunshine and cologne, the quiet steadying beat of his presence.

"Don't want to."

I laughed, a real, full laugh, and felt his lips curve against mine as he kissed me—slow, certain, like we had all the time in the world.

Erik

"I'm busy," I called when someone knocked at my door. I was sitting in my office at King Enterprises, the bright sun shining through the windows trying to coax me out of the building.

Any other day I would have loved to be outside with the rest of town, getting some air, but…the mess in front of me. I had to fix it. That was my responsibility. And it was starting to feel like Mama was slacking in her responsibilities as president of the board more and more lately.

Fuck, will I ever get a break?

No. If it wasn't Mama, it was Gigi. If not Gigi, then Laurene or the board or a fucking email with someone demanding something.

So, no, I didn't have time for—

Knock.

I didn't bother looking up. "I said I'm busy."

The door cracked open anyway, followed by the click of heels against the hardwood.

"I know," came a soft voice. "But you didn't come to brunch. So I figured I'd bring brunch to you."

My head snapped up.

Noelle.

I inhaled, sitting back and watching her enter. She had on a bright yellow dress, with the straps and shit that go behind her neck, the color contrasting with her deep caramel-brown skin. Her dark auburn curls were twisted up, with messy, soft tendrils falling loose around her cheeks. Her hazel eyes met mine with that same tentative smile she always gave me when she wasn't sure I still wanted her around.

As if I could ever stop.

"You came back," I said thickly.

"Yeah," she said gently. "I brought you a chicken caprese sandwich and a cappuccino. There's no pesto. I know you hate pesto, and I double-checked before I left."

"You didn't have to do that," I said still remembering our altercation, she'd been avoiding me. I didn't like it when Noelle did that; it felt like someone stabbed me in the chest.

She shrugged, that beautiful mouth curving slightly. "I wanted to."

God.

I wanted to kiss her right then.

It felt like my eyes couldn't drink enough of her in. From the top of her head, down to her feet, I took in Noelle. My little sister's best friend. She'd always been the girl next door. The nice innocent one. She probably was the best one out of all of us. She didn't do the bullshit tit-for-tat like the Kings did. Somehow in this crazy world of Lush, she kept her soul.

"What kind of chaos are my sisters getting into?" I asked.

She stepped closer, and I could smell the citrusy scent of orange and champagne clinging to her skin. I could see the slight flush on her chest, the way her throat moved when she swallowed.

"You have a new niece," she told me.

I furrowed my brows. "Don't tell me Laurene's pregnant again already? Shit, Ashbourne won't give her a break? I need to speak with him."

Noelle laughed, light and airy, like champagne bubbles bursting against my ribs.

"No, fool! Serena and Miles got a new cat."

I sighed, and shook my head.

Her gaze dropped to my shirt—still half-unbuttoned—and she raised a brow.

"Are you hiding?"

"I wasn't hiding."

"You sure?"

Another step brought her closer. I could feel the warmth of her skin now. See the shimmer on her collarbone. Her fingers brushed the edge of the table like she wanted something to hold, to stop herself from reaching for me.

My phone buzzed on the desk behind me. I ignored it.

"This doesn't change anything," She pushed the food to me. "Make sure you eat this time. Don't let it sit there for hours and then throw it away. You can't just have tea for dinner. It's not healthy, and you'll get a headache."

"Don't worry about me. I told you that before."

"I don't need your permission to care."

That hit somewhere I didn't expect.

"I just want everyone to be okay," she said, hands folding in front of her. "You too. Who takes care of you, Erik?"

My phone buzzed again, insistent. But I didn't move.

She stepped closer, hands brushing against the edge of my desk, looking behind me, voice barely above a whisper. "Answer it. Your mother's going to start sending people."

"I don't want to talk to her right now."

"Is it about the board meeting?"

I said nothing.

Noelle sighed, then reached up without thinking and gently smoothed her fingers over the crease between my brows. "You're always frowning. You need to smile more."

"You shouldn't do that," I said hoarsely.

She blinked. "Do what?"

"Touch me like that."

"Why?"

I didn't want to say it, didn't want to have to go down that path.

My life was calculated. All of us Kings didn't have total free will. I couldn't put that on Noelle. She deserved a life filled with joy, not the turmoil I knew bringing her into our family would cause—a fate I wouldn't wish on my worst enemy.

If an action didn't increase profits for King Enterprises, it was inconsequential, a waste of time and resources. I knew that. She did too.

I had to nip this shit in the bud now.

I reached up and caught her wrist—gentle, but firm enough that she stilled. Her skin was warm, soft as silk, the pulse at the base of her hand fluttering beneath my thumb like a trapped bird.

My palm engulfed her wrist easily, but she didn't pull away. Her lips parted slightly, her chest rising and falling rapidly as she stared at me, her eyes wide. I let my hand drift slowly down her arm, feeling the goosebumps rise on her skin. Over the soft bend of her elbow, along the inside of her forearm.

I swallowed, forcing the words out. "Thank you for the sandwich, really."

Noelle was something I'd never be able to have. And I had to be fine with that.

God help me. I wanted to pull her closer. Bury my face in her neck.

But the phone buzzed again.

"Erik..."

"I have to take this," I muttered.

It took her pulling back for me to release her. I felt myself ensnarled in her hazel eyes before I forced myself to turn around and walk to the other side of my desk. I didn't bother being cordial when I picked up the phone. "What?"

Some analyst started rambling about margins, stockholders,

the upcoming acquisition. Words that once used to mean everything.

Noelle didn't say anything at first.

She waited. Watching. Seeing if I would eat.

I bit into the sandwich. It was actually the first thing I'd eaten all day. Out of the corner of my eye, I saw the slight curve of her lips.

A smile. Small. Satisfied.

"Good?" she asked.

"Fantastic," I said, and the analyst paused.

Then she started to back away.

Her hair swung over her shoulder, a cascade of auburn, as she turned to the door. She opened it slowly, her eyes sparkling as she gave me another one of those sweet smiles, a smile that crinkled the corners of her eyes, before she stepped out.

And when she was gone, the door clicking shut behind her, her faint perfume lingered in the air.

I stared at the door.

I should have stopped her. I should have told her she was the only thing that made this all bearable.

But life was fucked up like that. Life doesn't bend for men like me, even with the money and cars and access. Men like me don't get to want.

Want more of the Kings?

The King Family Saga Begins with…

Lush

Power, ambition, and an old flame Laurene can't escape.

Sign Up For My Newsletter!

Would you like to see deleted scenes, character interviews, new releases, and exclusive character art? Sign up for my newsletter: https://tiniamontford.com/newsletter/

Connect With Me!

You can connect with me on:
Website | Facebook | Instagram | Pinterest | Tik Tok :
@tiniawritesbooks

Want the full Serena & Miles experience? Listen now: http://bit.
ly/4lcUbvz

There's more to explore!

California King Series

Lush – A forbidden affair. A family feud. A marriage neither of them wanted—but can't resist.

Pacific Grove University Series

It Started with a List – A bucket list, a loner, and an unexpected romance.

It Started with a Dance – A fake dating deal that turns into something real.

Standalone Romance

The Last-Minute First Lady – A whirlwind marriage, political scandal, and family drama.